DATE DUE

EMBERS & ECHOES

Also by Karsten Knight

WILDEFIRE

EMBERS & ECHOES

Karsten Knight

SIMON & SCHUSTER BFYR

NEW YORK LONDON TORONTO SYDNEY NEW DELHI

SIMON & SCHUSTER BFYR

An imprint of Simon & Schuster Children's Publishing Division
1230 Avenue of the Americas, New York, New York 10020
This book is a work of fiction. Any references to historical events,
real people, or real locales are used fictitiously. Other names, characters, places,
and incidents are products of the author's imagination,
and any resemblance to actual events or locales or persons,
living or dead, is entirely coincidental.
Text copyright © 2012 by Karsten Knight
Photograph copyright © 2012 by Ashton Worthington
All rights reserved, including the right of reproduction
in whole or in part in any form.
SIMON & SCHUSTER BFYR is a trademark of Simon & Schuster, Inc.
For information about special discounts for bulk purchases,
please contact Simon & Schuster Special Sales at 1-866-506-1949 or
business@simonandschuster.com.
The Simon & Schuster Speakers Bureau can bring authors
to your live event. For more information or to book an event,
contact the Simon & Schuster Speakers Bureau at 1-866-248-3049
or visit our website at www.simonspeakers.com.
Book design by Laurent Linn
The text for this book is set in Arrus BT.
Manufactured in the United States of America
2 4 6 8 10 9 7 5 3 1
Library of Congress Cataloging-in-Publication Data
Knight, Karsten.
Embers & echoes / Karsten Knight. — 1st ed.
p. cm.
Summary: In Miami, Florida, seeking her younger sister, sixteen-year-
old Ashline Wilde, a Polynesian volcano goddess, joins forces with other
reincarnated deities, but trickster Colt's diabolical plans threaten them all.
ISBN 978-1-4424-5030-1 (hardcover)
[1. Supernatural—Fiction. 2. Sisters—Fiction. 3. Goddesses—Fiction.
4. Gods—Fiction. 5. Tricksters—Fiction. 6. Miami (Fla.)—Fiction.] I. Title.
II. Title: Embers and echoes.
PZ7.K7382Emb 2012
[Fic]—dc23
2011046357
ISBN 978-1-4424-5036-3 (eBook)

FIRST
EDITION

To my niece, Victoria:
It's amazing how one laugh from a three-month-old can give
you clarity and perspective that twenty-seven years could not

EMBERS & ECHOES

CONTENTS

Lovers' Quarrel, *Monday* 1

Treacherous Waters, *Limbo* 18

PART I: THE SUN AND THE MOON

The Humidor Prisoner, *Tuesday* 45

The Scarecrow Murders, *1924* 83

Vines and Vengeance, *Wednesday* 100

The Tiki Bandits, *1927* 150

Hacienda Party, *Thursday* 162

PART II: THE CULT OF THE FOUR SEASONS

The Ice Sculpture, *Friday* 213

Blizzards and Squalls, *Saturday* 253

Weeping Willow, *Sunday, Part I* 287

Streetcar Sunrise, *1929* 316

PART III: THE SPARK, THE FUSE, AND THE FLAME

The Glass Sarcophagus, *Sunday, Part II* 333

Burning Blossoms, *Monday* 362

The Sibling Pyre, *1934* 382

The Candelabra, *The Netherworld* 388

The Molten Cure, *Tuesday, Part I* 427

Over the Edge, *Tuesday, Part II* 447

Embers and Echoes, *Epilogue* 457

Ashline Wilde lay battered on the side of the Pacific Coast Highway and watched her boyfriend emerge from the fiery car wreck, back from the dead.

She heard the sickening crunch as Colt twisted his broken neck back into place.

She waited as he swatted the flames on his jacket until they died away.

She listened to him tell her that he was a reincarnated god—just like her—who had been impersonating a mortal for the last month and a half of their relationship.

As far as breakups went, this had to be her worst.

She thought back to his lips on her lips. To his hands on her body. To his moments of vulnerability and the three separate occasions when she'd thought she was fighting to save his life.

All lies.

She retched.

Colt's smile crumbled as he watched her vomit onto the dusty road. "I don't get it. I thought you'd be glad that I'm like you."

Ash wiped the spittle from her mouth and tried to pull herself up onto her knees. Explosion of pain in her lower back. She fell back onto her hands. "Get the hell away from me, Colt."

"Oh, come on!" Colt shouted. "It's just dandy for you to be a Polynesian volcano goddess, but we're going to have a nuclear meltdown because I'm a Hopi trickster?" A queue of cars was slowly forming behind him, obstructed by the blazing wreckage. Several people were rushing toward the scene of the accident with cell phones in hand, and Colt lowered his voice as he reached down to help Ash up. "You weren't exactly forthcoming with me about having powers either."

Ash swatted his hand away. "Well, the appropriate time to tell me might have been after I *evaporated a tsunami to save your life*—a life that apparently didn't need saving!" She managed to get onto one foot, then the other, and slowly extended her spine until she was completely upright. A reservoir of hurt opened up on the side of her rib cage. "How much of this has been a game for you? Were you pretending to be unconscious when the poachers tagged you with that tranquilizer dart? Did you *let* Eve catch you and chain you to that rock?"

Colt looked out to sea.

It was all the answer that Ashline needed. After everything she'd learned from dating the wrong guys in the past, how could she have gone and let someone so manipulative into her life? "Was it real?" she whispered. Colt opened his mouth, but nothing came out, so Ash staggered up to him and shoved him roughly by the shoulders. "Was any of it real? Tell me, you coward!"

She went to push him again, but Colt grabbed her by the wrists hard and pulled them into his chest—how had she never noticed his strength before, the power simmering behind his eyes?

"It's real now," Colt said quietly. "And that's what matters."

Ash tried to break his hold, but his grip held true. "It's real *now?*" Ash echoed. "But it wasn't always? Is that some euphemism for 'I used you'?"

A man with graying hair lingered near them on his way toward the accident. "Is everything okay here?" He meaningfully eyed Ash, whose wrists were still in Colt's vise grip.

Colt released her and took a threatening step toward the older man. "How about you go help the dead guy in the crumpled SUV instead of interrupting roadside conversations?"

Ash took the opportunity to flee down the sandy highway embankment, heading for the trees. The sound of sirens picked up from the north. Ash could only hope that someone from the accident had survived, but there was nothing she could do for them now. She just needed to get away.

Colt's footsteps trailed behind her. "I needed your explosive little sister," he explained hurriedly. "I *still* need her. I can't explain to you yet exactly how I know this, but the youngest Wilde is capable of creating explosions *so intense* that they can rip right through the fabric of space and time. She's barely six years old now and hasn't mastered her abilities, but with the proper training not only will she able to create a rift between any two places in the world, but she may be able to open a doorway into the Cloak Netherworld as well. With your sister's abilities I'd finally have a way to destroy the Cloak, on their home turf, where they least expect it, and they'd never be able to take our memories or our immortality from us again."

"The Cloak Netherworld? Those creatures have a *home*?" It was hard to imagine what sort of dark underground lair belonged to the Cloak—the oily-skinned, fiery-blue-eyed monsters that had been stalking Ash for months, manipulating her, sending her cryptic instructions on how to prevent the apocalypse.

The same monsters that had swallowed Eve Wilde alive not two months earlier.

Wherever it was, "Netherworld" was probably a fitting term for it. "Couldn't you have just used my bat-shit crazy older sister for your dirty work?" Ash asked.

Colt laughed darkly. "I tried to use Eve, but in the

end I couldn't control her, precisely because she *was* bat-shit crazy. Sure, she shared my hatred for the Cloak, but Eve was a loose cannon. When I found out that she wanted to go all *Brady Bunch* and run off with you and the little Wilde . . . well, I had to cut her loose and find a new way to track down the little girl." He paused. "In this case, you."

"Oh my God." Ash stopped at the edge of the trees and bent over, preparing to dry-heave again. She had burned her sister and let the Cloak drag her to an oily grave . . . all while Colt had watched from his spot, chained to the rock. She'd done everything that he'd wanted, thinking that she was doing it for her own good, of her own free will.

"So to answer your original question, yes, I intended to use you. Yes, I thought the visions of the third Wilde that you and Eve shared could lead me to the little one." Colt took a step toward her. "But what I never intended . . ." He paused. "Was to fall in love with you."

She felt his arm slither across her back. For a moment she relaxed at the familiar touch, took pleasure in the solid, masculine grace of his hand and forearm, let his warmth radiate through her road-shredded tank top.

But then it began to feel different, poisonous, like an acid drip to the small of her back. A familiar heat burgeoned in the furnace of her chest.

A siren whooped back in the direction of the highway, and the trees overhead flickered with the pulsing red and blues of the arriving state troopers. "Come on."

Colt tugged her arm. "We have to clear out of here; I don't think you want to be around when the police try to figure out whose motorcycle shrapnel is lodged inside that flame-broiled SUV."

Ash didn't budge. She had her hands planted on her knees and was watching the thick trail of dark smoke drift down the hillside from the accident. "If you hadn't orchestrated all of this, Lily never would have killed Rolfe," she said finally. "He'd still be alive, without a hole in his heart."

"Lily was a bomb waiting to explode, and it was your crazy sister who lit the fuse." This time Colt wrapped his arms entirely around her waist and succeeded in pulling her a step, but Ash wasn't about to let Colt keep touching her. *You've pushed me around for the last time,* she thought. The heat that had been building in her chest started to rise to the surface of her skin, fueled by Colt's betrayal.

Colt yelped and released her. "Jesus, Ash, you're burning up."

"Good to know that you still feel something." Ash's hands started to vibrate.

"I'm indestructible, Ash. That doesn't mean I'm incapable of feeling. I still experience love, and I can still experience pain."

Ash spread her shaking fingers, a blossom of misery and wrath unfurling its petals. "Good," she said. A flame ignited in her open palm like a flint catching propane. "I was counting on that."

Her arm arced around, and her open palm slammed into his cheekbone. The fireball burst on impact, showering the two of them with sparks. The resulting blow sent Colt staggering back into the hillside with a pained roar, where he dropped down onto one knee and covered his cheek. As he removed his hand from his face, Ash saw the blackened, festering welt across his cheekbone. But even as it still seemed to shimmer with heat like pavement on a summer's day, the wound began to lighten and fade right before her eyes.

"Come near me again, and we'll find out what else you can regrow." She pointed at his crotch.

Colt's expression gradually returned to placid. The gash in his cheek fused back together, and the skin zippered closed over the wound without even the whisper of a scar. "You really want to do this now?"

"Is there ever a right time to break up?" Ash asked. "Good-bye, Colt. And don't follow me."

Ash turned on her heel and walked briskly into the copse of trees. She allowed herself just the slightest of last looks over her shoulder as she passed into the forest. Colt was standing, unmoving at the edge of the woods, his chest rising up and down as he watched her go.

As she carved her way through the trees with no particular destination in mind, she reached up and wiped the tears from her eyes. She was leaving behind the only anchor she still had in this world outside of her hometown. What few friends she had left were scattered around the western hemisphere. Ade, the Zulu thunder god, was down in Haiti rebuilding after the earthquake that had devastated his home country. Raja, the Egyptian protectress of the dead, was off somewhere coming to terms with the fact that she was carrying a child who would never meet his father. And as for Jackie and Darren—her nice, normal, mortal friends—well, they were at some commune farm in Alabama for the summer, and it was kind of hard to explain her situation to them while omitting the "I'm a Polynesian volcano goddess" part.

Back in reality, strong arms seized Ash from behind in a bear hug. It wasn't hard enough to hurt her, but firm enough to say *You're not going anywhere.*

With her arms pinned to her side no matter how much she strained, Ash had never felt so violated. The familiar scent of leather and ginger from Colt's cologne was so strong, she could taste it on her tongue. What had always smelled sexy to her before was now only repulsive.

"I can't just let you walk away from me like this," Colt whispered into her ear. "Everything I'm doing—searching for your little sister, destroying the Cloak—it all comes back to you. You might not see yet where you fall in the big picture, but I promise, in time—"

The fire streamed out of her pores easily this time, just above the elbows and wrapping all the way around her biceps. Colt screeched and staggered back. He held up his hands, which had blistered crimson from the insides of his thumbs all the way across his swollen palms.

Ash took advantage of his distraction and spun 180 degrees. Her foot connected hard with his sternum, with more force than she'd expected. The blow picked him up off his feet and carried him into the trunk of a nearby cedar. His arms shot out to either side as his spine collided with the trunk, and he dropped to the ground, landing with his blistered palms facing down in the dirt and pine needles.

Ash touched the leg she'd kicked him with like she was just noticing it for the first time. Tennis hadn't toned her legs *that* much; apparently being a volcano goddess came with some side effects in the muscle department. Even though she'd started coming into her powers weeks ago, it felt like there were other supernatural facets of her godhood that were still waiting for her beneath the surface. . . .

Colt wrenched his back roughly, and Ash swore she could hear one of his discs popping back into place. "Even despite your attempts to maim me, I have to point out how much better you're getting at controlling your abilities. Last month you practically needed oven mitts just to make out with me, and you barely summoned the fire in time to stop that tsunami."

Ash shrugged. "What can I say? I guess kicking your ass comes more naturally to me than saving it."

"What is your flawed logic?" Colt snarled, and clapped the debris off his healing hands. "Would you have preferred that I'd been mortal and died in that motorcycle accident?"

"I wish you hadn't pretended to be some creepy cartoon Prince Charming in the first place, and I *definitely* wish you hadn't swept me off my feet while you were really just looking to kidnap my little sister for whatever weird quarter-life crisis you're experiencing now," Ash said. "Come to think of it, I wish I'd just never met you at all." Even as the words twanged between them like a bowstring pulled taut and then released, Ash wondered whether she really meant them.

This time as she walked up the hill away from him, she kept her gaze trained on him over her shoulder the whole time, lest he get the jump on her again. He remained at the base of the cedar, slouched with defeat and melancholy. Gradually the forest thickened, until Ash lost sight of him altogether, his face disappearing behind a curtain of cedar and dusk.

Forty yards later she crested a hill and started down the opposite slope. Here a floor of rock emerged through the soil, cascading down the hillside like a waterfall of stone.

And then she heard the chord.

She stopped to listen.

It was neither entirely human nor instrumental, but a composite of the two, like breath passing over the lip of a bottle, with a deep male voice lingering somewhere beneath it. The virile chord was dissonant yet beautiful. She found herself turning and relaxing, despite the nagging sensation that she should continue down the hill, away, away, as far away as she could go. Somehow that urge to flee was slipping under the tides of warmth and security that washed over her.

Standing at the summit of the hill, backlit by the sun so that its rays trickled around his silhouette, was Colt. His mouth was agape, letting the strange and gripping chord fill the forest.

He closed his mouth finally, but the music continued to echo in Ash's ear, swimming in circles and keeping her feet rooted to the ground.

"In the myths about Kokopelli," Colt said without moving from his perch atop the rock, "he wasn't just a trickster. He was a tempter as well. A seducer. He would sweep into a village and impregnate whomever he desired."

Ash somehow found the resolve to reach down and grab hold of her leg. *Move,* she willed it. *Move!* But her legs might as well have weighed a few metric tons apiece. Besides, it felt so good just to stand here, not to have to run anymore. . . .

"He also had a flute," Colt continued. "I didn't have to join a choir to discover that the 'flute' was just a figurative reference to my voice."

Ash managed to get her foot to move a fraction of an inch, but Colt must have noticed, because he opened his mouth again. The chord doubled in her ears, and suddenly she'd forgotten why she'd attempted to flee in the first place.

Colt gazed directly into her eyes. "You should know—and this is very important—that my voice isn't *total* mind control. It can't make you do anything your subconscious doesn't already desire. It just strips away logic and inhibition. Which means that when I say, 'Come to me . . .'"

The weight lifted from Ash's feet, and she marched forward up the rock. One step, two steps, over the fallen branch.

"Deep down you *want* to come to me. Deep down you don't want to run away from the man you still carry a torch for."

The distance between them closed until she had joined him on the summit, half an arm span apart.

"It means that when I say, 'Put your arms around me . . .'"

Ash edged closer until her breasts just barely touched his chest. Her arms rose up from her sides, delicate and light like the fronds of a fern. They slipped around his charred shirt and onto the muscular small of his back.

"Deep down you *want* to put your arms around me. And when I tell you, 'Kiss me . . .'"

Her grip on his back tightened. She raised herself up onto her toes. Her head tilted back and her lips parted in anticipation.

Colt leaned his head down to meet her. His fingers found their way to either side of her cheeks as he cupped her head in his hands.

He kissed her.

As their noses touched, as his rough stubble scratched against her satin skin, and his tongue slipped into her waiting mouth, the echo in her ears faded just enough that she slowly began to see everything around her for what it was.

The way the light peeked out around him like the aura of an eclipse.

The impossibly tranquil expression on his face.

The way it would be easier just to shelve her reservations, forgive the past, and follow this familiar stranger into the north on whatever crazy errand he really had in mind.

But beneath the house of lies that he'd constructed, she saw all the cracks in the foundation.

That he had used her.

That he had just hypnotized her into forgiving him.

That she'd had to scatter a sixteen-year-old's ashes at sea because of the games Colt had played and the webs he had spun.

A scream erupted in Ash's throat and poured out into Colt's mouth. It broke whatever spell she was under, and Colt took a shocked step back.

That was all the time and distance Ash needed.

Ash had spent the last two months feeling like an amateur with her new fiery abilities, but now something snapped inside her, and in her rage she tapped effortlessly into her own raw, seething power. She howled and pointed at the rock beneath Colt.

He barely had time to look, confused, at the quivering ground before the rock under his feet liquefied into molten lava and he plunged all the way down to his thighs.

With his legs steeped in the scalding hot pool, it was Colt's turn to scream—another dissonant chord like the one he'd used to hypnotize her, but this one reeked of torture and pain and tasted bloody metallic in her ears. His hands fumbled around the lip of the well in an attempt to pull himself out.

Ash drew her hands back. The smoke and lines of heat rising off the lava instantly funneled toward her palms, as though she were the exhaust fan over a stove. The stone cooled rapidly until it hardened around his legs, locking him into place.

When it was all finished, Colt was half-buried in the rock, starting six inches above his knees. His screams had died down to a furious growl, and Ash realized that this was the first time she'd ever seen Colt truly angry.

"You little bitch!" he shrieked. "Do you know how much that hurt?" He twisted violently from side to side and tried to lift himself out of the rock.

"Tell that to the boy who took a mistletoe spear through his heart." Ash spat on the ground next to him; the ground was still hot enough for her saliva to sizzle on the rock. "You can find Rolfe's ashes at the bottom of the Pacific and tell him yourself, once someone comes along to jackhammer you out of here."

Through the look of pain on Colt's face a lascivious

smile suddenly broke through the gloom. And he began to laugh.

Ash crossed her arms. "What's so funny? Does the rock tickle?"

Colt snorted. "No. I was just thinking that you're the second Wilde to chain me to a rock in the past month."

"I assume that because you heal quickly you can also survive a while without food," Ash said. "But if you get hungry before help arrives, there are a couple of pine cones within your reach."

Ash started to walk away. She heard the familiar, dissonant chord as Colt opened his mouth and sang. This time it caused her only to stumble a little, although afterward something felt fuzzy in her brain. Her vision blurred and she had to shake her head to clear it. "You can sing all you want, Colt—I'm not going to free you."

He shook his head. "I was just leaving you with a last little present for those lonely nights ahead of you."

She could still feel the echo of the chord, no longer just in her ears but planting itself in a lobe of her brain. She tapped her head a few times with the heel of her palm, trying to prevent it from taking root. Miraculously, the ache in her head quickly faded away.

"What, no good-bye kiss?" Colt goaded her. "Well, chew on this before you walk away: Eve is still alive."

Ash narrowed her eyes at him. "I watched the Cloak devour her."

"Not devour," Colt corrected her. "They transported

her to their Netherworld, where they're holding her prisoner. She was too dangerous to them topside, but I'm sure they've kept her alive. She's too fascinating for those little pricks to let go of."

For the first time since Eve's final betrayal, Ash felt the murmurs of uncertainty, deep in her stomach like a growing, gnawing hunger. In many ways Ash felt as though her sister had died when she'd run away from Scarsdale the first time, and the Eve who'd returned had left behind only a legacy of burned wreckages and body bags. And while Ash had never felt good about letting the Cloak take her sister, in her heart she'd always known it was a necessary tragedy. Eve had nearly drowned her in that cove. If Ash hadn't stopped her, there was a very good possibility that Ash could have ended up a piece of bloated driftwood in the California tide.

But now knowing that her sister was alive and at the mercy of a dark beast—

Now knowing that Colt had been the real maestro orchestrating the symphony of terror and suffering back at Blackwood—

Well, it may not have changed everything, but it certainly sent a ripple through still waters.

Ash tried her best to mask her inner turmoil. The last thing she needed was for Colt to see that his manipulations had gotten to her. "So let me guess," she said. "You want me to use my visions to help you find my little sister, so we can open up a portal, save Eve, and destroy the Cloak?"

"You can't do it alone." He grunted as he made another futile attempt to pry himself from the rock. "That little girl has more power than all of us combined, more power than a six-year-old can know what to do with. That's why powers usually lie dormant until our teenage years. She could incinerate even you, her own flesh and blood, if you approach her the wrong way."

Ash looked out to the eastern horizon, where a menacing cloud mass was gathering over the mountains. "Looks like a storm's coming," she said. On cue the sky grumbled. "On the bright side, at least you won't go thirsty."

With that, Ash worked her way down the slope with no destination in mind, only to put at least a few miles between her and Colt.

But just like every boy she'd ever known after every breakup she'd ever had, Colt of course wanted to have the final word. It was one sentence, and he screamed it down the hill to her before she was out of earshot:

"I'll be seeing you in your dreams, Ashline Wilde."

Ashline didn't let herself cry until she'd locked herself in a stall in the airport bathroom.

She'd been on the run for hours, making her way out of the forest and back to the highway, eventually hitch-hiking to Portland with a hippie couple who'd taken pity on the ragged-looking girl on the side of the road. As long as she'd stayed in motion, it had kept at bay the reality of what had just happened with Colt. But now, sitting on a toilet seat with her knees hugged to her chest and a plane ticket back to New York tucked in her pocket, Ash could barely stifle her sobs.

Not only had Colt pretended to be mortal all that time while Ash and the others had been discovering their own godhood—

Not only had he manipulated Eve to do his bidding, only to let her be condemned to the Cloak Netherworld when he was done using her—

But he'd finessed Ash into developing feelings for him as well.

Even worse, Ash was just starting to remember the instructions the Cloak had given her, the three words on her scroll that were supposed to prevent some sort of cataclysm between the gods:

Kill the trickster.

After today it didn't take a crystal ball to figure out who the trickster on her hit list was supposed to be.

Just when Ash didn't think she could bear the stillness of the airport bathroom any longer, her phone chimed and vibrated in her pocket. The screen was cracked from her fall off the motorcycle, but she could still read the name on the caller ID:

Home.

Her first instinct was to press ignore. When she'd flown out to California to meet Colt for their ride up to Vancouver, she'd told her parents only that she was "visiting a friend." What was she going to do now—try to explain to them, between sobs, that she'd had a horrible breakup, nearly died, and fled the scene of an accident? Pass.

But if it was already after midnight in Oregon, that meant it was three a.m. Westchester time . . . and her parents were by no means night owls. It could only be some sort of emergency. She picked up on the third ring.

"Ashline?" It was her father, and he didn't even wait for her to say "hello" first.

"I'm here, Dad," she said. She tried her best to swallow

the lump in her throat, but her voice still sounded nasal from crying.

There was a long sigh on the other end, whispering over the receiver. "Ash, baby, there's something we need to tell you." His words sounded taut and trembling—had he been crying too? "It's . . . about your sister."

Ash leaned forward on the seat. *Please don't say that her body washed up on shore somewhere.* After hearing the news that Eve might be alive in the Cloak Netherworld, and experiencing the strange swell of hope that came with it . . . well, she couldn't bear it if that turned out to be just another one of Colt's lies. "What about Eve, Dad?"

"The Oregon State Police called. Eve's motorcycle was . . . recovered from a horrible accident that happened earlier today."

The bathroom's overhead lights flickered. Ash cursed her own stupidity. She had been so caught up trying to get away from Colt, she'd overlooked that the motorcycle's license plate might have survived the crash.

"For better or worse," her father continued, "she was nowhere to be found when police searched the area . . . but one man said he'd seen a girl matching her description talking with a guy about her age." Was that hope Ash now heard in his voice? Hope that would be dashed in so many ways if she told him that she was the Polynesian girl spotted at the scene of the accident? "Your mother and I . . . we just hope that she's not hurt, wherever she is. You haven't heard from her, have you?"

Ash wanted to shout, *When do I ever hear from her?* But the lights flickered again, and this time the bathroom around her went completely dark.

The door creaked open, and footsteps echoed over the tile. "Dad," she said quietly into the phone. "I'm going to have to call you back." She flipped the cell closed before her father could protest.

Whoever had just walked into the blacked-out bathroom moved with deliberate, heavy steps, and her first crazed thought was that Colt had somehow found her and the blackout was his doing.

Then she saw the blue light. The fiery, flickering sapphire glow that she'd come to associate with the dreaded Cloak.

Ash pulled her knees back up against her chest. She tried to soften her breaths, but they came out ragged and fearful anyway.

Its footsteps lumbered across the tile with calculated patience. Ash wanted to close her eyes so badly, but she couldn't keep herself from watching the narrow gap between the stall door and the wall.

Moments later, as the glow intensified, the creature passed right in front of the gap—first the single blue flame it had for an eye, then the rest of its massive oily body. Underneath the door its squat legs visibly slowed, then stopped, just in front of her stall.

It rapped on the plastic door. *Oh, God, this is it,* Ash thought. The creature had devoured her sister, and now it had come back for her as well.

The door thundered open, bringing Ash face-to-face with the Cloak. She screamed at the same time it gnashed its bear-trap teeth and roared. Then her gaze was drawn hypnotically into the iris floating in its blue flame, and she felt her consciousness ripped away to the edge of the universe.

To a place she'd been before, where your memories are no longer your own.

To limbo.

The jungle fronds slap against your face, and it's nearly impossible to see where you're going. The rain forest is so dense here, you could run off the edge of a cliff and not know until you'd fallen halfway to your death. But you can hear the barking of the hounds now, closer than they've been in weeks.

You are running for your life.

Ever since the explosion of that village more than a month ago, you've hidden in the trees, fed off leaves, berries, and whatever raw animals you can catch, all while avoiding the dogs and mercenary patrols that have been making vigilant sweeps through the brush. But no matter how far you journey away from the crater where the village used to be, no matter how often you roll in the mud, no matter how high you climb into the trees, the hounds never completely lose your trail.

Finally you have to stop—your little six-year-old legs are about to give out beneath you—and as you lean against the tree, broken to the point of almost giving up, that's when you hear another sound.

The sound of hope.

The whisper of the ocean tide.

You throw caution to the wind once more and sprint through the jungle, ignoring the scrapes on your cheeks and legs as you tear through the underbrush. Even the threat of the hounds and the military men can't stand between you and the water, the ocean that calls to you.

You stumble out of the jungle and across the narrow beach until you're kneeling in the surf. You cup your hands beneath the silken water and bring several handfuls up to cleanse your face. The brine stings your eyes, but you don't care. You begin to weep, from exhaustion, from joy that you're out of the jungle and into the water . . . and from nostalgia because the gentle lapping of the ocean reminds you of the distant island you once called home.

You wade in deeper, let the mud and grime and leaves and soil slough right off you. For a heavenly minute you float weightlessly in the ocean and feel as though maybe everything will be okay if you just drift out to sea.

The first bee stings your shoulder, and you let out a cry. You reach up and pluck out the stinger. No, not a bee at all. This stinger is long and metal and cylindrical and . . .

Another one slips into your opposite shoulder, closer to your neck. This time you can only whimper while your strength fails you and you struggle to reach up and yank it out. Soon your whole body has lost sensation. You float belly-up.

Though you can feel your consciousness beginning to

fray and unravel, your blurry, paralyzed eyes settle on a tall woman wading up beside you, wearing overalls. You can barely make out her features under her wide-brimmed hat.

You try to move your mouth to speak, but only a gurgle comes out. You can only hope she's come to save you from the soldiers, and the dogs, and now the metal bees with stingers that make you sleepy, so sleepy . . .

"Shh," she hushes you gently. Her arms support you, cradling your small delicate body in the tide. "You're safe now. And among friends."

As the last of your consciousness unwinds, you see three shadows—two boys and a girl—wade into the shallows too. One word bobs to the surface before your world goes black completely:

Friends.

When you wake up, the world beneath you is squirming.

You lie faceup in the dark, your eyes trained on what you believe is a ceiling fan. You can hear it whirring. You can feel its gentle breath against your face. Yet you still can't make out its shape, because the room you're in seems to be impenetrable to light.

Well, not quite. As your eyes struggle to adapt to the darkness and you turn your stiff neck, you see a faint glow trickling under the door across the cabin.

Beneath your fingers you can feel rope weave, which means you must be lying in a hammock like the one between the two banana trees at home. When you try to slip out of the swaying berth, you immediately fall flat onto your stomach. Your back tingles where the criss-crossing mesh of the hammock has embossed a waffle pattern into your flesh. Your joints feel like they haven't moved from this position in many days. How long have you been out?

The door opens with a resistant groan. You peel your face off the moist metal treads on the floor.

The woman in the door is backlit by a harsh spot-light. Her long shadow stretches all the way across the floor, but even in silhouette you know this must be the same woman who saved you from the metal stingers in the water.

"Good. You're awake," she says. She crosses the room in a couple of quick strides, and then very tenderly slips her hands under your armpits to help you up. "There are people that I want you to meet, Rose."

You don't remember ever being called that name before—Rose—but you sort of like it. She has her hand held out for you, so you slip yours gingerly into hers. The two of you walk hand-in-hand out the door.

Immediately you smell the ocean and understand that the world moving beneath you wasn't just your ham-mock.

You're on a boat. Like the one that brought you to the jungle and the stone castle where the men in white starved you. Will this be the one to bring you home?

You stop to look at the room in which you've been sleeping—it's some sort of rusty metal box, labeled in white painted letters: HV-48967-1.

At the end of the hallway, you can see the ship's forward railing, and beyond that the dark ocean. The strange woman guides you up to the prow of the boat, and the two of you stop there, with her gripping the upper railing, and you, so much smaller, holding the lower.

"Beautiful view, isn't it?"

At this time of night the water and the sky almost fuse into one, a dark mass of clouds above the horizon and the churning seas below. And just at the lip of the horizon, sandwiched between them, is a dark line . . . land. And the ship is moving steadily toward it.

Someone clears his throat behind you. It's an enormous boy with long dreadlocked hair and earthen skin, not unlike yours. His red-eyed gaze darts from the woman to you, then back again. "Lesley," he says.

"Yes, Rey?"

"The ship is approaching from the southwest." His eyes seem to dance wildly like two flickering candles even when they are still. "They will be within range soon enough."

Lesley waves her hand. "No matter. We have their cargo." She leans over and wraps her arm around your waist and ushers you away from the railing. The three of you journey toward the stern of the boat, with the boy, who is twice your height, making occasional glances at you.

Two others already stand at the aft railing, looking out over the trail of foamy white the ship is carving in its wake. Another ship looms off in the distance, visibly larger than the one you're on. It's getting close enough that you can see the outlines of people standing onboard its well-lit deck.

Lesley doesn't look too disturbed. She doesn't even spare a moment for the approaching boat. "Rose, this is Rey, Bleak, and Thorne. Everybody . . . this is Rose."

Rey, the one you met before, is smiling at you. His eyes continue to flicker red, and the corners of his lips won't stop twitching. He fidgets uncontrollably, and as a result his dreadlocks wiggle around his face like a nest of snakes.

The girl, Bleak, wears a flowing white floor-length robe with its hood pulled back, and her skin and French-braided hair are as pale as virgin snow. Unlike Rey, she does not smile at you. In fact, it doesn't look like she's ever done much smiling.

Thorne, the other boy, also doesn't look tickled by your presence, but he doesn't seem irritated by it either. He's a head shorter than Rey, and much leaner, too. He can't be any older than sixteen or seventeen, but he has a cigar gripped between his fingers. He appraises you for a moment, while idly tapping the ashes from his cigar onto the deck of the boat.

Finally he flicks the cigar into the water, kneels down, and sticks out his free hand. You suppose that means you should take it, and you do. It's cold.

"Nice to meet you, Rose," he says.

The name still sounds strange and wonderful, sugar to your ears.

Lesley unclips the box on her belt and clicks a button. "Cesar, kill the engines."

Almost instantly the motor below grumbles and then whines to a halt, while the frothing wake behind the boat dissipates off into the black.

Meanwhile, the boat behind you makes incredible gains. A spotlight shines out from its perch on the front of the ship, and it dances over the water until it finally pins the five of you standing on the deck. You squint and raise your arm to block some of the light.

"I think they've come close enough," Lesley says. "Let's show our newest passenger what you can do. Want to get us started, Bleak?"

Bleak rolls the sleeves of her robe up to the elbows. When she reaches out with her arms, just above her wrist you notice a tattoo of a circle, divided into quarters—white, green, red, and gold.

She closes her eyes. She lets out a deep breath, and despite the relative warmth of the summer air, you see her breath fog from the cold.

With a sudden groan of metal that's loud enough that you cover your ears, the other ship instantly grinds to a halt. The abrupt stop sends two crew members over the railing and plunging toward the water below.

But it's no longer water they're falling toward. Instead

the two men strike the ring of ice that has crystallized around the boat. The ice floe crackles some more, and long prismlike icicles extend vertically out of the surface, locking the boat into place. Slowly the icy fingers twist the boat around and the ice floe with it, until the broad side of the vessel is exposed to you and the others. The soldier manning the spotlight swivels it around to keep you illuminated. You wince as the glare momentarily blinds you.

"That spotlight is insufferable, Rey," Lesley tells the mountainous boy. "I think it's lights-out for our adoring followers."

Rey grins his crazy grin and brushes past Bleak to get a good spot at the railing. He cocks his head to the side at what looks like an uncomfortable angle.

The spotlight bursts, spraying the man operating it with glass confetti. The other lights on the main deck pop one by one until the ship falls into darkness.

Lesley clucks her tongue. "Too dark. I need to see what's happening on board."

Rey cocks his head to the other side. Fire bursts out of one of the portholes on the main deck, then another. This sequence occurs all the way down the row of portholes. One of the plumes of fire ignites a crew member. His shrieks echo over the divide, and he spills overboard. He smashes into the ice, where he briefly flails around until his body goes still.

You feel a strange admiration for the boy with the

dreadlocks. He's a creator of explosions—just like you.

As the flames consume the deck of the boat and men with fire extinguishers scurry madly to quell the growing fire, Thorne steps up to the railing.

"Yes," Lesley purrs. "Blow out the fire for those boys. Pretend their ship is a birthday cake."

Thorne's hands unfold as though he's about to conduct a symphony. His fingers swirl in the air, tracing concentric circles, small and slow at first, then gaining in speed and diameter.

Howling winds pick up over the stern, louder than any jungle storm that you've weathered. The clouds over the ship pulsate and twist until two gray daggers emerge. Their funnels grow thicker and longer, and soon the tornadoes touch down on the water's surface. Instantly the gray vortexes grow dark and pregnant with the ocean waters . . . and then converge on the ship.

The water from the dueling waterspouts does nothing to extinguish the growing fire. Instead, as the waterspouts gyrate and sweep over the deck of the ship, they snatch members of the crew one by one, sucking them up into the heavens. The two tornadoes approach each other on a collision course, and one man who had managed to cling to the railing now leaps overboard.

He makes it only halfway to the ground. His body hangs midair, his descent stopped abruptly as his limbs continue to flail. Then his course reverses as the two vortexes combine into one, and with one last scream he is ripped skyward. You wave at him as he vanishes behind a wailing screen of wind and water.

Lesley kneels next to you as the devastation continues. "Now, Rose, I'm sure this all must come as a shock to you and can't be easy to watch. But there's something you should know."

You want to tell her that it's not strange to watch at all. To you, death and destruction feel . . . natural.

"Remember the men who captured you from your home? Remember the days when you were forced to starve in that stone castle? Remember the men who chased you day and night through the jungle so you couldn't even sleep soundly?" Lesley looks sadly into your eyes, and then turns you by the shoulders so that you're facing the ship again. "The men who are responsible are on that ship." She pauses significantly. "And they're coming to get you."

The other three are watching you now. With their attention diverted, the vortexes are retreating into the sky, and the ice around the ship is melting, and the fire on deck has begun to die. Part of you wants to run, terrified, back to your cabin and cocoon yourself in the hammock for as long as you can.

But then you realize that if the other boat continues to pursue you, you may never be safe. You may never be free.

You may never get home.

And while part of you is crying out, *I don't want to hurt anyone . . .*

. . . there's a second voice even deeper, even louder, even more compelling saying, *Yes, I do.*

Thorne approaches you now, though he doesn't kneel next to you like Lesley did. "I've heard about you, you know," he says. "I hear you have quite the gift, that you can open a door between worlds." His face disappears behind a cloud of cigar smoke, but when it reappears, his eyes are gleaming. "Why don't you send those men someplace else? Somewhere . . . scary?"

Yes, you think. Somewhere *scary.*

You step around Thorne, and then past Rey. Bleak moves aside as you approach the railing.

You focus on the residue of hunger, the knot in your stomach from all those days as you starved in the fortress, the feeling of being caged within the concrete walls. You remember the nights when you were curled up in a tree, trying to sleep without a blanket while the jungle rains hammered down on you.

Then you draw in a deep breath and seize control from the wrath of war that has until this moment always been the master of you, pulling your reins whenever it wanted, to punish those both wicked and innocent.

Today you are the master.

Today the wicked shall be punished.

You blink.

Somewhere from deep in the water you hear a muffled *boom*. For a moment the air around the other ship shimmers and the melting ice trembles. The flames crackle and the breeze goes still.

A glow pulsates beneath the ice. Slowly the other ship begins to spin on an unseen axis, like a whirlpool has opened up beneath it.

But this is no whirlpool. The light shining up from the depths explodes outward, puncturing a hole between this world and the next. Where there had been water before, there is now just a jagged rift in the air, a portal to someplace even darker than here.

The hull of the enormous ship drifts uncontrollably toward the black hole, along with all of the water around it. When it reaches the gash in the universe, the ship folds in on itself, metal and wood and flesh imploding into one ball of wreckage.

Then the nugget of destruction vanishes into the depths, carried over the falls into the oblivion below. The rift closes behind it so quickly that a plume of water jettisons upward in its wake, licking the underbelly of the sky. You don't even flinch as the water rains down on you and the others.

Lesley's moonlit shadow falls over you. She kneels on the floorboards beside you, wraps her arms around your waist, and squeezes you gently. "Good girl. They'll never hurt you again. With us you'll always feast until you're full, sleep until you're renewed, and live safely with people who are just like you. You'll have a place to call home with us in Miami." She taps you once on the shoulder for each of the last three syllables. *Mi-a-mi.*

Lesley leans in closer until her breath washes over your tangled black curls. "You have a family now, Rose. And pretty soon, when your big sister, Eve, learns that we've found you, she'll come to visit too." Lesley smiles uncontrollably. "Yes, she'll come to see our little Rose Wilde." She pats your hair, and her last words tickle your eardrum as she whispers:

"Our Wilde Rose."

Ash woke up with her face pressed against the tile floor.

The airport bathroom rematerialized around her, and her mind migrated from the Gulf of Mexico back to the terminal. From underneath the stall door she could see a pair of—thankfully human—feet standing in front of the sinks. Unless the Cloak had taken to wearing high heels, Ash was probably in the clear.

Ash was grateful to be lying next to the toilet, in case she lost what was left of her food court dinner. She still felt queasy, though she didn't know whether it was from seasickness or her sudden return from the dream in limbo.

Or maybe it was from seeing her little sister again for the first time since May. The littlest Wilde had appeared to Ash in visions before—all of them visions of destruction like this. But Ash had never actually entertained the possibility of searching for "Rose," if she was to adopt the admittedly catchy name that Lesley had chosen for her. Young as she was, Rose was clearly more dangerous and capable than the average six-year-old. And even if Ash could trust these visions of a girl she'd never seen with her own eyes, there was the fact that Rose had been in a different country until now, and Eve—crazy Eve—had been so adamant about finding her.

But those had all really been excuses, hadn't they? Ash had spent the end of her semester trying to preserve the normalcy in her life, and that had selfishly meant finishing out the school year, not scouring the globe for a sister she'd never met.

This new vision only complicated things. One moment, seeing the world through Rose's eyes, Ash had felt helpless and vulnerable; the next, she'd been forced to watch Rose open up a portal into God knows where, then crumple an enormous boat like a piece of paper.

Paper, Ash thought, rubbing her eyes. She bolted upright and burst out of the stall. The middle-aged woman at the sink jumped when the stall door slammed noisily against the wall. Ash probably looked crazed, coming right at her out of the stall, but she didn't have time to apologize. "Do you have something to write with?" she frantically asked the lady. "Or write on? It's an emergency."

The woman's hands fumbled nervously in her pocketbook until she produced a Sharpie and a crossword puzzle that had been torn out of a newspaper. She passed them over to Ash and then held up her hands as she backed away. "Just keep them," she said. Then she disappeared through the bathroom door.

In the yellowed margin of the newspaper, Ash doodled the number that had been on the outside of Rose's crate on the ship: HV-48967-1. It wasn't exactly a solid lead, but it was at least a starting point. Ash folded the cross-word once, twice, and then slipped it into the pocket of her dirty, torn jeans.

Ash had just exited the bathroom back out into the terminal when the intercom crackled on: "Now boarding rows one through fifteen on Flight 683, nonstop to JFK."

Ash pulled her mangled ticket out of her jeans. She was row fourteen, but made no move toward gate seven, where the other New York–bound travelers were lining up to board the plane.

Ash knew she stood at a crossroads. On the one hand, she held a plane ticket back to "reality," back to a pastoral life in the suburbs. There she could live out a predictable, hopefully mythology-free summer, playing bocce with her parents, languishing by the community pool, and forcing some boring but welcome normalcy back into her life.

On the other hand, the Cloak hadn't provided her with the vision of her little sister for nothing. Rose's future rested in the hands of Lesley Vanderbilt, a wealthy megalomaniac who had already interfered with Ash's life once back at Blackwood Academy. In just the short time Ash had interacted with her, Lesley had already proven herself to be both unhinged and violent. As far as Ash could simplify the eighty-year history between the Wilde and Vanderbilt families, Lesley had parasitically suctioned herself to Ash's life in three not so simple steps:

1) Lesley had inherited the legacy of hunting down Eve, to avenge the grandfather Eve had murdered in the 1920s during her previous life.

2) After mistaking Ash for the Polynesian storm goddess she was looking for, Lesley had endangered Ash, along with Raja, Rolfe, Ade, Lily, and Colt. (Although, in retrospect, Ash wouldn't hold endangering the last two against Lesley.)

3) And now, because Ash had refused to collect Eve for her, Lesley had kidnapped Ash's *other* sister—in hopes of luring Eve out into the open.

Who knew what Lesley had in store for the youngest Wilde? And if those three sadistic gods in the vision were on Lesley's payroll, who was to say their dark influence wouldn't mold and corrupt Rose into the same tortured soul Eve had become?

Now Eve was supposedly suffering in the Cloak Netherworld, imprisoned and alone. If Rose could really open a portal into their world like Colt had said, then finding Rose might be Ash's only hope of rescuing Eve.

Going back home to Scarsdale now would be to forsake *both* of her sisters. But going to Miami . . .

Change of plans, Ash thought. She unconsciously reached toward the floor for her bag before she remembered that she didn't have one. Everything she'd brought with them had been in Colt's saddlebags on the Nighthawk, probably destroyed in the car wreckage.

Ash flipped open her phone, which had two missed calls and a voice mail from home. Her father picked up on the first ring. "Ashline, where the hell did you go?"

"I know where Eve is," she blurted out. It wasn't entirely the truth, but it was close enough that Ash felt only the first rumblings of guilt.

There was a long pause on the other end. "Is she okay?"

Well, she's potentially trapped in hell with some oily creatures that no one seems to understand, but other than that . . . "She's fine." After all that the family had gone through, it hurt Ash to have to bend the truth like this. But if she was going to obtain her parents' blessing to go looking for the other Wilde, she would need to sell this convincingly. "Granted, the lead I have isn't much—just a city—but I need to go right now."

"Just tell me everything you know." Thomas Wilde's voice bubbled with an excitement Ash hadn't heard since before Eve had run away the first time. "I'll take the week off and buy a plane ticket immediately."

"Dad," Ash tried to interrupt him.

But her father just kept going. "Gloria," he said to her mother on the other end of the line. "I need a notepad and a pen!"

"Dad!" This time Ash screamed it, and her father went silent. "I have to go alone. Eve is skittish enough already. If we all show up at her doorstep wearing matching 'Welcome Home, Evelyn' T-shirts, she's going to run again."

"I'm her father." He sounded almost angry now. "I'm *your* father! I'll be damned if I let my sixteen-year-old daughter go scouring whatever dangerous streets your sister has stumbled into. Now, where is she?"

Ash took a deep breath. This next part was going to hurt. "When Eve came back to Scarsdale, who did she come to first? To you? To Mom?" She paused long enough to let it all sink in. "No. She came to school. To find *me*. Eve's been on the lam so long that she's grown to fear the word 'home.' If you don't let me do this—and now, before she runs again—we will lose her forever."

"I've lost one daughter already. I will not lose another one." His voice broke, but Ash could hear his will breaking too.

Ash knew she just needed to hammer the last nail home. "Dad . . . without Eve, without my big sister, I might end up lost too." A tear slipped down her cheek, because between all the lies and half-truths, this much was true.

This time the pause on the other end of the line was interminable. Finally her father's sigh of defeat was so loud that the receiver crackled on Ash's end. "You better call your mother and me every five minutes to let us know you're okay. Just tell me where I need to make the plane ticket out to."

"I love you, Dad," she whispered. "The ticket should depart from Portland, Oregon." She stopped in front of the flight prompter, and couldn't help but smile a little at the irony—the three-letter acronym for her new city of destination was "MIA."

M. I. A.

Missing In Action.

"Destination: Miami, Florida."

PART I:
THE SUN AND THE MOON

When the plane finally landed, Ash was still mentally back in the late spring cool of the Pacific Northwest. That is, until the airport's electronic door whisked open and the wall of hot air billowed inward. She staggered back into a family of four, who quickly skirted around her and walked into the outdoor oven as though they didn't notice the abrupt climate change.

"Out of the ice cube," Ash said, "and into the kiln."

On the bright side, she thought as she walked out into the humid high-ninety-degree air, she could at least be grateful not to have a bag to cart around.

By the time she finally flagged down a taxi, her body had gradually embraced the saunalike conditions, and she reminded herself, *You're a freaking volcano goddess. This weather should be your element.*

"Where to?" the taxi driver asked as Ash clambered

into the backseat. He peered around her, perhaps looking for a bag, and then seemed to appraise her dirty clothing. He raised his eyebrow.

"Um . . . ," Ash said. She hadn't even thought that far in advance—probably something she could have taken care of on the seven-hour flight between restless naps. And it wasn't like the taxi driver could just type "Explosive Little Girl" as a destination into his GPS. No, she needed a home base first. "A hotel would be a good place to start." It sounded more like a question when it came out of her mouth.

"Ah, yes." The driver narrowed his eyes at her in the rearview mirror. "I will take you to the *one* hotel we have here in Miami." The driver sighed, flipped his Hurricanes cap around so that it faced backward, and then slammed his foot on the gas.

Twenty minutes of awkward cab silence later, they arrived in Miami Beach. The driver only smiled once he'd counted his tip, and he screeched away from the curb as soon as she slammed her door closed.

He had dropped her off in front of a high-rise, next to the Ritz-Carlton, that overlooked the ocean beyond. After a few minutes of exploration, she was in love with the hotel. It was beautiful, luxurious, and attentively staffed, and had its own tropical grotto in the back. But even though her fake ID listed her as twenty-five, she knew a nice place like this was likely to take one look at her rumpled clothing and see through her ruse. The fifteen hundred dollars remaining in her bank account—all the money she'd hoarded last summer working as a paralegal at her parents' firm—wouldn't go far at a four-star affair like this, and there was still food, clothes, and transportation to think about. And asking her father for money was just inviting him to get on a plane, if he hadn't already.

Instead she wandered across the street to a shady, run-down motel. The owner there barely looked away from his soaps on a little flat-screen, which looked modern and strange next to the peeling fleur-de-lis wallpaper and the yellowed ceiling fan. He just ran the card through the machine, pulled a key down off one of the hooks behind the desk, and handed it to her as though it were radioactive.

The room smelled like an ashtray, but she kind of liked it, a fresh break from the suburban comforts of Scarsdale and the pristine Blackwood dorm rooms. *Sad*, she thought, when a beachside motel felt like "roughing it."

Next on the priority list: replacing her belongings that had been incinerated in the car wreck. Ash felt the vaguest pangs of guilt that she had to spend half of the money left in her bank account on a new wardrobe. Everything—from jeans and tank tops right down to underwear and socks—was just as expensive in South Beach as she remembered it being in Manhattan. The one luxury item she did splurge on was a nice swimsuit, a red two-piece that cost practically as much as all of her jeans combined. She wrote it off as blending in with the locals and passed the cashier her plastic.

On the walk back to the hotel, it occurred to her that she'd left her cell phone off since the plane had landed. She juggled her bags until she had a free hand to withdraw the phone and power it on. Sure enough, to her expected horror, there were five voice mails in her in-box, four of them from her mother, along with a text message from her father that simply said, "Call your mom."

The fifth voice mail was from Ade. It began with a long silence during which she could hear only the patter of rain and canvas—the thunder god must have been calling from his tent on the construction site in Haiti. When he finally spoke, his voice was as deep as a chasm, and as hollow, too: "Today would have been his seventeenth birthday." Another long pause. "I miss him." Then he hung up.

Ash closed her eyes and tried to imagine what Rolfe would be doing today if he were still alive. She pictured him at the beach, sitting on the hood of his station wagon, watching the first rays of dawn spilling over the Pacific. There was still so much about the Norse god of light she didn't know. So much she would never know. All because of Lily.

With Rolfe dead; Lily rogue; and Serena, the blind siren, as strange as ever; Ade and Raja were the only two gods left who could understand what Ash was going through.

In the end Ash could only bring herself to text Ade back: "I miss him too."

Ash allowed herself a shower and a change of clothes back at the motel before she headed off to Ocean Drive in search of some dinner—and answers. Ocean Drive, true to its name, was a long strip of restaurants on one side of the palm-lined road, with the beach and ocean beyond on the other. At five p.m. many people were just getting up from their lunches at the sidewalk bistros, polishing off appetizers and oversize mojitos.

Ash found a club down by Tenth that was fairly empty, and slipped into a bar stool directly beneath a ceiling fan. The bartender, a middle-aged Cuban man, was hunched over the counter, staring off into the rafters. Despite his age he had a symmetrical beauty and a chiseled body that seemed to come standard with anyone who worked this part of the strip. A tattoo of a crucifix on his neck poked just above his collar, and he wore a name tag that identified him as Osvaldo.

When he finally noticed her, he asked with his slight accent, "Just here for a drink, *chulita,* or do you want to see lunch specials too?"

"Lunch specials?" Ash echoed. She pointed to the wicker clock that was half-hidden behind a row of multi-colored vodka bottles. "It's almost six!"

Osvaldo grinned. "Still on New York time? Things run on a different schedule around here."

Ash threw up her hands. "I give up. Is my accent that obvious? Am I really that transparent a tourist?"

"Relax—everyone's basically a tourist in South Beach.

And when I say that, I include half of the people who live here." He slipped a dinner menu in front of her. "In any case, once your jet lag wears off, commit this to memory: breakfast at noon, lunch at five, dinner at ten, sleep at dawn."

"That a rule, or just a general guideline?"

"I can give you some lessons on how to better blend in. For instance, when I ask what you'd like to drink, you say . . ."

Ash bit her lip. "I'll have a Diet Coke?"

Osvaldo sighed. "I know a lost cause when I see one. At least order something with a lime in it next time." He scooped ice into a pint glass and pressed a button on the back of the soda nozzle.

Now that they were building a rapport, Ash figured it was a good time to fish the waters for some answers. "So if I can ask some more touristy questions, I was just wondering . . . if I were a cargo ship coming into harbor in Miami, where would I go?"

Osvaldo looked up. The cola overflowed. "You call *that* a touristy question?" He dried the sides of her glass the best he could before he slid the soda across to her on a coaster. "You come to the most beautiful city in America in the middle of the summer, while half-naked gorgeous people walk up and down the beach across the street, and your first thought off the plane is, *Where can I find incoming cargo ships?*"

Ash sipped her cola with the most innocent expression she could muster, then shrugged. "I'm a sucker for sailors, I guess."

"Well, if you want to go chase deckhands, I guess you can lurk around the Port of Miami. That's where all the big ships come in. Maybe you'll come to your senses and decide to take a cruise instead."

"And what if I were a smaller ship?" She stirred the straw counterclockwise. "Maybe one that wanted to fly under the radar."

"Listen," Osvaldo said, suddenly serious. He checked on the few stragglers still at the bar—a couple canoodling a few seats down at one end, and a middle-aged man in a Hawaiian shirt—before he leaned over the counter. "I'm not an idiot. I see a girl like you come through the door, and I don't bother to check your passport, because I know a lost soul looking to have some fun when I see one. But I'm not about to let some high school student go prancing about in seedy areas by herself like some sort of mouse that wandered into the cat's lair."

Ash pushed her drink aside. Nothing ever went the easy way. "Give me your hand," she said impulsively.

"Are you . . ." Osvaldo shook his head. "Are you coming on to me now? Because you're my daughter's age, and Mrs. Osvaldo has a *nasty* temper when she gets jealous."

She held out her hands, palms up. "Just do it."

Osvaldo toweled off his wet hands, and with a last self-conscious look at his few remaining customers, he placed his sun-freckled hand delicately into her own, so that this fingers just barely tickled her palm. She took her other hand and placed it on top of his so she was cupping it between them. She closed her eyes.

Just as she had been learning to do over the last two months, she reached into her soul and found the magical valve. Only this time, rather than wrenching it on, she was careful to tweak the valve just a little bit.

When she opened her eyes again, the warmth radiated out of her palm onto Osvaldo's hand, just the first whispers of heat, like the sun emerging from behind the clouds. The bartender's face contorted with surprise, and he instantly started to retract his hand. But then he suddenly relaxed, and allowed it to bask in the strange warmth.

She blinked, and the valve twitched off. She opened her hands to allow Osvaldo to take his own back, but at first he just let it linger there. When he finally pulled it away, he held it out in front of him like he didn't know what to do with it. "You hear of such things, but you never . . ." He trailed off and peered at her as though he'd forgotten that the world could still have surprises in store for him.

Ash could see the condensation that had formed on the outside of her Coke glass, like a liquid kiss. "Not everything is as it seems," she said. She hoped that she'd done the right thing, revealing herself to this near stranger. She'd always thought she was a good judge of character when it came to whom she should and shouldn't trust, but if Colt and Lily were any indication . . . Still, she was here to find her sister, and she didn't have the time to sweet-talk answers out of reluctant bartenders. "Now," she said, "I need to know where I can find those little boats."

Osvaldo held up a *One minute* finger to the customer in the Hawaiian shirt who was trying to flag him down. "Miami River," he told her after a brief hesitation. "Parts of it are nicer now, but some smaller boats still dock in marinas upstream, closer to Little Havana. But I swear to God," he said with intensity, his accent thickening, "if I turn on the news tomorrow and I see your face among the missing . . ."

"Thank you," she said. "You've been both helpful and knowledgeable."

He held up his cell phone. "Your dinner is on the house if you'll call Mrs. Osvaldo and tell her that."

But at the mention of food, her own hunger made her think of Rose again, the persistent throb of starvation Ash had suffered while seeing the world through the little girl's eyes. It was hard to complain about her meal of airplane cookies and soda when her six-year-old sister had spent a month roaming the jungle and scavenging off the forest floor. With Rose potentially only a few miles away, dinner was going to have to wait. Despite everything that had happened with Colt yesterday, having a sense of direction felt . . . good.

Osvaldo caught her smiling. "For someone who's skipping the beach to hang out by the docks, you sure are grinning like a jaguar child." He chuckled. "You happy to be here, or are you just happy not to be somewhere else?"

"A little of both, Osvaldo. A little of both." She dropped a five on the counter and stood up. "How long do you think the taxi ride to the river will be from here?"

"Not long . . ." He tapped his chin. "But if you'll allow me, can I make a suggestion for more creative transportation?"

As the wind billowed through her helmet and the crisp bite of Biscayne Bay washed over her, Ash couldn't help but have flashbacks to just yesterday, sitting on the back of the Honda Nighthawk with Colt. But now she was on the opposite coast, on a motorized scooter alone, and cruising over a long bridge into who knew what sort of trouble.

This is the way I like it, she realized. *On my own.*

She didn't want to have to ride through life on the back of a bike, with her arms strapped around someone else. She wanted to be at the helm.

To the south of the causeway, on her left, a mountain of cargo containers glowed in metal bouquets of blue, green, and red under the low angle of the setting sun. Beyond that she could see a few mountainous cruise ships at dock. The ship she was looking for was probably more on the petite side, and hopefully docked on the Miami River where Osvaldo said it might be.

But where to begin? The boat could have already

pulled into dock and unloaded its cargo: Rose. Ash still had both sides of the five-mile-long river to canvas in her search. The odds certainly weren't leaning in her favor.

The causeway wound to the north until her phone's GPS indicated her upcoming exit, and she snagged the off-ramp. Music blossomed from Bayfront Park's amphitheater on her left—a concert that Osvaldo had suggested as a last-ditch attempt to derail her mission. She tapped her toe on the footboard to the rhythm of the song, a tune she recognized from the radio. Some stupid pop number with lyrics that basically boiled down to getting hammered and throwing yourself at every man in the nightclub.

She was almost glad to be scouring the river instead.

Ash had pored over a map of the city as she was renting the Vespa back in South Beach. To the south side of the river was Little Havana, a sweeping neighborhood that was apparently home to a large population of transplants from Cuba and Latin America. Directly north of the Miami River were a university, a hospital, a college, some hotels, and a convention center. Neither side of the river screamed "crime-ridden" to Ash, but the boat *had been* coming from Central America, and if she were smuggling a six-year-old war goddess into the country, she'd probably avoid the side in plain view of a convention center.

Much to her annoyance, there wasn't just one road that ran the full length of the river's south side. Instead she had to tediously carve her way in and out.

After four continuous miles of weaving roads and silent docks, she was beginning to feel like she was running a fool's errand—and she wasn't just thinking of her combing the Miami River in search of the boat, but her journey to Miami in general. Yes, Lesley had her little sister, and yes, Rose was just a little girl. But Ash had come to Florida with only two leads: the number on the boat's container, and the port of destination. She might as well have been searching for a coconut shaving on a glacier.

She was about to turn around and call it a night, maybe even have takeout delivered to her motel, when her eyes abruptly began to boil. The heat escalated until her vision grew bleary with tears, and she jerked the Vespa over to the side of the road.

When her line of sight cleared, she found herself standing in a world without color. Everything that lay in front of her—the shipyard, its compound of metal-sided buildings, the yachts and speedboats in the marina ahead—had been muted to shades of gray and brown, and even the dusky sky had been poached of its color.

No, not everything, Ash realized as she leaned her Vespa against one of the dock buildings. In the gravel there were two parallel lines of fading orange, trailing off into the marina grounds beyond.

Ash couldn't spot any dockworkers in the empty shipyard, so she followed the ember trail all the way to a boathouse in the back, where the lines stopped just behind the tires of a waiting van. The moment she touched the van, color leaked back into the world around her and the heat trail in the gravel faded into the stone.

Ash rubbed her eyes. Hopefully the weird heat vision was a sign that she was on the right trail, and not an indication that she was going completely insane. It was increasingly hard to tell these days.

The main door to the boathouse was locked from the inside, so her only way in was through the opposite end, where the boats exited. She had to skirt along the thin ledge between the dock walls and the river beyond. Up this close, the river water below had a green and brown tinge to it like mossy tree bark, and Ash prayed that she wouldn't fall in. Even fire wouldn't protect her from river pollutants.

Once inside the boathouse, she slipped quietly down the row of white midsize boats.

Four boats later, she found it.

It looked exactly as it had in the dream, and as she stared up at the two-bar railing, she had a flashback to her vision, to staring out of a child's eyes as the pursuing ship balled up into a nugget of steel and death and was swallowed by the wrath of a war goddess who didn't know any better.

Ash had to be sure, though. A metal gangplank had been extended from the starboard side of the boat down to the dock. She cursed the hollow clanging of her footsteps against the metal treads.

Once she had boarded the ship, Ash crept down the

hallway until she was standing in front of a familiar crate. She took the crossword clipping with the numbers and held it side by side with the actual numbers to make sure they matched. As she brushed the stenciled numbers and letters with her fingertips, it occurred to her that at one point her little sister had walked down this very hall.

For the first time since she'd had the original vision of Rose, Ash's sister seemed like a reality, not just some borderline nightmare that lay outside her realm of responsibility. In fact, Ash was beginning to feel down-right ashamed that she'd chosen to brush off the visions in favor of tennis matches, the school dance, and Colt. All of that felt so frivolous now.

Maybe she'd needed to lose one sister before she realized how important it was for her to save the other one.

She was so deep in reverie that it took her a full minute to realize there was a conversation happening inside the crate. She pressed her ear to the corrugated metal.

There were several voices, actually, and shuffling, too. Groans of exertion and deep breathing. It sounded as though the men inside were moving something heavy.

And they were coming for the door.

Ash scurried down the row of crates as quickly as she could, toward the port-side railing. The door to the crate slammed open behind her, and the voices exploded outward into the marina. She lost her footing on a slick section of deck and ended up scampering the remaining few lengths to get around the corner in time. She leaned against the outside of one crate and tried to listen as best she could.

"You resist again," a loud voice with a thick Hispanic accent shouted, "and I'm going to start cutting off fingers." There was the muffled sound of a fist striking flesh followed by coughing and sputtering.

Ash allowed herself a quick glance around the corner, hoping the shadows would hide her face.

Four men had emerged from the crate—one of them with a thick mustache and a suit, and three others with white button-down shirts rolled up to their elbows.

In their midst, restrained by the three underlings and shackled in heavy chains around his arms and legs, a figure in jeans and a dark black T-shirt was hunched over, recovering from whatever blow he'd just suffered. When he straightened up, Ash could see that he was tall, even taller than Colt—pushing up on six and a half feet. The giant had a solid, muscular build, and his tattered black T-shirt strained around his chest and arms. A dark mesh bag had been fitted over his head and cinched around his neck. Even without seeing his face, one thing was crystal clear:

This was not Rose Wilde.

"It's almost seven thirty," the man in the three-piece suit said as he checked his watch. "Should be plenty of time to get him to the factory before sundown."

"Sundown," Ash mouthed. Clearly some sort of hostage situation was afoot. Wouldn't it have been to their benefit to transport him at night?

"Do what you need to do to get him to the van." He made a shooing motion to the other men, two of whom secured the prisoner by his arms while the other steered him by his shoulders. "But remember, boss wants him conscious, so avoid the Chicano's face, eh?"

Ash was just starting to lean closer to the scene when she felt fingers slide through her hair and twist. She tried and failed to stifle a squeak as a hand yanked her to her feet by the top of her head. The follicles of her scalp screamed in pain.

She turned around just far enough to see her attacker. He wore a sleeveless T-shirt and couldn't have been older than twenty-one or twenty-two. His goatee was scraggly where his facial hair had yet to come in fully. But Ash was forced to take him seriously when she noted that his free hand had unholstered the gun from his hip.

"Whatchou doing here?" he grilled her in an accent that matched that of the man in the suit—Cuban?

She tried to untangle his fingers from her hair, but his grip tightened and he twisted her head roughly to the side.

She had to bite her lip to keep from squealing out again. "What the hell, bro?" she growled. "Can't a girl watch a sunset from a boat without getting scalped?"

"Wait a minute." The guard's eyes grew wide, and he released her hair, though to Ash's horror, a few of her dark hairs came away with his fingers. "You're her, aren't you?"

"What?" Ash asked, massaging her scalp, then realized she was asking the wrong question. *"Who?"*

He gestured quickly around the corner with the gun. "His little girlfriend. I've *heard* about you."

"Wait, I'm not—"

"I want to see them," he said.

Ash glanced down at her shirt. "Are you talking about my—"

"I don't got all day and I'm not playin'." He raised the gun and trained it directly between her eyes. "I *want* to *see* them. Take off your shirt."

She opened her mouth to argue, but he flicked the safety on and off to tell her that he meant business.

The bile crept up Ash's throat. She hadn't even removed any clothing, and she already felt violated by this little bastard. She didn't know who he thought she was, but she could only assume what he was after. Her choices, however, were limited. She didn't trust her abilities enough to melt a bullet in the chamber, and heating up his hand could cause him to misfire.

Her hands were shaking as they made their way down to the first button, and then the second. Strangely, however, she noticed he wasn't looking at her breasts. He was staring intently at her shoulders. In fact, he was so focused on the nape of her neck that his gun was just ever so slowly drifting off target.

When she hit the third button, she couldn't take it anymore—she struck.

She lashed out with her mind at the handle of the revolver. The guard screamed and dropped the gun. He held up his now crimson palm, which was bleeding in patches. Some of his skin was still stuck to the red-hot handle of the gun.

Ash seized the opportunity and landed a kick to his knee, dropping him. Then she followed up by slamming his head into the railing.

However, the blow to his head didn't put him out like she thought it would. He snaked his arm around the back of her leg and ripped her feet right out from underneath her. She landed hard on the unforgiving wood, and the air exploded out of her lungs.

The guard started to crawl toward her, and Ash lashed out on pure instinct. Her boot caught him square in the nose. His eyes had a moment to look at her, startled, before they lost focus and his eyelids drooped. His head landed on the wooden deck with a sickening thud.

Ash slowly lifted herself off the wood and massaged her side. The rib she'd broken during her confrontation with Eve in May was still tender.

She peeled the guard's face off the deck. He was breathing, but his nose was visibly bent and there were splinters now protruding from his forehead. After what he'd done, she had to resist the dark urge to roll his body into the water to see if he floated.

The four men and their prisoner were nowhere on the deck of the ship when she looked back down the row of metal crates, nor were they even in the boathouse any-more, she discovered after a little exploration. She took off running past the line of boats and exited out into the dockyard.

The van was just pulling away down the gravel drive. At first she just watched it barrel down the alley toward the main drag. Reflecting back on all the trouble that had ensued a month earlier, after she'd rescued Serena out-side the Bent Horseshoe Saloon, she couldn't help but ask herself, Was she really about to interfere with yet *another* kidnapping in a windowless van?

Yes, she realized, and dashed around the building to where she'd stowed her scooter. *Yes, I am.*

She snapped her helmet on and twisted the key in the ignition, and the little scooter rocketed off, sending a fountain of gravel and dirt pluming out from under the tire and onto the boathouse wall.

Almost as soon as Ash pulled out onto the river drive, she had to veer to avoid an oncoming SUV. The driver blared his horn, and Ash offered him an apologetic wave as she cut across both lanes to keep up with the van, which was disappearing down a back alley.

Ash tried as best she could to take a cue from all of the espionage movies that she'd seen, and kept the Vespa a few spans behind the van, but never took her eyes off the license plate. When the van barreled down a narrow side street, Ash slowed to let it extend its lead. The Vespa rattled over the uneven stones, and she earned her fair share of looks from the local residents, who were enjoying the summer heat outside of their apartments and houses. A few women crossed their arms in their fold-out chairs and appraised her like a king might regard a beggar in his court. A circle of five men in wife-beaters was throwing dice against a wall and into a chalk-lined circle, where the results caused one cheer and four groans.

Ahead the van rolled to a stop in front of a corner building with a low archway. Ash let the scooter drift to the right and parked in the shadows. Two boys clucked their tongues at her as they walked past. Ash avoided eye contact and gave them the finger.

At first she wasn't sure how the men in the van were going to do the unloading. The street was far from desolate, and if the locals considered a Polynesian girl on a Vespa worthy of their attention, then a giant bound and shackled like a medieval prisoner would definitely pique their curiosity as well.

The van did a three-point turn so that its tail end rolled right into the overhang. The fit was so snug and the van maneuvering so graceful that Ash figured this wasn't the first time they'd used this covert method of unloading.

When no one emerged from the van after a minute, she edged down the plaster wall. The glare from the streetlamps moved off the windshield enough for her to see that there was no longer anyone sitting in the driver's seat. They must have all slipped out the back.

The sign over the archway read ROJA'S CIGAR FACTORY, and a half-size statue of a butler smoking a cigar guarded the entrance. The same ROJA'S CIGAR emblem decorated the van's windowless side paneling.

Ash took one moment outside the van door to ensure that no one was watching her. She also acknowledged that what she was about to do outshined anything else she'd done in her life in terms of stupidity. And then she opened the driver-side door, slipped in, and crawled out the back.

The metal-striped wooden door to the cigar shop was still ajar, and Ash squeezed through the opening, for fear that the door might squeak if she pried it open any farther. Inside, the front of the shop was completely dark. A soft glow emanated from the computer screen above the cash register, illuminating a glass container that housed a collection of stainless steel lighters and cigar clips. The shop had an earthy sweet smell that would probably cling to Ash's clothes and skin long after she left.

The voices were coming from around the corner (not to mention the faint clinking of chains tapping together). She passed the wall of cigars for sale on her way toward the passageway in the back, which was cloaked with a single drape. The curtain was backlit with a neon blue glow, and Ash prayed that the kidnappers weren't working for the fiery blue-eyed Cloak.

Ash lowered herself onto her belly and crawled forward until her head poked under the curtain's other side.

In the spacious room beyond, a series of circular velvet booths lined the wall to the left. But the real attraction was on the right side of the room. It was a humidor, a special room with controlled humidity and temperature designed to store and preserve cigars, which Ash knew about only because her father was an aficionado (a habit her mother loathed). This one in particular had two glass walls and a glass door that was open a pinch.

Presumably the humidor's other two walls were lined with cedar and housed a high-end cigar collection, but Ash couldn't tell, because she was too distracted by the scene happening inside.

The prisoner dangled from the middle of the room, upside down. The chains around his feet had been strapped to a hook on the vaulted ceiling, and he swung helplessly back and forth.

The three thugs stood at attention in the corners of the room, and the man in the suit was pacing circles around the prisoner. But most interesting of all, Ash finally discovered the source of the buzzing and the blue light. They had set up a network of ultraviolet lamps around the humidor, all facing up and onto the prisoner to spotlight various levels of his body.

The man in the suit knelt down, loosened the bag over the prisoner's head, and tugged it off.

The prisoner—the giant—was a teenage boy. It was hard to tell in the eerie UV light, but Ash approximated him to be close to her own age and possibly of Mexican descent. He had long shaggy hair that formed a floating mane around his upside-down head. Even though his life was clearly in jeopardy, there was something about the two-tiered dimples to either side of his mouth that made him perpetually look as though he were about to laugh.

The suited man slapped the prisoner's face lightly. *"Oye, amigo,"* the man said gently. "We know that you and your little friend have been very curiously looking into our employer's affairs for the last month." He gestured around at the tanning lamps. "We even clearly know your weaknesses. All I want to know is why you were snooping around Mrs. Vanderbilt's boat like a little bloodhound before we caught you."

"Mrs. Vanderbilt's boat?" the boy said with mock surprise. "Shit, I thought I'd climbed aboard a Disney cruise."

His interrogator actually laughed. "You're a funny man, stranger." He slipped on a pair of brass knuckles that he'd taken from his pocket. "It almost pains me to have to knock some seriousness into you."

He turned fast and slammed his armored fist into the prisoner's stomach. With a spasm of pain the boy's body convulsed upward into a macaroni shape before gravity ironed him back out into a straight line.

"Okay, okay . . . but first . . ." The boy wheezed between breaths. "Just . . . answer me . . . one question."

The man leaned closer so he could hear the boy.

The boy cocked his head upward. "How long . . . did it take you . . . to grow . . . that mustache?"

This time the man struck him across the face. The prisoner's head twisted ninety degrees, and when it came back to the front, blood dribbled out onto the floor.

The man took off his jacket and draped it casually over one of the back tables. "You know," he said as he rolled up his sleeves, "I really have no pressing engagements to go to. *Mi esposa* is giving me headaches about choosing a high school for the kids, so between you and me, I'd much rather be here than at home . . . and I don't mind working on my tan under these lights."

Ash knew she had to intervene somehow, and soon. She wasn't entirely sure what the UV lamps were for, but they seemed important. Besides, they were the only things lighting the windowless room. A cover of darkness would give her an edge if she was going to make a move. Scorching the circuitry to one of the lamps wouldn't be a problem, but were her powers fine-tuned enough to sabotage all five of the lamps simultaneously?

Then Ash noticed the electrical cable snaking out of the humidor's entrance. It plugged into the wall three feet to her right.

It looked like a more conventional approach was in order.

Ash slithered across the floor and wrapped her hand around the plug. Before she pulled, she hesitated long enough to ask herself—was this really her fight? She could crawl safely away, place a call to the police, and then take the Vespa back to her hotel.

It occurred to her, however, that these men were on Lesley Vanderbilt's payroll, and therefore at least *some-how* related to her sister's kidnapping. And if that wasn't enough incentive for her to get involved, the man in the suit was now lumbering toward the prisoner, ready to strike again. He pulled back his fist.

Ash ripped out the plug. Instantly the electric buzz of the UV lamps hissed off and the humidor flickered into darkness.

The panicked shouts started almost immediately. The man in the suit yelled, "Get those lamps back on, you fools," and Ash heard slapping along the glass as his three underlings struggled to find the door.

Then she heard the rattling of chains. Something snapped.

A silhouette appeared in the door frame. One of the men had found his way out and was following the extension cord like a lifeline, heading right to where Ash was crouched. She saw him stop and squint into the darkness, finally noticing Ash's outline in the shadows.

A massive hand clamped down on his shoulder and dragged him back into the darkness. The door slammed closed behind him.

Ash took a few cautious steps toward the lightless humidor. Inside she could hear muffled shouts, growing more frantic, and then the *thwack* of fist on flesh. A gun discharged once, twice, in successive loud pops, and when it fired a third time, the glass in front of Ash shattered.

The bullet buried itself in the cigars not far from her head.

Shortly after, a man flew through the air and landed at Ash's feet, out cold before he could feel the glass shards stabbing into his back.

Ash's eyes gradually adjusted, and she stepped closer to the humidor, where she could just barely make out the brawl inside. A second underling was already draped, unconscious, over a bench in the back. The boy prisoner grabbed the third by the hair on his head and smashed his face into the glass, which spiderwebbed on impact. Meanwhile, the boss came at the prisoner, swinging with his brass knuckles, landing two hard blows on the boy's spine.

He might as well have attacked a brick wall with a Popsicle stick. The boy just laughed, grabbed his attacker by the throat, and carried him across the room. The boss's heels dragged limply beneath him until the boy forcefully sat him down against one of the cigar shelves. While the man struggled to get free, the prisoner quickly tethered a length of broken chain around the boss's neck and one of the shelf's support beams, tightly enough to secure him in place, loosely enough that he could still breathe.

"Hey, guardian angel."

It took Ash several seconds to register that the boy was talking to her. She pointed stupidly at herself. The boy must have been able to see her well enough through the darkness, because he laughed and continued, "Yes, you. Think you can find a light?"

"Sure," she managed. She groped around the wall near the door for a bit until she found the switch, and winced as the halogens over the humidor sizzled on.

In the short time it had taken Ash to locate the lights, the prisoner had blindfolded the man in the suit and bound his hands behind his head with another chain. The large boy gave her a comical wave, far too casual for someone who'd just been tortured, and Ash laughed when the remaining links of his broken handcuffs jingled. She caught him giving her a quick up-and-down while he leaned against one of the cigar shelves.

Then again, her first instinct had been to check him out as well.

Prisoner boy was hot.

He grabbed a handful of cigars and forced them between the boss's teeth, and when he was done, the man had a tobacco bouquet blooming out of his mouth.

As the boss attempted to spit out the cigars, the boy said, "Oh, come on. I gave you the expensive ones. You're just going to waste them like that?"

The man coughed the last of the cigars out onto his lap. "Vanderbilt won't just let you get away, you know."

"Then you can pass along a telegram, from me to her," the boy said. "That I'll snoop around her boat whenever I damn well please, and if she has a bone to pick with me about it, we'll find out how solid the construction is on that three-million-dollar hacienda of hers."

"Who's the bitch with you?" The boss allowed himself

a smile as he turned his blindfolded eyes in Ash's direction. "That your pet canary I've heard so much about?"

"Pet canary?" Ash mouthed to the boy.

He shrugged, which Ash hoped meant *I'll explain later.* "Don't own any pets," he said. "And I have an allergy to feathers."

"You two will pay for this," the boss said. "Nobody treats Raphael De La Cruz this—"

The rest of his words were lost as the boy cupped his hands on either side of Raphael's face, and whispered, "Sleep. . . ."

Raphael's mouth opened, but nothing came out. Whatever magic the boy possessed passed from his hands into Raphael's body. With a small shudder Raphael's chin dropped to his chest, and he fell silent, except for a light snoring and a whistle through his teeth. He was out cold.

Something buzzed to life behind Ash. One of the underlings had regained consciousness and was now wielding a single UV lamp he'd somehow gotten hold of while they'd been distracted with Raphael. He had the lamp aimed in the boy's direction, and the man's legs quivered as he waited for the boy to react.

Ash was instantly offended that the trembling man standing beside her didn't consider her a threat. So she reached across, put her hand on the back of his leg, and promptly set his pants on fire.

The UV lamp slipped out of his hands and shattered

on the floor. He shrieked and sprinted off into the store-front. It wasn't long before Ash heard the chug of the van's ignition and then the rumble of tires on uneven stone. She wondered whether he'd bothered to even extinguish his burning pants before he drove away.

"Well . . ." The boy was staring at her faintly smoking palm. "I guess that answers my first question."

"Your first question was whether or not I could light people on fire with my bare hands?" Ash leaned around him just to make sure that Raphael was actually asleep before she introduced herself. "I'm Ashline Wilde, by the way. Ash for short."

"Wesley Towers—Wes for short." His hand engulfed hers, and Ash was disgusted with herself for feeling a trickle of excitement when his other hand gently touched her elbow. "Actually," he continued, "my current ques-tion involves whether or not you have a getaway vehicle. Because I think our flame-broiled friend might be calling for backup as we speak."

Ash nodded. "Follow me."

Outside, the night had finally descended on Miami, but the oppressive summer heat was only beginning to vent into the clear sky. Once they had stepped out onto the street, Wes tilted his head back to the stars. As he drew in a deep breath, his skin pigment darkened ever so slightly. When he opened his eyes again, they swam with an inky black before the white coalesced again.

"Oh, no," she said with mock concern. "I've saved

a vampire. The UV lamps, the way you were hanging upside down, your murky eyes and almost erotic fixation with the night—"

Wes snorted. "I'm the Aztec god of night—Tezcatlipoca."

"Texting a cat with a what?" Ash asked.

He ignored her. "I draw all of my power from the night sky, power that increases the closer we are to a full moon. But during the day, and in environments that mimic the sun"—he jerked his thumb back at the cigar factory with the UV lamps—"I'm just like everyone else."

"That's not a bad gig, you know," Ash said. "To get to be human part-time."

"Yeah, well . . ." He touched his stomach gingerly where the brass knuckles had pounded him. "Not when someone's trying to make mashed potatoes out of you. Where's your ride?"

Around the corner two teenage boys and an apprehensive-looking girl were admiring the Vespa a little *too* fondly, but when they saw Wes approaching the scooter, they quickly changed direction.

Wes climbed on the front. Given his enormity compared to the tiny scooter, he looked like a bear riding a unicycle.

He held out his hand patiently for the keys, but Ash just fixed her hands on her hips. "Who made you driver?" she snapped. "Are we going to have to have a talk about how sexism is alive and well in the new millennium?"

"Or we can have a talk about how practicality and logical thinking are alive and well. I know where we're going, while you're *clearly* a tourist." He passed her the half-helmet, like it was a basketball.

She caught it and slipped it onto her head. "I have a GPS on my phone," she grumbled. But she slipped onto the back of the scooter and handed him the keys in silent agreement. "Where are we going, anyway?"

"To where I parked my Cadillac before I was abruptly captured aboard that stupid boat." He angled the Vespa away from the curb, and it began its *put-put-put* up the bumpy road. "Speaking of which, can I borrow your phone?"

She handed it to him, and he tapped in the numbers with one hand while he steered with the other. When the person on the other end picked up, he said, "Yeah, Aurora, it's me."

An anxious female voice echoed through the receiver loud enough for Ash to almost make out the words. Wes winced and held the phone away from his ear. It sounded like she'd been worrying.

"I got careless," he admitted, finally interrupting her tirade. "But I'm safe now, thanks to a little help from a friend." He glanced over his shoulder, and his eyes bubbled black again when he met Ash's gaze. "Yes. Like us."

Like us.

That was the exact moment when Ash had an

epiphany: When she'd left the West Coast for Miami, she hadn't escaped the insanity.

She'd just traded one supernatural stomping ground for another.

How many gods and goddesses could there possibly be? And wasn't there *anywhere* in the country she could go that wasn't overcrowded with them? Like the mall, or a ball game, or . . .

"Meet me at rendezvous point C in ten minutes," Wes finished saying to Aurora—whoever she was. He flipped the phone closed and passed it back to Ash.

"So," he said. They turned a corner out onto the parkway, and Ash recognized the Miami River alongside them. "You want to tell me how you ended up in the right place at the right time to be my guardian angel?"

"The short version," she replied. "Lesley Vanderbilt—who it sounds like you know already—kind of rescued, kind of kidnapped my six-year-old sister from Central America. When I went searching for her on the ship they used to smuggle her into Florida, I found you instead. The end."

"A story to tell the grandkids," he mumbled. "Well, I guess we're looking for the same person. My partner and I have been tailing Lesley and her cohorts for a while now. We knew she was looking to bankroll another god . . . but I would have never guessed it was a child."

"Bankroll another god?"

They turned onto a bridge, heading toward the north

side of the river. To the east she could see the tall, sleek skyline of downtown Miami, stalagmites of glass rising up to the sky.

"That," he said, "is a story that will take longer to explain than a five-minute Vespa ride. Your sister, is she a fire goddess like you?"

"Volcano goddess," Ash corrected him. "And no, she's some sort of war goddess, I guess. But more like a fifty-pound ball of destruction. She blows things up, and opens portals into hell. . . . You know, typical six-year-old behavior."

He was looking at her again, and frowning this time. "You okay back there, Pompeii? You're looking a little queasy."

And she was. She swallowed hard. Being on the back of the scooter again . . . "Last time I was riding behind someone, we got into a bad accident." She omitted the part about it being only twenty-four hours ago.

"Jesus," he whispered. "Was the other passenger okay?"

"Unfortunately, yes," she blurted out.

He shook his head. "You and the short versions of your stories."

They rolled up over a curb and into a little park that was boxed in by palms and shrubs on three sides but open to the south with a view out over the river. As they climbed off the scooter a ship was making its way under the bridge, a small yacht with people partying so heavily that their voices carried over the water into the park.

But Wes was looking up at the stars. "Ah," he said calmly. "Here she comes."

Ash couldn't help but scream as the girl fell out of the sky. Like a human meteorite, she landed in the dirt with such startling velocity that earth and grass spewed out from beneath the heels of her knee-high leather boots.

When the dust cleared, Ash was looking at a girl with a striking Mediterranean face, a Rapunzel-length braid, and a curvaceous body that might have made Ash envious.

That is, if Ash hadn't been too busy gawking at the girl's wings.

Not large fluffy light ones like the goose-down wings an angel might have, but sharp-edged demonic things, webbed like a bat's. They were speckled with dark patches, like the fur of a snow leopard, but when they passed in front of one of the gas lamps, they glowed slightly translucent.

Instantly Ash recalled Raphael's reference to the "canary," and how the boy guard back at the dock had wanted to "see them," while staring intently at her shoulders. (Ash still didn't feel bad for knocking him out; he was just a *different* kind of pervert.)

The winged girl didn't even notice Ash at first. She just took three giant strides across the park and struck Wes across the face with a hard slap.

"What were you *thinking,* sneaking aboard that ship during the day?" she snarled.

When Wes turned around, he was cupping his cheek gingerly but smiling. "You Italians and your quick tempers."

She crossed her arms. "Don't even start with the stereotypes. You don't see me blaming all of Mexico for your persistent ability to make rash decisions and *worry me to death*."

Wes cleared his throat and nodded to Ash.

Aurora turned. "Oh." Her wings slowly deflated and folded onto her back like a convertible retracting its hood. "Company."

"Aurora, this is Ash," he said. "She's a volcano goddess."

"Of course. Pele, I'd guess." Aurora smirked. "Ash, huh? Is your name just a cosmic coincidence, or did you burn down the house when your parents first adopted you?"

Ash shrugged. "Haven't seen any baby pictures of me melting coffee tables yet."

"Count yourself fortunate. I discarded the name on my adoption papers for my true name—Aurora, the Roman goddess of the dawn. My adoptive parents gave me an old family name that, to this day, I *loathe* and refuse to share with anybody."

"Alma," Wes mouthed to Ash.

"What brings a volcano goddess to our sunny beaches? And more importantly, to the rescue of this careless moron?"

"Ashline's little sister is the goddess that Vanderbilt smuggled in on that ship," Wes explained.

Aurora cupped a hand over Wes's mouth. "Unless you're Morgan Freeman, why don't you stop narrating the girl's story and let her tell it herself?"

"You guys make a cute couple," Ash said, hoping it didn't sound like she was fishing. Part of her really did hope they were together. The last thing she needed the day after a violent breakup was to entertain any sort of attraction to another god—tall, dark, and handsome though he might be. She was in Miami to find her sister, not to indulge in a rebound.

"We're *not* together," Aurora said.

Wes flicked her braid. "You know, when you deny it so quickly and make that same scrunched-up disgusted face you do when you see cheese, you hurt my feelings."

Aurora swatted his hand away.

Wes crossed the grass so that he loomed over Ash—Towers was definitely a fitting last name for him.

"I have to go debrief the canary on a few things." His hand touched her wrist, and she had to actively stop herself from taking a step forward. "There's something I think you should see, though. Tomorrow. Which hotel are you staying at?"

Ash told him, and he wrinkled his nose. "Really? That place? I hope you chose a second-floor room with a good dead bolt. Anyway, keep your evening wide open tomorrow and lay out a white dress if you have one."

"Right," Ash said, "because I always pack a wedding

gown for my trips to the beach. Why, are you taking me to prom?"

Aurora laughed so hard that she snorted. "I like this one, Wes. Can we keep her?"

"Never mind," he said. "I'll take care of everything. Just promise me"—that touch of his again, this time her shoulder—"that you'll scooter home safely."

She winked at him. "You're the one who ended up chained and masked in a cigar shop, getting a nice tan. I don't think it's me you have to worry about."

"*Mañana,*" he said. He backed away, allowing their eye contact to linger before he and Aurora started toward the opposite end of the park. "You're not going to fly back to the apartment?" he asked Aurora.

"As if I'd let you out of my sights again . . . ," Aurora said, before their voices faded off into silence.

Rather than heading straight home, Ash crossed the park until she was at the river's edge, and sat down, with her legs dangling toward the water below.

And as she looked at her hazy lamp-lit reflection in the water, she began to laugh. This was the second time recently she'd saved a boy from being chained and tortured.

"Let's hope I don't regret saving this one," she whispered to no one at all.

Back at the motel Ash climbed onto her stiff mattress, ready to put her first day in Miami to rest. Between the crappy AC unit in the window and the extreme heat of the Miami summer, it was far too hot to sleep under the covers, which was probably for the best. The quilt on the bed crinkled disgustingly whenever she moved, like it was stuffed with a layer of rice paper and shredded plastic bags.

She closed her eyes, but as she descended into slumber, she felt something strange taking shape in her mind. Maybe she was just delirious from exhaustion, but it sounded a lot like the echo of that final, eerie chord Colt had sung to her before she'd abandoned him in the forest. Whatever he had planted in her brain, she could now feel it digging its roots deeper into her memory, growing branches, unfurling leaves. And through it all the chord grew louder until it unfolded into a haunting melody, twinkling softly and assertively while it carried her off to sleep.

While the song played, Ash felt herself being drawn into an island of memories in a dark corner of her mind, a part of her brain she never even knew was there. Her last sensation before she drifted off was that she was falling, falling toward a single, stranded memory. It was from a day nearly a hundred years earlier, during her last reincarnation—

Back when she still had the same face, the same copper skin.

Back when she had a different name, a different life.

Back when a familiar fire still smoldered within her.

THE SCARECROW MURDERS

You always come back to look at this
scarecrow because it's not like the others.

All the others sag on their wooden posts, made tender by the rain of a thousand New England storms, wilted from years in the wet summer heat. Their flannel and denim have faded, and their stuffing spews out of holes pecked by the very crows they were sworn to protect against. Worst of all, they always seem to be facing slightly down, even though their winged foes come from the sky. Whether they're ashamed of the job they're doing, or just downright depressed, you'll never know.

But this one stands tall with intrepid lines, pulled taut arm to arm on its cedar crucifix. Its corduroys look freshly pressed, and the tartan could have come straight off the clothesline. The straw pokes out only at the knees, where the corduroys are knotted, and at the throat, puffing proudly out like a mane of chest hair.

Perhaps this is why this scarecrow looks arrogantly up and to the west, toward the setting sun.

Perhaps this is why Horatio McGrath has the most spotless crops in all of York County.

Perhaps this is why you almost feel guilty that you're about to burn this scarecrow alive.

"Are you absolutely sure he's gone to church?" you ask your older sister, who at fifteen years old—one year older than you—is boss in this jurisdiction.

Violet smirks. "He's a good Baptist. Now get a move on, Lucy, and throw some wood on that little stove of yours."

You stare at the scarecrow one last time and silently apologize to it. Then you drop down onto your hands and knees in the dry grass, which crackles under your weight. It's been an exceptionally dry summer, and it's been weeks now since there was a good rainfall. Even Horatio McGrath's famous maize, the sea of corn husks behind you, is seeing the first invasions of yellow and brown on its normal healthy green, the onset of wither.

Violet stands at attention beside the scarecrow. She begins in the theatrical voice that you've heard many times before—twelve times, in fact, once for each scarecrow that you've consumed in flame in the towns of Limerick and nearby Cornish.

But those scarecrows were just practice.

"Horatio Arnold McGrath." She holds her arms out as if she's reading from an imaginary parchment. "Otherwise known in these parts as the Big H.A.M., a man as ugly as his crops are spotless, flaunter of wealth, husband to a shrewish wife, and father to insufferable offspring." As she says the last one, you glance back at the McGrath residence, an imposing white farmhouse on the hilltop, and pray that Melinda and Mary are both at church with their father.

"The court of the Sisters Whitney has summoned you before us on charges of giving dirty looks to your neighbors, coveting your neighbor's wife"—your mother—"and leading a generally unpleasant existence. How do you plead?"

The scarecrow says nothing. It twitches in the breeze.

"Then on behalf of the tribunal convened, we find you guilty and condemn you to burn at the stake." Violet's eyes flash white. "Executioner ready?"

You slide your hands into the dry brush and take a deep breath. A wisp of smoke rises almost instantly from the base of the post. The heat comes with greater ease each time you tap into that vein of power you discovered running through you last year.

The fire catches and you take a step back. As you concentrate, the flames march up the post toward the crucified scarecrow. You watch with guilty delight as the fire sinks its claws into the knotted corduroy knees and starts a slow crawl up the flannel.

The process is too slow for Violet; she steps in and rips open the flannel shirt, sending the buttons showering over the nearby grass. The fire ignites the straw within, and the slow burn transforms quickly into a blaze, no longer your careful creation but a savage and uncontrollable beast.

"We deliver you unto the all-consuming fires of hell," Violet shouts over the blaze. The scarecrow's once-proud face wilts and turns its attention to the ground as it passes into the great beyond. "May God Almighty have mercy on your soul."

Then something happens that has never occurred during any of your previous executions: The fire has grown so hot that it has somehow devoured the middle of the scarecrow's post. The post cracks in half loud enough to send birds soaring off from a nearby tree in an explosion of black wings. Your victim crashes headfirst to the ground, and the grass around him ignites, tinder for the burning.

"Violet!" you shriek. "Put it out!"

Violet reaches for the sky and bunches up her face.

"Hurry up, Violet!"

"I—I can't," she stutters. "It's too dry! The rains won't come! Can't *you* control what you've made?"

You stagger back. The fire continues to creep out through the grass, an ever-widening bull's-eye with the blazing effigy at its center. "Maybe if it were a candle flame on a wick," you snap. "I can't contain *this*!"

"Then it's time to go," Violet says quietly. She tugs at your dress.

You point to the old stone well on the other side of

the blaze, and the metal bucket propped against it. "We can still douse it with well water before it hits the fields!" You start to skirt your way around the blaze.

Violet catches you by the elbow, her grip so fierce that you're sure it will leave a handprint on your skin. "We both know that it's too late." She stares deep into your eyes the way only Violet can. "Think about it. This never happened in any of the other executions. Maybe we should take this as a sign that God *wants* to punish McGrath for what he's done."

For what he's done.

Violet must be referring to your family tragedy last summer, but of course you have no proof that McGrath wronged your family. What you do have is suspicion. Memories. Dark possibilities. You picture the festival last year in the town center. You picture the hazy, distant but ill-intentioned sheen over McGrath's eyes after all that whiskey.

Mama's strange silence and insistence that you all leave.

Finding her crying in the barn later that night.

Finding her hanging in the barn a month later.

Violet's grip on your arm retracts. Her hold on you does not.

You don't look down, but you can feel the heat of the flames that are almost upon you. You nod at her. "Then let God's will be done."

The two of you scurry up the hill and past the imposing

McGrath estate. It's only when you're beyond the back of the house that one of the curtains parts and you see Melinda's sallow, sickly face watching you through the glass.

The dinner table is oddly silent tonight at the Whitney farm. Not that it's been all that chatty since Mama exited this world with the creak of a rope. Grace sits silently in the high stool Papa built for her. Papa moves the corn around on his plate. Even Violet seems to have retracted into grim silence—Violet, who normally laughs in the face of the law.

You always knew that Papa was the one who loved you more. The adoption had been his idea, when after five years of marriage he and Mama had remained childless. As the only surviving children from each of their families, they'd all but accepted that the Whitney and Carlson family trees had reached a mutual end.

Then a lobsterman, a family friend, was out setting traps just off Bar Harbor when he heard the crying. As his small boat approached a buoy, he found a wooden washtub snagged in the seaweed . . . and, inside it, two children who were clearly not Maine natives. One was nearly a year old and remained strangely silent even as the men pulled her up onto the boat. But you couldn't have been more than a few weeks old at the time, swaddled in an old stretch of canvas and wailing your little lungs out. The story goes that you had a mighty fever, that until they brought you below deck and out of the sun, your little body was burning up with a raging heat.

You wouldn't be able to appreciate the irony until thirteen years later.

When the lobsterman brought the girls to the Whitney farm (he never went to the authorities), Papa didn't consider how the color of your skin might change the way the neighbors treated the Whitneys. He didn't care that you and Violet were both girls; the farm was small, easy enough for Papa to manage without any strapping young sons. He just wanted a legacy in this world beyond his toils in the field before he ended up in the family plot across the road.

Mama did eventually grow to love you, though not in the unconditional way that your father did. She grew to love the sixth sense you seemed to have when it came to baking, how you knew exactly when the chicken or the bread or, on those lucky nights, the casserole had cooked properly. She grew to love the way that Violet's outlandish stories made everyone laugh, without realizing how that same skill would eventually allow Violet to blossom into a masterful liar.

Little Gracie was a different story, one that made even your buoy rescue sound like a typical adoption.

You were ten at the time. Papa always told you not to play hide-and-seek in the cornfields, but you played anyway. You had just found a gap in one of the cornfield lines and wiggled your way through, not bothering to think of what Mama would say about the dirt clumps on your dress.

You heard rustling through the stalks in front of you. Knowing that Violet would soon catch you, you decided to get the better of your older sister by scaring her first. So you plunged through the leaves and hurled through the last row of stalks with a battle cry, prepared to strike.

You nearly stepped on the baby. She crawled—no, slithered—soundlessly, naked, through the dirt, weaving between the stalks. Even as your foot came down next to her, she didn't even look up at first to see what monster the foot belonged to.

But then her eyes tracked up and saw you, and she rolled onto her back and gurgled. She had the same clay skin as you and Violet, the same sharp eyes, and even the beginnings of the same ebony curls you would never be able to control on humid summer days.

Without knowing where she came from, or how she ended up in this field, you knew one thing for certain.

The girl your adoptive parents would eventually name Grace was, just like Violet, your blood sister. And she'd found her way from faraway shores to the bowels of Maine to reunite with you.

Now the three of you sit with Papa at the squeaky little table with just the light of the setting sun filtering through the open window. These days you're the remainder of a strange and eclectic family that once felt whole but was left disjointed and sterile when you found Mama in the barn. It's like the one woman who'd always felt like the odd one out had somehow been a linchpin to your family's happiness.

"You're awful quiet," Papa says in the thick Maine accent the three of you somehow failed to adopt when you learned English. "All three of ya."

In the silence that follows, you and Violet exchange a look over the corn and potatoes. Grace gurgles. For a four-year-old, she's always acting more like she's two, and even though she does talk on occasion, you wonder whether she's really all there.

"Just at the end of my wick from playing out in the fields," Violet lies. She reaches for the butter. "I think I got a bit sunburned on my neck too."

This at least gets Papa to chuckle. "My island girls—a darker shade than the Maine natives, but still not impervious to the sun." His grin fades when he turns to you. He hasn't smiled at you in a long time. Does it have something to do with the fact that you were the one who found Mama? Sometimes you even have to wonder if he secretly blames you. But you know that's absurd. Papa has never looked on you with an ounce of resentment, even when you snapped his fishing rod in half.

"And what about you, darlin'?" He leans over the table. His hand finds yours, which is closed in a fist on the table, and he shakes it gingerly. "Did you sell that charming voice and quick wit of yours to the devil?"

You can't help but smile. "No, sir." You pat the top of

his hand, and then pull yours away so you can reach for the carafe of milk in front of Gracie. "The only way I'd let the devil at my voice," you say as you bring the carafe over your empty glass, "is if he pried it from my unwilling hands."

The bullet hits the carafe. The glass shatters over the table before you can even register that the deafening bang from across the room was a gunshot. The milk splashes over your face, and Papa cries out when a sliver of glass pierces his cheek.

Horatio McGrath stands in the open doorway with a rifle snug against his breast. The bloodshot eye that gazes down the sights of his barrel twitches uncontrollably. When he smiles, his teeth burn red from the wine. If the man weren't such an impeccable shot even when he's drunk, the glass carafe could have very well been your head. You drop the broken bottle neck onto the table.

"Horatio!" Papa shouts. He stands up and kicks the chair out from behind him. "What the hell do you think you're—"

McGrath flips the rifle from trigger to barrel, wheels back, and strikes Papa hard across the face with the stock. Papa hits the table on the way down. He grabs his head and moans on the floor, but he's still conscious.

"None of y'all move," McGrath says, returning the rifle to its perch against his shoulder.

Even Gracie stops fidgeting in her high chair. You're

too terrified to even wipe the milk from your face.

"Now, Phillip," Horatio says out of the corner of his mouth. He always speaks that way, even when he isn't chewing tobacco. "This community stood by you when you decided to adopt Satan's offspring, not once, but twice. We sympathized with your fruitless efforts to yield some real salt-of-the-earth children. I even allowed my girls to play with yours in the hopes of teaching your girls the fineries of American so-ci-e-ty."

Papa seizes the back of the chair and winces as he raises himself to a knee. "Save your sermons for mass," he wheezes, "and tell me why you've barged into my house, endangered my daughters, and cuffed a man who never raised a hand to you."

"Never raised a hand to me?" Horatio growls. "Maybe you haven't; but the fire-lighting hounds of hell that you call *daughters* managed to burn through half my harvest."

Papa immediately stops trying to get up and turns his gaze on you. He says nothing, but his eyes whisper, *Is this true?*

"Now justice has come to collect." Horatio stumbles a little bit on a loose floorboard, but his aim stays true. "You know, Phillip boy, if you'd just given Clarisse the child she wanted, like a real man, none of this would have happened. . . . Shame I had to fill in for you."

Your breath catches. Papa's grip on the chair tightens so much that you can hear the wood splinter beneath his hand.

Horatio sneers. "You mean you didn't even suspect?"

Papa draws himself up to his full height.

"When Clarisse sent herself back to her Maker in that barn," McGrath says slowly, "she took one of mine with her."

Papa screams and lunges for McGrath.

McGrath opens fire.

The impact folds Papa's body in two and carries him across the room into the stove, where he shudders once and lies still. His unseeing eyes glare up at McGrath.

At once Gracie is wailing and Violet is screaming, and you want to join them, but the heat within is devouring your voice. Instead you dive for McGrath yourself.

He doesn't have time to properly aim his rifle, but he shrugs you off hard with his shoulder, knocking you back into the kitchen table. It flips over along with you, sending corn and the extinguished lantern down onto the wooden floor.

The cold barrel presses into the side of your neck. "Any last words before I show you the same courtesy you showed to my scarecrow?"

"The same thing we told your scarecrow," Violet says from behind him. *"Burn in hell."*

McGrath hollers, and the rifle clatters out of his hands. You turn in time to see McGrath clutching his bloody thigh where Violet has plunged in the broken milk bottle. Before he can reach for the fallen rifle, you snatch the lantern. In your mind you picture a bonfire in a field. Instantly the wick inside the lantern ignites.

Then you smash the lantern against McGrath's face.

He howls again as the glass and fire torch his cheek, and he tumbles to the ground.

Unfortunately, he lands right on top of the rifle, and to try to pry it out from underneath him is just asking to get shot. So you cast one last tear-filled look at Papa's still form, slumped against the stove. Then you push Violet out the back door—it's safer if you split up for now—and pull the squealing Gracie out of her stool. With one arm curled around her little body, you hurdle over McGrath's moaning body and run out the front door onto the porch.

You start for the road, but you hear the kitchen door slam open behind you, so you change course for the shelter of the barn. A bullet hits the WHITNEY FARMS, EST. 1796 sign next to your head, doing to the Whitney name what it had just done to Papa.

Inside the high-roofed barn you drop Gracie and heave the massive door closed as two more rounds slug the wood next to the handle. Twilight streams through the holes.

McGrath's leg may be wounded, but with Gracie slowing you down, there's no way you can outrun him. You'll have to hide and hold on until Violet comes back with help.

You hoist Gracie onto your back so that her arms wrap around your neck, and you climb up to the loft using the rickety ladder. Up top the two of you scamper over the hay until you've found a nook in the straw. The last dregs of daylight stream through the gaps in the wooden walls. You press Gracie, who has fallen silent now, flat against the floorboards, and you make a small hole in the hay in front of you so you can peer down at the barn floor.

It doesn't take long. McGrath hauls open the century-old door, which squeals disagreeably on its track. His eyes take in the barn—the broken carriage in the far corner that hasn't been hitched to a horse since before the Civil War, the collection of old hoes and shovels lining the walls, the ungainly tractor that Papa purchased secondhand and never found use for in the fields.

Then McGrath's gaze slowly shifts to the loft. When he smiles, fresh blood dribbles from the gaping wound the lantern left on his face.

As you listen to his footsteps plod patiently across the barn floor, you tremble under the weight of the decision you have to make. If you try to take Gracie and flee, McGrath will catch and kill both of you.

But if you lead the monster away from her . . .

"Gracie," you whisper as the first step of the ladder creaks. You press your face into her hair, letting your tears wet her beautiful dark curls. "I will come back for you." A second creak. "And I love you very much."

You spring from all fours out of the hay and off the edge of the loft. McGrath stops climbing when he sees you. He lets loose a round with his rifle hand, but the bullet goes wild and pierces the roof.

You hit the floor behind the tractor, and now this steel beast is the only thing that separates you, the prey, from the predator. You press your back up against the chassis and risk a peek around the tractor's back wheel.

A shot hammers into the tire, which lets out its air with a defeated *poof*. A second round grazes the fuel tank. Gas begins to pour out onto the floor.

You hear jingling. McGrath must be reloading from his pocket, and you know this is your moment. You give one look back at the loft. Gracie is peering out at you, with her lip quivering and her face framed by the straw. You try your best to smile at her.

Then you swallow the vomit and fear and the memory of your dead father and kick off across the barn. The back door is so close, swinging loosely on its hinges, and you just have to make it outside before McGrath pushes another round into the chamber. . . .

Then the explosion.

The flames hit you from behind in a wall and propel you off your feet. You crash through the flapping door. Even with your back to the explosion, your vision glows white.

Next thing you know, you're outside on the grass, rolling in the dirt to try to put out the fire on your dress, which you can't extinguish with your mind because there's a dreadful ringing in your ears. Wooden debris rains down around you.

When you finally flip onto your back, you see the

ruins where the barn used to be. Fire streams up the one remaining wall like it's coated in kerosene. The top half of the barn, roof and loft included, has blown completely off. McGrath's bullet must have hit the tractor's gas tank or the leaking fuel—nothing else could have caused this sort of devastation.

There is a hand on your arm, pulling you back. "No," you shout at Violet, though your words sound strangely muffled in your own ears, as if you're screaming them through a pillow. "Gracie's in there! Let me go!"

But Violet just slaps you across the face with enough force to daze you, and then throws you over her back. You want to protest, but you're nauseous, and disoriented, and there's a flaming wreckage where the barn used to be, and Gracie is dead in the rubble, and Papa is lying on the kitchen floor. Oh, God, Papa . . .

Everything rolls to black.

You come to just a few minutes later in a sickeningly familiar cornfield—McGrath's plot. You're still slung over Violet's back. The field is a mess of blackened, flattened corn husks. Embers still burn hot in pockets everywhere, like fireflies nesting in the wreckage.

It's only when you see the charred remains of the scarecrow that you squirm until Violet is forced to set you down in the field. "We did that!" you scream, pointing at the scarecrow. "This is *our* fault! We have to go back for them, Violet! We have to go back! We . . ." You wrap your arms around your sister's ankle and then fall into sobs.

Violet's hand affectionately slips into your hair, then both of her hands cup your face so that you're looking up at her. "I know you don't want to hear this," she says, "but it's just you and me now. We're back in that wash-tub, anchored to the buoy, only this time no one's coming to help us." She leans closer and forces you to make eye contact. "We can only help ourselves. If you trust me, I'll make sure we stick together—always." She releases your face and holds out her hand. "Do you trust me, Lucy?"

You gaze one last time back over the McGrath household at the steady column of smoke rising into the night, circling the summer moon over the trees.

When you turn around, Violet is waiting patiently with a concern you've never seen before.

You take her hand. Her grip is strong, but there's a resolve in your own that you never knew you had.

Ashline woke up in what smelled like a mushroom cloud of cigarette smoke and wondered whether she'd passed out on the floor of a seedy bar.

But it was just her motel room, with the lumpy bed, the comforter that looked like it had been balled up in the corner of a basement for a few years, and the browning water stain in the shape of Arkansas directly over the headboard. She touched her forehead, which was damp, and couldn't decide whether she'd been feverishly sweating in her sleep or something had been dripping onto her face.

Then came the vague whispers of her dream from the night before, the ugly patchwork quilt of disjointed images.

The scarecrow.

The farm.

The fire.

The pain.

Ash popped into the cramped shower and let the hot tendrils of water massage her face and extinguish the last images of the burning barn. But the shower couldn't cleanse her of the sickening feeling that the dream was somehow real, not just a twisted historical nightmare.

Almost as soon as she exited the bathroom, there was a knock at the door.

She wrapped her towel more tightly around her. The knock on the door could mean that (1) the landlord was coming to tell her that her credit card had been declined, (2) Lesley Vanderbilt was here to kidnap her, or (3) her father had broken his word and flown down from New York.

"Please let it be Lesley Vanderbilt," Ash whispered, and walked over to the door.

She peered through the peephole in time to see the landlord, with his mullet and ripped jeans, waddling back to the staircase like a satyr.

When Ash opened the door to see if he'd left anything, the package immediately landed on her foot.

At first she was hesitant to open it. She couldn't find the sender's name anywhere on the box, just her own name and room number scribbled on a Post-it note. But then she spied an insignia written in black marker on the upper left corner of the cardboard: a pair of wings, and a moon.

She smiled and carried the package into the room.

After a short-lived battle between the packing tape and her nonexistent fingernails, she tugged the top flaps open so hard that a handful of packing peanuts popped out and littered her bed. The first thing she found after she rummaged through the Styrofoam was a white knee-length dress. She unfolded it and held it up to her body in front of the grimy wall mirror next to her bed. It was going to take a much-needed steaming in the bathroom with the shower on hot, but it looked as though it would fit her perfectly. Either Aurora happened to be the same build or Aurora and Wes had correctly guessed her size.

Beneath the dress she found two more items. One was a new GPS. When she booted it up, there was already a destination plugged in, a little museum icon labeled "Villa Vizcaya" in Coconut Grove.

The last item was an embossed invitation, the fancy kind that people sent out for weddings. But this invitation was for a gallery opening—and it was dated for tonight.

The invitation was illustrated with a beautiful Renaissance-style Italian mansion sitting on the waterfront.

VANDERBILT VENTURES PRESENTS:
THE WINDS OF CHANGE:

*A journey through new discoveries in Mesoamerican mythology,
recently unearthed by Vanderbilt Ventures,
and how the ruins of one culture
may prophesy the ruin of our own.*

~

Please join us for light appetizers and cocktails
7 p.m.
Main House and Courtyard

~

Presentation to follow
8 p.m.
Mound and Gardens

~

White tie event, entrance by invitation only

The invitation seemed fairly harmless to Ash. That is, until she read the last line, written in fine red print and nearly hidden beneath the lace border threaded around the invitation:

The gods walk among us

Next to the final message was the blurred silhouette of a human in motion, which might have been almost comical had it not been for the single eye that looked suspiciously like a blue flame.

But that wasn't all. When Ash flipped the invitation over, she found a sticky note that was written in the kind of nearly illegible scrawl that could only belong to a man . . . in this case, Wes:

Call this number when you arrive,
and wait by the entrance for me to come get you.
DO NOT ENTER THE VILLA ALONE.

—W

"Overprotective much?" Ash muttered. She'd dealt with Lesley Vanderbilt before, and unless the woman had somehow fireproofed her skin since the last time they'd butted heads, it was Lesley who should be hiding. Besides, Lesley had Ash's sister somewhere. If push came to fire, Ash wasn't above dragging the eccentric millionaire into a back room and roasting her like a rotisserie chicken until she turned over Rose.

Ash dropped the invitation onto the rug. *Looks like the party doesn't start for another eight hours.* She cast a look at the dress on her bed, then to the corner where her sneakers were looking especially worse for wear after her trip to the docks and the cigar factory.

Guess I have no choice but to go pick out shoes that will do the dress justice.

After all, it was all in the name of good camouflage.

Ash would have gone with something with a flatter heel if she'd remembered that she was taking the scooter to the gallery event.

Instead she discovered—almost as soon as she mounted the scooter—that Vespas were designed more for shorts and sneakers, and not for evening gowns and heels.

Still, with her gown bunched up to her thighs and partially flashing the commuters of Miami as she rolled over the bridge, she managed to follow the instructions of the GPS's butlerlike voice.

In fact, the shiny new GPS reminded her of several questions that had been stewing since the night before, particularly about her two new friends. What sort of day jobs did Wes and Aurora have that they could afford to drive a Cadillac, purchase expensive gadgets for relative strangers, *and* reside in a city with such a high cost of living? How could they work and still find the freedom to participate in deity espionage at night? And, the guilty pleasure question of the hour, what exactly was the relationship between the two of them?

The two security guards checking invitations at the Villa Vizcaya's main gates both looked amused by her gown and scooter helmet combo. One of them attempted to flirt with her while the other scrutinized her invite with extreme care, as if she'd forged it, before they let her pass.

She parked between two news vans and paused to do damage control on her helmet hair, using the polished windows of a silver Mercedes as a mirror. She held up one strand and twirled it around her finger. How was she just now noticing how long her hair was getting? She hadn't cut it since well before the events at Blackwood in May.

She sighed. There hadn't been much time to look at her own reflection since the new life she'd tried to build for herself had started caving in around her, one ceiling tile and support beam at a time.

Ash followed the trail of newly arrived guests through the tree-lined pathway leading up to the west façade of the villa, which was much more regal and imposing in person than Ash could have guessed from the little image on her invitation. To either side of the villa's entrance, the building rose up three magnificent stories to top-floor balconies. Every window glowed with a soft daffodil light against the gradually darkening sky.

Ash paused beside the fountain and opened her cell phone. Wes *had* told her to call him first and wait out front until he could escort her in. But she wasn't about to wait in the gardens for Wes to show up fashionably late. *He* was the one who had gotten caught by Lesley's Cuban mercenaries. *He* was the one they would probably be on red alert for. So she texted him "See you inside, vampire" and made her way into the villa.

The entrance consisted of three archways that opened up into a long open-air foyer—the loggia, according to the map of the grounds she'd studied earlier. The walls were draped in blue curtains, with flowered vases on pedestals and a curved roof to shelter the stone floors. Two hostesses were distributing bright red masks to guests as they entered.

Just great, Ash thought. The last time she'd gone to a masquerade ball, Eve had kidnapped her date—Colt—and Lily Mayatoaka had speared Rolfe through the heart. At least these masks were different. Where the masks at the Blackwood ball had looked like souvenirs from Mardi Gras, these were bright red, and almost serpentine, with feathers gathered around the face. And on the bright side, even though applying the adhesive mask to her face conjured horrible memories, at least it would partially disguise her if she bumped into Lesley Vanderbilt.

She continued to follow the general traffic into the stately entrance room, which was adorned with oil portraits painted in muted greens, then through a pair of open doors out to the arcade, before she finally exited into the open-air courtyard.

Twilight was just starting to descend on the terrace,

which was packed with a sea of men and women, all in white and ivory, with the exception of their red masks. Much like the city itself, the guests hailed from a range of ethnicities, but she had a feeling that Polynesians constituted only a statistically small portion of the guest list.

Ash snatched a glass of champagne off a passing tray. Her nerves were already starting to flare up, and a survey of the courtyard on the tips of her toes failed to locate either Wes or Aurora. She wondered how Aurora could wear a dress and still manage to hide her wings.

Ash was just about to give up and join the walking tour of the grounds that one of the curators was announcing from the south arcade, when she spotted Lesley Vanderbilt.

Even with the mask covering the top of her face, the woman was unmistakable. Lesley looked as though she'd aged five years since their last encounter on the opposite side of the country. Her hair had very evidently been dyed a dark brown, and the lines around her mouth creased deeply when she smiled at the man standing next to her.

Whether it was worry or obsession that had aged Lesley Vanderbilt, one thing was clear when her eyes flashed between the guests in the circle growing around her—she hadn't lost the dangerous edge that had given Ash the shivers last month.

Ash was so bewitched by seeing Lesley again in the flesh that she bumped into a waitress. She apologized, downed the rest of her champagne flute, and grabbed another from the tray before the waitress could wander off.

Perhaps it was the warmth and liquid courage from the champagne, perhaps it was some jungle instinct in her summoned by the tropical night air, or perhaps it was the first bubbles of her own family revenge starting to burst within her, but suddenly Ash was consumed with a seething disgust—no, flat-out rage—for the woman standing in the corner of the garden. Lesley had taken a quarrel from another century, which could have died with the people involved, and had stirred up a shit-storm on this side of the new millennium. And although Lesley certainly couldn't be blamed for all of the events that took place at Blackwood leading up to Rolfe's death, she played a big role in the cosmic jigsaw puzzle. Worse, now that she'd brainwashed Rose, she'd gone from being a minor player in Ash's life to being a full-fledged villain.

That's when Ash made the decision to walk right up to her. After all, what was Lesley going to do in front of a crowd of wealthy Floridians and journalists? Shoot her? And if Ash missed her opportunity to approach Lesley now, who knew when Ash would find her next.

She made it only three steps before a tall waiter wearing a white button-down stepped in front of her with a tray. "Shrimp cocktail, ma'am?" he asked in his rich voice.

"In a minute," Ash said, and started to slide around him.

His hand caught her elbow to hold her back, and only then did she realize that the waiter was actually Wes. He had swept his long dark bangs down in front of his face, but his eyes were simmering beneath them through the holes in his mask. "This is *not* the time or place."

"This is *exactly* the time and place." Ash gently pulled her arm free. "We're in public. What could she possibly do?"

Wes stepped in front of her, just in case she decided to beeline it for Lesley. "*What could she do?* She can go back to her villa, ship your sister off to a place where you'll never find her, and then send all of her manpower after you. And in case you didn't notice last night, when it comes to handling gods and goddesses, her people come prepared."

Ash took another sip from her champagne flute. "Then, what do you propose that I do?"

"For starters?" Wes used his free hand to snap his fingers in front of her face. "Look at me and stop staring ninja stars at Lesley Vanderbilt. You're only in control as long as she doesn't know you've come to Miami."

Ash huffed. Then, as her way of waving the white flag, she grabbed a handful of shrimp off his tray. "Okay, *garçon*. You win. So tell me why you got a girl all gussied up to go to the prom, only to forbid her from exacting her revenge."

She went to dip her shrimp into the cocktail sauce on the tray, but he was already setting the tray down on the nearest table. He gave a quick look around to make sure the partygoers nearby were ensconced in conversation before he pulled on the jacket he had draped over his arm, instantly transforming from a waiter to an honored guest. "I have something to show you." She didn't follow at first, so he said, "You can bring the shrimp with you if you like."

She bit the heads off the last two shrimp and tossed the tails onto the table. "This better be good."

As they walked toward the south arcade, he allowed them to approach just a little bit closer to where Lesley's entourage was chatting. "Watch the guy under the tree," he instructed her. "But don't stare."

It was the large boy with the dreadlocks from Ash's vision of the boat. Even with his white khakis and button-down, rolled halfway up his forearms, he looked rough and unsavory for a soiree like this. His tie was loose, probably to accommodate his massive pro-wrestler neck.

"Bodyguard?" she asked.

"You got it." Wes directed her away as she edged in for a closer look. "The Incan sun god, Inti, but he goes by Rey—Spanish for 'king.'"

"He seems like a real 'Rey' of sunshine." Ash faked an obnoxious laugh.

"Oh, you'll be a hit at the after-party," Wes said.

They cut through the tea room first, which Ash thought was closer to a small ballroom with chandeliers than a nook for tea drinking. The temperature of the air instantly plummeted the moment they entered, and at first Ash figured it was just a very efficient cooling system.

Beyond a gaggle of women, who were all shivering, a familiar girl stood in profile with her back to the wall, gazing out the open portico onto the terrace outside and the gardens beyond. She wore the same hooded white robe she'd sported on the boat, and she was fanning herself despite the chill temperature. The cocktail glass in her other hand was lined with frost when she brought it up to her lips.

Wes cruised through once Ash had gotten a good look, but waited until they entered the dining room beyond to speak. "Skadi, Norse goddess of winter," he said. "They call her Bleak. I think she's a koi out of the koi pond, here in Miami, with the heat and everything."

The next set of doors opened up into a smaller music room. Ash instantly recognized the boy standing next to the antique harp, in conversation with a large group gathered around him. He had ditched his mask and was gesturing wildly with his hands, to the boisterous laughter of his entourage. Ash must have been staring too conspicuously, because Wes elbowed her in the ribs. She thought she caught the boy's eye before she turned away.

"And that," Wes said as they exited out onto the eastern loggia, where the air simmered back up to a sweltering ninety degrees, "is Lesley's right hand, Thorne, and the leader of the pack as far as I can tell. His true name is Quetzalcoatl, the Aztec god of wind." He paused.

"According to folklore, he's my nemesis and we have the same father. Brothers from different mothers, as they say."

"Your mom must have been taller, then," Ash said. "Probably prettier as well. So are they just hanging around Lesley for the free booze and dinner parties?"

Wes and Ash walked out onto the eastern terrace, where a multitude of couples had gathered at the railing, overlooking the Atlantic beyond. "I haven't quite figured out what their payoff is," Wes said as they started down a staircase toward the water. "As a rule, those of our kind don't work for humans unless they absolutely have to. It's against the natural order—gods working for mortals. And for people like Rey, Bleak, and Thorne, who could just burn or freeze or blow their way into a bank vault, money's not always a good enough incentive. Lesley must have some resource that they need, and in return they offer her protection."

"For such a well-known businesswoman to keep three gods in her entourage, in plain sight—it's got to be more than just ordinary protection," Ash said as she felt the dots slowly connecting in her mind. She thought back to Blackwood, and how the mercenaries that Lesley had sent after Ash and her friends had ended up fertilizer for the redwood forest. Lesley must have smartened up and realized that in order to shield herself from the supernatural, she needed to fight fire with fire. But it wasn't Ashline specifically that the businesswoman needed protection from. "They must be to protect Lesley from my older sister. Eve and Lesley have a blood feud that goes back nearly a century, to when my sister murdered Lesley's grandfather during her previous lifetime. Eve would easily electrocute her way through a wannabe Mafia guy like the one who caught you on Lesley's boat—no offense," she added when he looked a little offended. "But if Eve comes looking for Rose, expecting to find Lesley helpless, and she finds three violent gods waiting for her instead . . ."

After they reached the bottom of the stairs, they walked over to the edge of the terrace, where the stonework stopped and the water abruptly began. Out in the harbor a stone barge with elegant carvings sheltered the cove from incoming waves. The statues facing the darkening horizon looked as though they'd weathered their fair share of hurricanes.

"Aurora and I have been watching them for months," Wes said. "See, I've only lived in Miami for part of my life, but I've come to think of this city as my home . . . the only one I have." The word "home" made his eyes flicker black, but then he was back in the moment. "Given my special, uh, talents, I took it upon myself to protect the people of Miami. It started with mostly amateur superhero shenanigans—you know, stopping a mugger who was preying on tourists, monitoring the local Mafias. But then Lesley's new supernatural associates rolled into town and began consorting with a not-so-well-intentioned crime syndicate, so Aurora and I started devoting our nightly surveillance to the three gods, and eventually to Lesley Vanderbilt. I thought we'd gone unnoticed . . . at least until they captured me on the boat. We don't know much about these gods or their intentions, but lately they've been referring to themselves as the Four Seasons."

Ash snorted. "I thought you said there were only three of them. Can they not count properly, or are they a fan club for Vivaldi?"

"By my count, the three you saw in the villa—sun, wind, and cold—account for summer, fall, and winter." He shrugged. "Maybe they've recruited your little sister as their new spring."

Ash shook her head. "Spring is about rebirth and new life. As far as I can tell, Rose only brings the tides of death with her. There's nothing springy or rainy about her—other than the fact that I'm sure she could ruin an outdoor wedding."

"Well, there's a good chance that whatever 'discoveries' Lesley is presenting tonight have some correlation to your little sister," Wes suggested.

Ash pulled the invitation out of her purse and gave it a once-over. "I probably should have guessed from the words 'mythology' and 'ruin.'"

Wes turned her away from the horizon by her shoulders and held her out at arm's length. "Now that I've shown you what's going on behind the scenes, you should also know that I brought you here exactly so you *wouldn't* walk right up to Lesley in the middle of a party. You make a false move around here, and next thing you know, Bleak breaks into your hotel room and turns you into a human ice cube tray."

Ash rolled her eyes. "I've got a fuel tank full of magma that would like to see her try."

"I have to go rendezvous with Aurora now," he said. "She's been even more frantic and motherly than usual since I was captured yesterday. As for you, it will be better if we're not all sitting together when the presentation begins. In the meantime . . ." He snagged two more flutes of champagne from a passing tray and handed one to her. "Have some more champagne." He motioned to the empty eastern horizon. "Enjoy the backward sunset." He started to walk away, but came right back to her. "Oh, and go easy on the shrimp."

Ash attempted to kick him in the shin, but she got snagged on her dress and nearly fell backward into the water.

With Wes gone, Ash lingered at the edge of the bay. The third glass of champagne was beginning to make her feel a bit fizzy and warm. She hadn't touched a drop of alcohol since the infamous masquerade ball last month, and before that, the night of Serena's attempted kidnapping. She had begun to associate alcohol with trouble, and even now she was aware of how a gala hosted by her sister's kidnapper probably wasn't the wisest time to build a buzz. Time to slow down.

She was stirring her champagne with her ring finger and idly watching the bubbles when she felt a presence behind her. Immediately she had a brief flashback to the Bent Horseshoe, when Colt had introduced himself the exact same way, lurking silently in her shadow while she sat at the bar with her back to him.

Her conclusion: Men who quietly approached you in your blind spot were predatory and never to be trusted.

But when she turned around, there was no one at all—just a couple making their way up the stairs, a series of empty chairs and empty tables, and the lingering odor of a cigar.

Ash turned back to the horizon.

Thorne was standing next to her, a cigar in his mouth and a drink in his hand.

In her surprise the champagne flute slipped right out of her fingers.

Thorne, as quick as the wind itself, dipped and caught the glass before it shattered on the patio below.

"Shit, you spooked me!" she said, unable to compose herself in time.

He handed the champagne glass back to her and took the cigar out of his mouth. "Sorry about that. There's really no graceful way to approach a woman at the water's edge when she's not expecting you."

"Next time try announcing your presence first," Ash said. "Anything—even a friendly 'Nice bum, where ya from?' would go a long way." Ash's hand trembled as she took a long sip from the champagne to calm her nerves. It wasn't only from the way he'd startled her either. She was having flashbacks to her vision, to the two tornadoes he'd summoned from the sky and how they'd ravaged the disabled ship. While interacting with gods and goddesses was quickly becoming a staple of Ash's new life, she'd developed a particular phobia for those gods with weather-related abilities . . . like Eve.

"Hector Thorne." He extended his hand, which she hesitated to take. "Thorne is just a name," he said. "The hand isn't actually going to prick you."

Maybe not your hand, Ash replied silently, *but I know a prick when I see one.*

Better play along and improvise, she told herself. "Rebecca," she lied, and took his hand.

"Take a walk with me in the garden, Rebecca?" he asked.

She looked fleetingly to the villa entrance, where Wes had disappeared after he'd left her. This probably wasn't what Wes had intended by "lay low," but here was her chance to glean some answers from Lesley's confidant, who was hopefully just intending to flirt with her. "Fine," she replied. "As long as you get me back by curfew, or else Papa will get *real mad*."

He winked at her. "Don't worry; I have a way with fathers." He offered her the elbow of his expensive-looking suit. "Shall we?"

The formal garden was a long plaza consisting of a

center island surrounded by a stone-rimmed moat, and two lines of oak trees to provide general shade. The rest of the plaza was ornamentally landscaped with jasmine parterres, a series of elaborately designed hedges. In short the garden made the extravagant landscaping of Ash's neighbors back in Scarsdale look like a nest of weeds and crab apple trees.

"Do you know," Thorne asked as they walked along the stone path that cut through the parterres, "what the man who built this estate did?"

Ash shrugged. "Did he own Miami's most popular deli?"

"He made tractors."

They descended down into the statuary walk, a narrow side garden submerged in the shade of the native hammock trees. Ash felt her danger sensors tingling now that they were moving away from the bustling main villa toward the secluded fringes of the property. "You're quite the wellspring of facts," Ash said. "Does that mean you're a curator here? Or possibly a tractor salesman?"

"James Deering had a fortune, as you can clearly see," Thorne said, ignoring her questions, "but also the brains enough to know that tractors, much like the rest of us, have short life spans here on earth. A tractor's motor eventually burns out, and then it sits rusting in a shed for many years, until it gets recycled for scrap metal. The majority of us are one-and-done here after ninety years or so, if we're lucky. But a great man is someone who wants to leave a legacy, to be immortalized in some way . . . so rather than building just any ordinary home for himself, Deering sank a fortune into creating this villa."

Ash tried to pick up their walking pace a bit, but Thorne had slowed down to admire the white-stoned statues that lined the path. "Are you suggesting that he built Villa Vizcaya so he could 'live' longer?" she asked. "It seems much more likely that he just wanted a place to, you know, hang out and stuff. Have a nice little garden to sprawl out in and read a good book. Maybe throw some bitchin' parties in the courtyard."

The corners of Thorne's lips twitched. "Perhaps," he mused. "However, there's no denying that the villa *did* outlive the man who made it, and weathered a century against the elements after that." He glanced back in the direction of the villa. "Unfortunately, even this great house will eventually crumble. Maybe it will finally meet a hurricane it can't withstand. Maybe it will fall into ruin when we do, when there's no one around to keep up the grounds, and the gardens will become wild and overgrown."

This talk of mortality—and worse, the undertones of immortality beneath it—were seriously beginning to unnerve Ash. "Everything dies eventually," she said.

Thorne caught her eye out of the corner of his own. "So true. Yet there are some among us who waste their quickly expiring lifetimes seeking ways to live just a little bit longer."

"Among *us*?" Ash didn't like the way this conversation was proceeding at all.

He ignored her, and his arm tightened around hers, not threatening but enough to lock her hand against his side. He gestured with his cigar to the white statues they were passing on their right, which looked vaguely mythological in origin. "Immortality is like these Veneto statues. Three hundred years old, imported from Italy. Eventually acid rain will eat away at them down to the last pebble. But while the statues themselves may slowly dissolve, the gods and goddesses they depict have lived on in mythology for thousands of years. Flesh and stone may perish, but words, history, ideas—these are the things that live forever."

At this point Ash could barely stand the touch of his skin against hers as he led them back to the formal gardens, where several party guests were now making their way to the presentation. Ash was just happy to be in the presence of other people again, even if they were debutantes and journalists, distracted by the lush gardens and too human to protect her from a violent wind god.

Thorne stopped them in front of the limestone grotto next to the stairway, a fountain recessed into a little man-made cave. In the shadows she could see that the walls inside the grotto were decorated with jagged stone coral. Two sculpted women guarded the archway.

"The only way *we* can live on," he continued, and Ash noted the way he inflected the "we," "is through belief. The great religions can outlast even the civilizations that practiced them, so long as belief exists. Belief is beauty. Belief is power. Belief is immortality."

Ash attempted to smile politely at the megalomaniac. She wiggled her arm to see how tight his grip was and whether she had enough leeway to escape. "Riveting as this lecture has been, Professor Thorne, it's past my curfew." She raised her champagne flute in a salute to him. "Now it's time for me to return to my boyfriend."

Thorne shook his head. "No. Now it's time for us to stop pretending we're mortals."

She tried to lurch away, but Thorne caught her by the loose material of her dress, and he pushed her roughly through the archway of the grotto. Once inside, he slammed her hard up against the wall so that the sharp coral fingers jabbed into her back, and the breath deflated out of her on impact. With him pressing her up against the wall, they were both hidden from any passersby.

"Miami may be a diverse city," he whispered into her ear, "but the mask on your face didn't keep me from noticing the striking similarities between you and little Rose the moment I saw you across the room."

Ash's hand was still free, so she smashed her champagne flute against the coral. The glass and champagne littered the ground, but she had the daggerlike broken stem pointed at the side of his neck in a second. "Unless you can summon wind in these close quarters," she growled, "I suggest you *back off* before I shish-kebab you and serve you as an appetizer to the party guests."

Grudgingly Thorne released her. "I'm not here to hurt you. If I really wanted to kill you, I would have sent you into the waters back at the villa with a strong gust, and you'd be fish bait for the minnows of Biscayne Bay."

"That would have been a shame." Ash raised her makeshift dagger to fill the space between them. "To have my last breath of air be a whiff of ashtray and creepy cologne."

Thorne bent down and picked up his cigar, which had fallen to the stone floor. He didn't even wipe it off before he put it back into his mouth and took a long hit. "I don't know which of the other Wilde girls you are—Ashline or Evelyn—but Lesley Vanderbilt has charged us with finding Eve, so that Lesley can finally avenge her family vendetta against her." Thorne paused. "However, fortunately for the Wilde family, we have absolutely no intention of fulfilling our end of the obligation. You see, Lesley Vanderbilt is my stepping-stone to the Miami elite, and beyond that, the eyes of the nation—"

"Eyes of the nation?" Ash interrupted. "Do you guys have a sitcom or a variety show that you're trying to get syndicated?"

Thorne didn't look amused. "She and her national media connections remain available to me only so long as she doesn't find Evelyn Wilde, in which case she'll no longer need us. So here is my ultimatum: Stay away from Lesley, or I will bury you at the end of the earth. Lesley will never be the wiser and will continue to carry out her senseless grail quest to settle her family vendetta."

"Fine," Ash said. "Then give me back my little sister."

This made Thorne chuckle. "You can't get something 'back' that you never had to begin with. No, your little sister is the last cog in a machine I've spent the last two years assembling, and if you attempt to remove her, then—"

"Yeah, yeah, *you'll bury me at the end of the earth*," Ash repeated. "You should take some of the money you spent on that dinner jacket and buy some new lines."

"Enjoy the presentation." Thorne straightened the lapel of his jacket. "And just remember"—he spread his hands open threateningly—"that killing you would be a *breeze*." He vanished out of the archway, leaving Ash alone in the grotto.

It took a few moments of heavy breathing for Ash to realize that she still had the flute gripped tightly in her hand. "Great," she whispered to herself as she brushed the dust off the back of her dress and straightened herself out. Twenty-four hours in Miami and she'd already interrupted a Mafia interrogation, blown her cover at the villa party, and made quick enemies with a god who made Eve look like a graduate of charm school by comparison. With a long sigh Ash wandered out of the grotto and up to the moat around the central island, where she tossed the broken stem of the champagne glass into the water.

Ash joined the steady procession of visitors heading to "the Mound," where the presentation was about to start. With all the red masks and white jackets and dresses, they looked like a string of bloody pearls that had been scattered over the emerald garden. As Ash ascended the steps with the others, she spotted Wes on the opposite staircase. He gave her a quick nod but then broke eye contact and picked up his pace.

The Mound was a circular dais elevated above the gardens, sheltered by a ring of tall mangrove trees. The facility had set up enough chairs to accommodate at least two hundred people, and the chairs were all facing "the casino," a little white open-air house illuminated blue by a series of spotlights. In front of the casino was a projector and screen. But what caught Ash's eye was the mysterious nine-foot-tall object beside the projector screen, which was shrouded by a curtain. Looked like this presentation was going to be knee-deep in surprises.

Ash chose a seat on the outside, far enough back for her face to get lost in the crowd. On her way over she spotted Aurora. The winged goddess was wearing a white blazer over her dress, with no visible hump over her shoulder blades. Ash made a note to ask her later how uncomfortable it was to fold them up like that.

Thorne, however, was absent, even though the grotto where he'd attacked her was built right into the Mound. In fact, as she scanned the chairs, she couldn't locate Bleak or Rey, either. Unsettling, to say the least. The three of them *probably* weren't off playing Connect Four back at the mansion.

Lesley Vanderbilt stepped out of the casino. The

audience stopped chattering and began to clap. From the intensity of the applause, Ash guessed that the guests were all regulars at Lesley's galas . . . or were at least really psyched to be in the presence of free booze and appetizers.

"Thank you," Lesley said. The microphone on her lapel boomed her already commanding voice out across the Mound. Bathed in the blue, she was looking especially demonic tonight.

"It was nearly five hundred years ago that Hernán Cortés and his conquistadores landed in the Americas." An antique map of Mexico without its current borders flashed on the projector screen. "There, in what is now modern-day Mexico, they infamously laid siege to the Aztec empire, leaving its cities in ruins and its people in disarray.

"Years later," she continued, "when Cortés returned to Spain, he would claim that the Aztec people had received him as a deity—that they believed him to be their own wind god, Quetzalcoatl." The image on the screen transitioned to a yellowed painting of a warrior-like figure with the body of a man and the head of a snake. His garb was luxuriously adorned with feathers of every color. "But to the Aztecs, Quetzalcoatl was a symbol of life and resurrection, a good creator of the people. He was never intended to be a symbol of foreign invasion and a harbinger of doom."

Lesley crossed in front of the projector, so that the

gleaming image of the serpent warrior's eyes briefly overlapped her own. "What Cortés didn't realize was that Quetzalcoatl—the true Quetzalcoatl—was walking the earth at that time as a mortal . . . and that the two of them had actually met."

The screen transitioned to a picture of a stone carving. Much like the painting before, the relief was a sculpture of a fanged snake's mouth with a corona of feathers. "Using sonar technology, my archaeological team discovered this grave site buried under thirty feet of soil on the Yucatán peninsula. Within it were the mummified remains of an Aztec man, laid out on an earthen altar within. His hands and feet were ceremoniously staked to the four corners of the altar with the fangs of a large snake." She paused dramatically. "But that is *not* how he died."

The illustration on the screen morphed into a bloody battle in a large plaza. "According to the artifacts the team excavated, the man most likely came from the city of Cholula, and was one of the many *thousands* of unarmed noblemen massacred in the city plaza one night by Cortés and his men. His body shows evidence of two lacerations on his thighs and then a sword wound that penetrated through his back and exited the front of his chest cavity."

Ash pursed her lips. After her meet and greet with Thorne, the thought of him skewered by a conquistador wasn't so horrible an image.

"We believe that his body was secretly moved to the tomb by high priests from the cult of Quetzalcoatl, and the feathered serpent that marks the entrance identifies the man within as the wind god and creator himself." Lesley clasped her hands and grinned fiercely. "I'm pleased to announce that, thanks to the latest in preservation advances, Vanderbilt Estates has brought him here to you tonight."

She crossed over to the curtained object. With a grand flourish she ripped down the white sheet and cast it to the ground.

The audience collectively inhaled, Ash included. Encased in a clear unit with his arms and feet pinned at the four corners in the same way that Lesley had described, was a mummified corpse. Feathers had been gathered around his skull in a mane, and his jaw gaped open in an eternal scream.

"Recently my team has developed facial mapping software that allows us to scan the bone structure of any skull, full or partial, and develop an accurate representation of what the subject's face would have looked like in life." Lesley gestured to the projector screen, where a close-up of the mummified skull had materialized. "I give to you the face of a living god."

On the screen Ash watched as the skull's wrappings digitally unraveled, and the decomposing flesh beneath rotted away, leaving only the skull. Once the skull was clean and white, veins and muscle and cartilage quickly populated its surface, then on top of that, skin, lips, eyes, and hair.

When the digital transformation was complete, the image of Quetzalcoatl's face remained.

It was Thorne, and his dark eyes stared like lances out into the crowd. A murmur ran through the audience, and Ash heard someone a few rows back whisper, "It's like one of those paintings where the eyes follow you no matter where you go."

Lesley waved her hands to hush the crowd. "Now, moments ago I said that Vanderbilt Estates had brought Quetzalcoatl to you tonight. What you don't know is that I wasn't referring to the mummified remains from his tomb. I wasn't referring to the digital recreation of his face you see on the screen." She pointed to one of the blue-lit archways of the casino behind her. "I was referring to him."

The real Thorne emerged from the structure. No longer in his tuxedo, the wind god now wore full traditional Aztec garb. A loincloth, ornately woven with black, crimson, and gold, had replaced his tuxedo pants, and a similar cape covered his shirtless chest, knotted at his left shoulder. He wore a golden headdress with feathers, identical to the headpiece worn by the mummy.

There were rumblings of confusion in the audience.

And then the audience began to laugh and point.

Ash couldn't help a grin herself, especially seeing the impatient confusion written all over Lesley's face. True as her story was that Thorne was Quetzalcoatl in the flesh, how could she have possibly expected the audience to take her seriously?

Thorne, however, didn't look the least bit perturbed. He stepped calmly out to center stage, set his feet, and in a fear-inspiring voice shouted, "Silence!"

The blast of wind that accompanied it sent everyone's hair fluttering back, and the hysterical crowd died back to mumbling.

"You don't have to believe now," Thorne said, his voice quieter but still carrying over the Mound. "But in time you *will* believe. And for the present, you will hear the news that I've brought for you. A warning."

"Is this guy for real?" the woman next to Ash mumbled to nobody at all, but Ash noticed that she'd whipped out a handheld voice recorder—must have been a reporter.

"You see, my mortal friends, the gods *do* walk among us. I am not the only one. Hundreds of us, from mythologies around the world, from Egypt to Peru to the shores of Polynesia—are all here as flesh and blood. Some of us are here to protect you, while others . . ." He paused. "Well, to them you are ants beneath a magnifying glass to be burned, to be trampled . . . to be eradicated."

Some people even dared to laugh this time, but the cold silence was taking over the audience like a plague as Thorne continued. "Despite the imminent danger presented by these forces crushing in around you, I come before you tonight to tell you that there are four among us who have sworn to protect you. As the demons from around the globe assemble to wage war on the defenseless, feel safe in knowing that you can weather the storm beneath the umbrella of the Four Seasons."

One brave soul in the front of the audience, who hadn't yet heeded Thorne's steely warnings, stood up. "The Four Seasons?" he jeered. "I love that hotel!"

Thorne's head slowly rotated around to look at his critic. "No," he said finally. "I mean Mother Nature herself."

A heavy wind picked up over the casino and slammed into the heckler. He toppled back into his chair, flattening several of the people around him in a mess of limbs and folding chairs. Some of the audience nearest them rose to their feet, but nobody in the crowd dared to flee the premises.

"You may call me Fall," Thorne said, and nodded to the fallen heckler, "a name some will learn well. Let me introduce you to the other Seasons."

"Summer," a deeper voice called from the back corner of the Mound. Ash turned in unison with everyone else. Rey rolled his sleeves up and held his arms out over the audience.

It started as a pinwheel of light, floating over the central aisle for all to see, but it quickly spiraled into a burning orb. Soon a miniature sun blazed overhead, sending waves of heat fanning down onto the masses. Ash wiped her brow out of instinct, even though her own supernatural resistance to heat kept her from sweating. The temperature blazed hotter than even the native Floridians around Ash seemed comfortable with.

"Winter."

Bleak climbed out of the bushes in the northwestern corner and extended her hands toward the fiery sun. The air crackled, and the heat on Ash's face instantly cooled, then turned bitterly cold. A collective shiver rolled through the spectators.

The white-hot sun quickly died through several shades of tangerine and red, until it was reduced to a soft glow. A shell of ice crept around the bottom hemisphere of the orb, starting at its southern pole, then working its way up to the equator. By the time the ice had coated the orb, the fire within had died to a single, pulsing baby star, a fiery nucleus gently glowing inside the floating glacial sphere. Ash caught Rey casting Bleak a lustful look from the opposite side of the Mound.

"And of course," a strangely familiar woman's voice announced from the back, "winter always turns to spring."

"Spring" finished climbing the stairs in the back, a middle-aged Japanese woman with dark hair, even darker circles around her eyes, and a lopsided grin. Though Ash had seen her face many times before, she'd seen it only once prior in its aged state, shortly after this same woman had murdered one of Ash's best friends.

Lily Mayatoaka knelt down in the central aisle, stopping just beneath the slowly rotating ball of ice. From this close Ash could make out the crow's-feet at the corners of the blossom goddess's eyes. Ash's hands tightened around the edge of her chair.

The ground rumbled. Shrieks erupted throughout the audience.

From the ground underneath the ball two tendrils of ivy penetrated the stone surface, sending rocks and soil showering over the nearby observers. The appendages blossomed leafy fingers that snaked around the orb, lashing around it from all angles.

When the vines stopped sprouting, the ivy had encircled the orb at every latitude and longitude. Then, as one, the vines all contracted, hard, and the ice shattered instantly, extinguishing the fire within.

The remains of the ball landed at Lily's feet, a mass of shattered ice, cinders, and withering plant life.

Even the crowd members who had stood up before now slipped back into their seats. No one seemed so eager to depart any longer with the Winter, Summer, and Spring Seasons blocking their path.

Ash was trembling. She felt the old tang of fire lapping at her innards, rage igniting within the deepest pockets of her soul. Nothing burned quite like the opportunity for vengeance. Her first priority was supposed to be rescuing her little sister, and deep down she knew that revealing herself now could jeopardize that . . . but Lily had caused so much suffering for Ash and her friends that Ash had become a slave to her vengeful instincts. With the taste of retribution on her tongue, the part of her that was still a normal sixteen-year-old drifted to the back burner, and Pele, the volcano goddess, seized control.

With the audience sitting, Ash knew she'd be instantly recognized the moment she stood up. Then she'd have only a short window of time to trample over the seated bystanders between her and Lily. Could Ash get her hands on Lily and incinerate her before the plant goddess realized something was afoot?

"Undoubtedly," Thorne said, drawing attention back up to him, "tomorrow some of you will write in your newspapers of the 'parlor tricks' that happened here today, chalking up the miracles you've just witnessed to high-priced special effects. Rest assured that this has all been real . . . and these *parlor tricks* will one day soon save your life."

Ash was going to need a distraction if she was going to get to Lily unnoticed. And if she could disrupt Thorne's presentation at the same time, all the better. What was this crap he was saying about "saving lives" supposed to mean, anyway? Given Thorne's personality, he seemed more likely to use a strong gale to blow someone in front of a speeding bus.

"A cold and merciless force is coming to Miami. In just a few nights' time, the Four Seasons will have to face the threat of another god, a god who would have you all suffer." Thorne walked out into the center aisle toward the mound of debris. "The world will watch as we neutralize that threat." His cape billowed out behind him. "And *then* you will believe."

Ash slipped off her heels. Fortunately the reporter

next to her was too transfixed on Thorne and Lily to even notice her. Ash gripped each of the heels in a separate hand. Turned the valve connecting her to the sacred fire. Felt the juices of a millennia-old volcano building within her.

The heels ignited. Fire lapped around the straps, spreading fast from the soles up to the clasp. Then, as inconspicuously as she could, she lobbed the first one over her head and into the crowd.

The projectile landed somewhere near the center aisle not far from Lily. It was noticed immediately, because it landed in a man's lap.

He released a girlish screech as he slapped wildly at the heel, interrupting Thorne's bombastic conclusion to his speech. The woman next to the heel's victim, in true helpful fashion, pointed at the heel and screamed "Fire!"

Everyone within a five-row radius stood up immediately, and then, like the wave at a baseball game, the rest of the crowd rose to their feet as well. This was exactly what Ash had intended. The standing audience would provide enough cover and confusion for her to make her way to Lily.

With two hundred people already on the precipice of panic after what might have been the strangest fifteen minutes of their lives, Ash fired the second heel over the crowd, toward the front of the stage. This time the crowd erupted into chaos, and they funneled into the center aisle, washing around the gods like an unstoppable tide.

Ash spotted Lily through the fray and began to weave her way through the shuffling masses in Lily's direction. If she could sneak up from behind the blossom goddess and wrap her flaming hands around her neck, Ash might even be able to kill her and escape unnoticed. Revenge propelled her through the maze of people and folding chairs.

But when she reached the place in the crowd where Lily had been standing before, there was only a strand of withered vine in her stead.

Ash searched around frantically. At first she spotted only Rey and Bleak attempting to corral the milling crowd back toward their seats. Toward the north end of the Mound, however, she noticed a head of dark hair fleeing down the staircase.

Ash bagged her stealth approach and shoved through the crowd. At one point she knocked over an oblivious reporter who was filming the chaos with his handheld camera.

When Ash reached the back of the Mound, she didn't even have time to take the stairs. She leapt onto the multi-tiered waterfall, dropping from platform to platform and sending plumes of water up behind her. She hurdled over the final pool and hit the stones below in a roll in time to watch Lily trailing off into the statuary walks.

Ash breezed by two stone sphinxes and then vaulted over the balustrade onto the grass below. On the opposite side of the path, Lily's dress fluttered down a narrow passage leading into the mangroves. Ash was gaining ground, but for a woman who was now in her late forties, Lily could still run damn fast.

The evening released its last scraps of daylight as Ash sprinted down the path. She didn't have far to run, however. The trail emptied out into a circular garden, a corral of dense trees with nowhere else to go but the harbor. Ash could hear the waves lapping at the roots of the mangroves.

From studying the villa map, Ash recognized that she was standing in the maze garden, named after the broad circular maze landscaped out of the low shrubs. In the middle of the labyrinth was a single lamppost.

Ash didn't hear the rustling until it was too late. By the time she turned, Lily had already cocked back the vine that had sprouted out of her wrist. The whip struck Ash right on the ear. The impact snapped her head to the side enough to give her whiplash, and her ear exploded with church bells.

The whip came down again, but, discombobulated as she was, Ash thrust out her forearm to protect her face. It absorbed the blow intended for her head. Then Ash wrapped her wrist around the vine before Lily could draw it back and pulled with all of her might.

Off balance, Lily stumbled toward Ash. As the two goddesses collided, Ash's hand clamped around Lily's neck. Thorn claws slipped out over Lily's fingernails, and she pressed the sharp tip of her pointer finger into the skin over Ash's jugular.

"Stalemate, bitch," Lily rasped.

"Making chess analogies?" Ash asked. "Shouldn't you be playing backgammon or bridge at your age?"

"Better to be in early retirement than playing dollhouse in that stifling hellhole you call a school. Speaking of which . . ." Lily looked around dramatically. "Where *is* the merry widow?"

"Somewhere safe." Ash curled her fingers just a little tighter and let the slightest breath of warmth tingle from her palm into Lily's throat. "I'm sure she'd be more than pleased if I turned your head into a teakettle. See if steam really *can* come out your ears."

Lily laughed from the back of her throat, husky and thick. "If I'd be a teakettle," she wheezed, "then I guess that makes Rolfe a pincushion."

That got to Ash. She pounded Lily in the chest with her free arm, sending her sprawling over one of the hedges and onto her back.

Ash touched her throat where Lily's thorn had been digging into the skin. She felt a drop of blood dribble down to her collarbone. "I just don't understand how you could go from the Lily we all went to the bar with to . . . to this! How do you take away a boy's life as though it were yours to take?"

Lily's entire face convulsed as she untangled herself from the hedges. "You don't know what he did to me!" she screeched. "The things I *let* him do with me, all in the hopes of a time when he wouldn't stuff me back into the shadows, back into silence. The quiet torture of the months I spent waiting for him to come around. Then that little death-monger swoops in, and in no time at all she has him practically lapping up the milk at her feet."

"It's called dating, Lily!" Ash screamed. "So Rolfe was a player. So you got played. You don't skewer a boy through the heart for that."

A new whip slithered out of Lily's palm, and she slapped the ground with it. Dust mushroomed up into the air. "I did to his heart what he did to mine. Broke the heart of his little bitch, too." Lily coiled the whip around her arm and pulled it taut. "And I'll rip out yours as well if I have to."

Ash cracked her knuckles. Lily would get no sympathy from her. "You're looking a little tense around the eyes, Lily. Too bad Botox can't fix your personality." She held up her hand, which had started to burn. "And it certainly won't fix what I'm about to do to your face."

Lily brought her whip cracking down, but Ash released the fireball at the same time. It sliced right through the whip, sheering it in half so that the green tendril wriggled harmlessly on the ground.

The fireball continued on and struck Lily's bare shoulder, spinning her around in a circle, before it vanished off into the trees.

So it was to Ash's surprise that a larger, faster fireball whizzed out of the trees, too broad and quick for her to avoid. She lashed out her arm and easily shattered the ball into a million embers—one of the benefits of having fireproof skin—but she had to quickly slap out the miniature fires that had ignited all over her white dress.

Rey sauntered out of the trees with the maniacal grin of someone who wanted to eat her for dinner. Ash was probably the size of his typical meal.

Bleak too marched out from the palms. She rolled up the sleeves of her ivory robe, preparing for battle.

Ash backed away across the maze. Three on one was a game that she would undoubtedly lose, particularly against three gods who were clearly more practiced with their gifts than she was. From what Ash had seen them do on the boat, she was still an amateur by comparison.

Their determined approach was interrupted by a bomb dropping from the sky. Aurora landed in the space between Ash and the three Seasons. She had shucked her white blazer, and her wings were spread at half-mast.

Meanwhile Wes had stealthily approached behind Rey. He tapped the giant on the shoulder. "I think you owe the lady a new dress," he said.

Rey spun around just as Wes cracked him right in the face. The Incan sun god plunged down onto one knee. Bleak and Lily both turned on Wes, and in turn Ash and Aurora converged on the two women, ready to fight.

"Enough."

Thorne stood at the end of the garden trail, shaking his head and massaging his face in frustration. "We're all gods, you know," he said. "There was no need to turn my garden party into a scene from *West Side Story*."

Wes backed away until he was standing next to Aurora and Ash, but he kept his attention locked on Rey, who was rubbing his sore jaw and no longer grinning. "*You're* the one who decided to expose all of us to the world," Wes said. "You're the one who turned it into good versus bad, *us* versus *them*. What were you thinking?"

Thorne waved his hand impatiently. "Smoke and mirrors. Any religion needs to provide three things if it's going to stick: miracles, answers, and protection from evil, whether it's real or imagined. Our religion provides all three. And I am its shepherd."

Aurora spat on the ground. "Sounds like a cult to me."

"Oh, please." Thorne rolled his eyes. "'Cult' is just another word for a religion you don't fully understand."

Ash blew out a small fire that had unintentionally erupted on her shoulder, this one her own doing. "Well, 'shepherd' is just another word for a poser who thinks he's the second coming of Christ. Admit it," she goaded him. "You started a religion because you wanted more Facebook friends."

"The gods were put on earth to be worshipped, not to be forgotten. For centuries the humans built shrines for us, made sacrifices to us . . . even fought wars in our names. And now?" Thorne took the cigar out of his mouth long enough to spit on the ground. "Now we're just a footnote in an ancient-history textbook for some ignorant teenager to sleep through before he goes home to his video games and his crack pipe."

"Then why don't you go back to school, become a history teacher," Ash suggested. "MTV can make an inspirational movie all about how you used mythology to save inner-city teens from drugs and gang warfare."

"Come." Thorne turned and motioned for the other Seasons to follow. His cape billowed behind him. "We have better things to do than bloody a century-old garden."

Rey pointed at Wes with a glowing red finger. "Next time, bogeyman," he said before he thundered off. Bleak tagged along after him, close enough to be his shadow.

Lily backed slowly away. "You should tell Batwoman and Hercules that friends of yours tend to have short life expectancies." Then she scampered off into the trees, acrobatically using a low branch from one mangrove to flip up into the canopy. It took all of Ash's self-restraint not to plunge into the foliage after her.

Ash, Wes, and Aurora stood quietly, bathed in the pale yellow light of the garden's central lamp. Finally Aurora shrugged and broke the silence. "Well, we can stand around and wait for them to come back . . . or we can go back to the apartment and order Chinese food." She flapped her wings a few times to stretch, bent her knees, and then launched up into the air. A breeze followed in her wake.

After they had watched her fly away, Wes turned to Ash. "You hungry?"

Ash continued to look at the gap in the mangroves where Lily had vanished. "I'll eat Chinese—just no fortune cookies," she said. "After tonight I don't need a slip of paper to tell me to expect old enemies in a new town."

Even after seeing Wes's Cadillac, Ash was unprepared for the luxuriousness of his South Beach apartment.

Actually, as he flipped on the lights to the suite—which took up an entire quadrant of the twenty-four-story complex's top floor—she thought that "apartment" wasn't a fitting word at all.

Penthouse. Wes lived in a penthouse.

Wes unfastened his tie and tossed his car keys onto the stainless steel countertop in his kitchen. Only then did he notice that Ash was lingering in the doorway. "What?" he asked. "You can come inside. The carpet isn't booby-trapped."

Ash ignored him and kept gawking, but allowed herself a few tentative steps into the penthouse. "It's just . . ." It was just that the Japanese import furniture, in combination with the interior designer who probably put the room together, might have cost as much as the apartment itself. It was just that the view of Biscayne Bay and downtown Miami out the floor-to-ceiling glass windows was breathtaking even from thirty feet away.

It was just that eighteen-year-olds, even of the super-hero variety, didn't live in places like this.

"What do you think?" he asked.

She shrugged. "It's okay, I guess."

He laughed. "Stop acting like you've never seen an apartment before and join me on the roof." He walked toward the corner where a narrow spiral staircase led up into the ceiling. "View's better from up there."

"View's pretty damn good from where I'm standing," she mumbled, but she followed him up the corkscrew and through the metal door at the top.

The roof terrace was more like an oasis than just a pool deck. The kidney-shaped pool was surrounded by live palm trees that bristled in the warm summer breeze, a breeze that Ash thought was far too pleasant and serene to be anything produced by Thorne.

The two of them walked past a row of beach chairs. Ash, who was still barefoot, gingerly dipped her foot in the pool and gave the back of Wes's suit pants a tiny splash. He just rolled his eyes and walked up to the glass railing that protected the edge of the roof.

"Crazy night, huh?" Ash stepped up to a piece of railing beside him. "Are you disappointed that you didn't audition to be one of the Seasons?" She made the mistake of looking straight down, and experienced a quick flash of vertigo. Three hundred feet was a long way down.

Wes smiled. "I'd love to sit in on their poker nights.

The Four Seasons are all just so . . . charming. Especially your herbal friend."

Just the thought of Lily disgusted Ash enough to spoil her view. She turned away. "Lily is a weed. When the time comes, I will happily pluck her for all the things she's done."

"No doubt," Wes replied. "But if she's the fourth Season, what's curious to me is what they have planned for the miniature Wilde."

"Maybe Rose is the god they're talking about neutralizing while the world watches." Ash shuddered. "Maybe they want to kill her in some sort of . . . weird performance art, like they put on tonight."

Wes shook his head. "Not a chance. Thorne may be a lunatic with delusions of grandeur, but if he and his three Mouseketeers want to be championed as heroes by the city of Miami, the *last* thing he would do is publicly murder a six-year-old—even a dangerous one like your sister."

"True. And Rose is Lesley's last poker chip to get Eve back, so there's no way she'd let that happen." It sounded more like wishful thinking than fact, but Ash couldn't bear the thought that she'd come all this way just to see her little sister sacrificed in cold blood.

"But that still leaves the question—if your sister isn't the 'cold merciless force coming to Miami' that they talked about, then who the hell is?"

Ash didn't respond to this. She had no answer either. Instead she sat down on the lip of the pool and slipped her legs into the water. The bottom of her dress was instantly soaked, but with the burns all over it from Rey's fireball, even Miami's finest dry cleaner wasn't going to salvage it.

Wes kicked off his shoes, then his socks, and rolled his pant legs up until they were cuffed just above the knee. He joined Ash at the water's edge. Even when he was sitting down beside her, the night god towered a head above her.

"Ashline," Wes said, and he clasped his hands in his lap. "I want you to move in here."

"Whoa." Ash was so blindsided, she nearly slipped off the edge and into the pool. She tried to cover her shock with sarcasm. "I promised Mom I'd have a rock on my finger before I'd move in with a man. Or at least know him longer than twenty-four hours. I'm old-fashioned, you know?"

He flicked water at her. "I don't mean permanently," he said, "I mean for however long you're in Miami." His tone shifted from playful to protective. "Listen, I'm not going to blame you for losing your temper and blowing your cover tonight, but now you're exposed. We're all exposed. And if we have four Seasons of trouble lurking around the city, clearly itching to rumble with other gods, I would feel less antsy if you were a room away from me, and not holed up alone in a seedy motel."

Ash crossed her arms. "As flattering as it is that you want to play the role of the big brother, I've single-handedly taken on a tsunami and come out the other side alive." She pulled herself out of the water, letting her legs drip onto the concrete around him. "I don't need the big bad Aztec sandman to be my gladiator. *And*, if you can remember way back to yesterday, I was the one who saved *your* ass."

Wes caught her by the wrist, firmly but affectionately, as she started to go. "Please," he said delicately. "Let me rephrase my invitation in a way that would appeal to an independent woman. I would feel a hell of a lot safer myself with my own lava lamp nearby to protect me. Strength in numbers, you know?" He grinned from the left corner of his mouth. "If it sweetens the pot, Aurora is an *amazing* cook when she's not flying five towns away to pick up takeout."

Ash glanced at the light coming out of the door to the apartment, which Wes had propped open with a cinderblock. "Fine," she agreed at last. She lowered herself back down to the lip of the pool, and couldn't help herself from sitting closer this time, so that their thighs were touching. She smiled to herself when she felt his muscles tense under the touch of her scorched dress. "But if the Four Seasons come knocking, I call dibs on throwing Lily off the roof."

"Done," he said. "I might need you to sponge up any of Rey's fire too, so I can take another crack at his face." He looked her up and down provocatively. "Might be nice to see how much clothes he can burn off this time."

She punched him in the arm. "Jackass. Don't make me reconsider being your roommate."

The mention of burning dresses sent her on a flashback to the night of the masquerade ball, the singed remains of her dress after she'd evaporated the tsunami, lying next to Colt on that wet stone. . . .

Don't, she cautioned herself. *Don't project any memories of Colt onto a guy you just met.* Especially one who was handsome and potentially interested, even though he was, regrettably, another god.

"I hope you don't mind if I ask," she said, changing the subject, "but how is it that you can afford such a ridiculous penthouse?" She gestured to the vacant chairs lounging around the pool. "And unless you're paying all the other tenants *not* to use this beautiful pool deck, I'm going to assume that the whole roof terrace belongs to you."

She expected him to at least crack a smile, but his expression sobered. He shifted over, putting just an inch between them. It might as well have been a mile. "This all belonged to my father," he said. In case the way he'd used the past tense had left any room for confusion, he added, "I inherited it."

"I'm sorry," Ash whispered. On a whim she reached over and touched his knee. "How recently was it?"

"Three years in August." He stood up. Ash was painfully aware that he wasn't offering her a hand to join him. "Make yourself at home. The spare guest room is yours, and you can retrieve the rest of your belongings from the motel tomorrow." He started around the pool and made it into the stairwell before he leaned out the door and added, "Oh, and tell Aurora to leave some of those crab rangoons out for me."

As she listened to his heavy footsteps retreat down the stairs, the water she was dipping her feet into suddenly felt frigid and uninviting.

On cue there was a whoosh in the air, and Aurora dropped through the palm fronds overhead, landing in a slight crouch beside Ash. Clutched in each hand was a brown paper bag that smelled enticingly of grease and saturated fat. She was wearing a loose-fitting T-shirt tucked into the waistband of her shorts. "Sorry it took so long," she apologized between labored breaths. "Our favorite Chinese restaurant is in Fort Lauderdale. Thirty miles, but the food is always worth the flight time, and . . ." She suddenly took notice of Wes's absence. "Where'd he go? He was sitting right here when I was circling to land."

Ash turned back to the door. "What happened to his father?" she asked.

Aurora set the bags down on the cement rooftop and sighed. "You asked him, didn't you?"

"I have a history of asking the wrong questions at even worse times." Ash added to herself, *Or in the case of Colt and Eve, not knowing the right time to ask the right questions.*

Aurora's wings sagged. "Wes's father was . . . killed."

"You mean *murdered*?" Ash asked, sensing Aurora's hesitation.

Aurora said nothing.

"Did they ever catch who did it?"

"They did," Aurora said. "And they acquitted him of any wrongdoing." A pause. "And now he lives in his father's penthouse."

THE TIKI BANDITS

You stand in front of the large vault door. The metal is cool to the touch as you caress it, but you leave a trail of warmth as you draw concentric circles around the two dials. You knock three times and let the solid clack of knuckle on metal pulse through the underground chamber. Just from the sound of the knocking, you try to envision the bank vault on the other side, the rows of safety deposit boxes lining the walls, the hoard of gold and cash, hopefully in plain view or stashed accessibly.

Not that accessibility has ever been an issue for you.

The barrel of a revolver presses into the back of your skull. "Not a move," the man behind you growls. "I got no problems painting that vault door red if it keeps you on this side of it."

You turn your head just slightly; you can recognize the

gun just by the sound the hammer makes when it snaps into place. "Colt Banker's Special," you say. "Thirty-two caliber? You're not messing around."

The night guard must sense the mockery in your voice, because he forces the barrel deeper into your neck. "Hands to the ceiling and turn around real slow," he orders.

You sigh and hold your arms up limply to give the appearance of weakness. You do a little bobbing dance as you turn around to face him. He's got a horseshoe mustache tipped with the first tinges of gray. His eyes widen when he sees the wooden mask covering your face, with only slits for the eyes and mouth. He can't be that surprised, though. Drawings of these masks have been appearing in the papers for months now, as far away as Saint Louis.

"So it's true, then," he says. His eyes dip to take in your whole body—as if he needs to see the curves hidden beneath your floor-length coat to figure out that you are a woman. "The Tiki Bandits are just a couple of costumed hussies."

"We're no suffragettes," you say, "but we do prefer 'costumed *women*'."

"Shut up," he barks. "If you're the door woman, then where's your torch?"

You cock your head to the side, hoping your wide eyes peering out through the mask will unsettle him. "Torch?"

He motions to the bank vault with his free hand. "All

the other vaults were seared clean-through with an acetylene torch," he says. "Don't tell me that you've just been using a book of matches and a—"

The dim and grimy lightbulb overhead suddenly flickers and dies, interrupting his sentence. The underground foyer falls into darkness. He takes his eyes off you for a moment to examine the bulb.

"Storm's coming," you say.

A hand snakes around his neck and covers his mouth. The night guard's eyes bulge, and he spins his revolver around to intercept his ambusher.

Violet's too fast for him. The electricity shoots out of her palm and into his open mouth. He instantly crumples to the ground. "Storm's already here," she corrects you. She reaches down with her hand to shock the convulsing man again.

You catch her by the wrist. "He's out already. What the hell took you so long?"

"Patrol was lingering outside. Had to send a lightning strike onto the apothecary to lure them away." Violet gestures to the vault door. "What's taking *you* so long?"

You pull back your mask so that you can see better. "Cast-iron door, probably two feet thick, clad in steel plating with a layer of copper buried in there to slow down a torch."

Violet toes the fallen night guard, who has finally stopped shuddering. "Will it slow down *your* torch?"

You slip off your overcoat and toss it to the ground.

"Just get the sacks ready and keep your eyes on the door, Vi."

"Yes'm," she replies, and heads down the hallway.

You roll up your sleeves.

You press your left hand to the metal vault door.

You feel the wheel turning in your mind, which, much like a bank vault door, requires the proper combination to unlock the abilities within you.

Then the metal slowly begins to give way.

Your fingertips penetrate the top layer first as your hand heats the metal to three thousand degrees Fahrenheit. Your powers of conduction continue to radiate through the door into the thick layer of cast iron first, then through the copper alloy, which your skin melts through. The copper pools around your hand like hot molasses.

When all is said and done, your hand sheers through the dual lock mechanism, and you're able to rip the lock piston right out of the hole.

You whistle down the hallway. "Vi—we're ready."

You pull your arm free of the destroyed door. The already cooling liquid metal coats your left arm. There will be time to melt and slough the rest of it off later, but for now you use your right arm to pry open the vault door.

The two of you make quick work of the bank vault, emptying the teller trays into your bags. Every bank vault is different, but given that this is your eleventh robbery in the last year alone, you've learned enough to survive—

like how much you can carry before the load will slow you down.

On your way out of the vault, you almost don't see the night guard stirring in time. His eyes are clearly struggling to focus, but he angles his Colt Banker's Special up at you.

You twist and thrust out your metal-covered arm right as you hear the bang. The bullet hits you in the palm, and the force sends you backpedaling into the mangled vault door. You regain your balance and kick him across the face before he can fire off another round. It's going to take a lot of moonshine for him to nurse that headache when he wakes up.

You try to shake off the remaining sting in your left hand, and hold it up to observe the bullet you caught at point-blank range. The round protrudes out of the metal like a wart, and you pluck it out with your free hand.

"Come on," Violet urges you. "Now's not the time for a palm reading." She kicks the fallen guard in the stomach for good measure.

Outside, your getaway driver, Brigid, has the car idling in the shadows across the street, but she wheels around and pulls right up to the curb just in time for the two of you to toss your bags into the trunk. Violet slips into the passenger seat and you take the back.

"What's the haul?" the wheel woman asks the moment you climb into the car.

"Enough to take a little vacation," you reply. "Save

the accounting for later and concentrate on putting some miles between us and the bank."

"Shit," Violet growls as she adjusts the rearview mirror. "Looks like the suits are already coming out to play."

Through the back window you watch as one police car comes blazing around the corner so fast that it nearly tilts onto two wheels. One of the policemen pulls himself out of the window and aims a pistol at your rear tires.

You reach beneath the backseat and withdraw the tommy gun concealed beneath. With your one usable arm you poke the tommy gun out the window and squeeze off a burst of fire, wide enough to intentionally miss the vehicle behind you, but close enough to frighten the policeman, who slides back into the car.

"My turn," Violet says. She straddles the door frame, so that her head's outside of the car while one leg remains inside to anchor her in place.

It had been a flawless warm Louisianan night before, but Violet telegraphs her usual prayers up into the clouds, and the maelstrom gates open. A heavy shower hammers down on the police car.

With the downpour obscuring the windshield, the passengers probably can't see that the storm is miraculously leaving the Tiki Bandits in peace.

Your pursuers forge blindly on, but Violet's not done yet. The precipitation shifts to freezing rain, which crystallizes into ice as soon as it hits the road.

The driver of the police car, unaccustomed to icy

roads in New Orleans, panics and twists the wheel hard in the opposite direction. As a result, their spinout worsens and they slam sideways into a lamppost.

With your pursuers incapacitated, Violet slips back into the car. From the wicker basket in the front seat, she produces a bottle of real French champagne—a gift from Vi's bootlegging contacts. She pops the cork and pours two glasses. "Sorry, Brigid," you say as you take a glass. "Somebody has to drive."

Brigid just mutters something about how you better save some bubbly for her or she'll send the Wild Hunt after you.

As you cruise past the eclectically colored residences of the French Quarter, Violet slides into the backseat so that she's sitting between you and the money. "We did it, Baby Sister," she says, and raises her glass. "Here's to another great heist."

You hesitate. Tonight was a close call. It was sloppy of you not to hear that guard sneak up from behind. And when you started down this path of thievery with Violet, you promised you'd take only as much as you needed to survive. Not only do you now have enough to live comfortably, but you've landed in a city that you've come to love—and best of all, found a man who adores you.

You reach up and tug off your wooden mask, which you cast out the window and into the street. It collides with a lamppost and falls facedown to the sidewalk.

You finally clink your champagne flute with your sister's and say, "Here's to my last."

For the better part of the next morning and afternoon, you lie in bed, drifting in and out of sleep—because you know that the moment you climb out from beneath your covers, your life of adventure is officially over, for better or worse. You also don't want to face Violet, whose silence when you got home last night can only mean she's taken your retirement personally.

Violet finally barges into your room closer to sundown and throws a dress onto your head. When you claw the fabric away from your face, Violet is already walking for the door. "You can retire all you want, Lucille, but you are *not* making me go to the governor's party all by my lonesome."

You spread out the dress on the bed and wrinkle your nose. You're still a country girl at heart, and you're starting to realize that when you threw that mask out the window last night, you may have only been trading one disguise for another.

The governor's soirees grow increasingly lavish every time he throws one. Tonight is no exception. When you get there, the old plantation's backyard blazes with a small galaxy's worth of lanterns. You and Violet have received regular invitations, much to the chagrin of the governor's wife, ever since Governor Dupre discovered the two of you walking down Bourbon Street—his "island ambassadors" he called you, "come to bring the sunshine to this great community."

You sit on the weathered picnic bench and watch the crowd of old-money husbands and wives, the New Orleans aristocracy, accumulating on the sweeping lawn. "I wonder," you say, "how welcome we'd be here if the governor knew we were stealing his money from a bank just last night."

Violet snorts. "Consider it payment for the fact that the weather is always immaculate at his parties. If it weren't twenty degrees cooler than everywhere else, he would have sweated through his Parisian suit four times by now."

"And judging from the glaze over his eyes when we came to the door, he probably has a bathtub full of moonshine, so he would be the last person to pass judgment on our unlawfulness," you say as you unscrew the cap of your flask and take a swig. "Not that I'd be the one to judge his temperance either."

You squint at a figure making his way around the side of the house, decked out in a black tuxedo. Is that him?

Violet notices your fixation on the newcomer and gives you a hard shove forward. You topple off the picnic bench and nearly land on your knees. "Go," she says. "Go find your strapping fiancé and *smother* him with affection, you card."

You smile and walk backward. "Only if you go find a rich widower or an unhappy husband."

Violet raises her flask to salute you. "Your will shall be done."

Sure enough, the handsome newcomer is walking your way—he's always been able to seek you out like an arrow to its target, even in crowds—and he wraps his arms around you as soon as he's within range. His muscular hands pull you tightly against his body and lift you off the ground, then spin you in a pirouette. Even when he sets you back down to earth, he never lets you go.

Instead he eyes your arms, which are encircling his neck. You melted the metal off your arm after the heist, but it didn't completely slough off in some spots—a few traces remain, delicate copper veins intertwining from your elbow to your wrist.

He releases you but gingerly unfolds your palm to inspect it. Your life line and love line, too, are still embossed with metal that wouldn't melt out of the groove.

"What were you doing last night?" he asks suspiciously, then his eyes grow wide. "Please tell me you didn't melt the—"

"Don't worry." You hold up your other hand, and the enormous ring glitters underneath the cloudless moon. "Gleams as bright as the day you gave it to me. Although if I ever catch you eyeing another woman, don't be surprised if I turn this ring into a puddle."

Your fiancé adjusts his lapel as though he's suddenly become too warm. "I'm pretty sure you'd turn me into a puddle first."

Before you can explain to him that he can expect a *far* more painful end if there's ever even a question of infidelity, the two of you are interrupted. The governor has spotted you. "Lucille," he purrs in his gruff and musical Cajun accent. He takes you by the left hand and presses his lips to your skin. You pray that he won't see—or taste—the residual metal.

"Governor," you reply, and give a slight bow. Such formalities always seem to please him, though you could probably spit in his face and he'd still be delighted. You've never seen him frown.

He gestures to the skies. "I swear every time you come, you bring your beautiful island weather with you. Our delta never saw such heavenly skies before you and your sister came to our shores."

You nudge your fiancé, who is now smirking wildly. "I like to think," you say, "that we find good fortune wherever we go."

The governor finally acknowledges the man at your side. "And this dapper, grinning fool must be the mountain man who stole my Lucille away."

"Not too many mountains where I'm from," he replies, and extends his hand.

"Well, even if you were from the plantations of hell, you're welcome here as long as you make this lady glow." The governor envelops your fiancé's hand with both of his own. "Do you have a strong name to go with that strong handshake?"

"I certainly hope it's strong, since it's soon to be hers as well." He winks at you. "The name is Colton Halliday. Call me Colt."

"Well, Halliday, you two dote on each other enough for them to feel the beating of your hearts in Baton Rouge." The governor takes Colt's hand and places it in yours. You're surprised that he doesn't offer to read your marriage rites then and there. "I have a feeling," the governor says, "that this truly is a love that will last a lifetime."

Colt touches the side of your face with his free hand. "I think we've got a good shot at lasting longer than that."

There was someone sitting on Ash's bed.

One moment she was in Prohibition-era New Orleans, the next she was awake in the artificial cool of an air-conditioned Miami condominium, with a very alert-looking Wes perched on her bedside. The sinking of the mattress under his weight must have woken her from the dream—the memory?—the reality of which she would have to save until later to deliberate. Wes was watching her intently, and as soon as she blinked and pulled herself up into a sitting position, he said, "I have a very important question for you."

Ash rubbed her hair, self-conscious that thirty-six hours into meeting her, Wes had now seen what a train wreck she looked like when she first woke up. Goddesses were not immune to the concerns of normal mortal females. "What is it?" she asked.

"Do you," he said deliberately, drawing out each word, "prefer white or whole wheat toast? We're fresh out of pumpernickel."

So he was making jokes now, his soft grin and sarcasm resurrected just hours after his sober departure from the roof last night. Still, she wasn't about to start asking about his dead father—whom Wes had apparently killed himself, though Aurora had left the details vague. So instead Ash said, "Aren't carbs illegal in Miami? Am I *allowed* to eat toast?"

His eyes unashamedly swept from her shoulders down to her waist. "Whatever your current diet consists of is treating you well, so don't go starving yourself on Miami's account."

She pulled the sheets back up to conceal her body and kicked him through the covers. "Thanks, pervert. Give me ten. Surprise me on the toast."

"As you wish." He gave an exaggerated bow and backed out of the room.

Ash collapsed onto her back in a human *T*, letting the pillows cushion her head as she went down. The current state of her love life was rapidly growing back into a tangled briar patch.

If last night's dream was a true echo of her last time on earth, then Colt wasn't just her ex-boyfriend in this life. He was her fiancé in the last as well.

Now she was potentially being courted by a night god she'd temporarily moved in with, even though she barely knew him. If their conversation on the roof was any indication, his flirtatious, carefree playboy demeanor was just the skim layer of an abyss of baggage.

Colt had tried to conceal his godliness from her, whereas Wes had been honest with her from the start. Did that mean she'd learned her lesson in the male department? Or was the fact that she was contemplating the affections of yet *another* god proof that she *hadn't* learned her lesson?

Days like this made her almost wish that she was back in Scarsdale, oblivious to her fiery powers and still dating juvenile yet predictable mortals like Rich Lesley.

Wes chose that moment to wander past Ash's open door on his way to the kitchen, and she caught a glimpse of his bare abs. Apparently he'd decided to cook shirtless this morning.

Maybe Ash *could* live with complexity.

And suddenly she was stomach-numbingly hungry.

Breakfast might have been delicious, but Ash couldn't particularly remember. For some reason most of what she remembered from the morning meal consisted of throwing her dignity to the dogs and sneaking glances at Wes while he made omelets.

Aurora, who had been snickering at Ash's wandering eyes, left as soon as she'd wolfed down her plate of eggs. She had a cooking gig at a restaurant on Ocean Drive, which, judging from the back-and-forth between her and Wes, was some source of tension.

Why Wes so adamantly disapproved of Aurora's job, Ash couldn't say. Aurora's loose-fitting white button-down totally concealed her folded wings well. It wasn't like she was waitressing in a low-cut tank top.

Besides, Ash thought, if she were living in Wes's pad full-time, she'd feel awkward just coasting on Wes's inheritance—an inheritance that was already shrouded in mystery as it was.

After breakfast Ash took the opportunity to call home to Scarsdale, since a small library of voice mails and texts from her parents had already accrued in her cell phone's in-box. She hoped that by calling the house she could get away with leaving a voice mail, but Gloria Wilde picked up almost immediately. It wouldn't have surprised Ash if her parents were taking turns working from home just to thwart her attempts at avoiding direct contact.

So for the next fifteen minutes, Ash improvised a wild story about following a lead that Eve had "enrolled in art school" somewhere in Miami. She was even able to work some half-truths into the tall tale, like how her search for Eve had led her to a white-tie event at a seaside mansion. Making the whole trip sound like a trip to the museum seemed to calm some of her mother's anxiety . . . but even then, Ash still had to spend the remainder of the conversation dodging her mother's insistence that she fly down.

"Everything's going to be just fine," Ash assured her mom yet again. "I'm staying with friends now, and they'll make sure I stay out of trouble."

"I didn't know you had friends from Blackwood who lived in Miami," her mom said, surprised. "And their parents are okay with them escorting you around the city?"

Ash peeked out the door at Wes, who was humming to himself as he rinsed off the breakfast dishes in the sink. Surely no one in the history of the civilized world had managed to look so sexy using a spatula to scrape burned egg off a frying pan. "Actually," Ash said, "the head of the household is all for it."

Once Ash finally hung up with her mother and returned to the kitchen, Wes cryptically mentioned that he wanted to take her to visit a friend, and that she should wear beach-appropriate shoes. Ash resisted at first. She had come to Miami to find Rose, not to socialize. But for the time being at least, she was out of leads. Maybe some fresh air would help her to generate a plan of attack.

She slipped into her sandals and watched Wes pile a brown paper bag full to the brim with groceries out of one of the cupboards. "Is this friend of yours . . . hungry?" she asked.

He sifted through the contents of the bag to make sure everything was there, comparing it to a handwritten list on a yellow piece of paper. "Let's just say she's sort of a shut-in."

Half an hour later they had pulled into a parking lot on Key Biscayne, an island south of the city connected by bridge to the mainland, and they'd set a course down a palm-lined walkway that led to the beach.

After a long trek down the narrow shoreline, which was sparsely populated with families and couples, Wes pointed toward the cape's southern extremity. At first Ash thought he was gesturing to the tall white lighthouse looming over the beach, but then he set out for a lone gray beach umbrella. A single occupant sat within its shadow, a Latina girl with aviator sunglasses that covered half her face, and black hair so long it brushed the sand when she turned to look at them. She wore a daffodil sundress, and her tan arms were sun-spotted from overexposure. Ash wondered exactly how long she'd been sitting out on this beach.

"I thought you said she was a shut-in," Ash whispered as they approached.

Wes shifted the bag to his other side. "I guess she's technically a *shut-out*. Call the grammar police, why don't you."

"If it isn't my personal grocery delivery service," the girl sang. She lowered her shades just slightly when they neared her.

Wes placed the groceries next to her beach chair. "Right to your front door." He kissed her on either cheek. "How's the view?"

He was of course talking about the unobstructed view of the Atlantic, but the girl was staring right past him at Ash. "The view is just beautiful. You brought me a girl toy?"

Wes exploded with laughter, which only intensified

when he saw Ash's rose-tinged ears. "She's not an escort, Ixtab," he said, pronouncing her name "Esh-tawb." "Ash is a new friend, and the goddess of—"

"I know who Ashline Wilde is," Ixtab interrupted him. "Or should I say *Pele*?"

Ash, who was growing more unnerved by the moment, took an uneasy step backward. "Have we . . . met?"

Ixtab slowly pulled herself to a standing position and stepped into the sun. "You haven't met me, but I've met you. Twice, in fact." Before Ash could even piece together a question, Ixtab's body stiffened all at once. Her expression melted into nothingness, and even though Ash couldn't see behind her sunglasses, she could tell that Ixtab's eyes were staring somewhere . . . else.

Ash waved her hand in front of Ixtab's unmoving face just to be sure. Then she leaned around and shot a frantic look at Wes for help. "Is she epileptic or something?"

Wes was frowning too, but he wasn't even looking at Ixtab. Instead he was watching Ash with some concern. "She's the goddess of the gallows," he explained. "She comforts those who have died from violence or suicide during their final moments as they . . . pass over."

At least that explained how she'd seen Ash before— once at the death of Lizzie Jacobs, and then again when Lily had murdered Rolfe. It also explained why Wes was looking at her as though she were a total stranger. "Do you have any *normal* friends?" she asked, hoping it would snap him out of it.

"Do you?" he shot back.

Ixtab bristled, back in the moment with them. She removed her sunglasses and massaged the bridge of her nose. Despite the ninety-degree weather of the beach, she was shivering.

"You were gone a long time," Wes said. "Was it a bad one?"

Ixtab answered by walking back under the umbrella and rifling through the bag of groceries. While they watched, she sorted through the items on top—a pint of strawberries, a box of granola—until she found what she was looking for beneath. "Aha!" she exclaimed, and held up a box of heavily processed cream-filled chocolate cupcakes. "I'll never understand why you continue to hide these beneath the healthy stuff. Just leave them on top."

Wes crossed his arms. "Because there's no god of good nutrition around to watch over you."

She unhooked a can of cola from a plastic ring and tossed it to Wes, who snatched it out of the air. "Take a walk," Ixtab said, and nodded to Ash. "Hot stuff and I need to have some girl talk."

"Fine." His can of soda hissed as he cracked the top. He held it up in a lazy salute and walked off. "Don't corrupt Ash while I'm gone."

"Oh, please." Ash kicked a clump of sand at him, even though he was already out of projectile range. "She can't do anything to me that six months of isolated boarding school life didn't already do."

Ixtab raised an eyebrow. "You sure about that? Even you look skeptical."

Ash pointed to the six-pack. "Just pass me a soda."

Ixtab laughed and did as she was instructed, prying one loose for herself as well, but Ash couldn't help but notice that Ixtab's smile was stale, as though her face would crack like mud under a hot sun if she laughed too hard. "You're funnier in person," Ixtab said. "But then again, they always are." She glanced down the beach, to where Wes was getting smaller as he headed for the lighthouse.

"You didn't exactly see me in my shining moments." Ash settled down into the sand, taking refuge beneath the relative cool of the umbrella's shade. "So how often does . . . *it* happen?"

"Depends." Ixtab sipped her cola and wiggled until she found a comfortable position in her chair. "Usually it's instantaneous, sometimes a couple of seconds. It will no doubt happen many times throughout this conversation, and you may not even notice. But if it's really bad . . . well, for those I'll be gone as long as a minute. It all really depends on how far the victim has to go to find peace."

"But where do you take them?"

"Darling." Ixtab coiled her long hair around her finger. "I'm not a flight attendant. I have no clue where my passengers are going. It's not like I'm sunnily announcing over the intercom, 'It's seventy-three degrees and cloudless in Tampa. Please watch your step as you de-board, and enjoy your afterlife.' In fact, it's more about helping them come to terms with leaving this life behind than it is preparing them for whatever the hell lies beyond it."

Ash slipped her fingers into the sand, through the warm top layer into the cool, moist depths beneath. Rolfe would have been in heaven here.

"I'm sorry," Ixtab said. She removed her sunglasses and studied Ash with genuine concern. "I'm sure you'd just like to know that Elizabeth and Rolfe have gone on to a better place now."

"You remember their names?"

Ixtab bowed her head. "I remember *all* of their names. When you've stood beside someone in their final moments, shared that sort of emotional intimacy with them . . . how can you ever forget?"

"Do you come out here to be alone?" Ash gestured to the beach, which was gradually filling up with families. "If that's the case, I'm sure you could find someplace more isolated than a public beach in Miami."

Ixtab shook her head. "When a person experiences violence, whether they're the victim, the perpetrator, or— like you—just a witness, they're indelibly marked by that moment." A little girl with golden curls, no older than four, skittered by just then, wildly swinging a sand pail as she went. Her mother trotted after her, laughing the whole way. Ixtab smiled faintly. "I don't come here to get away from everyone. Just to be around those who haven't yet been scarred. Also," she added, "the whisper of the ocean reminds me that I'm back, keeps me grounded in reality even while my mind is racing off to the corners of the globe to clean up humanity's mess every four seconds."

Ash drilled her soda can into the sand. "You must see our kind a lot."

"Sometimes, when sleep finds me, I see flickers of violence from my previous lives. Ancient wars, cities conquered, bloody crusades . . . and our people are always there. Sometimes on the front lines, but often in the shadows." Ixtab breathed deeply. "The gods are born with every power imaginable. The power to control fire, to control storms. Power over the night and over the day. The power of life and death. It seems like the only ability that we lack is the power to *not kill each other*. This has happened every generation, and if there's one sure thing I can tell you, it's that this will continue to go on until our sun goes dark."

Ash thought back to what Colt had said about the Cloak, that they were not only blocking the gods' memories from returning with each new life, but potentially interfering with their reincarnations as well.

Maybe, she thought, the world would be a better place without us.

Maybe we shouldn't come back.

"Funny," Ixtab continued, "how so many mythologies have gods of war, and so few have harbingers of peace."

"Just because 'peace' doesn't come in our job title, doesn't mean it's not in the job description," Ash said. "One of the reasons I came to Miami is because I'm tired of being a witness. Watching two people die while I stood by helplessly was enough for one lifetime. Hell, it's enough for all of them."

A figure approached from the direction of the lighthouse—Wes, who had apparently decided that their time for "girl talk" had expired, although their discussion had wildly departed from talk of clothing and boys.

Ixtab was watching him as well. "I sent Wes away so we could talk freely. It's not my place to share with him any details of your history that I've witnessed. But the two of you are kindred spirits in more ways than you can imagine. You both *seek* peace, and I fear that is why you both may never find it."

"I'll do whatever it takes not to make a third appearance in your visions," Ash said firmly.

Ixtab turned so fast on her that Ash flinched and tipped over her soda. "What I'm telling you," Ixtab said with authority, "is that for you to find peace, there may come a time when you will *have* to see me again. One way or the other."

Wes ducked under the umbrella. "You two need a few more minutes, or are the boys allowed to play now?"

Ash just watched the pool of spilled cola slowly sinking into the sand. The oval silhouette it left could have been a surfboard.

"Where's that beautiful songbird of yours?" Ixtab purred, her gloomy demeanor gone.

"Aurora's at work," Wes said. "And she's still straight."

"Damn." Ixtab slouched back into her seat and let out a long sigh. "One of these days that girl's going to realize what she's missing out on."

With a shudder Ixtab's hand went slack on the arm-rest and her head drooped to the side. Her sunglasses dropped to the sand. Something about the distance in her unseeing pupils led Ash to believe that Ixtab wouldn't be back for a while this time.

Ash stood up and reached into the grocery bag. She pulled out one of the plastic-wrapped cupcakes and set it down on Ixtab's armrest. "For when she returns," Ash explained to Wes.

On their way back to the car, Ash maintained a brisk pace, so much so that at one point the much taller Wes had to jog to catch up with her. "Wait," he said, and grabbed her by the arm. "Where's the fire?" He laughed after he said it. "I guess you would know if there was one."

Ash barely heard him. A plot was growing in her like a wild vine. "Where does Lesley Vanderbilt live?"

He squinted at her, then glanced back down the beach toward where Ixtab's camp was. "What exactly did Ixtab say to you?"

"She just reminded me that I'm not here for spring break. That I'm not here for me." And it was true. Back in California, Ash had been so inwardly focused, so preoccupied with preserving the last remnants of her normal mortal life, that she'd missed the little details that could have prevented so much pain—the poison building up in Lily before she cracked, all of Colt's red flags. If she'd taken action before the actions of others had come to her. Well, she wasn't going to make that same mistake again. "So where does Lesley live?"

Wes hesitated. "Coral Gables," he said quietly. "It's no secret where her hacienda is. But do you really think she's keeping your little sister in her own mansion?"

"I'm not going there to look for my sister," Ash replied. Finding her sister was the endgame, but what she needed for now was a starting point. She needed the element of surprise. And there was still one person in Miami who didn't know she'd arrived. "I'm going there to kidnap Lesley Vanderbilt."

Kidnapping Lesley Vanderbilt the same night she'd decided to throw a large dinner party was, Ash realized as they pulled up outside Lesley's hacienda, less than ideal.

After manipulating some of Wes's contacts within the Vanderbilt empire, they had gleaned inside information that Lesley was hosting a board of trustees dinner at home. So much for an in-and-out kidnapping.

"This is a horrible idea," Aurora reminded them for the third time as they walked around to the back of the van they'd rented. "Entertaining, possibly ingenious, but ultimately horrible."

Ash slipped the black apron over her head and pointed to the FORBIDDEN SWEETS BAKERY decal they'd applied to the side of the otherwise plain vehicle. "Why? You don't think Lesley has a sweet tooth?"

"I don't care if she's a *sugar fetishist*. She has four supernatural bodyguards who'd like to see you filleted and served for supper." Aurora opened up the back door of the van and pointed at Wes, who was sitting patiently inside next to a very elegant four-tiered tangerine-colored cake. "I can't believe you of all people are supporting this plan, Wes."

"Oh, come on." Wes nodded to the towering bakery creation next to him. "It will be a piece of cake."

"I can't believe you just said that," Ash said. "I'm actually embarrassed for you."

Wes responded by grabbing a handful of flour from the bag on the cake's pushcart and slinging it at Ash. It caught her fully across the chest, exploding in a fine white mist. When Ash was done coughing, she touched her hair and then looked down at her apron, which was coated in flour. "What the hell, Wes? Our plan didn't involve me looking like a powdered donut."

"Now it looks like you've actually been baking the cake yourself, and not that we took it off the hands of Miami's finest bridal bakery." He hopped down off the back of the truck and ran a finger along the side of her forehead. His fingertip came away white, and he sucked his finger for good measure.

"You are such a child," Aurora said. "He also puts his elbows on the dinner table, FYI."

Ash tried to shake the rest of the flour from her hair. "I bet he plays with his food, too."

Wes winked at her. "What do you think I was just doing?"

The cake cart, complete with the cake on top, must have weighed a hundred pounds easy, but since it was after nightfall, Wes was able to single-handedly lift the dolly and place it on the ground.

Aurora gave them a three-fingered salute. "I'll have the car idling for when you come racing out of the hacienda after this plan inevitably explodes in your face."

"Trust me, if there are any explosions," Ash said, "they'll be on purpose." She slammed the back door closed.

Ash and Wes, decked out in their aprons and baker's hats, wheeled the enormous cake up to the front entrance of the hacienda. The doors were wide open to let in the fresh Miami air, but there were two men in suits posted to either side of the entrance. Fortunately, neither guard was a member of the Four Seasons. As long as Thorne had kept his word and said nothing about Ash to his boss, they were safe.

One of the guards peeled away from the wall and stepped into their path. "Catering got here two hours ago," he said. "They didn't say they were expecting a cake."

Ash gestured back to the van. "This is a Forbidden Sweets delivery. A four-tiered tangerine-glazed dark chocolate cake for Lesley Vanderbilt, on behalf of Mario De La Cruz of the *Miami Ledger*. He sends his compliments on last night's successful—"

"Yeah, yeah." The guard yawned, stepped aside, and waved her through. "Just leave it in the kitchen and let catering divvy it up to the aristocrats."

"Let them eat cake," Ash said regally as they pushed the cart up the ramp and over the hump that marked the hacienda's threshold. Both the guards laughed.

Lesley's hacienda was like a smaller version of the villa where they'd held the presentation the night before—but not smaller by much. The walls of the entrance foyer curved right up into vaulted ceilings, made of adobe that looked as though it could have come straight out of a kiln. The hall was lined with plants potted in turquoise vases. Strangest of all, Lesley seemed to have completely shunned electricity, since the hallway was dimly lit by candles on tall brass candelabras.

Wes slowed the cart down to take in the clay-tiled hallway. "I'm just waiting for Zorro to pop out from behind a pillar," he whispered. "Does she have some weird fixation on the way things used to be?"

Ash ran her finger over the wick of a candle as they passed. It's something she'd always done for a thrill when she was a kid, an irony she could appreciate now. "Considering the lengths she's been going to to get her hands on Eve—all to avenge a grandfather who died eighty years ago and whom she never met—I don't think an obsession with the old days is out of the question."

They turned a corner and came to a sweeping staircase that ascended to the upper floor. If the second story had even half the square footage of the first, Wes would have a lot of ground to cover. Somehow she'd convinced him to do a sweep of the upper floors to search for any trace of the little Rose, or at least something that might point them in the right direction. In the meantime Ash would carry out her plan to wrangle Lesley Vanderbilt.

Wes rolled the cake cart to a stop and surprised Ash by seizing her hands. "You sure I can't convince you to switch roles with me?" Wes ducked down so that they were on eye level with each other. "Maybe it makes sense for *you* to search for your sister, since you know what she looks like."

Ash couldn't help but laugh, even though she was having trouble returning his intense gaze. "She's a six-year-old Polynesian girl who's probably on a leash. I'm sure there aren't too many of those hanging out in the hacienda." When he still didn't look appeased, she added, "And there's a chance that I can bargain with Lesley if I can get her alone. She has something I want, and I know the location of something she wants. If we can agree on an exchange, there doesn't have to be a fight."

He hesitated at first, but finally released her hands. "Fifteen minutes," he said. "Fifteen minutes tops and we meet back at the cart. Any longer than that and Tweedle-Dee and Tweedle-Douche at the front door are going to wonder where the bakers went." Wes leaned in and kissed her on the cheek, not far from her mouth. His lips lingered against her skin. "For good luck," he added. Then he loped up the stairs two at a time until he had rounded the corner out of sight.

Ash touched the hollow of her cheek where the shape of his lips still persisted. "That's going to make for some interesting dreams tonight," she whispered.

With any luck the bed-igniting-sex-dream phase was something she'd outgrown since she'd left Blackwood.

Ash slowly pushed the cake cart down the hallway, drawing closer to the voices that were echoing down the vaulted hall. She eventually stopped where the windows opened out into a central courtyard. At first she was afraid that she might be seen if she tried to get a closer look, but then she realized that Lesley's old-world lighting would work to her advantage. Ash passed her hands in front of the nearest candles and the flames extinguished immediately. Then she ducked down, shrouded in the new darkness, and stared out over the window ledge into the open-air courtyard.

In the torch-lined courtyard, in the midst of a tropical garden, Lesley sat at the head of a long table with twelve board members gathered around her, six to either side. She was gesturing recklessly with a wine goblet. From the glaze over her eyes and the trickle of wine that dribbled over the edge of her glass as she flailed about, it was clear that Lesley was really hitting the sauce tonight.

Ash counted the trustee members around her just to confirm that there were in fact twelve. What was this, the Last Supper?

Lesley's twelve "apostles" also seemed to have indulged, from the looks of the empty wine bottles that were now scattered around the table like fallen tombstones, and the trustees too were chattering excitedly.

That is, all except for one. A board member with a Fu Manchu sat rigidly in his chair near the end of the table. Unlike the others, he hadn't let out his tie or removed his suit jacket, and he was staring into his glass of wine, which was still decidedly full.

Apparently the man with the Fu Manchu had finally had enough, because he tapped his glass with a fork and then spoke commandingly so that his voice carried over all the others'. "As much as it pains me to dampen the spirits of this celebration over today's new acquisition," he said in a French accent, "I was hoping the madame would take this opportunity to talk about last night's gala at the Villa Vizcaya."

Lesley barely acknowledged him. "Please, Arthur, we've had enough talk of business for the day. Let's keep this gathering on the pleasure side of things, shall we?" This seemed to be a definitive answer for the other board members, and the pockets of conversation picked up again around the table.

But he wouldn't take "no" for an answer. "I'm just curious why it was necessary to spend six figures on a gathering that, insofar as I can tell, amounted to a circus of wizardry and has potentially transformed this company's name into tabloid fish food."

"Arthur." Lesley leaned over the table, and the conversation around the table died. "We're currently the number three defense contractor in the country. As of last night local media outlets witnessed that we now have a monopoly on a new, previously unrealized threat to *all countries* worldwide. We could be number one internationally by the end of the year. Check your numbers again when that happens, and *then* question my investments."

"Threat?" Arthur's previously restrained disgust emerged. "The way to run a successful defense contractor is to manufacture solutions to *real* threats, not to *fabricate* imaginary ones."

Lesley, who had been midsip, set her goblet down heavily. Wine showered the white tablecloth. "The only thing that's *imaginary* is the need for your concern, especially when it comes to my spending habits and marketing campaigns, unorthodox though they may seem to you."

"Listen to yourself rationalize. '*Marketing campaigns*'? Some days," Arthur said solemnly, "I look at you and I see your father's daughter." He stood up. "Today I just see a spoiled girl who likes to throw rocks at the hornets' nest."

Lesley rose out of her seat so fast that her chair slid backward. Its metal feet grated dissonantly against the stone patio before the chair clattered to the ground.

Arthur didn't look impressed. He picked up his wineglass and irreverently poured the remaining cabernet onto the ground, drawing lazy circles on the tiles. When the last drop had been poured out, he said, "I know a waste when I see one." Then he turned and stormed out of the courtyard.

Ash realized almost too late that he was heading in her direction, so she hustled back to the cake cart and pretended to apply more icing. Arthur, however, paid her no heed, and soon he was gone.

When Ash scurried back over to the window, Lesley was still standing in silence. She had a vise grip on her own wineglass, and Ash was surprised it didn't shatter in her hand.

Then Lesley's outrage slowly dissipated into the night, and she found her way back to a pleasantly intoxicated smile. "Frenchmen," she said, and pointed to the pool of cabernet on the pavement. "They never appreciate a good Napa wine."

The rest of the board laughed uncomfortably. "That laughter sounded far too sober." Lesley shook her head. "I have a great Chianti for dessert that should remedy that. In the meantime . . ." Lesley clapped her hands twice, and a swarm of caterers emerged from a second courtyard entrance, armed with pastry dishes. "Enjoy this white truffle cheesecake that my favorite chef made fresh this afternoon. I shall fetch the wine."

Again Ash hurried over to the cake cart and busied herself, with her back to the courtyard. If Lesley started down the hallway in her direction, then Ash would just have to improvise.

Instead Lesley hung a right out of the doorway and wandered with visible imbalance in the opposite direction. Ash followed close behind. All she needed to do to corner Lesley was wait until they were out of earshot of her party guests, and the millionaire wouldn't stand a chance.

They weren't alone for long, though. Lesley stopped at a door partway down the hall and pounded on the wood. Ash dove into the nearest alcove, and held her hand up to the torch over her head. Her volcanic powers siphoned off the flames until the torch was extinguished with a quiet hiss, cloaking Ash in shadows.

Not a moment too soon either. The door that Lesley had been so vigorously pounding creaked open, and Thorne's angular nose poked through the opening. As usual he had a cigar clenched between his teeth. "Well," he said, his eyes taking in Lesley, who was tottering from foot to foot. "Looks like someone's been hitting the sparkling water hard tonight."

Any merriment Lesley had shown to her board of trustees was gone. She waved her finger sloppily at Thorne. "Having a relaxing night off, are we?" Lesley barked. "Are you and the Four Seasons just *chilling* around the haci-enda, playing Monopoly?"

He lazily tapped his cigar ashes onto the floor. "Trust me, Lesley—we're using all of our resources to locate your Polynesian storm goddess, and we have some solid leads. But the girl isn't exactly writing her name in the sky with lightning."

"I don't care if you have to fly a kite in a storm or run down the street with a lightning rod to find her." Lesley leaned in closer. "I risked my reputation to put your little Four Seasons religion on display in front of some very important people, and now I'm about to put you in front of the world. So now that I've done what you've asked, it's about time that you get off your ass, do your damn job, and *bring me Evelyn Wilde!*"

Thorne leaned in and massaged Lesley's shoulders in a way that made Ash feel icky, even thirty feet down the hallway. "Just wait until Sunday," Thorne said calmly. "After that, wherever Eve is hiding, I'm sure she'll come storming into town looking for the little one. Then it's just a matter of following the trail of electrocuted corpses."

Sunday? Ashline thought. "The little one" was clearly a reference to Rose, but how did they think they could use Rose to lure Eve out of hiding? If only Lesley knew that the only way she could get Eve back was to storm into the Netherworld and steal her back from the Cloak . . .

Whatever they were talking about had obviously calmed Lesley down. "I've waited forty years to get my revenge," she mumbled. "I guess I can wait out the weekend." She patted the side of Thorne's face and then staggered away.

"If you're paying a visit to the wine cellar," Thorne called after her, "I recommend the '87 vintage. It's my favorite." Then he disappeared back into his room.

Ash let out a long breath and emerged from her alcove. At the end of the long hallway, Lesley hauled open a large oak door and descended uncertainly down the staircase inside.

This was it. With Lesley alone in the wine cellar, Ash couldn't ask for a better opportunity. She hurried past Thorne's door and followed Lesley into the cellar.

As Ash padded softly down the steps, she was grateful that the staircase wasn't truly as old as it looked. It didn't creak once, and neither did the door as she pulled it closed and locked it from the inside. No one was going to interrupt this conversation.

Down the stairs, under the dim wine-protective lighting, Lesley was browsing a wall that was filled floor to ceiling with a staggering collection of bottles. Down here the temperature had plummeted twenty degrees, and Ash tried not to shiver while she crept up behind the older woman. She stepped carefully over a white drop cloth that was partially unfurled on the ground. On the back wall of the cellar, some new stonework and a shiny stainless steel door had clearly just been installed for what Ash guessed was cold storage for Lesley's collection of chilled wines.

Finally within range, Ash slipped her hand around Lesley's mouth and whispered harshly into her ear, "Don't move. I'm not going to hurt you."

Rather than listening to her, Lesley let out a short scream into Ash's hand and then elbowed her hard in the chest. The blow was enough to make Ash release Lesley, who grabbed a bottle from the wine rack and swung wildly at Ash's head.

Ash caught Lesley's wrist just as the bottle came within an inch of smashing across her face. In that moment Ash panicked and lashed out with her free arm.

The punch connected solidly with the side of Lesley's head. Her eyes rolled back and she slumped back into the wine rack. The bottles rattled in their slots under the weight of her body before she collapsed to the floor.

Ash dropped into a squat and caught the bottle Lesley had been brandishing. Any later and it would have smashed against the floor.

Ash shook her head at the unconscious woman, then at her own hand, which was still balled into a tight fist. "So much for having a quiet, polite discussion."

At the top of the stairs, the door rattled. When it failed to budge, whoever was behind it knocked on the oak. "Lesley?" Thorne's voice called. "Lesley, are you in there? Why did you lock the door?"

Ash froze. This guy, *again*? The lock on the cellar door was just a big dead bolt. Thorne could break through it with a strong gale if he wanted to. Ash searched around the room for an alternate escape route, on the off chance that Lesley had built the cellar with a contingency plan. No dice. The oak door was the only exit.

Anxious from the silence, Thorne pounded on the door with a sense of urgency. "Lesley, what's going on?"

Ash cleared her throat and attempted her best impression of Lesley's voice, letting her voice drop half an octave into Lesley's husky alto. "Just looking for the dessert wines. Everything's fine. Return to your post." She held her breath. It would be a miracle if he actually bought it.

"Return to my post?" Thorne echoed. "Lesley, what the hell are you talking about?" He jimmied the door handle hard, and then began to slam his shoulder into the wood. On his third attempt Ash heard the door crack.

Ash grabbed the unconscious Lesley by her lapel and heaved her across the floor and onto the drop cloth. Lesley hadn't even finished rolling across the cloth before Ash grabbed the corner and dragged it into the shadowy nook beneath the stairs. The slamming against the door ceased, but Ash knew what was coming, so she piled on top of Lesley and folded the canvas cloth over her to conceal the two of them.

The door came right off its hinges when the gale struck it. Through the peephole she'd left in the drop cloth, Ash watched the door land just shy of destroying part of Lesley's wine collection. The ensuing wind nearly ripped the covers right off Ash's head and, worse, sent a plume of dust her way. Ash covered her mouth and tried her best not to cough or sneeze.

Thorne took the steps four at a time and landed at the bottom of the stairs in a crouch. His eyes vigilantly searched the room. Thankfully he glossed right over Ash's hiding spot.

Then she watched his posture relax as he straightened up, no longer on red alert. "Oh, now I get it. . . ." A carnal smile spread across his face. "You want to play a little game of hide-and-seek. Well, you know I'm always on board for some after-hour festivities."

Between the seductive way he was talking and the shit-eating grin on his face, it immediately dawned on Ash what he was implying.

Him . . .

Ash looked down at Lesley's regal but clearly age-worn face.

And her.

Ash's face convulsed with disgust, and she resisted the urge to retch right then and there. A teenage wind god "mating" with a forty-something bloodthirsty corporate cougar. Disgusting.

If she escaped the hacienda alive, Ash made a note to look up Florida's age of consent.

Thorne wandered over to the side of the wine rack and peeked behind it. "Where, oh where could you be?" His boots passed in front of the drop cloth, but he didn't give it a second look. Instead he seemed fixated on the steel refrigerator door, which was so new that it gleamed even under the dim light.

"I wonder . . . ," he whispered as he trekked across the stone floor. He pulled the lever and hauled the steel door open, which was so big it looked heavy even for him. Then he disappeared inside.

This was Ash's chance, and she knew she would get only one shot. Ash sprung from beneath the drop cloth and headed straight for the door. She grabbed hold of the handle and with all her strength heaved the door shut.

Almost immediately Thorne was back at the door, pushing and pounding from the inside.

While Ash pinned it closed with her feet and shoulder, she focused on last night's dream, how her hand had melted right through the bank vault door. She reached out with her free hand, tapped into her inner fire, and pressed her hand to the metal.

Like an acetylene torch, her fingers made raw, molten slices into the steel as she raked her fingertips from the top of the door, through the lock, and all the way down to the bottom. The igneous metal spilled out over the door frame and leached into the porous stone. The lock itself liquefied under Ash's touch.

And just as easily as she had poured the heat from her hand, her fingertips vacuumed the heat right up again.

When she was confident that the door no longer needed her support to stay shut, she stepped back and admired her handiwork. The entire edge of the door was warped, bubbled, and now cool to the touch. It was going to take another torch to cut Thorne out of there. She could hear his weak attempts at wind already thudding up and down the interior of the door, but in such a confined, nearly airtight space, it was going to take some real ingenuity for Thorne to get out.

"I know it's you!" he screamed from the inside. "I can practically smell your kerosene *stink* from in here."

"You might want to crack open a bottle of that over-priced wine in there to stay warm," Ash suggested, and patted the metal door. "Oh, and I'd conserve your air if I were you. You're going to need it."

The thumping against the metal door picked up with renewed vigor.

Ash crossed the room and grabbed all four corners of the drop cloth where she'd concealed Lesley. "I'm going to apologize in advance for this," she whispered.

With Lesley cocooned in the drop cloth, she pulled her up the stairs one step at a time, then out into the long hallway, like a net full of fish being hauled out of the sea.

Fortunately, the trustee members out in the court-yard were too involved in their raucous conversation to notice Ash towing her load down the hall, or to hear the hiss of the drop cloth against the adobe floor tile.

When Ash finally reached the tangerine cake, she rolled Lesley's body up into the underbelly of the cart, where she would be concealed by the long tablecloth.

With impeccable timing Wes jogged down the stairs

right as Ash began maneuvering the cart down the long hallway. "No dice," he whispered. "No sign of any Polynesian orphans *or* any arrows pointing us in the right direction."

Ash sighed. "So much for the days when crooks kept a paper map on their wall with pins in all the locations you should look."

Wes pointed at the cart as he walked alongside her. "Did you . . ."

"Uh-huh," she said, and kicked the cart's bottom shelf.

"How are we going to explain to the guards why we still have the cake?"

"Push the cart and leave that to me," she replied.

They switched places, and Wes slowed the cart down enough so that Ash could cut two big pieces from the cake's lowest tier. She scooped them onto the serving plates they'd brought along just to further their ruse as bakers.

The two guards outside immediately looked perplexed to see the cake being rolled out intact, but Ash was on top of it. "Apparently Ms. Vanderbilt is allergic to tangerine," she explained. She snagged the two pieces of cake off the cart before Wes dollied it out into the street. "But there's no reason for perfectly good cake to go to waste. Enjoy, boys."

As she left, she overheard one guard say to the other, "Finally this job comes with some perks."

After they'd loaded the cart into the back of the van,

Ash buckled herself into the passenger seat. "Keep an eye on our hitchhiker," she instructed Wes. "She'll be stirring soon."

Wes lifted the edge of the sheet and peeked underneath. "Considering how hard you must have *negotiated* with her to knock her out this long, we might want to have some aspirin ready for when she wakes up. Or at least a slice of cake."

"Where to now?" Aurora flipped on the van's headlights as they rounded a corner and drove out of the Gables by the Sea neighborhood. "I suspect you'll want someplace quiet and cozy for your date with sleeping beauty?"

Ash rolled down her window and let the tepid Miami air wash over her face. "As a matter of fact, I know just the place."

When Lesley's eyes flickered open, Ash was patiently sitting across from her in a little wooden chair with her hands clasped between her legs.

"Where . . ." Lesley mumbled.

Ash gave Lesley a minute to lasso her senses back in—to recall the remarkably short-lived brawl in the wine cellar, to test the ropes that were tethering her to the stiff wooden chair, to take in the fact that she was sitting face-to-face with the volcano goddess whose family she had vowed to destroy.

Ash reached under her chair and held out a pastry

plate. "Cake?" She pulled it back just a few inches. "Or are you *actually* allergic to tangerines? Because that would be a hilarious coincidence."

Lesley responded only by jerking her hands, which were tied to the chair's wooden armrests, eventually pulling hard enough that the legs of the chair lifted off the ground. When that proved fruitless, she looked around the inside of the metal container. Then her gaze fell to the floor itself, the soggy carpet over the steel flooring.

"Ah, yes. This room looks familiar, doesn't it?" Ash pointed to the hammock that was still swaying in the corner from the sea's gentle undulations. "This is the four-star cruise ship bedroom that you holed my little sister up in after you kidnapped her."

Lesley groaned and attempted to blow a strand of hair out of her eyes. "You say 'kidnapped.' I say 'rescued from certain death.' Without me Rose would either be jaguar food or target practice for the rain forest militia."

"Yeah, and then you inducted her into a cult with sociopathic gods who have lost all touch with reality. At least one of whom is a murderess."

Lesley snorted. "Sociopathic gods . . . murderers . . . You could be describing the Wilde family, for all I know."

Ash stood up and hurled her own chair at the container wall, where it splintered on impact. Then she seized Lesley by the throat and shoved her back. The chair balanced up on two legs and then crashed back onto the floor, taking Lesley with it.

Lesley gritted her teeth and squeezed her eyes closed.

"See what I mean? You've come *so* far since the days of Lizzie Jacobs."

"Where is my little sister, you cradle-robbing psycho?" Ash shook Lesley by her lapel and slammed the back of the chair against the ground again.

"Where's your *older* sister?" Lesley shouted back. "You know what I want. I'll hang on to the wrong Wilde for as long as it takes if it eventually leads me to the right one."

Ash straightened up and took several deep breaths. She thought she'd left her days of violent rage behind her in Scarsdale, but how easily it all came back when someone like Lesley Vanderbilt pushed the right buttons.

Ash lit a small, hot fire around the length of her pointer finger, and used it to sheer through the bonds that were holding Lesley's arms in place on the chair.

Lesley held up her hands, clearly surprised to be free, and rolled off the chair onto her feet. She massaged her rope-burned wrists and regarded Ash suspiciously.

"Come on," Ash said, and walked toward the door to the storage crate. "I have a business proposition for you."

The two of them walked out to the deck. At first Lesley kept her distance from Ash, as though she were convinced that the volcano goddess was going to incinerate her and toss her charred remains overboard. But as they approached the starboard railing, she seemed to notice that the boat was actually moving.

Ash leaned up against the railing. Wes had steered the boat out into the open water. The distant lights of South

Beach, and beyond that, the Miami skyline, glowed faint to the west. The moon blazed down on the Atlantic from the eastern horizon, sending a snaking oil trail of light over the swells.

"Eve isn't coming for Rose," Ash explained when Lesley finally joined her at the boat's edge, "because Eve is in hell."

"What?" Lesley's shrill voice cut through the night air just as the engine died.

"But not for good," Ash said. "And that's where I want to make a deal with you: one sister for the other. Eve Wilde for Rose. We believe that Rose can open a doorway into the underworld, and only through that rift can we extract Eve."

"That's convenient. You need Rose first before you can give me Eve. You chose family loyalty the last time over my original proposition. How can I trust you to turn the elder Wilde over to me once you've brought her back?"

Ash gazed down into the moonlit water that was lapping at the hull of the boat. From this close she could taste the salt of the sea, taste the subtle difference between the Atlantic, here, and the Pacific where she'd subdued Eve, where she'd allowed her sister to get dragged into oblivion by a monstrous entity no one fully understood.

Some tastes you never forgot.

"Because," she answered finally, "I was the one who sent Eve to hell."

"If I do this," Lesley said, boiling over from suspicion

into excitement, "it will be an open betrayal of the Four Seasons."

"But why?" Ash asked. "Rose may be powerful, but at the end of the day she's still a six-year-old girl. I understand why the Four Seasons needed you to get the attention of the media, but where does a clueless kindergartner like Rose fall into their big picture?"

"I . . . I overheard them saying something about using her 'to revisit the past.'" Lesley shook her head. "It doesn't really matter. As soon as she goes missing, they'll come for me. And then they'll come for you."

"Let us take care of them," Ash said. "Which brings me to the catch. I need you to do one other thing for me: The Four Seasons talked about neutralizing a threat, another god. I need to know what they're planning."

Wes and Aurora came out of the cabin just then and joined the circle. Lesley tucked her hair behind her ear as she studied the two newcomers. "They had me buy a small fortune in airtime on a cluster of television networks. From what I understand, they captured some god last week. While the world watches, they're going to drug and sedate him, so that he's just lucid enough to use his powers, but too out of it for it to be a fair fight." She paused. "And then they're going to sacrifice him."

Ash sagged. Gods killing other gods in cold blood? It was Blackwood all over again. New city, new gods, same backstabbing.

Aurora let her wings unfold and fill up like a sail with

the sea wind. "Establishing religion through terror and killing. Sounds like a new crusade."

"Where are they holding their victim?" Ash asked.

"Not even I am privy to that information," Lesley replied, then eagerly added, "but I can find out."

Wes handed her a black cell phone. "There's one encrypted number programmed into this. Once you find out where he's being held, pass the information along. Sooner rather than later, so we're not picking up an innocent god's corpse off a Miami sidewalk after the broadcast."

Lesley cradled the phone in her hands. "There's an old artesian well in Coral Gables, a public pool that my company has roped off for the week while we do restorations. When I have your bush child ready for you, I'll contact you and we can meet there."

"Wait," Aurora protested. "How do we know she's not just setting up an ambush, courtesy of her seasonally affected friends?"

"Lesley's too smart for that," Ash said in what she intended to be a half-statement, half-threat. "Because I'm the gatekeeper to what she's been looking for her entire life. And if she crosses me now, her descendants will have a new Wilde to hunt down . . . for incinerating their grandmother."

Lesley nodded absently, but her eyes had glazed over. Perhaps she was fantasizing what she would do when she finally had the prize she'd sought all these years. Or perhaps she was considering how she could possibly contain the untamable beast that was Eve Wilde once Ash delivered her. Either way, she was off in nirvana when she rested her elbows on the railing.

Only when they'd finally returned to the river marina and docked did the reality of Lesley's kidnapping seem to sink in. "My people must be on red alert by now. You did," Lesley reminded Ash, "kidnap me from the middle of a trustees meeting."

"Make something up," Ash suggested. "Tell them you got drunk and went out joyriding in your boat. You seem like a convincing liar." Ash slapped Lesley on the back with enough force to make her stumble all the way down the gangplank to the marina deck. "We'll see you and Rose at that old pool at midnight tomorrow . . . and not a minute later."

The three of them watched Lesley go, before Wes asked the one question Ash had been thinking herself. "Do you really intend to trade one sister for another?"

Ash pulled out the cell phone she'd be using for her communication with Lesley. "Not if I don't have to. I wouldn't be too worried about Eve, though. If there's one thing you should know about my sister, it's this:

"Even hell is too small to hold her for long."

Celebration was in order, if only because Ash had successfully completed her first kidnapping and no one had ended up dead.

Although, the thought of Thorne possibly freezing to

death in the wine cellar was an admittedly pleasant one.

The thought of Thorne and Lesley "together," however, was not.

Aurora dragged Ash and Wes to a small club in Little Havana called El Cielo Cristal, a Venezuelan bar along Calle Ocho. The interior wasn't much to look at—a long bar in front of a dingy mirror—but the true appeal was the salsa band performing on the small stage. The open-air seating had all been pushed aside to form a dance floor, where a large mass of dancers was churning to the sultry music. Overhead the metal rafters were strewn with a thick webbing of white holiday lights.

To Ash the romance of string lights had long since faded. Now they summoned only flashbacks to the Shelton Inn and the night of the fire and Rolfe's death, a memory that kept resurfacing like an apple bobbing to the top of a dark barrel. No matter how hard she pushed the memory down, the littlest triggers kept buoying it to the front of her mind.

Wes almost immediately spotted somebody he knew—from the way the other man carried himself, Ash guessed he was the owner—so Ash and Aurora sidled up to the bar by themselves.

Aurora tapped on the bar to get the bartender's attention. *"Tres avocado coladas, por favor."*

The bartender snickered a little bit and said, "But of course."

Aurora puckered her lips when she turned to Ash.

"I've lived in Miami four years, and my Spanish still makes the natives laugh."

"At least you don't get carded," Ash said.

Aurora tugged at the black cardigan over her shoulder. "Probably because hiding the wings requires an elderly fashion sense sometimes. Tough to look stylish and sexy when you have a nine-foot wingspan that needs to go unnoticed."

Ash clinked martini glasses with Aurora in a toast and said, "On the bright side, wings make it easier to pull off the angelic look."

Aurora shook her head and laughed under her breath. "Do you carry around a book full of these jokes, or do you pull them all out of your ass?"

Ash took a sip of the colada, which, between the pea-green complexion of the liquefied avocado and the coconut shavings on top, could have been sludge from the Miami sewers. So it was to her surprise when she liked it—the soft chill, the sweet kick of lime juice. But then the harsh undercurrent of rum hit her and she began to cough.

Aurora clapped her on the back a few times. "Easy there, tiger. I was just trying to give you a little liquid courage before Wes drags you out onto the dance floor."

"I am *not*," Ash said determinedly as she cleared her throat and pointed to the throbbing mass of people, "going out there." The last time Ash had danced with a boy, Eve had crashed the party. Even though this bar seemed safe enough, she still equated dance floors with hostage situations and death.

"Oh, yes, you are," Aurora said. "The looks that you and Wes have been exchanging the last forty-eight hours are so hot that I'm surprised you don't need sunglasses to keep from getting pregnant."

This time Ash spit her colada all over the bar top.

Aurora smiled at her. "Protest all you want like the delicate fire flower that you are, but when he finally comes up behind you and asks you to dance, we both know you're going to accept with a nervous giggle, and then you're going to set fire to the floor."

Ash waved apologetically to the bartender, who had trudged over to swab her spewed colada with his dish-rag. "Careful when you use fire metaphors," Ash said to Aurora. "When I'm involved, they end up less figurative than you'd think."

Aurora twisted in her bar stool. Her attention seemed to be gravitating toward the far end of the bar, where a younger Hispanic man, maybe a college student, was casting unabashed glances in her direction.

"I'm surprised you and Wes don't date," Ash said. "Two gods, both attractive, under the same roof, good rapport."

"Love is not a checklist, and love is not convenience," Aurora said whimsically. "Maybe in a different time. But sometimes people know far too much about each other for romantic feelings to ever take root."

Ash frowned. "What do you mean?"

Aurora finally took a break from her amorous eye

contact with the dark stranger. "When Wes and I first met, I was a sixteen-year-old girl in a bad relationship with a forty-year-old man. An . . ." She struggled with the word that came next. "Abusive relationship. Wes was convincing me to get out of there, but I was a teenage girl in a big city with nowhere to go. And once I make the decision to let a lover see the wings, to know the truth about me . . . well, that's a lot to walk away from."

"You don't have to go into this if you don't want to," Ash said.

Aurora just waved her hand and peered into the mirror behind the bar. "The night when I finally tried to leave, it got ugly. He hit me. I blacked out. But when I woke up . . . I was lying in a bed in Wes's bungalow with a cold compress on my head. All my stuff—what few things I owned—was all moved in. Wes never said a word about what happened back at my ex's place, or how he'd known where to find me. All I know is that when I worked up the nerve to stupidly go back to the old apartment—just to see, you know?—a Realtor was showing it to a family. He was gone."

"I've found myself in some sticky situations with boys before," Ash said slowly, as Colt's face flashed through her mind, "But nothing even *remotely* as traumatizing as that."

"I'm still here," Aurora said, "and I'll never again take for granted finding a good man like Wes . . . especially one that you can confide in about your supernatural shit without him threatening to call *The X Files* or *Men in*

Black. So go ahead and play hard to get if you want—a little HTG never killed anyone—but for crying out loud, when he asks you to dance, *take him up on it*."

"Speak of the devil," Wes said delicately from where he had snuck up behind them.

"I'll leave you two kids alone." Aurora handed Wes his drink and abandoned her bar stool. "There's a beautiful Cuban man at the end of the bar who seems to want to tutor me on my Spanish. Lord knows I need it."

"Yes, you do," Wes agreed, and Ash wasn't entirely sure he was referring to her Spanish fluency.

He took a sip of his colada and made a face. "Every time we come here, she orders me the same damn thing. Aurora is the type of person who wants somebody to like something because they should, not because they will . . . even if they don't care for it in the first place."

Ash prodded the coconut shavings in her drink with her straw and smiled softly. "I'm not convinced her radar is as off as you think."

The band started up with an up-tempo number. The brasses made a triumphant entrance by themselves before the bass and congas began to thump away beneath them.

"This is my favorite song." Wes pushed the remainder of his nearly full drink across the countertop and proceeded to drag Ash out to the dance floor.

Ash let her feet drag only a little. It was a half-assed protest, and she knew it.

The other dancers graciously let the large night god

and his companion through, but then sealed back in behind them. Wes didn't stop until they were completely encapsulated by the crowd. Ash looked anxiously at the wall of shoulders surrounding them. "Gah—no exit!"

"Just relax," Wes replied, and added in his best cheesy voice, "Let your body succumb to the rhythm of the music!" He concluded his sentence with a flourish of his hands.

"Oh, my God. First of all"—Ash glanced around, embarrassed—"never do jazz hands in public ever again. And second, the only salsa that I know is the kind that goes on tortilla chips."

"No one here is studying to see if you trained in Latin ballroom." Wes circled around the back of Ash. "The good news is that if Polynesian women and Latin women have anything in common, it's this: They're both known for their almost paranormal ability to move their hips."

"I'm from Westchester County," Ash reminded him. "We're not exactly overflowing with classes in traditional hula, so unless my island ancestors miraculously possess me while we're dancing, I'd recommend keeping low expectations."

Wes moved suddenly up behind her so that his chin loomed over her shoulder. His hands found the notches of her hips. "Guess I'll have to give you a crash course in rhythm, then."

Wes spun her around, and from there on out he took

control. One hand slipped into hers, while the other guided her from her back. He exuded strength, with his abilities at their peak now that it was nearly midnight. In fact, under his guidance her feet even began to move to steps they'd never learned, and she realized that she could read every intention of every move that he was about to make, simply by maintaining eye contact. His eyes said it all.

And it was only measures from the end of the song, as her racing heart rivaled even the machine-gun rhythm of the congas, that Ash knew:

Somewhere in the disconnected centuries of her previous lives, she'd met Wes before.

The song released its explosive last breath, and the band trickled into a slower song. Ash tried to latch on to that ghost of a memory, to dig further for a vision like the ones she'd been having over the last few nights. But the phantom slipped away from her, and she was left only with Wes holding her, unmoving, watching.

Ash cleared her throat and gestured toward the Calle Ocho. "Let's get some air, eh?"

They moved to the edge of the crowd, where they had a view of the street. Ash pulled Wes close as they danced. The top of her head barely reached his chest.

Wes smoothed his thumb over her hairline. "You've been conveniently tight-lipped about your life before Miami. How many kidnappings of CEOs and brawls with Japanese blossom goddesses am I going to have to participate in before you fill in the rest of your backstory?"

"At least three more of each," Ash said.

"Ash," he said, turning serious. "I can't know how to fully help you if I don't know what you left behind."

"Left behind?" Ash shook her head marginally against his collarbone. "When my sister ran away—for the first time—my mother sat down with me and said that there are two kinds of people. The kind that run to their future, and the kind that run from their past."

"And which one are you?"

"As someone who has run twice in her life, I can tell you this: They're the same damn thing. You can't run someplace new and not fill up the new space with the old stuff. The things you want to leave behind are the very things you can't."

Wes had gone silent, and Ash's first thought was, *Oh, shit. I've run my mouth again and pushed him away. Now I'm the chick with baggage.*

But Wes had turned his head away from Ash and was looking over the rope that marked the boundary between the café and sidewalk. "It looks like somebody else is waiting in line for a dance with you."

"Huh?" Ash lifted her head off Wes, since his chest was blocking her view of the street.

And she immediately wished she'd kept her head glued to him.

Colt stood on the edge of Calle Ocho, waiting for her. He wore a smile that was infuriatingly calm, attentive, and patient.

"Shit." Her hands fell away from Wes's shoulders like a spring rain.

Wes's attention alternated tensely between Ash and the newcomer in the street. "I'm going to assume from the look of horror on your face that you know that guy."

"I guess you could say we have a history," Ash replied. "A couple of them, actually."

PART II:
THE CULT OF THE FOUR SEASONS

It wasn't until Colt actually started walking toward the stanchions that Ash was able to move her feet. She stepped protectively in front of Wes. "It took you only four days to get out of the rock," she said. "And I'd hoped it would take *at least* two weeks."

"Three days to escape," he corrected her. "And one day to track you down."

Wes was trying to step around her, but Ash moved in front of Wes again to box him out. It was like a gender power struggle of who should protect whom.

"Relax." Colt opened his hands. "I'm not here for revenge, and you're in no danger—at least from me."

"I'll believe that as soon as you get your Adam's apple removed," Ash said. "Or at least a soundproof muzzle."

Colt lifted his head to regard Wes, who with his height and size could never truly be "hidden" behind Ash.

"I'm sorry. I didn't mean to interrupt your date. Though I have to hand it to you, Ash: You sure rebound fast."

Wes finally managed to muscle past Ash so that his shoulder eclipsed her.

"Tezcatlipoca, Aztec god of night," Colt said. "You're not as big as I remember."

Ash put her hand on Wes's back. She could feel the muscles tense and harden into wooden boards beneath his shirt. "Have we met?" he asked.

Colt rubbed the fuzz on his head. "Not recently."

"Something tells me I didn't like the smell of you last time either." Wes made to step over the stanchions and out into the street.

"Wes." Ash grabbed him by his arm and tugged him aside before he could hike his leg over. "I . . . I need a moment alone with my old friend."

Wes chewed on his lip while he studied Ash. Finally he shook his head and gazed off through the crowd. He didn't look pleased. "I guess you weren't messing around when you talked about being followed by the things you leave behind."

"Even when you think they've been set in stone," Ash said. "Listen, you don't have to worry about me. *I'm* the volcano goddess. He's just some jackass with a persuasive singing voice."

"And remarkable hearing," Colt piped in.

Wes retracted himself and Ash into the crowd that was beginning to dance again now that a fast samba had replaced the slower song. "I'd say I like this guy about as far as I can throw him . . . but I could probably throw him pretty far. In fact, I'm happy to find out exactly how far that is if you give me your blessing."

Ash stood on her tiptoes and roped Wes by the neck to pull him down. She kissed his cheek just by the mouth. "Believe me," she whispered into his ear. "If I have any trouble, he'll be swimming in the asphalt on Calle Ocho."

Wes slipped his finger along the edge of her jaw and then tilted her head upward. "It's really tough to play the protective, territorial alpha male when the girl you want to defend is potentially more powerful than you are."

"At least around UV lamps and tanning beds," Ash said. "I'll see you guys back at the apartment."

"I'll be waiting up," Wes said, and slipped into the crowd. She watched his head cut through the dancers all the way to the bar, where he interrupted the conversation between Aurora and her suitor. She wondered whether Wes had any younger sisters, because he definitely played the protective older brother part to a T. Only, maybe not so much a *brother* when it came to Ash. . . .

Ash ducked under the rope and met Colt out on the sidewalk. "You've got three minutes, Halliday."

Colt smiled from the corner of his mouth. "Gives me flashbacks to the second time we met in this lifetime, when you would let me ask only three questions. You and your conversation limits."

"That wasn't an invitation to be nostalgic," Ash said.

"We're not reminiscing about the good times. We're not trying to rekindle a spark."

Colt steered them down the road and away from El Cielo Cristal. "Actually I'm here to reminisce about a different time. Have you by chance been having any interesting dreams?"

Ash blanched. The way he'd said it made it clear that he already knew the answer to his question, which meant that either he was their architect or, worse, he was sharing the visions too and they were real. She didn't know which possibility was more horrifying. "You . . . you're the one who designed these . . . visions?"

A street cigar vendor came up to hassle them, but Colt brushed him away. "I didn't design anything; they are *very* real. When you left me back in the forest, the final note I sang to you opened the door for them. Peering into your yester-life is essential if you're ever going to understand why I've done the things that I've done."

"I thought we couldn't remember memories from our former lives," she said.

Colt tapped the front of his skull. "All the memories from our former lives are up here, stored and waiting for us. The Cloak just did something to destroy the bridge that connects us to them."

"That chord . . ." Ash remembered the last thing Colt had sung to her before she'd left him imprisoned in stone, the strange feeling in her brain like the lid had been pried off an old tomb. And then Colt's final words: *I'll be seeing you in your dreams, Ashline Wilde.* "So, what—you repaired the bridge?"

"Not fully," he said. "What you're seeing are just echoes of many memories that are beginning to bleed out, like a hole that has burst in the dam. But the trickle is slow. Your brain is no longer accustomed to handling memories from multiple lives, thanks to the way the Cloak tampered with it—so your subconscious is sorting through the old memories, cherry-picking just the ones that it thinks you need to survive."

Ash stopped under a streetlamp. "I needed to know that we were engaged in my last life to survive? It only complicated what should have been a clean break."

"Unless your mind is telling you that you can't live without me," he suggested.

"If my mind is genuinely convinced of that, then I'll volunteer myself for a lobotomy now." She leaned against the lamppost. "So you helped me tap into the echoes so that I'd eventually realize how much I missed you? It's going to take more than a couple of amorous looks at a garden party that happened eighty years ago for me to honestly believe you care for anyone but yourself and your crusade."

Colt's eyes caught the light of the streetlamp, and Ash was surprised to see them sincerely wistful. "The garden party . . . ," he whispered. "That was a good night."

Ash took a deep breath. Whether Colt was still here to play her, or whether a piece of him did *truly* miss her—the "her" from this life or one from the past—it wouldn't do her any good to remain constantly on the offensive . . . especially when she had the opportunity to manipulate some answers out of him. "So how much of the last life do *you* remember?"

He bowed his head. "All of it. My regenerative abilities eventually repaired whatever brain damage the Cloak performed to separate us from our old memories. As far as I can tell, I'm the only god among us who can remember all of it . . . and not just the last life. All of those that came before it. Let's just say you figure prominently in the last five or so of them."

"Oh, God." Suddenly Ash's stomach ached under the weight of her own history. "We're one of those on-again, off-again couples."

"Ashline." He placed his hand on her shoulder. "We have the longest love affair in the history of the world."

"I don't understand." She looked at his hand, but noted her own reluctance to brush it away. Was she supposed to feel the exact same things this time around just because she had four times before? With only brief glimpses of the last life, how could she ever be sure he hadn't been using her for something else back then, too? Was he even the same person now that she married before? Was *she* the same person? "If you knew all this— if you remembered everything when you came to me at Blackwood—how come you didn't just tell me then? Or even show me?"

Colt's hand slid off her shoulder and fell limply away. "That's the difficult part. You see, I never intended for us to reunite for a fifth time."

Despite all the ill will that they'd exchanged since his emergence from the fiery car wreck, despite that she'd sworn off Colt for the rest of this life, it still stung. "Even sitting on four lifetimes' worth of memories with me, you were considering not *trying*? Were you just bored with me? Were you ready for a new flavor?"

"No." Colt look surprised. "That's not it at all. I was trying to protect you. Last time didn't end so well for either of us, to put it delicately."

"At least we lasted until our engagement in the last life. This time we barely made it a month." She held up the back of her right hand. "Now instead of an engagement ring and a fiancé, I have a dead friend and an ex who refuses to let me move on."

"I clearly couldn't keep away, though, could I?" Colt argued. "At first, in this lifetime, I somehow convinced myself that it was all about finding your little sister, even if deep down I knew that was bullshit. I convinced myself that we'd meet and my heart would be safe, because you wouldn't remember me. That maybe this Ashline Wilde from Westchester, New York, wasn't the Pele I'd fallen for over the last four centuries. But from the moment you told me to stop blocking your sunlight at the bar, I knew that, even without your memory, you were the same girl who captures my heart every time."

A yellow convertible cruised slowly past them, a couple joyriding through the cloudless Miami night. Ash was tempted to jump into the back of the car just to get away from Colt; she was beginning to feel the first ripples of sympathy for the manipulative bastard, and that was a very dangerous thing. "Two people can't have a real relationship when one of them is holding all of the cards, Colt. It was like I was falling for three weeks' worth of you, while you'd already fallen in love with a few hundred years' worth of me. A 'me' that I don't even know *is* me." She clutched her head. "Shit, this reincarnation thing is confusing."

"That's why I'm here. To level the playing field." Colt fished around in his back pocket and pulled out a white hotel key card. "This is a spare key to my room at the Delano. Room 432. I've booked my stay here all the way through the weekend. If you come, I can help you with these echoes that are bleeding through, and then you can make a decision for yourself whether I fit into your life. If you don't come after the week is over, then I leave and you'll never see me again."

"Really? You'll just leave? You won't sing at me until I come with you?"

A young Cuban girl with a bouquet of flowers wandered up to Colt with a sheepish smile. She rocked on her feet and held up the carnations. Colt smiled and exchanged a bill for one of the flowers, and she skittered back to her father, who watched stoically from his cart of flowers that he was pushing along the road.

"Hard as it may be for you to believe," Colt said, and cupped the flower in his hands. "There are no strings attached this time. Besides . . ." Colt tucked the carnation behind Ash's ear. "There's always the next life." He turned and walked away.

Ash plucked the flower from her ear. "Colt," she said, her voice breaking.

He paused and looked over his shoulder.

"Did we . . . Was there ever a happy ending for us?" she asked. "Any of the times?"

Colt wet his lips and gave her the smallest of smiles. "The odd thing about living forever is that the word 'ending' doesn't apply to us. But just because there are no happy endings doesn't mean you can't hope for a 'happy-for-now.'"

Then he was gone. Ash was left standing on the street corner, looking back and forth between the key card in one hand and the carnation in the other. As she watched, one of the flower petals dropped to the concrete.

Ash woke up to her first Florida thunderstorm.

Up until now the weather had remained relatively warm and tranquil, if not occasionally overbearing when it got too humid. But now an eerie gray-green light filtered through the floor-to-ceiling windows, through the blinds, and the rain hammering against the windows could have been Satan himself drumming on the gates of hell.

The clock read well past noon; they'd had a late night, so Ash wasn't surprised that she'd slept in so late. However, what bothered her was the relative silence of her sleep.

She hadn't dreamed once.

Jarring as it had been to relive the trail of death and fire at that farm in rural Maine, confusing as it had been to watch herself rob a bank, Ash had actually started to look forward to the echoes. The memories, after all, weren't just Lucy's. They belonged to Ash as well. The dreams so far had just been the taste of a millennia-long backstory waiting to be retold.

Now she was experiencing the first pangs of withdrawal. Especially after Colt's cryptic visit, she was dying to know what he'd meant when he'd said the last time around "didn't end so well" for them. Was it his fault? Was it hers? Were they destined to cross swords time and again because that's how they were programmed to be?

Ash rolled onto her side and gazed at the carnation that was wilting already on the nightstand. Or was this exactly what Colt had planned? Maybe he wanted to tease her with a taste of the last life, and then somehow take it away again, so that she would feel like she *needed* him to keep those memories alive.

Either way, it was sure working.

Even now she was starting to see the appeal of restoring the memories to all the gods and goddesses.

Even now—if they were truly at fault—she was seeing the appeal of destroying the Cloak.

Ash wandered into the kitchen with the carnation in hand, where Aurora was hunched over a bowl of cereal with her wings at half-mast over the bar stool behind her. She took a long slurp of milk and then jabbed her spoon at the flower. "What's that for? You going to play a game of He Loves Me, He Loves Me Not?"

Ash fished an empty soda bottle out of the recycling and filled it halfway with water. "No sense torturing an innocent flower over questions that don't matter." She put the carnation and its makeshift vase on one of Wes's glass coffee tables. Outside, a spear of lightning darted down from the clouds. The thunder that rumbled shortly after vibrated the building. Even to this day, when Ash saw lightning flash in a window, she always swore she could see Lizzie Jacobs's reflection in the pane. She shook the image off and turned back to Aurora. "You're not going to spend this beautiful day on the beach?"

"Yeah." Aurora's wings twitched. "I'll just throw on my three-piece swimsuit."

"I met a Mayan goddess the other day who seemed like she'd *really* love a visit from you."

Aurora choked on her cereal. "Oh, Ixtab. Girl's a sweetheart, but I think she's waiting for my love life to get bad enough that I switch teams." She paused. "Given my track record, it's not the most absurd prediction she could make."

Ash eyed the folded newspaper on the sofa, and

the film of orange juice pulp on a recently used glass. "Where's the man of the house this morning?"

"Gym in the basement," she said.

Ash raised an eyebrow. "Wes is lifting weights? But doesn't he already have . . ."

"I know," Aurora said. "He's been working out down in the cave for three hours already. That's long even for him."

"Should I check on him?"

"Yes," Aurora replied. "But leave the carnation here."

Ash cringed.

It took minimal searching to find the gym in the basement, a blessing after two days of operations that required her to know floor plans in enemy territory. In fact, Wes was one of the gym's only male occupants, and the only person at all who was actually using free weights. The rest of the residents were on the treadmills and ellipticals that lined the wall, everyone hypnotized by their iPods and the wall of flat-screen televisions.

Wes, however, was without an MP3 player. His concentration instead remained on a fixed point in the ceiling as he lay flat on a bench doing flies with dumbbells. After observing firsthand his strength and stamina over the last few nights, it was odd to see him breaking a sweat doing something so . . . human.

"Need a spot, brah?" Ash asked as she stepped into his light.

Wes finished his last rep and then dropped the sixty-pound weights to the floor. The thud of the dumbbells against the foam mats made Ash jump.

"Depends," Wes said. When he sat up, his sweat-glazed shoulders bulged under his black muscle shirt. "Do you think you can handle these iron weights without smelting them?"

No, she thought. *In fact, if I keep looking at you, those weights will be syrup on the floor by the time I'm done with them.* She kept this thought to herself and averted her eyes. "My control is getting better by the day." She toed the dumbbell and let it roll across the mat. "Speaking of powers, isn't all this weight lifting sort of . . ."

"Overkill?" he finished for her.

"I was going to say 'pointless.'"

Wes picked up the weights and waddled over to the weight rack to return them. "Summer nights in Miami last ten hours. That leaves fourteen hours a day when I am powerless and abandoned to my own 'natural' defenses."

Ash snorted. "Christ, you *are* a vampire."

"What?"

"Nothing." She cleared her throat. "So as soon as the sun sets, you get this absurd strength from the moon—"

"Night," he corrected her.

"But you actually have to bulk up and retain your own muscle for as long as the sun is overhead. Even when you're indoors in the garden level gym of an apartment complex, safe from the UV rays."

He stretched his fingers toward his toes. Even folded

in half, he was still practically Ash's height. "Listen," he said. "You can't try to find a compromise between the gods and science. Science don't want nothin' to do with us, ya hear?" he added with a twang.

"Easy there, varmint," she said. Ash felt weird just standing around while Wes was clearly intent on working out, so she wandered over to the weight rack and picked up a dumbbell to do some curls. Even though she hadn't been to the gym since she'd left Blackwood, the weights felt strangely feathery in her hands. "There's some coexistence of science and gods going on," she said as she began to curl. "My sister can summon storms, but on a day like today Mother Nature produces the thunderclouds all by herself, the good old-fashioned way. Still . . . you never know."

She noticed that Wes had stopped stretching to gawk at her while she lifted.

"What?" The rhythm of her movements slowed down until she lowered the weights to either side and tossed them to the floor.

"Just reconsidering letting you spot me." His eyes dropped to her arms. "You're handling those like they're made out of paper. What sport did you say you played again? Bodybuilding?"

She drilled him in the arm with a quick punch, enough to make him stagger back. "Varsity cage fighting," she replied.

He rubbed his arm and laughed. "Guess I better stay

on your good side, at least as long as the sun is up. You must have broken a few hearts *and* heads back where you're from."

The mention of broken hearts conjured a chilly silence. Ash shivered in the gym's heavy air-conditioning. No doubt Wes was picturing Colt's appearance the night before as well. As if to confirm this, he lumbered over to the rack that had the heaviest weights.

Ash stepped in front of him to block his way. "Look, I'm sorry about last night. Goddess or mortal, it's every girl's nightmare that her ex will show up while she's hanging out with another guy."

"You don't owe me an explanation or an apology," Wes said. "I've known you for four days." He tried to head for the bench press again.

She cut him off. "Wes, we can play the game where we pretend that there's nothing going on between us; it's not like I haven't played it before. But this is me offering you a free one-way ticket past the bullshit."

Wes ran a hand through his hair, and when he finally made eye contact, the whites of his eyes clouded dark. "I'm not pretending like I don't feel anything. I'm not pretending that, from the moment you saved me from that humidor, I haven't been thinking about you as something more than just my rescuer. But seeing that guy last night reminded me that four days—no matter how much feeling they bring with them—can never compete with what I suspect is a long history." He paused. "A very long history."

"Everything begins with a few days, Wes," she said. "And besides, whatever happened between Colt and me, it's . . ." Somewhere in her throat a whirlpool opened up and sucked the word "over" down into the abyss.

Ash's pocket vibrated, saving her, and the cell phone chirped out the familiar ring tone of "In the Hall of the Mountain King."

"Someone calling for a second date?" Wes asked.

"No." She flipped open the top, silencing the music, and read the text message on the screen. It was an address for somewhere in north Miami Beach, along with a floor and room number. There was no explanation provided, but no explanation was necessary.

"Lesley just coughed up the location of the Four Seasons' sacrificial victim," she said. "Good thing freeing imprisoned gods is my specialty. You ready to break a few laws?"

He smiled for the first time since the conversation had turned to Colt. "Kidnapping . . . grand theft boat . . . What's one more breaking-and-entering charge at this point?"

"Better sharpen your crowbar, then," she said. "We strike at nightfall."

They didn't wear all black, or panty hose masks, or, for that matter, bring crowbars with them on their mission to rescue the sacrificial god. Ash decided that since they were striking just after dark, it was probably best if they dressed normally so they could at least play the "oblivious teenager" card if caught. Their plan was fairly straight-forward: Ash and Wes would enter the building from the ground level, while Aurora would do aerial reconnaissance outside in the rain, which had unfortunately developed into a downpour just as they'd arrived.

Given that Lesley had supposedly sent them to the location of a captured, sedated god, Ash expected the address to belong to some sort of maximum-security fortress. Instead Lesley had directed them to the top floor of a luxury condominium, not unlike the one where Wes lived. There were no guards at the building's entrance, unless you counted the concierge, who didn't even look up from her desk as Wes and Ash walked through the lobby to the elevators.

The two of them stood in the elevator in silence. Ash was watching the numbers over the door light up one at a time, while Wes was boring a hole in his own warped reflection in the brass doors. Their conversation had suffered all afternoon. It could have been nerves about the rescue mission that they were blindly walking into, with no advance knowledge of the room's floor plan or security. Or maybe he was still picturing where he fit into the equation with her and Colt—watching helplessly from the outside? Or lodged somewhere in between?

"Isn't flying around outside at window-level just asking for someone to see you?" Ash asked, breaking the silence.

"With the weather like it is, hopefully not too many

people are staring dreamily out at the Miami skyline," Wes said. "And Aurora has a few years of practice flying stealthy."

"Should we be worried about lightning?"

"Trust me." Wes drummed his finger against the brass doors. "She currently has the least dangerous job of the three of us."

The elevator chimed and the doors parted.

The hallway was completely quiet except for the tap of the rain on the skylight. They followed the red stripe in the carpet to a fork in the path, where a sign that read 3805–3810 directed them around the bend. They were looking for 3807.

But they weren't alone when they turned the corner. At the far end of the corridor was a glass window with the downtown skyline framed within it. In front of that was a man in a suit, who stirred as soon as they came into view. The door he was standing next to could only be 3807.

Wes's reaction was to let out a laugh—a love-drunk laugh if Ash had ever heard one—and he seized her by the waist and pressed her up against the wall. His lips found her neck, but she heard him whisper, "Pretend you're attracted to me."

It was tempting to explain how little acting that would actually require. She let out a theatrical groan instead.

The guard, however, was undeterred by their performance. His pace didn't even falter as he approached the lovebirds. "Can I help you?" he asked hoarsely. Through

Wes's long hair Ash spotted a gun holstered in plain view on the man's hip.

Wes pulled back just long enough to look around the corridor. "Sorry, mate," he apologized. "Guess we got off a floor early." He then returned to Ash's neck and playfully bit her earlobe.

"This is the top floor," the man reminded him. He reached out and put his hand roughly on Wes's shoulder. "Now, I'd suggest—"

Wes seized the hand on his shoulder and twisted until the man's wrist joint audibly crackled. The guard dropped to his knees about to cry out, but Wes drilled him across the face, and the man slumped to the carpeted hallway floor.

Wes grabbed him by the legs and dragged him down the hall. Ash jogged after him. "Think he's from the same mob that was playing piñata with you the other night?"

"Not mob," he said quietly. "Local syndicate for hire." He nodded to the door to 3806, through which they could hear a baseball game blaring on the television, and several voices shouting at it. "If I had to take a guess, I would say that this is their barracks, and this"— he stopped when they reached the door to 3807—"is the safe house."

"Well, let's hope the 'safe' in 'safe house' extends to us." Her pocket vibrated, and she pulled out her cell phone. A text from Aurora. She held it up so Wes could read it too.

"2 Rooms. Entry clear. Package + 1 keeper in back room. Must be something good on TV."

"Thank God there's a Marlins game tonight," Wes said, and now that he mentioned it, Ash could hear the same game piping through the door to 3807, albeit softly.

She touched the doorknob tentatively and gave it a soft twist.

It turned without a hitch. No lock.

"Guess they put too much confidence in that guy," Ash whispered, and indicated the unconscious guard that Wes had slung over his shoulder.

The apartment was lavish, and was the last thing that Ash would have expected to act as a detainment center for gods. It wasn't a stainless steel cage but a warmly furnished penthouse, complete with sprawling crimson oriental rugs and a large dining room table. Then there was the enormous fish tank that took up the middle of the room, teeming with football-size tropical fish. There was even a room service cart—room service, in an apartment building!—abandoned next to the fish tank. Ash's best guess: If you were a person with a lot of money who needed to disappear for a few weeks, but also wanted to live like a king under the protection of professional soldiers, this was where you paid a small fortune to hide out.

Or, Ash thought as she eased toward the archway that opened into the other half of the suite, where you paid a small fortune for mercenaries to keep an eye on a sedated but potentially lethal god.

Wes propped the unconscious guard against the wall and then locked the door behind them, but Ash's curiosity propelled her across the room. Without waiting for him, she moved stealthily to the threshold between the dining room and the common area. She nearly yelled in horror when she came within sight of the scene in the den.

The god—for it was a "he"—dangled from the ceiling in what looked like something out of a science fiction movie. Fifteen, maybe twenty, thick cables snaked down from a steel contraption that was bolted to the ceiling. The cables wrapped around the god's thick torso and neck like an overzealous anaconda. More cords sprouted from the bottom, connecting him to a similar steel device on the floor. In essence he was being suspended in place by a series of rubber bands.

Then there was the IV—a thick needle plugged into one of his forearms, both of which were strapped to his sides. The intravenous tube led to a column of liquid supported by a metal tower beside his "cage."

But it wasn't the horrific prison or the industrial-strength anesthesia that caused Ash's heart to sear hot in her chest. It was the fact that she knew the Haitian thunder god that the Four Seasons had selected as their sacrifice.

Just seeing Ade like this brought bile to her throat. His eyes were closed in a sleep that was far from peaceful, while he dangled from the ceiling like a broken marionette. How had they even found him? Had they kidnapped him from his native Haiti, where he was supposed to be helping his people rebuild after a devastating earthquake? Then smuggled him into Miami just like they had Rose?

Ash found herself wandering carelessly into the other room, but Wes slipped a hand around her waist and gave just the gentlest "Shh" into her ear.

On the other side of the room was, as Aurora had warned them, just one guard, who was deeply engrossed in the baseball game. He had his back to them, and he didn't even stir until Wes was right behind him. By then it was too late. Wes wrapped his forearm around the man's neck and tightened.

The guard started to flail, but rather than choking him completely, Wes cupped his free hand over the man's eyes. "Sleep," he whispered. "Sleep."

The guard's hands, which had been trying to pry Wes's other hand away, dropped impotently to his lap, and his head lolled forward.

"Jesus, what are you, the sandman?" Ash said.

"One of the perks of being a night god. Only works on the weak and the willing." Wes released his hold on the man's neck, and the guard slumped sideways onto the couch.

Ash sized up the enormous guard that was now snoring soundly on the couch; he didn't look too weak to her, at least physically. "That guy was *willing* to lose consciousness?"

"His survival instincts probably reminded him it was better to sleep on the job than fight a losing battle with my arm and die of asphyxiation."

Ash wanted to ask him how he'd even figured out he could do something like that, but seeing Ade wrapped up in the machine distracted her. She reached up and brushed a strand of hair away from his face.

"I take it you know this guy?" Wes asked. "You must be really popular among the gods."

Ash scowled at him, sensing the acid beneath his words. This was the wrong time and place for jealousy to rear its head. "A good friend from school. His name is Ade, and he's a Zulu thunder god."

Wes crossed his arms and examined the device that Ade was cocooned in. "They weren't taking any chances with your friend, I guess."

Ash plucked at one of the cables. Despite its metallic appearance, it was elasticized. When Ade bobbed up and down in the harness but didn't wake up, Ash suddenly got it. "Much as I hate them, can't say I'm not impressed. This whole thing is like the shocks on a car—meant to absorb any vibrations in case he starts to quake in his sleep."

Wes whistled. "So they put the thunder god in a big Slinky?"

"To keep the neighbors oblivious, or, knowing Ade, the whole city block." Ash gently withdrew the IV needle from Ade's flesh, and a drop of greenish liquid spilled onto the carpet. The cables holding Ade in place held fast against her tugging.

Wes reached down and yanked the same cord. With just a little bit of oomph, the cable came free in his hand.

"Show-off," she muttered. "You're in charge of getting my friend down. I'll stand watch."

Starting with the bottom, Wes ripped out the cables one at a time as though he were plucking weeds from a garden. Meanwhile Ash wandered over to a wall hanging that was rippling even though there didn't seem to be a visible air vent or open window nearby. When she passed her hand over the cloth, she could feel a cool draft blowing through the weave. She pulled the tapestry aside.

Behind the wall hanging was a door constructed of steel mesh, like the doors to an old-fashioned elevator. Through the mesh she could see a stairwell on the other side. Ash unlatched the lock and folded the door open. "I guess a syndicate safe house wouldn't be complete without its own secret exit," she said.

"At least we know how they got your friend up here in the first place," Wes said. "Though the bored concierge downstairs probably wouldn't have looked twice if they'd dragged an unconscious 250-pound thunder god through the lobby and into the elevators." With a grunt Wes ripped free the final two cables at once and caught Ade in his arms.

It wasn't a second too soon. Someone was rattling the safe house's locked front door, then pounding when it wouldn't open. "Lorenzo," a man's voice shouted. "You know you're supposed to keep this door unlocked!" More rattling, more pounding. "Lorenzo, answer me, damnit!"

Wes slung Ade across his shoulders in a fireman's carry, and Ash shoved them through the secret door and into the stairwell. He turned and waited for her, expecting for her to lead the way.

But Ash grabbed the mesh door and slammed it shut from inside the apartment. While Wes watched in confusion, she used the heat from her hands to weld the door shut.

Wes shrugged Ade onto one shoulder and used his free arm to tug at the door from the other side. "Ash, what the hell are you doing?"

Ash's eyes grew teary just seeing Ade so vulnerable, knowing that he'd been just days away from execution. "You may be a superman with the sun down, but the boy slung over your shoulder isn't. This isn't his fight. Thirty-eight flights of stairs is going to take even you some time to travel down. So I'm going to give you a head start."

The pounding on the front door intensified, and Wes smashed his fist against the metal. "Damnit, Ash. I *will* break this door down. Those guards may not be fireproof, but you aren't bulletproof, either. We can all make it."

"Wes, this sacrifice could have been you if I hadn't stumbled upon that boat Tuesday night. Now it's one of my best friends, and . . . I don't have many of those left. I'm done pretending this isn't personal." She touched his knuckles that were blanched white from gripping the steel mesh and let just a lick of warmth touch his skin reassuringly. "You have thirty-eight floors. Get moving." With that, she pulled the tapestry back over the escape door.

By now the guard at the front door had returned with the keys. Ash could hear him madly trying them in the dead bolt to see which one would work. Ash started across the room, hoping to surprise him when he entered, but he burst into the apartment when she was only half-way to the door. She spun quickly and tried to look busy with the fish tank.

"Who the hell are you?" the guard barked.

Ash tried to assume her best innocent "This isn't what it looks like" face when she turned around. "I'm with aquarium services, here to clean your fish tank, and . . ." She stopped talking when she saw the guard's face. It was the same man-boy she'd kicked in the head three nights ago on the deck of Lesley's ship.

"You?" he said. He reached up and tenderly touched his mangled nose, which was in a splint.

"Shit," Ash said. "Just my luck they didn't fire you after Tuesday."

The guard's spell broke, and he reached out for the gun at his side. Ash panicked, and in the heat of the moment, she went for the only cover in sight. She seized the edge of the tall fish tank and pulled herself up to the rim, intending to hurdle over to the opposite side. Her leg, however, got stuck in the process. As a result her body flopped into the water and dropped like an anchor to the bottom.

A piece of coral ripped into her shoulder, but she barely had time to process the pain, because there was a sharp crack from the guard's gun, muffled by the water around her. Her eyes shot open in time to watch the blur in the water as a bullet torpedoed past her face.

The wall to the fish tank exploded under the impact of a second bullet. Ash rode the cascade of water and glass out onto the red carpet. Through her water-blurred eyes she saw the guard's arm twist around to line up a shot. He wasn't taking any chances.

Ash palmed a handful of the water that was still pouring out onto the carpet. She ignited her hand and slung the water into his face at the same time. It turned to steam by the time it hit him square in the eyes, and he erupted in a series of high-pitched shrieks.

Ash rose up out of the water and cracked him in his already broken nose. He fell flat onto the carpet with a heavy squish, landing in a bed of fish tank debris, including the poor aquatic casualties of the firefight, which were now drawing their final breaths on the carpet.

Footsteps rumbled up the hall. Ash slammed the door closed and threw the dead bolt just before the other sentries from the next room could get inside. She scooped the gun off the waterlogged carpet.

Without any keys the guards outside began to shoot

at the lock on the door. Apparently they weren't concerned about noise complaints from the neighbors. Ash scrambled across the room, heading for the secret metal door. With any luck Wes had had enough of a head start with Ade that the hidden stairwell was okay to use. She reached out to pull aside the tapestry so she could melt her way through the door.

Then, over the gunshots at the front door, she heard more footsteps. These ones coming up the stairs. She backed away from the tapestry just as a new set of guards began to pound on the metal door.

With no exits left, Ash ducked behind the broken fish tank's wooden base. Keeping her back pressed against the new cover, she whipped out her phone and speed-dialed Aurora. She hit the speakerphone button and dropped the phone to the ground so she'd have both hands free.

The phone rang twice before Aurora's voice crackled from the speaker. "Ashline? Where the hell are you?" Rain spattered the receiver on the other end.

"Trapped in the penthouse, and I have two very important questions to ask you." Ash held the gun up in front of her face. Even though she had no intention of actually shooting anyone, the sound of gunfire was something the guards would recognize and hopefully fear if she needed to buy herself time.

"I'm listening," Aurora said.

"First, how much weight can those wings of yours support?" Ash asked. "Another person?"

Behind her a final gunshot took care of the lock, and the door splintered in after several kicks. Just as the door burst open, Ash popped up over the base of the fish tank just long enough to fire a wild warning shot. It splattered the wood of the door frame, and the point man ducked back out into the hall. Ash dropped back into a sitting position as a barrage of gunfire from a semiautomatic drummed against her cover.

"Is that gunfire?" Aurora yelled.

"Yes or no, Aurora?" Ash shouted back.

"I . . . I don't know," Aurora said.

"Good enough," Ash said. "Second question—I need to know how good your hand-eye coordination is. Did you ever play any sports where you had to catch something?"

There was a long pause, then Aurora stuttered, "Oh, n-no. Ash, you're not thinking of—"

Whatever Aurora said next was drowned out by a wave of cover fire. Ash could hear the heavy footsteps of the point man as he dashed into the room and dove for cover somewhere near the entrance, probably behind the dining table. Ash fired another two bullets over her own cover to warn them, but a teenage girl wielding a pistol wasn't going to keep away a roomful of trained mercenaries for long.

"Look for the broken window," she instructed Aurora. "I'll see you in ten seconds. Have faith." On the other end it sounded like the cell phone clattered to the rooftop.

Ash hoped that meant Aurora had understood the message loud and clear.

This was going to take more courage than anything else she'd done in her life. Ash reached out to the room service cart and ignited the white tablecloth with the hottest blaze she could. Within seconds the cart had transformed into an inferno. Ash mustered all the strength she had left and shoved the cart. The fiery vehicle rattled across the wet carpet on a collision course for the front door, just as a second syndicate member was trying to slip inside.

With the guards hopefully distracted, Ash fired one last bullet—this one intended for the balcony window. The whole pane shattered, and a torrent of rain and wind was sucked through the opening and into the apartment.

Keeping her whole body low to the ground, Ash sprinted across the floor. She dashed over the broken glass onto the outdoor balcony.

At the last moment she wasn't sure she had the nerve to make the jump.

A bullet sizzled past her ear, giving her just enough blind courage to maintain her momentum.

And she dove headlong over the edge of the balcony.

In the brief seconds that followed,

Ash spread her arms as though they were wings,

felt her body succumb to free fall,

felt the blistering wind suck the moisture right from her open eyes,

and instead of her life flashing before her eyes,
she really just kept wondering how long she had
until she hit the road below,
but behind this curtain of
wild,
choppy,
random thoughts,
she heard a steady chant pulsing through her mind,
two words,
two little words:
Have faith.

Hands caught her under her armpits, which then slid down into the crook of her savior's elbows. There was a flutter sound like a parachute opening—Aurora's wings billowing out. Aurora grunted in pain with the addition of the extra weight. Ash's shoulders felt ready to rip free of their sockets and leave the rest of her armless body to plummet to its death, but her descent slowed significantly.

Still, Ash knew that Aurora's wings couldn't be accustomed to supporting the weight of two people. Sure enough, even as the leathery appendages flapped, the two girls continued to descend at a steady pace to the street. The cement loomed beneath them, close enough now that Ash could make out the spaces between the yellow stripes in the road, the headlights of the cars driving either way down the street. Ash was quickly sliding down the length of Aurora's rain-slick arms. In a last-ditch attempt to hold on, Aurora grabbed Ash's arms with her fingers—

But there was only the horrible sinking feeling of wet flesh failing to grasp wet flesh.

Ash dropped free of Aurora's hold with fifteen feet left to go. Her body rotated enough for her to watch the wind whip Aurora back up into the skies as though she had a bungee cord strapped to her back.

Ash hit the grassy median hard enough to knock the sense completely out of her. Her body bounced right off the curb and into the middle of the road. Dazed, she struggled to make it onto her hands and knees.

A light—

No, two lights—

Twin lights—

Side by side—

Approaching her.

She peeled her head off the asphalt and had to cover her eyes. A tractor trailer was rattling toward her. She knew she should crawl out of the way, but after the hard fall her body wouldn't cooperate. Directions blurred. The truck's horn blared. Hope died.

A streak crossed the avenue like a comet. Strong hands slipped underneath her body. Lifted her off the road. Carried her out of the path of the truck.

Wes dove with her onto the median just in time. They landed in the grass, with his arms and chest cushioning her fall. She felt a heavy vortex swirl around them in the wake of the tractor trailer as the truck barreled past the nearby curb.

Ash couldn't remember much of the next few minutes. One minute she was draped over Wes's back, wondering how she could still be alive. The next they were in the Cadillac with Aurora behind the wheel and Ade asleep and strapped into the passenger seat. Wes was leaning over Ash, touching her face tenderly. "Ashline," he whispered. It may have been the first time he said her name. It may have been the fiftieth.

"We did it?" she whispered. Trying to collect her wits was like wrangling an entire bag of marbles as they scattered across the kitchen floor.

Wes smiled and nodded to the unconscious Ade. "We'll take him back to my penthouse and watch over him until he comes to."

"No," Ash blurted out.

Wes frowned. "I don't think taking him to a hospital is a good idea."

Ash leaned around Wes. "Go to the train station," she instructed Aurora.

Aurora shrugged and did a sharp U-turn around the median.

"If Ade wakes up in your penthouse and finds out what's going on," Ash said, "he's going to want to stick around and help." She turned to the rain-tracked window so she wouldn't have to see Wes scrutinizing her. "Sometimes being a good friend is offering to fight your friends' battles with them. And sometimes being a good friend means refusing their help so they stay out of harm's way."

Wes lingered for another minute before he accepted that the conversation was over and slipped back into his seat.

Ash was lodged in a memory of Blackwood Academy, when Rolfe was still alive, when they were all still just mischievous kids with an addiction to breaking curfew.

By the time they got to the Amtrak station, Ade was already beginning to toss and turn as the sedative wore off. Together Wes and Ash managed to get Ade's hulking body on board the Silver Service train and comfortably into a seat. Ash turned his head so that it was looking out the window and then tucked his one-way ticket halfway into the pocket of his shirt so the conductor could punch it on his way down the aisle. It was a six-hour train ride to Tampa. Hopefully Ade would eventually wake, disoriented but alive, and find the water bottles Ash had left next to him.

She gave Ade a last look as the conductor outside made final call and the train's whistle blew. Ade's eyes flickered open for just a brief moment before they drooped closed again, but Ash swore that he had seen her.

She met Wes back outside on the platform. Her phone buzzed, and she was grateful for the distraction so she wouldn't have to watch Ade's face through the window while the train chugged away, or wonder whether she was doing the right thing keeping him at a distance like this.

It was another message from Lesley. This one read:

"Red Rose in hand. Midnight, tonight, at the Venetian Pool."

"Lesley again?" Wes came up behind her shoulder, attempting to read the screen.

She flipped the phone closed. "Yes. She's ready to give us Rose."

"When?"

Her mouth started to form the word "midnight," but it twisted and mutated until what came out instead was: "Noon. Tomorrow."

When they returned home, Aurora's stomach was growling something fierce—as was Ash's—and the winged goddess demanded that they go out for a "slightly late" dinner, since an eleven p.m. supper wasn't unheard of in nocturnal Miami.

"Can't we do takeout instead?" Wes whined from the couch, where his body had already molded into the cushions. "After that jailbreak, I'm completely exhausted." He rubbed the spot on the couch next to him, and raised his eyebrows meaningfully at Ash.

"Nice try, Wes," Aurora said, "but the whole exhaustion excuse? Doesn't really fly when you're a night god. Ash?"

Ash, who had been resisting Wes's attempts to coax her over to the couch, shook her head. "You two go out and have a nice dinner. I could use some alone time here to touch base with my parents." It wasn't a total fabrication, after all, even though she had no intention of calling them once the other two gods left. Her eyes darted to the clock on the kitchen wall. She had barely an hour to make it to the drop point where Lesley intended to deliver Rose.

Unfortunately, when she tore her eyes off the clock, she found Wes watching her carefully. "Got a date?" he asked. Any warmth that he had been showing toward Ash before melted off him and dripped between the seat cushions. Wes's moods were every bit as transparent as Ash's, and it sounded like he might be under the impression that she intended to go meet Colt.

Ash wondered what would make Wes angrier, believing that she was visiting her ex-boyfriend's hotel room, or finding out that she was purposely walking alone into what could be an ambush. She managed a smile. "Yeah," she said. "I have a date with one cell phone, two angsty parents, and a shot of cold medicine to help me sleep."

Aurora, who had been trembling uncontrollably with jitters since they'd gotten home, took a shot of something clear and then pointed the empty shot glass at Wes. "You don't need drugs to knock you out when you live with Miami's resident sandman."

"Can you promise good dreams, too?" Ash asked. Her eyes unconsciously flitted to the clock again.

"Only the dreams about me." Wes stood up. "Let's go, Aurora. I'll call for a table at Atlantic Liberty when we're on our way. A table for three in case Magma Maggie here decides to join us later on." He didn't even look at Ash as he said it, and the tension as Wes and Aurora finally filed out the door was enough to sandpaper a bed of nails smooth.

Mood ring that she was, lying had never been Ash's strong suit, especially when it involved lying to people she cared about.

Even when she was doing it to protect them.

Ash had originally been filled with a blind sense of excitement about meeting Rose for the first time, but by the time she pulled her Vespa into the deserted lot outside the Venetian Pool, her anticipation had diluted into fear and uncertainty. As she walked down the palm-lined path to the pool, questions buzzed around her like she'd just smashed a hornets' nest. What would she do when Lesley handed Rose over? Would they have anything to say to each other? And where the hell could Ash even *keep* her? Short-term, she supposed they could stay with Wes. But beyond that, would Ash bring her back to Scarsdale?

Try explaining that to the Wildes. *I know Rose doesn't have a birth certificate or any proof that she actually exists, but believe it or not, she's my long-lost sister, and I really hope she helps to fill the void your oldest daughter left when she ran away from home and then got imprisoned in hell.*

She was so preoccupied with these daydreams of having a new sister that she almost didn't notice the change in the air. The hot Miami night seemed to cool a few degrees with every step she took toward the gates. Even more concerning, where the air had been humid before, Ash felt her slick skin instantly dry, as though all the vapor had been sucked clean away.

Ash came to the black metal gates. One side swung open with an ominous creak under her touch.

Ash had never visited the Venetian Pool before, but it was apparent from the get-go that something wasn't right. The rain had since died away, but the overcast clouds blotted out the stars and moon so that the only light came from a few candy-striped lampposts that rose out of the pool like skinny gravestones. Under their faint glow everything appeared far too still, all the way across the pool to the stone fortress in the back. Stranger even, the temperature continued to plummet with each step forward she took.

When she toed up to the pool's edge, it all made sense—the stillness, the cold.

The pool was frozen solid from end to end. In the distance, as Ash's eyes adjusted to the light, she could see where even the waterfall had frozen, a curtain of icicles dangling like butcher's knives over the icy expanse.

Most unsettling, however, was the tall structure rising out of the middle of the pool, where the meager light from the lampposts failed to penetrate and darkness triumphed. It was like a totem pole made of ice, maybe twenty feet high, and at the top there was some sort of design that Ash couldn't quite discern from this distance.

Ash's skin tingled as she stepped down onto the ice. The needles on her internal threat detector were tracking off the charts, but she had never been one to turn away from a sinister cookie crumb trail.

The tall structure was still a mystery when she approached it. It started narrow at the base and then slowly widened as it grew higher until it fanned out at the very top. It was as though a two-story geyser had exploded out of the center of the pool and then frozen instantly.

Ash held up her arm and let the fire blossom from her fingers down to her wrist, transforming her hand into a makeshift torch. Her eyes adjusted to the tangerine light, and she lifted the torch higher, until the aura extended up to the top of the ice sculpture.

As soon as the orb of light revealed the top of the totem pole, Ash nearly fell over backward.

Lesley Vanderbilt was encased within the ice, at its very top, with her arms spread in a twisted human cruci-fix. Her fingers were curled into claws and her eyes had been frozen wide open, but there was no life left behind them. Her mouth hung open in a last-gasp scream. Maybe in her final moments she'd known that she was only a half-inch layer of ice away from the air she so desperately needed.

Ash dropped to one knee. The Four Seasons had dis-covered Lesley's plan to betray them. Rose's rescue had been compromised, again, just when it had been within reach of Ash's fingertips. Now her only link to her sister had been brutally murdered and put on display in a tortured ice sculpture that was clearly meant for Ash to find.

Then she felt the presence behind her.

Ash spun around and let the warmth from the torch on her arm wash over the figure lurking behind her.

Bleak wore the same floor-length hooded robe she always wore—did she ever wash the thing, or did she just have a closet full of them? She lingered back five yards from Ash, with her feet set and her arms slack. Hardly a threatening pose, but Ash still felt her hackles rise.

"It's funny," Bleak mused, "how we echo the forces of nature. The warm front collides with the cold front." Her voice was higher than Ash had expected; she had anticipated something huskier. Bleak had a vague hint of a Scandinavian accent as well, her inflection rising and falling musically with every syllable.

"I've met cold fronts before," Ash said. "You're just a cold bitch."

The winter goddess ignored her comment, and let her eyes float up to drink in the totem pole of ice and flesh. "Do you like my sculpture? I've never been much of an artist."

Ash was trembling. Involuntarily the fire burning in her arm flared up, showering the ice with sparks. "I would never have asked Lesley Vanderbilt to be my maid of honor, and the woman is—was—a complete megalomaniac . . . but did you really have to murder her?"

"Yes," Bleak said quietly. "She dishonored her vow to the Four Seasons. She attempted to lie and steal what is rightfully ours. And we needed to transform her into an example so you would know to stop looking for your sister."

A drip landed on Ash's shoulder, then another. In her frustration she was growing so hot that the ice sculpture was beginning to melt behind her. She tried to curb her growing anger before she burned a hole right through the ice beneath her. "What is my little sister to you anyway?"

Bleak rolled up her sleeves and cuffed them at the elbows, revealing the same divided circle Ash had seen in her vision. Up close, Ash could now see that each of the quadrants of the circle stood for one of the seasons. "The Four Seasons are very forward-thinking," Bleak said. "Surely you know by now that your sister is a portal-maker, and she has access to the Cloak Netherworld?"

"So I've heard," Ash muttered, thinking of Colt and his vendetta against the Cloak. "And I'd bet anything that you want to use my sister to invade their Nether-world, and destroy them so that you can get all of your memories back. What is with you people and your obsession with the past? I've revisited some of my old memories, and let me tell you, it just complicates the shit out of things, and it's much better—for everyone's sake—that we come back with a fresh start each lifetime."

"What good will it do for us in the long run to start a new religion and spend a lifetime recruiting true believers when we won't be able to remember any of it the next time we're reborn?" Bleak asked. "Without our old memories we might as well be filthy mortals like everyone else. Memory *is* immortality, and Rose is to be our savior, our miracle."

"Miracles don't leave craters in their wake." Ash took a brave step toward Bleak. "Rose is a confused little six-year-old who wouldn't know the difference between a handshake and blowing someone up if you showed her those images on flash cards. Hanging around your little cult isn't going to do anything to help refine her sense of right and wrong. Mark my words: If she stays with the Four Seasons, I guarantee you that people will die. She needs guidance. She needs family."

The temperature fell ten degrees, and a heavy wind hit Ash, blowing her hair out and knocking her back a step, until she could feel the ice tower against her shoulders. The palm trees surrounding the pool rustled. Bleak's patient, stoic façade was beginning to deteriorate. "You of all people would lecture *us* on what family means? Until we found her, Rose was an orphan wandering around a dangerous jungle, with mercenaries hunting her like a wild boar. And did her two older sisters come to save her? No. You brand the four of us as monsters, but your sister would be rain forest compost if it weren't for us, all while you contented yourself to live the life of a human. Rose will live a better life with us. She'll be revered by the humans, the way the gods were intended to be." Bleak shook her head, and the clouds above instantly blotted out the stars. "With you she'd just end up playing in the sandbox in some godless corner of suburbia."

It began to snow, and Ash experienced a vivid flashback to that day in the parking lot when Eve had barged back into her life. Why was it that dramatic shifts in weather around meteorological goddesses always meant bad news?

"I get no enjoyment out of killing," Bleak said, "and that's why I'm giving you a moment to resign yourself to the truth that you and your sister are not meant to be together in this life. If you tell me that you can walk away and live your life without interfering with the wishes of the Four Seasons—and if I believe you to be sincere—then our feud is over. But if you resist, then you better believe that I'll do what's necessary to preserve the interests of the Four Seasons. Now . . ." Bleak flicked out both hands. The thickening snow parted in front of her, forming a corridor between her and Ash. "Look me in the eyes and tell me that you're ready to walk away from this fool's quest."

Ash leaned in and stared directly into the grays of Bleak's eyes. "Go build an igloo."

Bleak nodded as though she'd expected that. She extended her right hand, and the snow swirling around her vacuumed toward her outstretched fingers. The snow packed, and lengthened, and sharpened. Moments later Bleak held a white curved saber in her hand. Ice crystallized over the outside of it until the edge of the blade gleamed.

Bleak ran her finger along the edge. A few droplets of her own blood beaded and glistened down the blade, but she didn't even flinch. "Just know that you could have avoided an early death if only you'd done what I asked."

The winter goddess propelled herself forward so that her leather boots skated over the ice. She extended the blade, its tip speeding on a collision course for Ash's heart.

But Ash's rage had been slowly boiling inside her throughout their conversation. The flames came easily this time. She pointed down and showered the ice between them in the hottest fire she could muster.

Bleak skated right into it, and after a heavy crack that made even Ash lurch forward, Bleak dropped like a boulder through the melted ice and into the pool below. Chunks of ice floated to the surface along with a single air bubble.

Ash stepped up to the edge of the hole, but it was hard to see anything. After a few moments with no signs of movement below, it was clear Bleak wasn't coming back up. "Just know," Ash said, "that you could have avoided being a Popsicle if you weren't such a psycho."

Ash began to walk away, but felt an ominous trembling of the ice beneath her. She jumped to the side just as Bleak's blade pierced up through the ice, where Ash's leg had been moments before.

Bleak muscled through the rift in the ice, forcing aside the frozen chunks until she could clamber up to the surface. Most disturbing was that she was dripping frigid water from her ivory robe but didn't even shiver. In fact, she looked more comfortable than she had before.

With no plan B in mind, Ash took off running across the pool, toward the dark waterfall in the back. Her progress was hindered by a snowy squall, which slowed her to one labored step at a time. She held one arm in front of her face like a visor to block the storm.

Meanwhile booted footsteps thundered behind her. Sensing danger, Ash threw herself flat onto her back just in time to watch Bleak's saber slice through the air above her. Bleak recovered quickly, flipped the sword around, and slashed downward at Ash's face.

Ash dug deep into that cauldron of heat within her, and when she raised her arm, a raging fire flashed hot down the length of her arm, instantly incinerating the sleeve of her T-shirt. When the ice saber struck her heat shield, it vaporized instantly, sending a plume of steam up into the air.

It was enough distraction for Ash to send a second

wave of flames up at Bleak's face. The winter goddess shrieked and staggered back as the fire singed past her eyebrows.

Still, Ash wasn't expecting it when Bleak blindly lashed out with a superhuman kick that drilled her in the ribs. The air deflated out of Ash's lungs, and momentum carried her across the ice like a hockey puck until she stopped under the umbra of the frozen waterfall.

Ache echoed through her chest. Ash couldn't breathe and was having trouble pulling herself out of the beached turtle position on her back. Overhead she could see the lethal razor-sharp points of the unnatural icicles the waterfall had formed when it had frozen.

Worse, a sheen of ice crawled out of the pool's surface, suctioning Ash flat onto her back, with her arms outstretched to either side. She tried to summon the fire to melt it, but the pain in her chest had shattered her concentration into a thousand ungraspable particles. The ice quickly won over, and Ash was all too aware that in a minute she'd transform into a human snow angel.

Bleak stepped patiently over her, straddling Ash's body where the ice had begun to draw her squirming legs taut to the surface. Ash shivered uncontrollably. With her internal temperature plummeting toward hypothermia, she could feel her fire power drifting farther away, like a lantern lost in an Arctic sea.

Between her fingers Bleak was twirling the remnants of her saber's handle, which had unfortunately formed a convenient dagger. "I'm truly sorry," Bleak began.

Ash fixed her eyes on the row of icicles overhead. *Just one fire.*

"Just as I got no enjoyment out of Lesley's departure . . ." Bleak glanced back at the ice totem pole. "I shall get no satisfaction out of this."

Ash narrowed her eyes. She roved the tundra of her mind for that last scrap of tinder she had left. She felt the flint catch once, twice, felt the spark. *Just one little point of light.*

Bleak knelt and lowered her knife toward Ash's throat. "My only prayer is that you are the last obstacle on our way to power."

Then Ash could see the tiny point of light, the prick of fire, ignite at the top of one of the icicles overhead. "I am . . . ," Ash managed to say through her chattering teeth and frost-chapped lips, "your last obstacle . . . on your way to *hell.*"

A heavy crack like a splitting tree trunk was Bleak's only warning. The tiny point of fire chewed through the top of the icicle directly over her, and the icicle dropped straight down. Bleak didn't even have time to turn before the razor tip sank into her back and plunged into her heart.

The ice dagger clattered from Bleak's hand and landed point-down inches from Ash's cheek.

Bleak's hands tried to find their way to her back, where the icicle had penetrated her body, but the wound was hopelessly out of reach. With a long wheeze she collapsed onto her ribs beside Ash.

Ash was able to wrangle control of her internal furnace again, willing herself back from hypothermia. She felt a raging fever, the type she always used to get when she came back inside after playing in the snow for too long. At last she ripped her arms and legs free of their icy shackles.

It might have been the residual anger from knowing that Bleak had killed Lesley, her only link to Rose, or it might have been shock that for the first time in her life, Ash had actually killed somebody. But Ash could think only to drag herself to her stiff-jointed feet and begin the trek across the ice toward the gate, without looking at Bleak's body.

"Wait."

Ash stopped. She turned.

Bleak reached out with a shaking hand. "Please . . . just stay . . . with me."

Ash hesitated. She didn't want to get within attacking distance of the girl she'd just condemned to death. Pity swelled in her heart, however, along with remorse that it had come to this. She had taken a life, taken the future from a girl she barely knew and would never know. The fact that it had been in self-defense wasn't important right now.

Ash knelt beside Bleak, whose cheek was pressed against the ice. Water immediately soaked into Ash's jeans. With the spell broken, the snow had transformed to rain, and the surface of the ice was already slowly melting. Ash made sure to stay out of the path of the dripping icicles, so that she wouldn't share Bleak's fate.

"I just . . . didn't want . . . to be alone," Bleak whispered. "At least . . . you're one of us."

Hesitantly Ash reached out and brushed the hair away from Bleak's eyes. A thin trail of blood rolled out of the corner of Bleak's mouth. It was strange sharing this moment of intimacy with a girl who, by all accounts, had been her enemy. But when Bleak opened her eyes, which were fading into white, there was no malice as she gazed up at her killer. Only sorrow.

"So this . . . is what it's like . . ." Bleak's eyes were now staring right through Ash. "So this . . . is what it's like . . . to feel cold."

Her lips lingered open but her breath had expired. Ash waited there until it was clear that the Norse goddess had passed on. Then she gently drew the hood over Bleak's head.

On her way back to the main gate, Ash had to hustle. The ice was rapidly melting and separating into floes beneath her feet. When she'd safely reached the edge of the pool, she gazed back over the scene as the ice rink, Bleak's last work, succumbed to the tropical heat. With a mighty, trembling crack, the ice totem pole with Lesley at its crest broke apart at its narrow trunk and crashed through the ice. The resulting suction dragged Bleak's body under with it.

Ash couldn't help but wonder whether Ixtab had been there in Bleak's final moments. The words Ixtab had spoken just two days earlier echoed in Ash's ears, ringing all too true as she stood at the water's edge, where the night's body count had tallied to two.

It seems like the only ability that we lack is the power to not kill each other.

Ash sat on the edge of the condo roof with her legs folded beneath her. It was so late that even the tropical air threatened to stumble into chilly territory, and Ash hadn't exactly bothered to buy any hoodies or cardigans when she'd restocked her wardrobe for Miami.

Although the eastern face of the building offered a beautiful view of Biscayne Bay and the ocean, Ash was facing west, landward. Her gaze was transfixed by one of the more prominent skyscrapers in the Miami skyline. It wasn't the tallest, but it was lit top to bottom with golden lights through all of its nearly fifty floors. (Ash had counted.)

She was trying to count the floors again when Wes slipped down beside her. He was wearing a pair of plaid drawstring pajama pants and a gray T-shirt that looked like it had seen ten years and a thousand washings.

He wiggled his butt over so that they were directly side by side. With his legs out in front of him and hers bent underneath her, the two of them were almost at eye level for once.

"Miami Tower," he said, and pointed to the building on the horizon that had been the object of her attention for the last two hours. "They change the lights to celebrate certain holidays throughout the year. The gold is a new one, to celebrate the summer solstice. It will go red, white, and blue for Independence Day soon enough."

"Did you wait up for me, Dad?" she asked.

"What? No." His attempt to sound surprised was one of the worst performances Ash had ever heard.

Ash rubbed her hand through his shaggy hair, which was somehow still immaculate. "Despite your pajama attire, it's pretty obvious that your hair hasn't seen a pillow all night."

"Or maybe flawless hair is one of my supernatural talents." He picked up the blanket he'd carried outside and tucked it around her shoulders. But the real warmth she felt came when he slid his arm around her waist. Her face flushed red when she realized that even through the blanket he could probably feel the sudden rush of heat coming from within her.

"You went to meet Lesley on your own," he said calmly. Not a question.

"Yes," she said.

"You lied to me."

"Yes." She paused. "Why don't I sense a rant coming?"

He squeezed her waist playfully. "I spent a good part of the night pacing while I was waiting for you to come home. Then when you finally got in, I figured I'd pretend like I wasn't waiting up for you, even though I just ended up pacing some more. But I felt no anger when I heard the door open . . . just relief."

"That's it? No lectures about deceiving you, or about being a team player?" She elbowed him in the ribs through the blanket. "No macho rants about how it was foolish to show up for an ambush without my big strong male protector and his flawless hair to stand between me and harm?"

"You're alive," he said simply. "Although, I'll have you know that this hair has saved many a maiden in its day."

Ash settled her hands into her lap and turned her attention back to the golden tower. "I killed somebody tonight."

Wes's thumb, which had been affectionately drawing concentric rings on her lower back, stopped in its tracks.

"I've seen people die before," she said quietly. "I thought I'd seen the worst. But it's another thing altogether when it's your own hand that takes a life."

"You also saved a life tonight," Wes reminded her. "Ade is safely waking up on a train somewhere, hopefully far from here, because you risked your life to extract him from that building."

"It's not a checkbook," Ash said. "You don't save a life, take a life, line it up in the margins, and everything adds up. I feel . . . dirty." Ash took a deep breath. "It's like because we know we have all these past lifetimes behind us and future lifetimes in the pipeline, it's okay to treat each other like we're disposable. Like we're only ripping a page out of someone's book rather than burning the whole thing."

Ash chanced a look at Wes. He was looking wistfully off to the north. "My father was a bastard," he said finally. "But he wasn't a killer. You'd think a man who was wealthy and successful, who traveled the world, couldn't possibly be unhappy enough to lay a hand on his wife. On his kid." A pause. "I guess you just come home to San Antonio after spending the weekend with your mistress in your Miami penthouse, and you realize that none of your lives—at home, abroad, in the arms of family, in the arms of strangers—are the ones you saw yourself living. Or, worse, maybe you *are* living the life you thought you would, and it's still not enough."

"Wes," she whispered, offering him an out in case he didn't want to relive the pain.

He continued anyway. "He comes home after a long trip. Sees that we forgot to take out the garbage. My chore. Throws me down the basement stairs and locks the door. I remember watching the sun going down through the garden windows. Remember my face on the dusty cement floor as I listened to what was going on up in the kitchen. Then as the last shadow faded on the basement wall, I remember something boiling up in me like a dark spring. Walked up the stairs. Ripped the door off the hinges. Dad raises the cordless phone clutched in his hand. Couldn't hear a word he was screaming at me. Then I hit him. Once." Wes paused again. "Just once. And the noise stopped. And my father fell. And he never got back up."

Ash, who didn't realize she'd been holding her breath throughout the entire story, let out a long breath. "You did nothing wrong, Wes. You know that, right?"

"The court absolved me of any wrongdoing," he said robotically, like the excuse had been programmed word for word into his brain—like everyone believed it but him. "When you have a mother and a kid who are visibly bruised and scarred, apparently it's difficult to argue that it was anything but self-defense."

She was thinking back on the visions she'd seen of the childhoods of other gods. Ade's earthquake bringing the chapel down on the pastor. Raja locked in a funeral home while her foster father's corpse reanimated. Lily's cutthroat father. Ash's own sister, a murderess and an outlaw; her other sister, a fugitive in the Central American jungle. And now Wes. "Let no one say that gods live charmed childhoods," Ash said at last.

This seemed to snap Wes out of his dark reverie. In fact, he almost seemed relieved to have gotten it off his chest. Lighter. "What I was trying to say is that every choice we make has two sides to it. And you're right. It doesn't always add up. Just because you saved your mother doesn't mean you didn't kill your father. Just because you protected your friend doesn't mean people won't get hurt along the way."

"Then what do you do when the math doesn't add up?" she asked. "What do you do when doing the right thing *doesn't* make things right?"

He held out a hand toward the skyline. "You make a decision whether you want to spend your life staring at dark horizons . . ." He turned. Ash followed his gaze over her shoulder, to the ever-brightening eastern sky. "Or whether you want to spend it catching every sunrise that you can."

They didn't even need to discuss it. Ash and Wes rose as one, and her hand slipped into his fingers, which had curled in anticipation. Together they wandered over to the condo's eastern railing.

They waited.

Something about staying up until the point of exhaustion always allowed Ash the deepest sleep. Thus she shouldn't have been surprised when, after staying up past the sunrise, she woke up at nearly four the next afternoon.

Wes must have either been monitoring her or had an acute sense of her sleep patterns—he popped his head in the doorway before she even had time to pick her head off the pillow. "Oh, good," he said. "You're up in time for lunch."

Ash attempted to sweep aside the hair that was matted to her forehead, but sweat had cemented it in place.

"I could live in Miami for a hundred years and not get used to your bizarre meal schedule," she said.

Wes shook his head. "We eat lunch at the right time. Everyone else in the country just eats four hours early."

Ash rolled over. "Wake me up before dinner, then."

She heard his footsteps plod across the room. Then Wes ripped the covers off the bed. She squeaked and curled up into a ball as the air washed over her bare legs. Wes's grin was barely apologetic while he stood over her, with the down comforter still in his talons. "Nice boy shorts," he said. "Get dressed. And pack a bathing suit."

"Get out!" Ash shrieked. She tugged the comforter out of his clutches to cover up her exposed legs.

He held up his hands apologetically and backed out of the room. But he poked his head back in almost immediately, "For the record, red is a *great* color on you."

"Out!"

Once Ash had finally dressed—and made sure she wasn't wearing a single item that was red—she sauntered out into the kitchen, where she caught Aurora, who was halfway out the door. Her eyes widened when she spotted Ash, and her wings visibly fluttered underneath her button-down. If Ash didn't know any better, she would have thought that the winged goddess had been trying to sneak out of the apartment.

Ash raised an eyebrow. "You're not coming to the beach with us?"

"I'd love to," Aurora said, "but I, uh, have to . . ."

"Did Wes tell you to make yourself scarce so that he could take me out one-on-one?" Ash interrogated her.

"Don't be silly," Aurora said as she gradually edged out the door. "I have a . . . hair appointment. At the salon." She pulled halfheartedly at her hair, which had clearly been recently cut and colored.

"I'll be the girl not looking surprised when your hair looks the same the next time I see you," Ash said.

"Gotta go!" Aurora gave a short playful wave, and the door snapped shut behind her.

"So." Wes walked out of his bedroom just then carrying a wicker basket with a stack of beach towels folded on top. "Ready for a picnic on the beach?"

But Ash just shook her head at him. "Smooth, Wes. Real smooth."

At the beach, as she spread out their towels and Wes planted their umbrella, Ash felt a twinge of guilt. She'd slept the day away already, and now she was going to spend her evening lounging on the beach? She was here on a mission to find her sister, not for a vacation—or a tropical romance, for that matter.

The more she thought about it, however, the more she resigned herself to an evening of leisure. Lesley Vanderbilt had been her last tether to Rose; for better or worse, Lesley's corpse was probably still thawing out in a Miami mortuary. Without the Lesley connection, Ash didn't know where to find the Four Seasons. They could have a lair next door to Wes's condominium, for all she knew. Now that Ade had been rescued, the Four Seasons no longer had a god to sacrifice for their national broadcast. Hopefully, whichever god they went after next would incinerate them in the process. With Bleak dead, they were already down a Season. Maybe the cult would fall apart altogether.

Ash dug her toes into the warm sand, and for the first time in a week let her anxieties melt away under the low evening sun. She'd give it a night, she decided as she bit into one of the artichoke sandwiches Wes had made. Then, if she needed to, she'd start early tomorrow taking the city block by block. Maybe if she got close enough to where Rose was being held, the same strange heat vision that had directed her to the dockyard four nights ago would lead her to her sister as well.

From behind the stealthy privacy of her sunglasses, she allowed herself a long moment to drink in Wes out of the corner of her eye. He was lying facedown next to her, in the volcano-covered swim trunks he'd worn for her amusement. His body was so long that his knees didn't even fit onto the beach towel.

At least there were some perks to sticking around Miami while she was searching for her sister, with or without leads. Though the fact that Wes was even partially weighing into her desire to stay in Florida concerned Ash. She'd known him for four days—four days!—and wasn't a week out of her "relationship" with Colt. It had all the makings of a rebound train wreck . . . yet she couldn't help herself.

Wes opened his eyes and shielded them from the low-angle sunlight with one of his hands. He squinted at Ash. "Were you watching me nap?"

Ash just smiled and adjusted her sunglasses. "You'll never know."

Wes rifled through the contents of their wicker basket. He held up the empty sandwich wrap that used to contain their homemade paninis, then pointed to the third empty wrapper at Ash's hip. "Either I'm a four-star chef or you were really hungry."

Ash tucked the sandwich wrapper under her towel. "Shut up."

Later, once the sun was setting and the white sands were clearing out, the two of them got dressed and indulged in a long meal at an Italian restaurant along the main drive. Ash felt particularly sluggish by the time Wes asked for the check, but he still insisted they ditch their sandals and go walking on the beach.

The conversation had been fairly constant through all of dinner, but now, alone on the moonlit Atlantic shoreline, they fell into an impenetrable silence. They'd been surrounded by bustle and movement all day, from their fellow beachgoers to the hordes of people dining on Ocean Drive. Now the background static had descended to a distant hum, and the beach was empty save an occasional couple as they wandered by.

When Wes was clearly beginning to fidget as the quiet persisted, Ash laughed.

"What?" Wes shoved his hands deeper into his jeans pockets. "What's so funny?"

"When we first met," Ash explained, "four nights ago, you told me that your nocturnal powers increase as the full moon approaches. Between everything you've organized for us today—the one-on-one time, the beach picnic, the dinner for two, and now a very clichéd but enjoyable moonlit stroll—I'm starting to wonder if it's your sense of romance that waxes with the moon."

Wes visibly slouched a few inches. "You just seemed so glum last night that I thought a pick-me-up was in order. If anything—"

Ash stepped in front of him and placed a hand on his chest to stop him. "Hey, I didn't say that so you'd get defensive. There's no need to apologize for a night that I'm enjoying every minute of. Nor do you have to feel like a stretch of silence will make me enjoy it any less. These last few hours have been exactly what I needed."

Her words summoned Wes's confidence again, and one of his hands found its way out of his pocket and into her hand.

The two of them cut across the dry sand until they hit the water. The tide lapped at the bottom of Ash's jeans, which she didn't bother to roll up. Even at night, even as the surface of the sand expelled a day's worth of heat, the water here remained so much warmer than the Cape Cod beaches where Ash had vacationed growing up.

"Aurora has this getting-to-know-you game she likes

to play," Wes said. "She says you can never really know someone fully, but there are three questions you can ask that can help you to understand them *right now*. I've seen her play it with strangers she just met at the bar; once upon a time she used to play this game with me, too. Do you mind if I ask you those three questions?"

Ash splashed a little bit of water at his jeans. "As long as you're not disappointed if I choose not to answer."

"Question number one," he said. "What is something you secretly wish but that you probably wouldn't tell your best friend?"

"Wow." Ash whistled. "That's a pretty personal question. Aurora gets strangers to answer that at the bar?"

"She's a very persuasive girl when she wants to be. You and I hardly qualify as strangers, but I'm also not the charmer she is. . . . So I guess you'll have to ask yourself whether you're willing to take a chance and share something personal with a sort-of stranger who you sort of live with."

Ash realized they were walking north along the shore. Somewhere a thousand miles in this direction, her parents were at home, probably worrying sick about her, about Eve, too. Ash bowed her head. "Sometimes I think that I would give all this up—the new friends, the adventure"—she snapped her fingers, and a jet of fire sprung from the tip of her thumb like a lighter—"my powers, if I knew that it would heal my broken family. I would give up a thousand fast-paced, violent lives as a goddess in exchange for just one life of happiness and stability with the people who swore to love me, even though I would never be their daughter by blood." She snapped again. The fire extinguished. "And sometimes I remember life in high school before all this, and I think that I'm full of shit, that I'm selfish, that no matter how many people I see get hurt, no matter how much pain I feel myself, I wouldn't have the strength to return to a 'normal' life."

"I guess the sand is always whiter on the other beach," Wes mused. "Second question: What is your greatest fear right now?"

This one came more easily to Ash. It was something that she'd spent a good chunk of her time on the roof last night thinking about. "For the last few days I've been afraid that I'll never find my younger sister, and that I'll never bring Eve back. But then last night, when I thought I was *this* close to Rose, I realized what was most terrifying to me is the thought that I'll get both of my sisters back . . . and it won't make everything okay."

"Well, at least the third question is on the lighter side," he said. Ash could tell he was wondering whether his thought-provoking three-question game had taken a harpoon to the romantic gaiety of their date. "The last question is this: If you could be anywhere in the world right now, where would you be?"

But even this question, which she knew was supposed to be fun and inspire her to describe a dream vacation, took on a new sense of gravity. Did he expect her to say "here"? Was he wondering if her desire to give it all up for a normal life in Scarsdale included giving up meeting him as well? Was he wondering whether there was a place for a ninety-six-hour romance in Ash's ideal life?

Rather than answering, Ash said, "I want you to answer those same three questions. Since you've just put me on the spot, it's your turn to psychoanalyze yourself."

Wes's expression soured. "The easiest of the three questions, and you're just going to skip it?"

Ash pouted right back at him. "God, give a girl a second to come up with a thoughtful answer."

"Fine." Wes stopped walking and set his heels in the wet sand as he formulated his answers. "My secret desire," he said, "is that I hadn't inherited everything that I own—the money, the car, the condo—but that I'd worked for it. At the moment my secret fear is that, even if what you and I have between us is something special, when all this ugly business with the Four Seasons and your sisters is over, you won't be able to remember me without thinking of all the pain along the way." He paused to take in the moonlight. "But despite all that, if I could be anywhere in the world right now, I'd be right here standing ankle-deep in water with you."

Ash's ears were growing hot, to the point where she thought they might ignite. She tried to blow the flames out by looking out over the ocean. In fact, the warm Atlantic waters were looking particularly inviting. . . . "If

I could be anywhere in the world right now . . ." she said playfully, "then I would be . . . right there!" She pointed to a patch of water twenty feet out, where a trail of moonlight reflected off the surface.

Wes cocked his head in confusion, but by then Ash was already stripping off her pants. Soon she had tossed her T-shirt into a pile in the sand with her rumpled jeans. Now in just her bikini, she took off running through the water and dove gracefully into the waves. The water was warm, yes, but even then she still had that moment of cold shock as her body slipped into the velvet touch of the ocean.

When Ash resurfaced, she flipped her head back to get the wet hair out of her face. After she'd cleared the salt water from her eyes, she saw that Wes was still dawdling on the beach, fully clothed.

"Seriously?" Ash said. "The girl you just poured your heart out to stripped and jumped into the ocean, and you're just going to stand sheepishly on dry land? Are you Tezcatlipoca, Aztec god of night? Or are you a barnacle?"

Wes laughed darkly, almost as if to say *You asked for it*. Then he stripped off his shirt and tossed it onto Ash's clothes pile. It wasn't until she heard the gentle jingling of his belt as he unclasped it that she felt the familiar heat returning to her ears. Still, she couldn't look away.

Wes loped into the shallows and dove, though not gracefully like Ash had done. His massive body sent a plume of water right into Ash's eyes and mouth. By the time she'd finished choking and had wiped her eyes clear, Wes had vanished.

A hand tugged on her ankle, and she screamed, even though she knew it was Wes. Sure enough he popped out of the water behind her and slipped a wet hand over her eyes. "Guess who?"

Ash elbowed him in the ribs and swam a few strokes away. On the beach a rowdy group of teenagers was stumbling along, possibly drunk. Some privacy would have been nice. "I want to try something," Ash said.

Ash closed her eyes and extended her arms so that her fingers just grazed the water's surface. She let the heat radiate out of them in a thin net intended just for the skim layer of the water. As always, she found her powers easier to control when she was actually touching the object she wanted to heat, rather than from a distance—conduction versus convection.

The steam began to waft off the ocean's surface lightly at first, then thicker, until a fine vapor had fully enshrouded them. The cloud continued to thicken, and Wes slowly faded into the veil of mist. Too late Ash realized that her makeshift sauna might cause flashbacks to that awful night back in California with the—

tsunami hitting her wall of fire, the

acre of mist settling over the cove in the aftermath,

then

Colt chained to the rock, his

shirt ripped open and his

eyes blinking open as she

approached, an angel in the mist come to—

Ash shook her head to dislodge the shattered memories. Before any more could resurface, she paddled through the mist. Wes's image reemerged through the haze. Just for this one night, enveloped in their own outdoor steam room, Ash would try to forget the world outside, the violence, the fear, the uncertainty of the future. Just for this one night, she'd pretend like it was just the two of them, swimming in their own little private universe.

Ash closed the remaining space between them, sending a ripple out toward the edges of the mist. She stopped floating and let her feet touch the ocean bottom so that she was standing once more. "Ask me again," she whispered to Wes. Underneath the water her legs pressed against his.

Wes's hands glided around to the small of her back, and he pulled her against him. He bent his knees so they were closer to the same level. His lips started to travel toward hers, but stopped just shy of their target. "Ask you what?" he whispered back.

Her fingers slid up his chest and finally came to rest so they were on either side of his neck. Their lips came together, and they kissed softly at first, then harder. Ash sucked on his top lip for good measure before she pulled away. With an inch between them she gazed at him until he opened his eyes and looked back at her expectantly.

"Ask me again," she whispered, "where in the world I'd rather be right now."

Ash couldn't be sure how long they were out in the ocean. Could have been ten minutes. Could have been two hours. But for some time they just listed idly in the water like driftwood, with Wes's arms wrapped around her from behind. Together they floated, looking up at the stars, as the mist slowly dispelled into the sky.

Eventually they extracted themselves and took the long walk back to the towels and sandals, bumping flirtatiously into each other along the way. While they'd been "lost at sea," Wes's beached cell phone had received a text from Aurora, inviting them out to a nightclub where they could use her "bouncer connections" to bypass the line. Wes left it in Ash's hands whether or not to go. She juggled her options. The devilish part of her wanted to take things back to Wes's condo. But she was afraid that she might get carried away in the heat of the moment if they were alone and near a bed. Who knew what other tools of seduction the Aztec night god had?

"I don't want this night to end," she told him finally. "Especially since I know your moves on the dance floor are as sharp as your game in the water."

He leaned into her and kissed the wisps of her hair just below her ear. "Then let's hope it's a dark bar with even darker corners," he whispered.

She curled a finger under his chin. "You're the god of night. I'm sure you could make a dark corner on the surface of the sun if you had to." With that, they suited up in club-appropriate shirts they'd packed in Wes's Cadillac and walked two blocks over to the nightclub.

The line of people waiting to get into CHAOS ran nearly a quarter mile long, well past the stanchions, which were guarded by four burly men in tuxedoes. Half of the people in line barely looked old enough to be out clubbing (not that Ash was one to judge). Many were hopping up and down to look over the line and see if it was moving at all. As far as Ash could tell from their restlessness, the line hadn't budged in a while.

Much to the disdain of the others waiting on the street, Wes ignored the stanchions and walked right up to the tallest and widest of the bouncers, who was still shorter than Wes. The night god whispered something into his ear that Ash couldn't hear, but she caught the name Aurora, which instantly brought a smile to the bouncer's lips. He shook hands with Wes—in the middle of which Ash saw a few green bills exchanged—and he pulled aside the red ribbon to let them through. Ash heard the angry protests of a gaggle of girls at the front of the line before Wes ushered her inside.

The volume of the music was so loud inside that the club could have been the interior of a jet turbine. Wes took her by the hand and led her past the coat check onto CHAOS's massive dance floor.

"Whoa," Ash said, though she could barely hear her own voice over the thumping bass line.

"Yep!" Wes shouted back at her.

The huge room, which was the size of a small airplane hangar, had been constructed to look like it was upside down. The ceiling was decorated wall to wall with tables and chairs that had been bolted into place, complete with tablecloths, plates, silverware, and even electric candles. At the far end of the ceiling was a music stage complete with an upside-down drum set, a grand piano, and a series of mounted guitars.

Beneath the stage—or above it, depending on how you chose to view the room—there was a long wrap-around bar clustered with dancers going up for another round of drinks while an overworked staff of bartenders moved around behind the bar like windup dolls in black T-shirts.

Ash and Wes maneuvered through the packed dance floor, where a large spinning disco ball completed the illusion that the dancers were on the ceiling. It was uncomfortably hot even for Ash, who could practically taste the cloud of perspiration in the air.

Aurora somehow spotted them almost immediately from the high top she'd secured by the bar. She waved them over. She wore a very professional-looking suit, but with the white dress shirt unbuttoned halfway down— the sexy businesswoman look?

They were far enough from the speakers that Ash

could at least make out what Aurora was saying. She pulled Ash over by her elbow and pointed her empty mojito glass at the bar. "See those three guys?" she asked.

At first Ash wasn't sure who she was referring to—the bar was an absolute zoo. But as her eyes roved the barflies, she managed to pick out one guy, another, and then a third, who were all casting amorous glances in her direction.

"Which one should I let buy me a drink?" she asked Ash.

"Must be nice to have that many options," Ash shouted back over the music.

Aurora corralled her in closer, and Ash could smell the rum on her breath. "I'll let you in on a little secret," she yelled loudly enough for the tables around them to hear. "Men like a little mystery. They come into a bar, and they automatically know what to expect from the three hundred hoochies here who look like they're wearing trash bags and lingerie." A girl at the high top next to them, who was wearing a revealing black top, scrunched her face in Aurora's direction, but the goddess ignored her and continued. "I, however, come in here dressed like a CEO—thanks in part to these deformities on my back—and men can't resist. Conservative fashion means power, power means mystery, and mystery means challenge."

"Well." Ash examined Aurora's three suitors again. "Guy number one looks a little nervous and keeps checking his cell phone just to seem like he's busy. Guy number two has an umbrella in his drink—a drink that I'd like to point out is bright blue." She turned to the man on the end who was dressed in a suit as well and grinned a little when he noticed them checking him out. "But guy number three is looking over here without mercy or shame, which means either he's very confident . . . or he's a total creep."

Aurora slapped her on the back. "My thoughts exactly." She pointed to Wes. "Now take this loser dancing for a couple of songs so Señor Confianza will see me alone and bring me a mojito."

Ash laughed and saluted Aurora before she followed her orders and seized Wes by the arm. Wes's long sigh was audible even over the dance music.

A spicy Latin song with a quick beat and frenetic guitar strumming rattled out of the nearby speaker once they hit the dance floor. Ash halfheartedly moved to the rhythm for a few measures before she leaned into Wes so he could hear her. "I'm really not in the dancing mood. Is there a corner we can go sulk in while Aurora woos her man?"

Wes's shoulders relaxed. "I thought you'd never ask." He pointed to a pillar in the corner, between two hanging plants. "Let's just go sway over there."

Within the privacy of the fronds, Ash felt a little more comfortable being a stick in the mud while the rest of the club undulated to the music. Up at the bar she could see Aurora's well-dressed suitor make his way casually over to her high top with a drink in either hand. "Can I ask you an awkward question?" Ash asked Wes. "Aurora seems really into . . . male attention. But with the wings how does she . . . when they . . . ?" She let her sentence trail off.

Wes covered his mouth as he laughed. "In the dark?" he joked, then added, "Aurora's little flings never leave the bar. As to why she finds them endlessly entertaining . . . You can read into Aurora's behavior all you want. She could just be young and having fun."

"Or?"

Wes shrugged. "If you meet somebody new every night, you get a taste of romance without ever having to get close to someone. Whatever her reasons, after a relationship as crappy as she suffered through, she's entitled to play a little cat and mouse at the bar."

"We all heal in different ways," Ash said. Some people, fresh out of bad relationships, seduced strangers at the bar.

And others, Ash thought, *fly halfway across the country with no game plan to rescue a girl they've never met.*

Ash snapped back to reality, hoping that Wes hadn't been studying her face or reading the dark thoughts that lurked behind it. Colt had already come between the two of them enough already.

Wes's attention, however, was fixed over her shoulder into the dance crowd. "I thought this girl was checking me out, but if I didn't know any better . . ." He looked troubled. "I'd say she was staring at you."

Ash twirled around. It didn't take much scanning to pick her out of the crowd—a teenage girl in a black tank top and jeans standing barely five yards from them. Statue-still and rigid, she had her gaze pinned on Ash.

It was Eve Wilde.

Ash got lost in the eyes of her sister, the eyes that she thought she'd seen for the last time as they'd vanished into the belly of the enormous Cloak creature almost two months ago.

Now here she stood in the flesh, not only breathing and alive . . . but smiling.

Amused.

Gloating.

Despite everything the Wilde sisters had been through, Ash had spent the last week doing everything in her power to get Rose back, so she could in turn rescue Eve from the Cloak. But this wasn't the happy reunion Ash had imagined—Eve leering at her across the nightclub floor, with her teasing grin flickering under the strobe lights. Even a goddess like Eve, who could make a career out of her dramatic reentrances into Ash's life, didn't just break out of hell and come back with a smirk on her face.

Something was very wrong.

Wes stepped into her view so that Eve, still unmoving, drifted out of focus behind him. "Tell me I don't need to be jealous."

"That's my sister," Ash whispered, then repeated herself louder so he could hear her over the music. "My sister!"

Wes took a second look at Eve. "I see the resemblance, but she's a little on the, um, mature side for a six-year-old."

"Wrong sister!" Ash snapped. Wes leaned over just enough to block her view of Eve. Ash leaned around his shoulder . . . and discovered the back of Eve's head receding through the crowd. She had a red backpack slung over her shoulder and was cutting a path for the front entrance.

Ash brushed past Wes, and he was too startled to even make a grab for her until she had plunged into the fray, out of reach. With one shoulder forward as a battering ram, Ash muscled her way through the trance-music pandemonium. Most people were dancing so frantically that they didn't even stop to see who had shouldered past them. Even over the music Ash could just barely hear Wes shouting her name.

There wasn't time to apologize that, for the second time, a face from her past had shown up unexpectedly while they were dancing.

Ash sprinted past the coat check and out onto the street, past the bouncers. "The music's that bad?" a girl at the front of the line asked her.

Down the street Ash spotted Eve making a break for a couple who were parking their Vespas at the curb. Eve roughly shoved the man off his scooter before he had a chance to withdraw the keys. He flopped onto the curb while his girlfriend shrieked and tried to take a swing at

Eve. But Eve drilled a hard kick into her attacker's stomach, and the girl tripped back-first over her own scooter. Eve revved the engine and rocketed onto Collins Avenue.

Ash took off toward the curb, where the Vespa-robbed couple were just climbing to their feet and brushing themselves off. The boyfriend looked like he was in shock as the taillight of his Vespa disappeared down the avenue, while his girlfriend collapsed into hysterics, trying to fish her cell phone out of her purse.

Much to their added confusion, Ash hopped onto the second Vespa. "Are you kidding me?" the girl shrieked. She sauntered toward Ash with her bag raised, ready to strike.

"I'm going to get your boyfriend's scooter back," Ash promised as she flipped up the kickstand. "But I need to borrow yours first." Ash took off, and the girl chased her only a few steps before she stopped, helpless, and watched the second Vespa sail away.

Ash isolated the other Vespa's taillight, a small red dot a block up the avenue, and set a course for it. Well aware that she had only a few days' experience on a scooter, she pushed her chariot up through thirty miles an hour, then past forty. She veered around a Porsche that looked fresh off the lot, and caught a yellow light in time. Up to fifty miles an hour. She shot through another light and dodged a slow-moving joyrider in a convertible, who laid on the horn.

Sixty miles an hour and she was flying perilously toward two SUVs that were shoulder to shoulder, blocking both lanes and obstructing her view of Eve's taillight. Her vision was growing blurry as the hot and humid Miami air drilled into her face. Overhead the stoplight shifted from green, to yellow, then to red.

Ash was sick of watching her leads drift away.

She was sick of having two sisters who existed only as visions and memories.

She sure as hell wasn't going to let Eve come back from the dead only to run away again.

Ash punched the engine up to seventy. She sucked in her breath. And she held the handlebars as steady as she could.

Somehow she kept the scooter on a straight enough line to navigate the tight gap between the two SUVs. Only by ducking at the last second did she prevent the side mirrors from taking off her head.

As soon as she popped out into the dim intersection, a pair of headlights sliced across her. The harsh blare of a horn startled her so badly that she nearly toppled off the scooter. She twisted the handlebars to the right just as the swerving BMW squealed past her back tire, missing her by only inches.

Ash surveyed Collins Avenue ahead, expecting to have lost her sister in the chaos of running the red light. Instead Eve was directly in front of her, still cruising forward but at a relaxed speed, allowing Ash to steadily catch up. Eve glanced over her shoulder and smiled again before she finally accelerated.

She's not trying to get away, Ash realized. *She's waiting for me to follow her.*

But where was Eve leading her to? The Cloak underworld? Off the edge of a cliff?

After Ash had followed her at a cautious distance for several blocks, Eve took a sharp right into a driveway leading up to a large, expensive-looking hotel with a long, white curved façade. Eve plowed up the drive and only slowed when she rolled under the roof of the porte cochere. There she abandoned her scooter on the curb and dashed through the revolving door to the lobby.

Ash pulled in just a few seconds later. She tossed her keys to the very perplexed-looking valet as she dismounted the bike. "Park it next to my Ferrari," she said, and stormed past him before he could protest.

Ash burst through the revolving door and followed the collective gazes of the confused hotel guests. Eve was sprinting through the crowded lobby, which was lit blue like the inside of an ice cave. The guests must have been even more startled to see a second Polynesian girl—who looked so much like the first—in hot pursuit.

Ash was still just a month fresh out of tennis season, and rapidly gained on the less-athletic Eve now that they were on foot. Perhaps sensing this, Eve grabbed the golden luggage-packed cart from a bellhop and spun it in Ash's direction.

Direct hit. The cart toppled over onto Ash, and heavy luggage cascaded down onto her.

By the time Ash had unburied herself from underneath the luggage, Eve was at the end of the blue-carpeted corridor and turning the corner. Ash waved away the bellhop, who was trying to help her up, and charged after her sister again.

When she rounded the corner, the door directly in front of her was slowly listing closed. The spa beyond lay in darkness, but Ash wasn't about to let a little trespassing stop her. The hotel staff was no doubt already on red alert to find the suspicious girls who'd transformed the hotel lobby into a violent foot race, but after squaring off against bloodthirsty gods and gun-toting mercenaries, the threat of being caught by underpaid security guards was laughable.

Inside the spa's waiting room the only light was what filtered through the opaque spa doors, but it was enough for Ash to make her way to the steam room beyond. A thick steam was already beginning to fill the space, its hissing echoing off the tile walls.

Ash's caution had returned, now that her sister had corralled her into a dark and cloudy enclosed space. She ignited one of her hands enough to form a halo around her, a lantern in the mist. At least her torch could double as a weapon should Eve launch herself out of a dark corner. "You know, Eve . . . ," Ash called out. Her words echoed with a twang off the tile. "You could have just asked me to go to the spa with you. Hell, between my fire and your storms, we could have just *made our own*."

There was no answer from the shadows.

In the next room, which was even narrower than the steam room, Ash spotted a series of drains on the ground. What the hell was this room for?

Something clicked at the end of the hall. The spouts overhead pulsed on. It was a rain room, sending a network of light showers, cold and hot, hot and cold, down onto Ash, drenching her shirt and jeans within seconds. "Come on," Ash shouted again. "Flipping a switch to make rain? That's far too conventional for the sister I know."

And that, Ash realized, was a problem. None of this chase was like Eve. Sure, between Scarsdale and Blackwood, Ash's sister had always enjoyed making dramatic entries back into her life. But Eve was also in love with the sound of her voice and prone to grandiose speeches whenever she reappeared. Eve was the type of girl who cornered her opponents, *not* the type who led them on a wild sprint halfway across a city in the dead of night.

Ash's blood began to pump faster when she reached the third room, which contained a long mineral pool and a parade of reclining beach chairs. It also had some ambient light, courtesy of the moon as it streamed through the French windows that opened out onto the spa's patio. Ash let the flames of her torch peter out to a soft glow.

One item was out of place in the mineral pool—Eve's bright red backpack, which was tucked against one of the beach chairs. Another warning flag. Eve, label snob that she was, wouldn't have been caught dead (or in this case, alive again) wearing a knapsack the color of a fire engine.

Ash pried open the rope clasp and withdrew the soft contents within. The backpack contained a black shirt and jeans, the same clothes that Eve had been wearing just minutes ago. Ash held the shirt up to the light. *Unless Eve is running around the resort naked somewhere . . .*

A hand clutched her elbow.

Ash screamed and brought her fist around to attack, her whole hand bursting into flames on sheer survival instinct.

Wes caught her by the forearm. "Jesus," he said, eyeing the ball of flames that had nearly seared his face. "Let's try not to burn down any billion-dollar four-star resorts. Or me, for that matter."

Ash huffed, but let her arm cool until the flames extinguished. "One word of warning could have prevented you from becoming a human barbecue," she snapped at him. "How the hell did you even find me here?"

He took a cautious step away from her. "I nearly didn't, thanks to your Indy 500 race through half of Miami Beach," he said. "Thankfully I just kept my eyes peeled for two abandoned scooters and a valet who looked like he was on the verge of a panic attack, and—"

Ash held up her hand to cut him off. She was staring through one of the French doors out at the sky, which was still immaculate, as though the moonbeams had vaporized any clouds over Miami. "The weather . . ."

"Is perfect?" Wes finished for her. "It's exactly the same as it's been all night."

"That's the problem," Ash replied. "A cloudless star-filled night? If Eve is truly back, Miami should be either in the middle of a category-twelve monsoon or under two feet of snow. States of emergency are how she celebrates." She cocked her head back and smelled the air. "That girl I just chased was *not* my sister."

"Why are you sniffing the air now?" Wes put a hand on her arm. "It's dark here. Let's get back inside where we can at least see a little better."

Ash pivoted on her heel, grabbed Wes by the lapel, and used all her strength to heave his enormous body toward the pool. With Wes caught off guard, his foot snagged on one of the beach chairs and he crashed into the water.

Ash was at the mineral pool's edge before he could even resurface. She plunged her arms into the water up to her elbows.

When Wes bobbed to the top, he floundered and attempted to swim for the opposite side of the pool.

"Don't move," Ash growled at him, "or I will happily bring the temperature of this water up to boiling in a matter of seconds."

"A-Ash," Wes stuttered, treading water. He was blinking uncontrollably. "It's me. It's Wes—"

Ash balled her hands into fists and sent a lance of

heat that torpedoed through the water. When the trail of hot water hit Wes's legs, he screamed.

And then he transformed.

His face shuddered with a violent seizure before it melted into blankness. His arms, which were still thrashing about in the water, shortened by nearly six inches, withdrawing back into his body while the bones beneath them rearranged.

When his face restructured itself, the person it revealed underneath had a broad, flat nose and slicked-back hair. It certainly wasn't Wesley Towers.

Ash opened her hands again and allowed the water to simmer. "You should remember next time that no self-respecting Aztec night god is afraid of the dark. Also," she added, "whatever fragrance is coming off you certainly isn't Wes's cologne. You're good, but you're not that good."

Gradually the shifter stopped floundering. He floated and said nothing.

"You have ten seconds to tell me who you are, who you're working with, and why you're impersonating my sister," Ash said. "Otherwise you better transform yourself into a lobster or a deviled egg. Ten—"

"My name is Proteus," the shifter blurted out. "I work independently, but I lend my unique . . . services to those willing to pay. In this case I was e-mailed a file with orders to carry out tonight."

Ash let the temperature of the pool rise a few degrees,

literally turning up the heat of her interrogation. "What sort of orders?"

Proteus cast a panicked look at the simmering water. "They sent me everything I would need to carry out their wishes. Full-body and facial close-up photos of you, Wes, and Aurora. Approximate height and weight measurements. MP3 samples of your voices."

Ash frowned. His yet-to-be-named employers—the Four Seasons, no doubt—had provided Proteus with all the information to forge their identities, yet he'd appeared in the nightclub as her sister, who, imprisoned in hell, was nowhere around to be photographed or wiretapped for a vocal sample. "Then why did you come as my sister?"

"Only Aurora was supposed to be at the nightclub. When all three of you showed up, I received an auxiliary plan from my employer—a series of old photos of some Polynesian girl—your sister, apparently—that I would use to lead you away from the mark."

"Auxiliary plan? The mark?" Ash felt her temper rising. Her blood was turning to lava, starting at her heart and pumping out through her bloodstream. "What the hell was the original plan? *What was it?*" She drove another spear of boiling water into the shape-shifter's torso.

This time Proteus wrapped his arms around his stomach and sank for a few moments before he resurfaced, gulping for air. After he'd spit up the hot water, he stammered, "I—I was supposed to pretend to be you or the tall guy, and lead the winged one outside. But when you showed up, they changed tactics. My new instructions were to get you as far away from the night-club as possible. They said if you left, Towers would follow, which would allow them to . . ." He trailed off and went still.

"Allow them to what?" Ash echoed, then louder, "To what, Proteus?" Her rage was billowing out of control, and she had to force herself to withdraw her hands from the pool so she wouldn't boil the shifter to death before he could tell her what she needed to know. "TO WHAT?" She ignited her arms and moved to plunge them into the water again.

"To extract the winged girl!" he confessed. "She's the one they wanted."

Ash dropped back onto her haunches. It all made sense now.

The Four Seasons had planned their sacrifice for tonight.

Ash, Wes, and Aurora had stolen their sacrificial victim from them.

Ash had killed one of their own.

And now they were going to retaliate.

If they truly intended to televise the murder, then Aurora made the most sense. Whereas Ash and Wes had powers that made them dangerous to the Four Seasons, Aurora had only a pair of wings. Not only would she be no match against the more powerful gods, but the wings would also provide convenient, visible evidence to any viewers that Aurora was in fact a goddess.

With Ash temporarily distracted, Proteus was stealthily making a move for the edge of the pool, but Ash pointed a flaming finger at him. "Don't you dare move." She pulled her cell phone out of her pocket. Three missed calls from Wes. She hit the callback button.

Wes picked up before it finished ringing once. *"Ash, where the hell are you?"*

"Where are *you*?" Ash said. "Please say you're still at the club." The silence on the other end of the call said otherwise.

Wes paused. "I came out looking for you. I'm in the Cadillac driving north now, and—"

"You have to go back!" Ash dropped her face into her other hand. "You have to go back to the club *right now*."

"It's too late," Proteus said quietly.

Ash held the phone away from her mouth. "What did you say?"

Proteus cleared his throat. "It's too late. They drugged Aurora's drink before you even left. If the big guy left for even a minute . . . then it's too late."

Ash slowly brought the phone back to her face, her eyes glued to the shifter in the pool. She could hear Wes asking questions about who she was talking to, but she was having trouble hearing him over the intense ringing in her own ears. "Come pick me up outside the Fontainebleau resort as soon as you can," she instructed him, her voice hollow. "I have to go right now."

She clicked the phone closed. It immediately started to vibrate again. She ignored it and knelt down next to the pool. "Where are they taking her?"

"I—" Proteus's eyes shifted, like he was about to lie, but then he stopped himself. "They told me I could lead you anywhere, as long as it was in the opposite direction from some condemned movie theater. Palmetto Bay, south of the city. I swear that's all I know! I—"

"Get out of the pool," she said calmly. "Get. Out. Now."

Now that she actually *wanted* him to climb out of the mineral bath, it was the first time he looked like he wanted to stay put. His hesitation broke when she made a *come hither* motion with her finger, and he reluctantly paddled to the edge.

He had just put his hand on the rim of the pool when Ash flashed over. She seized him by the wrist, and with a strength that came to her only in moments of true rage, she lifted him out of the pool by his arm. He squirmed in the air like a cat that had been caught in the chicken coop and was dangling by the scruff of his neck.

Ash channeled all her heat into the hand holding him up. Proteus screamed as the fire bit into his skin. She let the heat smolder against his flesh for several seconds before she tossed him onto the pool deck.

Proteus writhed on his back, gripping his burned forearm, just below where Ash's fingers and palm were now branded deeply into his skin.

"Since you're a shape-shifter," Ash said, "you may be able to cover up that scar with a little bit of concentration." She took three steps forward until she was standing directly over his body. "But now every time you have to erase the scars, every time it takes that much more effort to transform into someone else, you're going to think of me. And if I *ever* see you again, a little second-degree burn will be the least of your problems."

Then she stepped over him and didn't look back as she made a run for the French doors leading out of the spa. Before she closed the door behind her, she heard a splash and a whimper as Proteus rolled into the pool to submerge his branded arm in the mineral water.

Wes was just swerving into the drive leading up to the Fontainebleau when Ash emerged around the side of the building. The two abandoned scooters still lay in front of the valet, who was looking twitchy. Ash sprinted past him, threw open the door to Wes's Cadillac, and slipped in. The Cadillac never even fully stopped moving as it whipped around the circular drive and back out onto the road.

"There's an old . . . condemned movie theater . . . south of the city," Ash said between breaths. "Someplace called . . . Palmetto Bay."

Wes, who had just come to a hard stop at a red light, stalled the sport utility just shy of the intersection.

"There's an antique theater that just got purchased last month . . . with plans to turn it into a steak house." He paused. "It was bought by the Vanderbilt Estates. But why? Aurora's back at CHAOS waiting, and . . . " His words trailed off, as though he could sense that something was terribly off.

Ash put a hand on his wrist. "We don't have much time, Wes. If I'm wrong and Aurora is back where we left her, we can all have a drink about this and laugh." She didn't have the heart to go down the path of *But if I'm right* . . .

Wes studied her for several moments, and when she wouldn't meet his gaze, he sped through the red light, heading west—toward the highway.

Ash just rolled down her window for fresh air that she knew didn't have a chance of clearing her mind.

After the initial explanation of what was going on, Wes and Ash fell into tense silence. There wasn't much to discuss.

Proteus had no reason to lie, with no loyalty to the Four Seasons and under the threat of being boiled to death by Ash.

Aurora wasn't answering her phone.

They both knew this could be a trap.

They both knew they had no choice but to go anyway.

Twenty-five minutes later, after they'd flown down

the South Dixie Highway in record time, Wes swerved onto an off-ramp so fast that the Cadillac rocked briefly up onto two wheels. Soon they were blowing red lights through the suburbs of Palmetto Bay, down narrow palm-lined avenues and past a parade of uniform one-level Spanish houses.

At last, when all the streets were blending together to the point where Ash thought they might be driving in circles, Wes tugged the steering wheel toward a weed-filled parking lot. The Cadillac bucked hard as they popped up over the curb, and then rumbled over a minefield of pot-holes before Wes threw the car into park in front of the old theater.

It may have once been regal, but the white art deco theater looked like it was half a century past its heyday. A long chain was braided through the handles of the decrepit front doors. For a moment Ash thought they may have been duped. But then she tugged on the chain. It slipped free of the door, not padlocked, and then coiled on the ground with a series of clinks.

Inside, a dingy backlit menu flickered over the concession counter. The popcorn machines were lined against the back wall, empty coffins of glass, the soda fountains dry and silent as well. The NOW PLAYING sign over the ticket counter listed movies that hadn't seen the inside of a movie theater since Ash was in middle school.

In the hallway beyond, between the old framed movie posters, there were three doors, one for each screen. But as Ash listened carefully, a faint mechanical whining could be heard from the far door.

Theater number three was small compared to the megaplexes Ash was accustomed to back in New York. A light shone out of the booth window in the back of the theater, projecting a shivering black mass onto the screen.

Eeriest of all, when they reached the front row of the empty theater, two of the chairs had been folded down as though people had already been sitting in them. A soda cup had been tucked in each of their cup holders, and a big bucket of popcorn was balanced on the armrest between them. The smell of butter and salt was fresh, and Ash could hear the soda carbonation still crackling.

On the screen the black background switched to the image of a man's face. As the projectionist, hidden in his booth, focused the image on the screen, the distorted pixels gradually refined until Ash could see Thorne. He wore a subdued smile, and his twenty-foot-tall face was looking down at them as if he knew exactly where in the theater they were standing.

"Ah, you made it," Thorne said around the cigar clenched in his teeth. "As you can see, I've reserved two front-row seats for you to watch tonight's entertainment. It's just a shame that you're in the wrong place to enjoy it live and in person."

"Where is Aurora?" Wes growled at the screen.

But it must have been a one-way transmission, because Thorne's only response was to blow a smoke ring into the camera lens. "You see," he continued, "this plan could really only be a total success if the two of you—and not just Ashline—ended up at that movie theater. Because that means that Wesley Towers, our beloved Aztec god of the night, has chosen to protect the girl who didn't need protecting, while the *other* one . . ." He trailed off, and stepped out of the frame.

Thorne had been dominating the foreground, but now the background took over the screen. It was a garden courtyard with archways in the distance, lit by firelight. At first Ash thought they were broadcasting from Lesley's hacienda, but Wes drew in a long breath. "Wait," he said. "I recognize that place. That's the old Spanish monastery. It's *north* of Miami." He pounded his fist against the nearest armrest so hard that it snapped clean off. "They sent us to the opposite side of the damn city!"

So Thorne had intended for her to catch Proteus. And, more disturbing, he had banked on Wes leaving the nightclub to find Ash, which could mean only one thing.

Someone had been watching Ash and Wes together.

The situation got worse as the camera panned over. In the center of the courtyard, Aurora was squirming on her hands and knees. She had been chained to a post that had been driven into the ground. Her wings fluttered weakly as she pulled against her restraints with excruciating futility. When she looked up at the camera, there was a drugged film over her eyes, which flickered as they struggled to stay open.

Ash jumped as Thorne slid back into view, once again eclipsing the image of Aurora behind him. "It didn't have to be this way." He took another drag from his cigar. "We could have all gone our separate ways after the night at the museum, but you've continued to meddle. You freed my sacrifice. You attempted to turn Lesley against us. And then you killed one of our own, killed my Winter."

"We have to get to that monastery," Wes said quietly to her. "If we start now—"

"No doubt you're making your way to the exit by now," Thorne said, "clinging to some last fiber of hope that maybe you can make it here in time to stop this sacrifice from happening. But the doors have all been locked. And for the next ten minutes, you two will be reduced to mortals."

Behind them the doors through which they'd entered crashed shut, and the click of the lock echoed through the theater. A grating sound announced the metal bar that was being threaded through the handles on the other side.

Then the lights hummed on.

The ultraviolet lights.

They had been installed everywhere—attached to the walls, bubbling up from the track lighting underneath their feet. The room instantly heated several degrees as the dark theater transformed into the arid floor of the desert.

Under the harsh lights Wes looked visibly weakened.

He would be useless to break through the door, which was spotlighted by a small galaxy of lamps.

Ash took a step for the door with her hand raised, prepared to burn a hole through the locked doors. Given the rage and turmoil bubbling inside her, she could probably get hot enough to walk right through them.

"I wouldn't if I were you."

Ash turned and looked at Thorne's patiently waiting image; he stared right back at her.

"Take a moment," he instructed her. "Smell the air."

Now that he mentioned it, there was something pungent in the theater's atmosphere, the growing smell of natural gas that she'd failed to notice before in her panicked state.

"This room is slowing filling up with a special blend of gases that, I'm afraid to say, are quite flammable. One burst filament from any of the UV lamps, or better yet, one spark from you, and the whole building will go up in flames, along with the nitroglycerin containers we've conveniently positioned around you." Thorne tapped the end of his cigar, so that the smoldering ashes rained down. "If you so much as think a fiery thought, this movie theater will become a crater. And while you may be fireproof . . ."

Behind her, Wes was violently pulling at the doors, but his strength was too sapped to move them.

"Your boyfriend isn't."

Ash stared at her hands. Thorne had done it. By

corralling the two of them into the same place, he'd managed to neutralize them both.

On-screen Thorne touched the Bluetooth in his ear and smiled. "Looks like we're ready to record the sacrifice. But before I go, there's somebody here who wanted to say hello to you, Ashline."

Vaguely Ash could still hear Wes slamming his shoulder into the door, and calling out her name for help, but she was hopelessly transfixed by the screen. The camera tracked down.

Rose Wilde stepped into the frame.

If anything the bags underneath Rose's eyes had darkened since the last time Ash had seen her; they were now a bruiselike shade of indigo. She wore a white cotton dress over her small, deceptively frail body. Her shoulders poked sharply through her skin. And the way she was looking into the camera . . .

It was as though she were already dead.

"Aren't you going to say hello, Rosey?" Thorne asked from offscreen.

Rose reached out and touched the camera lens. When she pulled her fingers away, she left the residue of one of her fingerprints on the glass. "Who?" she asked finally. Just one word in that innocent high-pitched voice, from the girl who had seen so much of the world already.

Thorne squatted down next to her and winked at the camera. "Just another person looking to take you away."

Rose didn't react. Her face was an empty canvas. But

after a moment the corner of her eye twitched. Somewhere in the distance there was a rumble.

Thorne finally rotated the camera so that Rose was cropped out of the frame. "The sacrifice won't broadcast until prime time tonight, so you get the unique privilege of watching this sixteen hours before everyone else. Enjoy the show," he said. "And possibly the fireworks after." He laughed.

Then the projection went blue. Ash shouted "No!" and reached out for the screen.

But when the feed returned several moments later, from the perspective of a new camera, Ash wished that the screen had stayed dark instead.

The sacrifice began with Lily unshackling Aurora's chains from the wooden mast. Immediately the winged goddess of the dawn stumbled forward to escape.

She nearly tripped right into Rose, who had tottered out into the courtyard. That's when Ash realized the full genius of the Four Seasons' plan. To anyone watching this who didn't know Aurora, she would look monstrous in her drugged state. Add that to the fact that she was lurching toward a six-year-old girl . . .

At last Aurora spread her wings and bent her knees, preparing to spring into the air.

The drugs in her system, however, had other plans, and her legs buckled beneath her. She landed on her knees, where she wobbled unsteadily and her wings wilted against her back. One hand braced her against the earth while the other one massaged the side of her head.

Then a look of courage came over her. Her back straightened with a little shiver. When she opened her eyes, they shone out like headlights on a midnight road. She glanced over her shoulder at Lily, who was very lazily approaching her on foot. Aurora retracted back onto her haunches and launched herself up into the air. Her translucent wings spread to their full regal wingspan, catching the firelight behind them in a blaze of tangerine and amber.

"Come on," Wes, who had come up beside Ash, whispered at the screen. "You can do it, Rory. I know you can. You're the strongest goddess I know."

Ash was clutching her legs so hard in anticipation that she was drawing blood. She watched Aurora take off with one stroke of her wings, then a second and a third, each one more powerful than the last as she fought her way into the sky above the monastery grounds. For a moment Ash felt a sapling of hope somewhere in her terrified heart.

Then a gust of wind ripped Aurora right out of the sky.

Her body, which had been rigid and determined, folded in two, and she crumpled like a sheet of paper on her way down. The camera followed her through the entire length of her quick plummet until she hit the grass. A second gust seized her wings, which involuntarily opened like a parachute.

She didn't stop sliding across the monastery courtyard until she hit the wooden post. She got to her feet, but by then Lily had reemerged from the shadows. Vines sprung from the soil and coiled around Aurora's body in vicious spirals. As more vines lashed out, they caught her wings and roped them flat to her back.

Meanwhile, as Ash and Wes watched, cemented to the theater floor, a different kind of plant life was beginning to rise up out of the dirt around Aurora's squirming body.

Roots.

Wood.

Bark.

The camera zoomed in to capture every grisly detail of the scene that unfolded next.

It started at her feet, a living sheet of wood pulp that coated Aurora's shoes, her shins, up past her knees. The bark grew thicker and coarser and darker and sharper. Aurora twisted. She gritted her teeth. With what must have been every last vestige of will to live she had left in her, she screamed the fiercest war cry Ash had ever heard.

Her wings exploded out of their vinelike cocoon.

It was too little too late.

As they flapped uselessly to lift her out of her botanical prison, the growing tree trunk had already climbed to her waist, locking her hips in place. No matter how hard she bucked with her wings, her lower half wouldn't budge.

The fury in her eyes dipped into panic while the tree

continued up her torso so that she had to raise her arms over her head to keep them free. The bark washed fluidly over her wings, which continued to fight until the plant matter convulsed inward with the strength of a trash compactor, flattening her crippled wings to her shoulders.

A sob burst out of Ash. Wes breathed raggedly beside her.

On-screen Aurora let the tears flow freely. She stopped fighting. She stared heartbreakingly into the camera while the trunk of the tree cemented itself around her neck, then her chin.

Then Aurora disappeared behind a shroud of timber and bark, buried upright in a living sarcophagus.

The dawn goddess had seen her last dawn.

The spell broke as soon as Ash lost sight of Aurora's face. Her arm burned where Wes's fingernails were now digging into her. "Get us out of here!" Wes yelled. "We need to get to her!"

"It's too late," Ash cried. "She's already—"

"Don't you dare say 'She's already gone.'" Wes's voice broke. "Don't you *dare*. Just work your magic and burn us a path out of here."

"And incinerate you in the process?" Ash shouted. "You don't think I wanted to scorch my way through a wall to get to her? No—I'm not going to lose you both in one night."

"Fine," Wes snarled. He released her arm and ran over to the wall. "Then I will tear this place apart with my hands." He reached up and grabbed hold of one of the ultraviolet lights. He tried to pull it off the wall, but his strength was depleted and the light held fast to its mounted bracket.

Meanwhile, on the screen, the camera zoomed out, showing Lily's horrible creation. Aurora had been just the start, the foundation, but now that the tree had matured in just a matter of minutes, Ash saw it for what it was, with its drooping curtains of green leaves that hung low enough to brush the grounds.

It was a weeping willow.

A shadow passed in front of the image projected on the screen. Ash whipped around. The face of the man in the projector window was blotted by shadow, but Ash recognized his enormous frame and backlit dreadlocks.

Rey held up what looked like a bottle of alcohol.

With a rag stuffed into the top.

The rag ignited under his touch.

He lobbed it to the seats below.

Ash could see it tumbling in slow motion.

She could feel the flammable air around her crackle with potential energy.

She could feel it waiting to ignite.

Ash made it to Wes, who was still trying to jerk the UV light free of its mast, just as she heard the bottle shatter on the floor.

She grabbed him by the shoulders.

Threw him into the corner.

Forced his head down so the giant was balled up into the smallest space possible.

Blanketed her whole body over his own.

Tucked her head down into his.

The heat was extraordinary when the blast happened, even for Ash. The fire ate through the back of her shirt almost instantly. Even with her eyes tight the inside of her eyelids glowed white-hot. Still, she focused her mind, trying to divide her body into two separate tasks—

The back of her, a raging river of lava keeping the probing fingers of the explosion at bay.

The front, as cool as the dark side of the moon to protect Wes.

Then the white light through her eyelids dimmed to a flicker. It was over.

She pulled her head back to make sure Wes was unscathed . . . and instantly realized she couldn't breathe. The massive explosion had consumed a chunk of the theater's oxygen supply.

Wes, too, put a hand on his neck when he discovered that his breaths were only taking in smoke. The explosion, however, had burst the UV lights. Wes pulled back his arm, which was blistered with minor burns, and sent a punch right into the boarded-up exit door.

The whole door buckled outward and slid across the pavement outside. Cool predawn air rushed in through the opening, and Ash drank it greedily.

When she'd inhaled her fill of oxygen, she crawled

over to the front row. Pressed her bare, charred back against the rigid metal seats. Stared at the movie theater screen.

The projector was still running, and the flames at the edge of the screen flared red-hot again as the oxygen billowed into the room.

Ash could only watch as the aperture of fire converged around the smoldering image of the weeping willow.

STREETCAR SUNRISE

You can't help but squeal as the man holding you kicks in the front door. It slams against the inside wall of the plantation manor. You bounce in his arms as he crosses the threshold.

He stops in the middle of the manor home's magnificent foyer, with its dual staircases running up to the second floor, and the enormous chandelier over your heads, crafted out of a series of antlers from animals from a distant forest. He pulls you so tightly to his body that you can feel the muscles of his chest even through the four layers of your white wedding dress. "Welcome home," he says to you. "Welcome home, *Lucille Halliday*."

You coquettishly slide a finger along his jawline, but just as he leans in for a kiss, you slip out of his arms and onto your feet. You sashay across the foyer, and your heels click on the floor. "Your home is quite lovely," you say, as though you haven't spent a hundred nights enter-tained in this house before. "If not a bit roomy."

"*Our* home." He steps up behind you and cups his hands over the points of your hips. "As for the abundance of space, it sure could benefit from a woman's touch."

You cluck and slap his hands away one at a time. "I fear to guess how many *women's touches* the Halliday estate saw before its master made himself an honest man."

"None that stayed till morning." Before you can pro-fess your disgust, his arms completely encircle your waist and he hoists you up into the air. You squeak in mock pro-test. He carries you to the staircase, and walks backward with you up the steps. "And darling," he says, slightly out of breath from the exertion of climbing the stairs for two. "You knew going into this that you were marrying a Hopi trickster. To 'make an honest man' out of myself would be to deny my trickster identity, and thus to be *honest* would in fact be a *lie*." He finally bears you up the last step and sets you down on the upper landing with a long breath of relief. "Do you see my conundrum?"

"A paradox, to be sure," you say sarcastically. You poke him in the sternum again and again, until you've backed him all the way up to the banister that overlooks the lobby floor thirty feet below. "You can continue to lie, cheat, and steal as much as your trickster heart desires. The only thing I ask"—you push him up against the dusty banister—"is that you do none of those three things to cross me. Especially cheating."

Colt laughs and sets his elbows down on the railing. "You don't have to scare me into fidelity, Lucy. Far as I'm concerned, there is no woman but you." He glances down at the foyer floor. "It's perplexing, given all that you know about my special ability, that you thought the threat of a short drop would scare me faithful."

You wink and back away. "Knowing that you'd live through the fall to feel the pain is what makes it a far more appealing threat."

"Where are you going?" he asks.

"To freshen up," you reply, and continue to edge toward the door to the bathroom. "That bed chamber of yours sure is drafty. I think I'll need to put on a few more layers before I'm warm enough to sleep."

Colt laughs from the back of his throat. "Darling, you've got more warmth inside of you than a thousand fireplaces could muster. I reckon you've never been cold a day in your life."

But he doesn't know that you *have* felt cold before, a deep and biting cold. The shadow of a smoldering barn drifts fleetingly over your face.

He walks up to you and stops with his face just shy of yours; you can smell the bourbon and tobacco on the ruffled white shirt beneath his tuxedo jacket. "Take your time. I'll wait for you in the bedroom with profound eagerness."

You stretch your arms over your head and fake a yawn. "Not too eagerly, I hope. I'm simply burned out from a long day of celebration, and I fear I might drift into slumber the very moment my head strikes the pillow."

"Then I shall hide all the pillows," Colt replies. The last thing you see as you close the bathroom door is your trickster husband's broad grin, which after three years of knowing him still brings your blood to a slow boil.

You let the faucet run, and splash water on your face until you've removed most of the ridiculous makeup the governor's wife applied before the ceremony. You've always felt like a doll wearing it. The cosmetics they sell in New Orleans aren't exactly targeted at Polynesian skin tones.

Once the last of the blush has bled into the sink, you stare into the pearl-lined mirror and tuck the curly tresses of hair behind your ears. The marriage and the celebration afterward at the governor's mansion were a blur of flowers, lanterns, and faces both familiar and new. But now fatigue slows everything down. You finally have time to see the one thing that was missing from the biggest day of your life.

Family.

Although they have long since left this world, you had expected to feel Mama, and Gracie, and especially Papa there in spirit to guide you.

But you did not.

You knew Violet did not take the news well when you traded your life of thievery with her for a life of domesticity with Colt, but you still expected her to be there in the flesh.

But she was not.

Through the beads of dew on the window, you can see the first whispers of dawn leeching up into the eastern horizon. Your husband is waiting for you. "My husband . . ." you whisper, waiting for the words to not sound alien.

There will be plenty of time to entertain all of these thoughts when you have another moment alone.

You fill a wash bucket full of water under the faucet and then tiptoe down the hallway toward the master bedroom, trying your best not to spill any. You came up with this idea during one of the many times you spent daydreaming about your wedding night ever since Colt proposed. (Who are you kidding? Even *before* he proposed.) You wanted to make your first night together as memorable as possible.

The door is just slightly ajar when you come to it. You take the bucket of water and slosh it so that the water streams under the door. Then you close your eyes and let the heat rise to the top of your skin. Your white dress, the one that cost so much yet you'll never wear again, smokes, and then crackles, and then ignites. You kick off your shoes.

You keep your eyes closed and push through the door. You step into the room, feel the cool puddle of water against the bare soles of your feet. Just the thought of what sort of pleased expression Colt has right now watching your wedding dress burn off makes you smile.

You open your eyes.

And you scream.

Colt lies bare chested on top of the patchwork quilt. Only he's not waiting in eager anticipation. He's not even looking at you.

He's staring at the cannonball-size hole in his chest. The one right where his heart should be.

Then, with shallow gasps, he reaches out to the man who's towering over the bed, squeezing Colt's bloody heart in his fist.

The assassin spots you immediately, and the sight of the flames rising off you is enough to get him to back away from the bedside. With his black eyes trained on you, he drops Colt's heart into a jar. Once he screws on the lid, he turns and runs for the far wall. He crashes shoulder-first through the balcony window, then drops over the ledge to the ground below.

You rush to the bedside. Your body has run cold, and the flames soon extinguish themselves.

Meanwhile Colt gropes around his chest, trying to hold the wound open. His regenerating flesh, however, has other ideas and rapidly closes over the gash, forcing his fingers out of the chasm as the ribs, and cartilage, and blood vessels knit themselves back into a living fabric.

You bring your face up close to his. "Look at me, Colt," you plead, even though his eyelids are fluttering closed. "Concentrate. You can survive this. You have the strongest heart of anyone I've ever met. You can grow it back if you just believe . . ."

Your teardrops land on his face, and that's when his eyes reopen. Dim embers still burn behind his pupils, but they're cooling fast. He takes your hands in his and presses them to the disconcertingly smooth patch of his chest where his heart is . . .

Or where his heart should be.

There is no beat.

Only an interminable silence that you will never forget.

"This heart ain't coming back, love," he whispers.

"No!" you cry out. You pound your fist on his chest.

"Shh." He musters the strength to open his eyes one last time. "Just remember," he says, "that you were the first person to steal it."

His eyes are no longer looking into yours. They're staring through you and into the next life.

Your husband is gone, and even his supernatural talents can't bring him back this time.

There is a time to mourn. There is a time to weep for the fallen. Part of you just wants to crawl into the bed next to him and pray that your own heart stops beating before the shock wears off. Before the real pain comes. Before you have to ask questions about what sort of enemies your husband had who would murder him on his wedding night.

But the fire in you takes over. Instead of looking at

Colt, your gaze gravitates to the broken window through which the assassin exited. Where your heart wants to choose despair, the smoldering magic in that primordial lobe of your brain awakens and chooses something else for you instead:

Vengeance.

You dive through the gaping, jagged hole in the window as though you were threading a needle, and land in a crouch on the lawn outside. You pause, unsure at first where to go. The assassin has already fled the grounds, somewhere beyond the mangroves at the edge of your lawn.

The air shimmers. The color bleeds out until the grass and the trees and the row of manor houses across the street mute into shades of gray. But faintly, heading in a thickening trail toward the south, a river of crimson floats in the air—the residual body heat left in the assassin's wake, like the blood trail behind a wounded animal.

This skill is new.

It took a killer to activate your killer instincts.

The hunter has awakened the huntress.

You follow the trail at a sprint between two of the neighboring houses. It takes you across the quad of Tulane University. When you reach Saint Charles Avenue, that's when you see him, crossing the grassy streetcar tracks. He jumps in front of an oncoming streetcar and waves his hands. The brakes screech and the trolley conductor stops the vehicle just inches shy of the killer.

Meanwhile you're running toward the trolley. Through the window you see the assassin toss the conductor out of the car and onto the grassy shoulder of the avenue. The streetcar takes off rolling before you can reach it. The dark stranger rotates his head to watch you through the window when he cruises past.

You have no intention of letting this husband-killer escape from your clutches. If you have your way, he won't live past sunrise.

Your legs ache, but you still close the distance between you and the trolley, enough so that you can catch the metal guard on the caboose. With the rail as leverage you vault yourself up into the air and impossibly slip through the open window in back.

At this early morning hour the trolley is completely devoid of passengers except for you and the pursued. Seeing him now in profile, there's something almost regretful in his dark eyes, beneath his mangy shoulder-length hair—something that you recognize. But before you can study him any further, he senses your presence, and when he spins around, he launches an object on a long chain in your direction.

You almost take the claw right to your face, but you dodge into one of the seats just in time to save yourself. The razor-sharp metal talons sink into the floor of the bus, and hold for a second. This close to the claw, you can see traces of blood on its blades—so this is what the assassin used to dig out Colt's heart.

So this is what you'll use to dig out *his* heart.

The assassin is already pulling on the chain to retrieve the claw, but you catch the other end before the talons can disengage from the floor. A quick pulse of heat shoots out of your hand, into the links, and conducts all the way up the chain. The dark giant roars and drops his end. He shakes his seared hand vigorously to soothe the burn.

He grabs for the chain with the other hand, but you're on top of him before he can reclaim it. Whereas he had showcased profound strength back at the mansion when he'd plowed a human-shaped hole through your window, he seems weaker now.

Your rage is caustic at this point, hot to the touch, and you easily subdue him, despite the fact that he's twice your size. He struggles, but you herd him back into the driver's seat of the streetcar, wind his own chain several times around his neck, and then knot it beneath the seat. A quick squeeze from your hand melts the links, securing the knot in place.

"Please," he rasps, pulling at the chains around his neck. He draws in a gulping breath. "It wasn't personal."

"Why did you murder my husband?" you demand. You try to withhold the tears, but they leak through anyway. "What did he do to you?"

"Please," he says again. His words are punctuated between sharp breaths. "It was . . . nothing personal . . . just a job . . . I was sent to do."

"Sent by whom? By whom?" You tighten your hand

around the chains and send a current of heat from one end to the other. The assassin's scream sounds more like a cough when the chains burn into the skin over his throat.

When he recovers enough to speak, he says, "There were . . . no names." You reach for the chain again. "Wait!" he rasps. "She looked . . . just like . . . you."

You stagger away from him, back to the door. It can't be. You knew Violet wasn't thrilled about your marriage to Colt. About breaking up the sister duo after all those years together on the road. About how nothing would be the same again.

But how could your own sister do this to you? How could Violet kill the one person who had managed to make you happy, truly happy, in a way that Violet never could in the years since you'd left the farm?

In that moment you know that you hate her.

In that moment you know you will do anything to find her.

To track her down.

To kill her.

Your dress ignites again, not on purpose this time. This is a dry, uncontrollable wildfire fueled by an ocean of dark thoughts. Your flesh turns to molten rock, cracking in places to let the magma fluoresce through. A corona extends from your body outward, outward, until the fire streams up the walls, over the seats beside you, over the dashboard controls. The assassin tries to move back in the seat as best he can, out of the radius of your flames, but the globe continues to thicken. The blaze is already chewing its way through the streetcar.

You stare out the front window. The streetcar has reached its maximum velocity with no pilot to slow it down. Not far ahead, you see the blocks across the railway where the track has been shut down for repairs. You'll be upon it in a minute.

"Do you have a family?" you calmly ask the assassin. "Do you have a wife?"

He nods frantically. He has pulled his feet up onto the seat. The flames are crawling across the floor toward him. "Yes!" he cries. "I have . . . a wife. Please let me . . . see her again."

He could be lying to talk his way out of the situation, but something in his voice tells you he's sincere. Somewhere in the world this bastard actually has a family who's waiting for him.

"Good," you say.

The assassin stops fighting against the chain-link noose around his neck and actually looks hopeful for once.

You lean just close enough that the hot surface of your corona brushes against his face. *"Now she'll know how I feel."*

You kick open the streetcar doors and jump down onto the green central avenue. You hear a long but broken "Nooooo!" echo out of the open doors.

Then the flaming streetcar, the steel-cased inferno,

batters through the barricade onto the disrupted track beyond. It flips onto its side and slides across the dirt until it smashes into a tree. The flames continue to burn. But the screaming has stopped.

Over the derailed streetcar the dawn sun simmers on the horizon to the east.

East, the direction of the last known place you heard from Violet.

East, toward Miami.

Ashline woke up facedown on the floor, screaming into the shag carpet. She was sweaty. She was breathless. She was faintly smoking.

She staggered to her feet and threw open the window, partially to catch her breath, but also to ventilate the room so her nocturnal smoking wouldn't set off Wes's fire alarms. The afternoon air that rushed in was hot and humid, and did nothing to cool her.

There was so much to take away from the vision.

She really *was* in love with Colt Halliday in her last life.

For better or worse he really did appear to love her back.

Despite all his regenerative abilities, he was not invincible.

Eve had been as violent and conniving as ever the last time around, maybe even worse.

And the man that had killed Colt Halliday—

The assassin that had taken orders from Eve—

The man that Ash had left in the flaming wreckage of the streetcar—

Left there to die in an infernal coffin—

Was the very man she'd moved in with.

The man she'd been fighting alongside this past week.

The man who, against all of her better judgment, she was falling in love with.

"Oh, God," Ash whispered to the afternoon sky. "I killed Wes."

PART III:
THE SPARK, THE FUSE, AND THE FLAME

THE GLASS SARCOPHAGUS

Sunday, Part II

It was a beautiful, spotless afternoon, which felt wrong in every sense, with Aurora having been dead only a few hours. Ash wanted to follow her pain up to the penthouse roof and sit by herself in hurricane weather, let the storm winds carry her to the edge, let the cold bite into flesh that was designed to burn.

Where was Eve to conjure a monsoon when Ash needed her?

Wes's bed was still empty when she poked her head in, the plaid sheets tucked immaculately into the edges of the bed frame—so he hadn't returned yet. He had dropped Ash off at the condominium in the morning, directly after their escape from the movie theater. Once he'd made it clear that he didn't intend to get out of the car to come inside, she'd pleaded with him to let her go with him wherever he intended to go. Instead he'd quietly leaned over and opened her door for her. The moment she'd climbed out of the Cadillac, he'd snapped the door shut and driven off without a word, leaving her only with a set of keys and a burden of grief that she didn't know how to deal with.

It was probably better this way. Grieving alone was somehow easier than the idea of grieving together with Wes. And now with the knowledge that Wes had died by Ash's own hand in the last life . . . well, that just added a layer of complexity that she wasn't prepared to deal with.

The truth was that Ash didn't know how to properly grieve for a girl who'd been gone only a few hours. In the past few days, Ash had gotten to know Aurora, had spent so much time with her, yet Ash still didn't *really* know the Roman goddess. Ash had witnessed only a few of Aurora's many facets—the saucy girl who'd reveled in attention at the bar, the winged athlete who'd showed fearlessness in battle, even when she'd been faced with certain death. There was both virtue and darkness from Aurora's past that Ash could never know, would never know.

And just like when Rolfe was taken from this life before his proper time, Ash's heart ached.

Everything felt wrong, no matter how she chose to spend her afternoon. Eating, trying to go back to sleep, going up to the roof to reflect . . . nothing felt big enough to fill the empty condo. Just the thought of planning another mission to rescue Rose or to confront the Four Seasons seemed blasphemous, when that same sort of scheming had ultimately led to Aurora's death. Who was next if they continued to fight back? Wes?

Lily's words from just a few days earlier echoed in Ash's mind. *Friends of yours tend to have short life expectancies.*

Ash savagely flipped one of the beach chairs into the pool and let a shrill scream bellow out of her. Hatred rose in her like magma leaching its way to the earth's surface. The desire to exact her revenge on the Four Seasons suddenly outweighed everything else.

Revenge on Lily for killing yet *another* one of her friends.

Revenge on Thorne for masterminding the execution in order to advance his sadistic cult.

Revenge on Rey for nearly burning Wes alive.

And even revenge on Bleak, because Ash had seen a shred of humanity in the winter goddess. Maybe if Bleak had survived her fight with Ash, she could have been a voice of reason and put a stop to the violence.

Everything else that had been a priority to Ash before—her desire to rescue Rose, her drive to retrieve Eve from the Cloak Netherworld, even the new feelings that she was developing for Wes—grew hazy beneath a film of dark urges.

Tangled in her brooding thoughts, watching the beach chair bob on the surface of the pool, Ash suddenly remembered the clarity she'd felt on the beach after her conversation with Ixtab. As gloomy as Ixtab's powers might be, the girl seemed to have a knack for imparting a sense of purpose to those who visited her. Ixtab was probably hurting fiercely right now too. Her abilities would have forced her to watch Aurora violently entombed within that tree, and if Ixtab was as keen on Aurora as she'd implied during Ash's last visit . . .

Ash took the Vespa to the store and picked up a few boxes of the processed cupcakes that Ixtab liked. Then she let her GPS navigate her south over the causeway and across the bay, until she reached Key Biscayne. Somehow she picked up the trail that Wes had taken across the island the last time, then retraced their steps down the beach until she spotted the familiar umbrella in the shadow of the lighthouse.

But when she approached, the chair was completely empty. Ash frowned and set the bag down beneath the umbrella. Surely Ixtab couldn't spend her *entire* day here, as Wes had suggested. Perhaps she'd just gone somewhere to eat, or to use the bathroom. She would return soon enough. Ash dropped into the chair and waited.

An hour and several cupcake wrappers in the sand later, Ash wasn't so sure. That's when she finally examined the sand and discovered a series of slight depressions—the imprint of sandals—leading away from the umbrella.

Ash followed them to the edge of the water, where the rising tide had begun to wash half of a barely visible footprint away. Standing in the shallows, Ash looked out to sea and wondered what had become of the goddess.

That's when she began to feel truly alone.

Aurora was dead.

Wes was grieving.

Ixtab was, for all Ash knew, lost at sea.

Ash dropped down into the sand and let the sweeping surf lap around her bare knees. For the second time in two weeks, Ash had lost all of her friends in the mythological world and was utterly alone.

Then the anger seized her. Just like last time, her godly friends hadn't deserted her by choice. They'd been taken from her. They'd been murdered in flesh. Murdered in spirit.

Vengeance would be her new friend. Vengeance meant that the Four Seasons, whom she'd already reduced to three, would shrink to two, and then one, and then none at all. Vengeance meant delivering a final blow for Rolfe, and for Aurora, and for all the gods who the Four Seasons had yet to harm on their rise to power.

Vengeance meant finishing what she'd started.

She opened her cell phone. If she was going to have any hope of tracking down Rose and finding the Four Seasons to bring them to justice once and for all, she needed someone with ears everywhere in the god world. Someone whose manipulative mind and elaborate trickery could keep them one step ahead of the Four Seasons.

Someone in Miami who might understand what she was going through.

She dialed the operator. Inside her wallet she found the key card she'd been avoiding since Friday.

The operator connected her to the Delano hotel in South Beach, and when the front desk picked up, she paused only a moment before saying, "Yes, I'd like for you to connect me to room 432. The guest's name is Colt Halliday."

Ash was on her way to meet Colt when they televised Aurora's execution.

She was walking down the Lincoln Road Mall, a long pedestrian avenue that crossed the entirety of South Beach between Sixteenth and Seventeenth Streets. It was a gorgeous mix of restaurants that spilled right onto the outdoor walkway, as well as trendy nightclubs that would start to see lines form around midnight. As if anyone on the Lincoln Road Mall could forget where they were in the world, a long center island of palm trees stretched end to end along the boulevard.

Just as she was passing a sports bar where a cover band was playing an old country hit, the music pumping out of the windows suddenly died. As the cymbals faded to a whisper and the banjo twanged into nothingness, Ash could hear a commotion inside. She ducked through the front door.

The bouncer didn't even notice her come in—he was too transfixed by the large flat-panel televisions over the bar. In fact, all of the bar's occupants, from the early diners to the waitstaff and even the band, had gathered in one clump to watch the grisly images on-screen.

It was just as horrible for Ash watching the execution a second time—even worse, in fact, without the flicker of hope that Aurora might escape her gruesome demise. Even though Ash knew that Aurora was the victim of the sacrifice, from certain camera angles it really did look like Aurora was staggering threateningly toward little Rose. The distant, drugged abyss of her eyes made her look crazed, dangerous, ready to snatch the six-year-old girl in her talons and carry her off into the clouds.

There was also footage Ash hadn't seen before. The Four Season had filmed additional shots of Thorne and Lily concentrating hard as they summoned their powers and dragged Aurora back to earth. Without context, without reality, it might appear to any viewers that the two gods were vanquishing some sort of evil winged demon who was trying to murder a little girl.

Ash looked away when the weeping willow finally swallowed Aurora. But when she turned back, through her bleary eyes she had to watch something just as nausea-inducing and horrific—a final close-up of Thorne dropping to his knees and wrapping his arms around Rose. Now that the bartender had pumped up the volume on the TVs, Ash could just make out Thorne's words to the little Wilde:

"You're safe now."

They'd done it, Ash realized. It was ghastly, it was scripted—but they'd almost managed to make themselves look like the heroes, at least to anyone twisted enough to buy what was happening on-screen.

Eventually the scene looped right back to the beginning. Some people wandered back to their dinners, while others remained at the bar to watch the execution all over again. The bartender was using the remote to try to find a new network, but it took several tries before he found a sports station that *wasn't* broadcasting the supernatural horror.

Ash felt a hand on her arm—the bouncer, peering curiously at her. "Hey," he said. "It's okay. It was just special effects. Must be some advertisement for a new movie." He actually sounded convinced too.

Ash didn't say anything. She just backpedaled out of the bar and power walked down the Lincoln Road Mall to get to her meeting with Colt. Like the bouncer, many other people would choose not to believe what they'd just seen. The world would not stop for the Four Seasons.

But somewhere out there, among the deranged and the fanatical, Ash knew that this broadcast would strike home. Maybe just a few loonies here and there, watching it over and over again, baptized in Thorne's madness. Eventually they'd come to the conclusion that the gods *were* real. Then the Four Seasons wouldn't have just followers . . . they'd have zealots. Extremists.

Worse, seeing Aurora's murder reduced to a Sunday night television spectacle made Ash think that maybe it was time to abort her quest to bring home Rose and rescue Eve. There was nothing she wanted less than for her younger sister to be raised in the arms of a murderous cult, like some sort of explosive messiah, but Aurora would be alive right now if Ash hadn't involved her. What would happen if more people died, only for Ash to finally reach Rose and discover that the little tyke *didn't want* to leave with her?

As the hostess escorted Ash to her seat at Machibuse, the upscale sushi restaurant where Colt had made reservations, Ash realized she'd actually warmed up to the idea of having dinner with her immortal ex. It would at least provide a welcome distraction from everything else.

So it was with a mixture of electricity and dread that she waited at the two-seater table, out in the warm clutches of the Miami night. Her eyes anxiously darted around, on the lookout for Colt, but also to familiarize herself with the restaurant should she need an escape route.

The nervousness of it all was causing Ash to drink like a fish, to the point that her poker-faced waiter had to refill her glass almost immediately. She was loath to admit that there was some element of excitement to meeting Colt—not necessarily in a romantic sense. But there was a certain unpredictability to him. Every meeting with Colt was like boarding a new roller coaster, and you never knew—

"Somebody looks deep in thought," Colt said.

Ash had been so busy scanning the pedestrians on the Lincoln Road Mall for Colt that she hadn't even noticed him slip into the seat across from her. "Just people watching," she replied.

"Looked more like people-examining."

The waiter came over, and without even looking at the menu, Colt rattled off something in Japanese that ended with "sake." Leave it to Colt, who looked ten years older than his actual eighteen, to order alcohol fluently in another language and not get carded.

Then again, Ash thought, although they were both teenagers in body, they were also millennia old in spirit.

"So you're fluent in Japanese, *and* a sake connoisseur," Ash said. Suddenly her ice water with lemon looked very plain.

"Don't worry. I ordered enough for two," he said. "And you don't travel the world for a thousand years without absorbing other languages and developing some more refined tastes."

"All the time to try new things, yet you keep coming back to the same woman." As soon as Ash said it, she was surprised at her own boldness—but there was no turning back now.

"Not *exactly* the same woman." Colt thanked the waiter, who had just brought a ceramic carafe and two glasses. "That's the interesting part about dating incarnations of the same goddess. It's like you start with the same mold, the same cup"—he pushed one of the glasses across the table and slowly filled it with sake—"but what you pour into it changes each and every time."

Ash took a cautious sip from her glass. "So Ashline Wilde is very different from Lucy Halliday, who was very different from . . . whoever I was before that. What was I like in the other lives you knew me?"

The question caught Colt off guard. She could tell because he spilled a little sake from his glass onto the table. "You were . . ." He searched for the word. "You were much more impetuous before. More explosive, and rash."

Ash laughed dryly. "Sounds like I had a little bit of Eve in me."

Colt choked on his sake. The comment hadn't been *that* funny, Ash thought.

He cleared his throat. "Something like that. Your temper made you violent at times. Let's just say I was very grateful for my regenerative abilities. But at other times that same explosiveness also made you more passionate. It was intoxicating. I couldn't get enough of it."

"Apparently not," she said. "Intoxicating enough that you lied just to get a fifth helping."

Colt's face tightened. He slipped his fingers through his bristly hair. "When the Cloak designed this mental block to separate us from our old memories—when they designed this *brain damage* for us—they overlooked the god with regenerative abilities. Never realized that his brain might slowly heal itself, too. Do you know what it's like to be the only one who remembers?" He turned away from Ash to watch the passing crowd instead—a group of dolled-up girls chattering rapidly about their night plans, two young lovers arm in arm heading to dinner. "To live and die like everyone else," he continued, "but to come back with a full memory of everything that happened before, while the people around you—strangers, friends . . . lovers—don't remember a damn thing?"

"So just to be clear, your argument"—Ash folded her hands and leaned over the table—"is that because you're the only one who *knows* everything, you also have to *lie* about everything."

"Travel back in time and space to that first day we met at the saloon, when I came up behind you at the bar." He tapped two fingers to his temple. "Now imagine that by way of introduction, I said, 'Hi, Ashline. You don't know me, but I was married to you in your last life back when your name was Lucy, and you were a farmer's-daughter-turned-bank-robber living in New Orleans. We had a beautiful love affair until an Aztec assassin ripped out my heart on our wedding night. Oh, and PS, you don't know it yet, but you're a Polynesian volcano goddess." He paused and let all that sink in. "I'm sure you would have *definitely* agreed to a second date after that."

"I really hate when you do that," Ash said.

Colt raised an eyebrow. "Do what?"

Ash sighed. "Make a good point that I can't argue with. Although," she went on, as Colt chuckled, "you could have used some of that singing magic of yours to convince me to believe you."

Ash's hands were still in the middle of the table from

when she'd leaned in, and Colt reached across to touch them. "Hey," he said, "I'm glad you came."

She withdrew her fingers just an inch. Damn this guy was good. A week ago she buried him thigh-deep in stone. Now she was unintentionally letting him back in. *This wasn't meant to be a romantic meet-up,* she wanted to tell him. With Wes still possibly in the picture, and all the death that was going on in Miami, the last thing she needed was a tropical love triangle.

Colt took his own hand back and averted his gaze as he refilled his sake glass. His eyes glistened in the moonlight. "I'm sorry," he said, and smiled into his glass. "Sometimes I expect relationships to heal as fast as I do."

"Even relationships that heal can scar, too," Ash reminded him.

Before the conversation could cascade further into awkward touchy-feely topics that Ash wasn't prepared for, the waiter graciously returned to take their food order. She panicked because she hadn't even opened the menu, but Colt jumped to the rescue. "Do you mind?" he asked Ash. He proceeded to order what sounded like enough food to invite half of the pedestrian mall to join their meal.

"Hungry much?" Ash asked.

He passed the menus to the waiter, who walked away. "I'm still catching up on the meals I missed when I was trapped in an Oregon boulder for seventy-two hours."

Ash narrowed her eyes. "How *did* you escape from the rock, by the way?"

He only smiled and sipped his sake. "So," he changed the subject. "What's the status of the hunt for your sister?"

"On hold, I guess." She slouched in her chair. "I thought that tracking down Rose was the right thing to do, but now I just don't—"

"Ash," Colt interrupted, "you're trying to rescue a kidnapped six-year-old. How could that be anything *but* the right thing to do?"

"In theory maybe. But I'm a night's sleep from throwing in the towel and going home."

"You can't give up!" When he said it, his voice split into three pitches at once in a terrible chord—his persuasive song-voice had leaked through enough that Ash could feel it tug on her marionette strings.

"What is your malfunction?" she asked him. "If you want Rose so you can go spelunking in the Cloak Netherworld, then go retrieve her yourself. I've tried my best, and because of it, three people are dead."

"Because of you," he reminded her, his voice back to normal, "Ade is alive."

He was right, of course, and Ash opened her mouth to agree with him. A pulse went through her brain, however, a beacon of warning that flashed once, twice, and then began to strobe outward through her body. Her stomach tightened. Her vision wavered, and nausea swept over her. Her survival instincts were alerting her that something about this conversation was terribly, terribly wrong.

That's when she figured it out. In the course of all this plotting, all the destinies of these gods and goddesses converging and intersecting in pursuit of their own selfish ends, it was often hard to keep straight who knew what exactly. But after a quick mental review of the last few days, double-checking where her last conversation with Colt fell in the chronology, she could say one thing confidently:

There was no way Colt Halliday should have known that Ade had been the Four Seasons' sacrificial prisoner.

"How did you know Ade was the sacrifice?" Ash demanded. "How did you know that we saved him?"

"I . . . ," Colt started. "You said that—"

"I didn't say *a word* to you about that, Trickster," Ash said. "How did you know it was Ade?"

He massaged his stubble nervously. His right eye twitched. "It's not what you think, Ash. You're jumping to conclusions that—"

"What did you do?" Her fingers curled around her glass, and the sake inside began to froth and boil. "What the *hell* did you do, Colt?"

"Fine." Colt threw up his hands. "You got me. The Four Seasons were looking for a sacrifice. I suggested Ade. I told them where to find him in Haiti. I knew you needed more incentive to stick to your guns, and the best way was to make it more personal." He glanced at Ash's glass, which had grown so hot that it was starting to steam. "He was never in any danger. I knew you'd save him."

Ash watched Colt's image swim through the steam curtain. "Should I even ask who told them about Rose and where to find her?"

He shrugged. "Why smuggle the little girl that I need into the country when I could trick a crazy billionaire and some hell-bent gods to do it for me? Trickery is what I do, Ash." He tilted his chin up and stroked the skin over his neck. "All I had to do was open up these special little vocal cords of mine, and the Four Seasons were willing to do *anything* to achieve their delusions of grandeur. Lesley, too."

The heat in Ash was growing so intense that she could feel the metal armrests of her chair beginning to soften. It was only a matter of time before she lost control completely. "How could you make them do those things, Colt? These aren't soapstone pieces on a chessboard. They're *real people*. You try to convince me that the Cloak are the evil monsters, but you're the one who puppeteers massacres and then sleeps well at night."

"I don't put evil in the hearts of men. My song, my vocal persuasion, didn't make the Four Seasons kill Lesley Vanderbilt and your friend. The ability to kill was always there in their blood. All I do is strip away inhibitions to let people do what their dark hearts truly desire." A smile twitched at the corner of his lips, and Ash could all but see the shadow of their kiss back in Oregon reflecting in his eyes. "You of all people should know that, Ashline Wilde."

Ash splashed her sake in Colt's face. He didn't even flinch as the scalding liquid splattered against his skin. The red welts it left quickly faded back to his copper Native American skin.

"In the short time I've known you," Ash said quietly, "you've put me and just about everyone that I know in danger. You set your plans into motion, and then you sit back and watch the body count add up. You may not be a murderer, but you might as well be. Get away from this table, and get the hell out of my life."

"I can't do that," he said.

Ash pointed out to the pedestrian mall. "I said get out!" she screamed. It was loud enough to draw the attention of all the nearby diners and passersby.

Colt downed the rest of his glass and stood up. He pulled a roll of twenty-dollar bills out of his pocket. "One day," he said, and counted out a stack of bills onto the tabletop, "you'll realize that I did it for you." He backed away from the table but never took his eyes off Ash. "I did it *all* for you."

"The next time I bury you in rock," Ash called out as he disappeared down the pedestrian mall, "it will be from the top of your head down!"

Once she finally lost him in the crowd, she let her head drop to the table. How could she have ever thought this meeting was a good idea? Moreover, how could Colt . . . How could he just . . . She'd known he was conniving before, and that his trickery had indirectly resulted in Rolfe's death, but to purposely place Ade on death row just so Ash would follow through with her plans . . .

This was the second time that the gravitational pull of Colt's plotting had latched onto Ash's life like a tractor beam, and twisted and tore at it until she had nothing—and no one—left.

"Miss?"

The waiter was standing next to the table, looking beyond uncomfortable. He was trying his best to stay focused on Ash, but his eyes kept darting to the empty seat across from her.

Ash flicked the sake carafe. "Just bring me another pitcher of whatever this is."

Thunder rolled down the strip, coming from the west, accompanied by a flash of light. "Heat lightning," the waiter explained. A second flash and more thunder, only louder.

With the third clap of thunder, she heard a different sound, indiscernible at first, but then growing into something recognizable.

Screaming.

Lots of screaming.

Ash stood up just as the first person came running past her. Soon a current of shrieking people came sprinting down the pedestrian mall, heading east toward the water, engulfing the bystanders in their path and carrying them away. Ash had to retreat toward the restaurant to avoid being towed away in the swift tide of people.

The fourth time she heard the thunder, she knew it wasn't thunder at all.

Explosions.

Explosions moving down the strip.

The remaining people who hadn't already been swept away by the mob joined it as soon as they realized what they were hearing. She heard the words "terrorist attack" thrown around by a couple rushing past her.

Ash knew better.

The pedestrian mall rapidly emptied of everyone— even Ash's waiter, who knocked her carafe of sake off the table in his rush to flee.

Then Ash saw the lone man coming determinedly down the strip. White-collared shirt unbuttoned halfway down his chest, sleeves rolled up to the elbows, dirty dreadlocks.

Rey.

Summer had arrived.

"Ashline Wilde!" he shouted.

He aimed his hand at the front of the restaurant a few doors down and across the street from Ash. A light blossomed in the air in front of the window, a miniature sun rotating rapidly, like a basketball spinning on an imaginary finger.

It condensed briefly.

Then it exploded outward.

The restaurant's tinted windows shattered from top

to bottom. The patio furniture near the explosion was blasted outward until it clattered down the Lincoln Road Mall. Somehow the diners inside had missed the chaos before, but they streamed out of the restaurant now, anywhere they could—some through the doors, and others through the gaping jaws of the windows.

"Ashline Wilde!" Rey shouted again. He was drawing near Ash's position now, and he angled his hand this time at the restaurant where she was.

Rey noticed Ash immediately and stayed his hand—no explosion this time. "Ashline Wilde," he repeated. "I am to escort you back to Villa Vizcaya, where you will meet your fate."

Ash felt the first pinpricks of anger dilating beneath her skin. "Wow, as much as I've been meaning to meet my fate recently, I have to politely decline." She pointed her thumb back at the restaurant. "See, I have a large sushi platter for two coming out any minute, and as you can see, I no longer have a date, so if you want to sit down and talk this out over some raw fish—"

Rey roared and thrust out his open hand. Another miniature sun detonated just in front of the sushi restaurant. The glass rained down from the window frame. The sushi chefs taking cover inside came sprinting out of the restaurant in a parade of white aprons and hats.

Ash winced and slapped her ear, which was singing from the explosion. "Look what you've done," she said. "How are they going to finish making our order now?"

"I figured you'd put up a fight," he said. An unhinged smile unzipped across his face. "If only your boyfriend had been more of a challenge."

Ash's breath caught in her throat. In all the time she'd spent waiting for Wes to come home, it had never occurred to her that he might be someplace worse than mourning. "Wes?" she choked out. "What have you done with him?"

"Caught him lurking around the Spanish monastery looking for his leafy little lass." Rey snorted. "Predictable. Now you get to come and watch him live out his destiny as our next sacrifice." His face darkened as he picked a cloth napkin off the nearest table. It erupted into flames, balled up in his hand. "Now I will roast him alive in front of the world, and bring him to justice for what he did to my girlfriend."

"To your girlfriend?" Ash started to ask. And then it all clicked.

Bleak and Rey. Winter and summer, together as one.

And now Rey was blaming Wes for the icicle-shaped hole in his dead girlfriend's back.

Well, it was time to set him straight. "Wes didn't kill Bleak," Ash said. *I did.*

"You?" Rey squinted at her. "You murdered my girlfriend?" Every time Ash had seen him before, he'd looked perpetually amused by nothing at all.

He wasn't laughing now.

"What was I supposed to do, Rey?" she argued.

"Bleak froze me to the surface of a pool and then came at me with a knife. Should I have just *let* her slit my throat?"

"Yes," Rey said tersely.

"Glad this is going to be a rational conversation," Ash mumbled.

He clutched his dreadlocks at the scalp level, like he wanted to rip them out, and his eyes scrunched shut in agony. When they reopened, his red eyes blazed with a deadly focus. "Then I can't take you back to the villa. If I do, Lily will want to horde you for her own private revenge. But it's Bleak's life that you need to pay for, and you'll pay for it right here, at my hands."

"Listen," Ash said. "I know what you must be feeling right now. I've spent the last week feeling my hatred bubble up for you people for kidnapping my sister and Ade. I've spent the last month thinking about what I'd like to do to Lily for killing my friend Rolfe back in California, and now for murdering Aurora last night. But as much as I'd like to set fire to those beeswax dreads of yours, let's be smart enough not to start a firefight in the middle of the Lincoln Road Mall." A chorus of sirens picked up from the north. "Hear that? Do you want to be here in ten minutes when the Air Force shows up on red alert because of your explosions?"

Rey unbuttoned his shirt and then threw it onto the ground. The guy was a mountain, close to three hundred pounds of sinewy muscle that could make most NFL linebackers run for the goalposts. "Do I look," he said, "like a man who gives a shit about making a spectacle?"

"So what are we going to do, Rey?" she inquired. "Gods of fire who are both *fireproof*. Sounds like a stalemate, unless you want to have a good old-fashioned brawl. Maybe we could throw some chairs at each other?"

Rey responded by picking up the metal chair nearest him, stretching it over his head, and launching it full speed at Ash's head.

She had to roll over a table to get out of its path. It hit the pavement and did several cartwheels until it smashed into the windows of the next restaurant over.

The table tipped over under Ash's weight and she spilled onto the other side. Her elbows slammed against the ground and cut open. The pain invited her internal furnace to flicker on, and her eyes sparked when she looked up at Rey. She climbed to her feet. Reason was battling it out with her blossoming temper.

On the one hand, entering into a brawl with Rey wasn't like her school yard brawl with Lizzie Jacobs last year. Rey was bigger and stronger and crazier, and, at least for the moment, more enraged than Ash.

But the scales of rage were quickly changing. Her temper flared. This man had helped expose the gods to the public, and life was about to become even more difficult because of it. He had taken her little sister. He had participated in a conspiracy that had resulted in Ade's kidnapping and Aurora's death, and now potentially Wes's as well.

Ash wanted blood.

Rey held out his hands. "Just because my explosions won't kill you because you're fireproof"—an orb of fire twinkled to life in front of him and started to expand—"doesn't mean the asphalt won't kill you when you land." The orb stretched rapidly, ready to burst.

Footsteps slapped across the pavement, and a figure hurled himself off the central island—Colt, who'd apparently been summoned by the sound of explosions. Rey may have weighed much more than him, but Colt struck him like a two-hundred-pound missile, and the larger boy went down. The sun that had been ready to burst fizzled out.

Colt turned to Ash, clearly straining to hold Rey's face against the pavement. "Run, Ashline," he ordered her. "Run!"

Colt's arrival snapped Ash out of her trance. Her temper deflated long enough for her survival instincts to kick in. If she were to stick around—even if her flesh could handle the fire—one blast from Rey could break her neck. She found herself backing away at first, then turning and running from the two gods, who were slugging it out on the ground.

She chanced a look over her shoulder. Colt had picked up a chair and held it out like a battering ram as he charged toward Rey. However, the Incan sun god wasn't to be bested by the trickster. From his crouched position on the ground, he flicked out a single finger, and an explosion detonated in the area in front of Colt. The trickster god flew up into the air, over the center island, and into a second-story window across the boulevard. Even despite all that Colt had lied about, Ash experienced a fleeting urge to turn around and see if he was all right. But he was the one with regenerative powers, not Ash, so she turned up the heat and ran faster.

Once she had safely crossed Collins Avenue and approached the terminus of Lincoln Road, she thought she'd made it safely away from Rey. Her trail was silent except for the growing wail of sirens and the fluttering of helicopters overhead, circling the mall farther inland. If only the authorities really knew what they were looking for.

She heard the explosion at almost the same time that the fireball hit her back. The impact carried her body up off the road, over the beach boardwalk, and into the trees. Her back bounced off the trunk of a palm before she tumbled out through its fronds and onto the beach beyond.

The impact against the beach was even worse. Sand splashed up around her, and by the time she rolled to a stop, she was unable to breathe. It felt like two cannonballs had replaced her lungs.

Her vision was blurry with tears, but she could still see Rey's burning upper body emerge through the palms onto the beach.

"You have an awful lot of men who want to fight your

battles for you," he called out as he approached. "But they cannot protect you. Just like I couldn't be there to protect Bleak before you ripped her life away from her. Now you'll die knowing that you were too late to save your love, your all-powerful Aztec night god, from sacrifice."

Ash staggered to her feet and launched a fireball at him, which he easily deflected away. It struck the white lifeguard tower, which erupted into flames. Rey followed up with an exploding sun that, with her injuries, Ash was too slow to dodge. The world rotated like she'd been trapped in a cement mixer.

When her body finally came to rest, she tried to open her eyes, but the vertigo was too much for her. She let her head rest on the sand, pressed against the cool grains, so that she could hear Rey's footsteps approach.

"Now as far as your final resting place goes . . . ," Rey said.

Ash kept her eyes closed. She burrowed her hands into the beach.

"Would you like to be buried on the beach for some kid with a sand pail to find?"

Ash reached out with her mind, deep into the earth. Searched for that thread of power somewhere beneath the earth's crust that she had tapped into for centuries. *If I can make islands,* she thought.

"Or would you rather I scatter your limbs at sea as shark bait?"

Then I can take care of this asshole.

Rey came to a stop on the sand just a few yards in front of her. She could hear his jeans stretch as he crouched down. "I thought I'd be humane and give you a choice," he said.

The sand beneath them trembled. Ash finally opened her eyes. "I'm not that thoughtful," she said. "You don't *get* a choice."

The magma, with the heat of a fledgling sun, penetrated up through the earth's surface, instantly liquefying the beach under Rey's feet. He didn't even have time to look surprised—his body just plunged deep into the fiery pool, where the heat had transformed the sand into molten glass.

The high temperatures, Ash knew, couldn't kill him. He managed to swim to the surface, his body a uniform, glowing orange form covered in the smoldering glass. Ash could feel the heat radiate off him while he blindly attempted to melt the goop off his body.

This wasn't a battle she was going to lose. She stepped up to where Rey was floundering to climb his way out. Bubbles were forming in the molten rock over his mouth as he struggled to breathe. His fingers clawed away enough of the liquid glass that he could burble out a single word for Ash to hear:

"Bleak."

"You'll see her soon," Ash whispered. She pulled back her hands, siphoning the heat swiftly away from the volcanic vent that had ruptured onto the beach.

The earthen cocktail of lava and glass cooled.

Rey's coating of glass dimmed from orange to beige to gray.

His movement slowed.

His articulations stiffened.

In his final moments, with his legs still halfway buried in the vent, he extended his hand out toward the ocean.

Then he was still. Rey died, an enormous glass statue frozen in time like some sort of twisted wax figurine.

Ash struggled not to fall to her knees exhausted, because there was no time. Across the dark moonlit beach she could see beachgoers converging on her location. The lifeguard stand was still burning and drawing the late-night walkers to it like a bug zapper. It was only a matter of time before they discovered Rey and his glass coffin as well.

She heard Colt screaming her name back in the direction of the street. He had bought her time just now, for sure, but the last thing she needed was him tagging along on her rescue mission to save Wes. As much as she didn't want to walk into a death trap alone, as much as his regenerative abilities might prove useful, Colt had been the catalyst for all the bloodshed that had happened in Miami, all so he could get to her little sister—and Ash had no intention of leading him right to Rose.

She fled back across the beach and onto the board-walk, and began to navigate through the streets of South Beach to the garage where her scooter was parked.

Rey had said they were holding Wes back at the Villa
Vizcaya.

And if Lily and Thorne were there waiting for her . . .

Well, she couldn't disappoint them, could she?

As Ash drove over the bay to Villa Vizcaya, the night sky was filled with lights. Helicopters buzzed overhead, circling the scene of the explosions back at the Lincoln Road Mall. Ash knew it was only a matter of time before the military and National Guard came to close off the bridge, and she might be too late to save Wes if she had to seek an alternate route.

Ash abandoned her bike just off the road. She wasn't about to waste time climbing over the front gates to the villa, so she burned herself an Ash-size hole right through them.

The villa itself was dark, its visiting hours long since over. But Ash knew that Thorne and Lily both seemed to enjoy putting on a show, and if they were going to film another sacrifice, the best place to do it was the same place where they'd performed for the media last week.

Up on the Mound.

Ash followed the path around the side of the villa to the gardens. Now that she was out of earshot from the sirens and helicopters, an eerie calm had descended around her. Even the fountains had been turned off for the night. Had Rey sent her to the wrong place? Was this going to be like Aurora's death? Was Ash going to stumble upon a big-screen television that would show her Wes dying, someplace out of reach, too far away for her to get to in time?

When she rounded the corner, however, she knew with a mixture of relief and dreadful certainty that she'd come to the right place.

The beautiful, well-manicured formal gardens, the ones that led the length of half a football field to the Mound, had been transformed into a wild, unkempt rain forest.

Ash wandered forward into the new wilderness and lit a soft glow on the torch of her hand, just enough to make sure she didn't walk into a snare or pitfall. All around her, tall tropical trees had grown at odd angles like crooked teeth, some of which looked like transplants from the Amazon. Then there were more familiar-looking trees—cypress trees, mangroves . . . and of course small redwoods and sequoias mixed in with the rest. As if Lily needed to leave a calling card for Ash to know who had done all this.

Things only grew stranger the deeper Ash penetrated

into this twisted little enchanted forest that Lily had put together. Spanish moss clung to the crisscrossing tree limbs and draped down in curtains, green cobwebs that made visibility difficult.

Then there were the flowers, so many flowers. Thick beds of violets clinging to the forest floor, where they had chewed through the stone path and pulverized it into loose gravel. Orchids crawled up the side of a nearby redwood. Ash had to skirt around a bed of Jurassic-size roses that had thorns so big and thick they could qualify as tusks.

All this time she'd been wondering how Lily's "construction" had gone unnoticed. Sure, the museum was closed for the night, and the police had their hands full at the crime scene across the bay, but wouldn't security have noticed this severe landscaping issue by now?

Ash stepped up to the moat that surrounded the central island. In between the leaves and lily pads that coated the water, she saw two lumps floating at the surface. Their bodies bobbed facedown, but both the corpses wore gray security uniforms and black utility belts. A silent radio drifted not far from them.

It was when Ash leapt over the moat onto the center island that she spotted the first camera. It had been crudely bolted to one of the trees, and must have had a motion detector, because it swiveled to peer at her, like a vulture gawking down from its perch at potential carrion.

The trees thinned out as Ash progressed across the

island, except around its periphery, where they eventually grew so close together that no person would be able to fit between them. In fact, now that she thought about it, they were sort of like the thick bars to a prison.

It's a fence, Ash realized. She spotted two more cameras, then a third, all pivoting to leer at her. By now she'd reached the far end of the island. Here there was a ten-foot gap in the fence of trees, but her passage through was blocked by a web of very angry-looking thorns. The thorns had been wrapped around the trees to either side and pulled taut, forming a tall net of natural razor wire. Through the mesh she could see the waterfall and the dual staircases leading up to the Mound, her destination. It was as though Lily wanted to tease her, to show her where she wanted to go but trap her in here.

Time for some landscaping, she thought. She ignited her hand, ready to burn her way through the thorn patch.

Then a second thought occurred to her. The cameras. The fence surrounding the island.

This wasn't intended to just keep her away from the Mound.

It was intended to keep her corralled on the island.

Because Lily had transformed the island into an arena.

Which also meant that Wes wasn't the sacrifice—

He was just bait.

"I'm the sacrifice," Ash whispered.

"Perceptive, as always," came the reply from the trees overhead.

Ash winged a fireball upward toward the voice, but the flames met only with branches and leaves. She let a second ball of fire simmer in her palm and waited for Lily to appear.

Too late Ash felt the vine snarl around her ankle. It tightened, sinking its little thorns into her skin and pulling her flat to the ground. The vine retracted across the island, dragging her with it through the grass and dirt. The wild ride slammed her into one tree and continued toward a bushel of Jurassic thorns in the shape of a jaw. The thorny teeth gnashed together, hungry, longing to devour her in a few quick bites.

Ash lit her fingers, bared her claws, and sheared right through the vine holding her. Her body skidded to a stop right before she could enter the giant thorny mouth. That didn't stop the jaws from lunging for her. She crab-walked backward, away from the botanical bear trap before it could turn her feet into its next meal.

She heard a rustling in the canopy overhead and looked up. In the center of the island, from the upper branches of the mangroves, Lily descended in a nest of vines. The vines had curled around her arms and shoulders and lowered her gently to the ground. She looked like a demented marionette, only she was her own dangerous puppeteer.

"Right on time," Lily said. She peered around Ash, looking for someone else. "But you didn't bring Rey with you? Good. I always thought he was a stick-in-the-mud."

Ash brushed herself off and stood up. "Yeah, he was looking pretty stiff when I last saw him too."

"I hope you're not camera shy." Lily nodded to the nearest camera, which twitched to follow her movements. "See, when we tried to play the heroes on the last broadcast, the viewers just laughed us off as some work of fiction. We live in a skeptical world, and we've realized that the only way for the public to *believe* in us is to first make them *fear* us. Once we capture your death on film, we'll take care of your nocturnal boyfriend. That will give us two more sacrifices to broadcast to the world. Should be enough to scare up a small following, before we start doing some *live* performances in cities across the country. Now, do you want us to air your death first? Or would you rather be the encore presentation?"

Ash shook her head, suddenly feeling more weary than vengeful. "What happened to you, Lily? You were my *friend*. I'll never fully understand what sort of internal torture you must have been going through at Blackwood to break this way, but I could have helped you if you'd let me in. Instead you had to go and break the rest of us too, when you killed Rolfe."

Lily's smile fell at the mention of Rolfe's name. "Don't." Spittle flew from her mouth. "Don't you say his name."

"His name is all that you left of him." In her rage Ash hurled a fireball at Lily. Lily quickly sidestepped the flames, which incinerated a bed of violets instead. "I've seen people take rejection poorly before," Ash said, "but what was it about getting played by Rolfe that made you snap like this?"

"The only thing that's going to snap," she snarled, "is your *neck*."

Only when she felt the caress around her neck did Ash realize her mistake. She'd been so concentrated on Lily in front of her, and the thorn jaws to the rear, that she hadn't paid any attention to what was happening above her.

A vine noose had slipped loosely around Ash's neck. As soon as she brought up her hands to throw it off, the noose fastened itself tightly, crushing her trachea and flattening her fingers to her throat. The vine retracted up into the canopy, and her white-knuckled grip on it was the only thing preventing her neck from breaking as the vine jerked her roughly off the ground.

Ash dangled ten feet above the forest floor, feeling the pressure build in her neck. She ignited her hands once again and tried not to panic—she should be easily able to sear right through the vines.

But the noose only tightened further in response. Lily was smiling up at her. "That vine is armored with redwood bark," Lily explained. "How strange that I was so eager to get away from Blackwood Academy that I never realized that the redwood trees surrounding campus actually have fireproof bark. If I'd known *that,* maybe I would have stuck around."

Ash's fingers were still clamped to her throat, but she aimed her elbow so that it pointed down at Lily's face. Lily's noose might be fireproof, but Lily wasn't.

Only a few impotent sparks streamed out of Ash's elbow. With the noose cutting off the oxygen supply to her lungs, it was like trying to run a furnace in an airtight room. Soon even the sparks stopped coming.

Lily rolled her eyes. "Come on, Ashline. You have to put on a better show for the cameras than that. Nobody's going to believe you're a god just because you can shoot a sparkler out of your elbow. Where's the fireworks display?"

Ash wriggled to get free. The more she moved, the more pressure she felt pull on her vertebrae. Her arms were bearing some of the weight for now, but even her tennis-toned forearms wouldn't be enough to hold on forever.

Lily extended her arm, and a new vine sprouted lazily from it, coiling on the ground. "I know in your heart you think you're the hero. That *I'm* the villain. And I'm going to admit there was a time when I felt conflicted about what I'd done to . . . him." Rolfe's name wilted in the air without ever blooming. Lily coiled the whip she'd created around her wrist. "But you know what I realized? He was a *taker*!" As she growled the last word, she unfurled the whip and lashed at Ash.

It caught Ash in the ribs. She might as well have been stabbed. The pain was so great that it caused her whole body to convulse upward, sapping some of the strength from her arms.

Lily reeled the whip back. "All of you are takers. But you and Raja are the *worst* offenders. You pretend to be friends with everyone, and you flash your pretty little smiles. . . ." She touched her aged face, perhaps remembering the youthful skin she once had before Raja got to her. "And then you take. You take any man that you want. You take thirty years from my life. You take *everything*!" Lily let the whip fly again.

The second blow from the whip was even worse. It was agony for Ash to have her hands tied, to be unable to reach down and soothe the wound. And her oxygen was long since used up. The world around her was starting to grow speckled with black. Even through the coming darkness, however, Ash turned her eyes up to the tree limb overhead. The one the noose was attached to. The one that looked like it was straining under her weight.

"That," Lily continued, "is when I finally understood—it's in your natures to take. Death destroys. Fire destroys. But I . . ." she spread her arms at the horrible arboretum. "I *create*! I bring life where fire brings only death." She wheeled back her whip. "Well, today is the day that the forest triumphs over the wildfire."

Finally Ash pried one hand loose and grabbed the vine over her head quickly so that her neck wouldn't bear the added pressure. Then the other hand. With the little oxygen she inhaled, she pulled herself arm over arm up the vine. In the canopy above she could see the branch that the noose was coiled around. All she had to do was keep climbing.

Meanwhile Lily's whip cracked in the space where Ash had just been hanging. The blossom goddess jerked it back in frustration, preparing to strike again.

When Ash reached the top of the vine, she wrapped her hands around the limb that had been serving as her gallows and let herself dangle. With the pressure off the noose, she could finally breathe a little. She knew that if she lost her hold on the branch, she'd fall and break her neck when the vine went taut, but she had a plan. So she mentally prepared herself for a long fall, delegated all her power to her arms, and then heaved down on the branch.

The limb cracked right off the tree. Together Ash and her scaffold dropped all the way to the grass below. She was too relieved to feel any pain when she hit the ground. She loosened the limp noose around her neck to let in the air.

Lily, who had dived away to avoid being crushed, came at Ash with thorny fingernails, ready to slice her apart.

Ash picked up the fallen limb with two hands and jumped to her feet. Just as Lily got within range, Ash assumed her best softball batting pose and smashed the branch across Lily's face.

The blossom goddess staggered back, stunned, giving Ash enough time to tackle her around the waist.

Lily maintained her footing, but Ash pressed on until she'd carried the girl all the way across the island. With their combined momentum Ash slammed Lily back-first through the thorn fence that was blocking the island's exit. Both girls tumbled through the air and struck the back wall of the shallow moat, before plunging into its leaf-covered waters.

The next few seconds were a blur. Lily somehow ended up on top, and her weight carried both of them to the bottom of the moat. Ash blindly thrashed out at first, connecting a few heavy blows to Lily's head and chest, but the other girl retaliated by pressing Ash's face down into the hard stone floor. Ash was already oxygen-deprived from the hanging, and if it came to a battle of holding each other underwater, Lily was sure to emerge victorious.

Sure enough the blossom goddess had reached the same conclusion. She slipped her hands around Ash's neck and squeezed Ash's already crushed windpipe. With Lily kneeling on top of Ash, no amount of floundering could break Lily's hold. As the last few bubbles escaped from Ash's mouth, a trail of embers sparked impotently out of her hands, illuminating Lily's face long enough for Ash to see it. After all her talk of how she would enjoy murdering Ash, there was nothing gleeful written in Lily's expression. Instead her eyes were knotted into something horrible as she wept, and her lips were trembling as the water silenced her sobs.

Something else was glinting under the light of Ash's dying embers, however. It was glass lying on the moat floor, just within her reach—the shattered stem of the champagne flute Ash had thrown into the moat the night of the white-tie party, the same one she had defended herself with when Thorne had attacked her in the grotto.

Ash used the last of her strength to reach out and grasp it by its flat base.

And then she plunged the stem into Lily's heart.

Lily's hands immediately went slack on Ash's throat, and her crying eyes shot wide open. A crimson ribbon of blood streamed from the wound in her chest and diffused through the water around them.

With little time left before she completely asphyxiated, Ash wriggled out from under Lily's limp body and kicked off the bottom of the moat. In a moment of compassion, for whatever humanity was left in Lily's soul, Ash grabbed Lily by her belt and dragged her to the surface.

Ash burst through the leaves and lily pads, and drew in several long breaths. Lily breached the surface with her, and Ash started to tow her toward the opposite edge of the moat.

"No," Lily croaked.

Ash stopped splashing and treaded water next to the dying blossom goddess. Lily floated faceup, with her hands folded over the mortal wound to her heart. Blood continued to pump up between her fingers, a ring of red expanding through her wet shirt.

Her half-opened eyes fell on Ash. "Didn't I tell you that you were all takers?" she whispered, every few words interrupted by the moat water she was still choking on. "First you took thirty years from my life . . . and now you've taken the rest."

Lily's final breath expired as a wet wheeze, and her eyes closed for the last time.

When she was sure Lily was gone, Ash paddled to the edge of the moat and crawled out. It was as much a relief to be back on dry land as it was to breathe fresh air again. There, she lay in a bed of flowers, trembling, until the drowning sensation had passed and she was well enough to climb to her feet.

Ash plucked one of the flowers in the bed around her and held it up to the moonlight. She recognized it—a black calla lily, a beautiful flute-shaped flower with dark petals.

She dropped it over the edge of the moat onto Lily's chest, which seemed like a fitting tribute.

After all, like the blossom goddess, the black calla was a lily with a dark heart.

Ash hiked her way up the stairs to the Mound. She felt sore. She felt haggard. She was physically and emotionally exhausted.

It was time for all of this to end.

The search for her sister.

Colt's schemes that he sucked everyone around him into.

The Four Seasons and their morbid quest for followers.

The rescue missions to save her friends from danger.

The loss of friends she couldn't reach in time.

The chasing.

The fighting.

The lying.

The dying.

At the top of the stairs, Lily's twisted landscaping
had transformed the Mound into its own cathedral. The
mangrove trees around either side had extended their
branches up, up, and over, until they braided and twisted
together above to form a high vaulted ceiling. On the
ground level six rows of shrubs had blossomed out of the
ground to either side of a center aisle to form pews.

At the front of the church, a thick knobby altar had
been erected. Wes lay on top of it, immobile thanks to the
IV tower pumping sedative into his veins. Thorne stood
beside the altar, frozen. This was the first time Ash had
seen Thorne looking unsure of himself—petrified, even.
A cigar smoked faintly from between his lips. He had his
hand on something beneath him, out of sight.

When Ash stepped closer to the altar, she could see at
last over the front pew.

Ash had to stop walking. Her stomach rolled up tight
like a window shade.

It's her, Ash thought. *She could be a ghost.*

Thorne rested his hand on little Rose Wilde's shoulder.

As Ash approached, Thorne's fingers curled around the little girl's collarbone like an eagle clutching a rodent in his talons.

It was so strange for Ash to finally see the girl—her own sister—in the flesh and not in some freakish vision of death and destruction. Rose wore a lacy white dress that hung unflatteringly over her body. If it were at all possible, she'd *lost* weight since her time half-starving in the Central American jungle. Despite her frail thinness, Ash now saw the uncanny resemblance she bore to pictures of Eve and Ash when they were in grammar school.

If Thorne's hold on her shoulder was painful, Rose didn't show it. She peered unblinkingly at the new arrival with her wonder-glazed brown eyes. Perhaps she thought she was seeing herself ten years into the future.

"So," Thorne said. He puffed on his cigar. His hand shook when he plucked the cigar out of his mouth. "The other Seasons have fallen, and now only Fall remains."

"The only fall remaining," Ash said, "is the one I'm going to help you take right off a cliff. Give me back my sister. Give me back my boyfriend. And go fly a kite someplace windy where I'll never see you again." Thorne was silent, so Ash added, "I can give you the name of a couple of deserts where you could start."

"I will have," Thorne said, articulating each word slowly, "my sacrifice."

"I just gave you one," Ash said. "She's floating in a bed of wet leaves and lily pads. I'm a short fuse away from dropping you in there with her. The pair of you will make a great compost pile."

"Better a compost pile than a weeping willow." Thorne brought his cigar up to take another drag.

Ash focused on the embers at the end of his cigar. The cigar exploded in a cloud of tobacco and ashes. Thorne screamed.

When the cloud cleared, Thorne was quivering with his teeth bared. His face was blackened with soot. "Fine," Thorne said. He glanced at the camera behind the altar. "I was going to save this finale for your night god lover, but you just earned your spot as my ultimate sacrifice." Thorne crouched beside Rose. He moved the hair away from her ear and whispered just loud enough for Ash to hear: "Do you remember what you did to that ship after we rescued you from the jungle? Do you? Well, I want you to do something even *worse* to this bad lady." Just so Ash was clear, he turned and mouthed the word "boom" to her.

Rose's eyes narrowed. The edges of her eyes grew red in a fiery corona.

Ash felt a queasy, sinking sensation in the bottom of her stomach. Was this how it was going to end after all she had survived? A gory, explosive death at the merciless hands of a six-year-old girl? Her own sister, her own blood?

Thorne grew impatient. "What are you waiting for?" he shouted. "This bad woman wants to take you back to the jungle. To take you away from me!" Thorne shook her by the shoulders. "Do you want to go back there and live like an animal? *Then do as I say*."

Rose turned her head to face the wind god who was ranting into her ear. Her nose wrinkled as though she smelled something foul. Her eyebrows caved downward into an angry V.

"Run," Rose said.

"What?" Thorne barked. "I don't want her to run. I want her to *die*."

"No," Rose corrected him. "*You. You* run."

Thorne's mouth opened. He looked back and forth between the two Wilde sisters. Ash watched Thorne's bravado quickly fall away. No more arrogance, no more megalomania, no more speeches about convoluted religions or a new world order—just sheer, liquid terror dripping off him like an ice cube under the Mojave sun.

Then he fled. Ash stuck out her leg as he passed, and he tripped and flailed, but righted himself long enough to plow his way out of the back of the chapel.

Rose waited until he was a good ten seconds away from the Mound. She smiled. And in the voice more of a demon than a child, she rasped to the unseen Thorne, *"I found you."*

A not-too-distant "Nooooooo!" echoed out of the gardens beyond. The long wail was overpowered and clipped short by the sound of a thunderous explosion. Through the branches that formed the roof of the chapel, the sky flashed red.

Silence.

Ash turned back around, expecting Rose to show some sign of anger or contempt for the man she'd just disintegrated. Instead the little girl had dropped into a sitting position on the ground. She was tugging absent-mindedly on a stray branch from the nearest pew, like she'd forgotten all about Thorne already.

Ash shivered and stepped over to the altar where Wes lay. She pulled the IV out of his arm. His breaths were shallow, and when she pressed her head to his chest, she could hear that his heart beat slowly. Still, he did not stir. She would just have to wait patiently for the sedative to wear off.

Well, she realized, maybe there *was* something she could do to accelerate the process. She extended her hands to the roof overhead and let her makeshift flame-throwers consume the mangrove branches in fire. Gradually the hole in the ceiling widened like an opening eye. She tried not to take too much pleasure in destroying Lily's final villainous creation, this perverse cathedral of pain and suffering.

When Ash had finished, the moonlight streamed through the new skylight in the ceiling down onto Wes's altar. He trembled under the light, and his eyes shot open. They were black to the corners. Whatever power he drew from the night coursed through his veins, usher-ing the sedative out of his system.

Ash couldn't help but remember the night of the

Blackwood Academy masquerade ball—it was barely more than a month ago—sitting next to Colt as he stirred from unconsciousness. Only, then it was Colt who'd had the bag of secrets.

This time Ash was the one with the dark skeletons in her cupboard.

This time Ash was the one saddled with the decision whether or not she should tell Wes the truth.

Tell him that she'd murdered him in the last life.

That she'd *enjoyed* murdering him.

Could their fledgling love survive all the baggage from their previous life?

And more important, could their love survive the baggage from the last *week*?

Wes interrupted her thought process from careening any further into dark territory. He groaned and stretched his arms way over his head. "This is going to make for one punishing hangover," he said in a groggy voice.

Ash laughed. "Don't be such a baby. A couple of Advil and a few minutes basking in the moonlight, and you'll be fine." She couldn't help herself—she leaned in and kissed him.

When the kiss ended, Wes's eyes dipped to look at her lips. "Or maybe I just need a few more of those." Then his eyes tracked to the empty spot next to Ash where Aurora might have been standing if she were still alive. The romance of the moment derailed in a fiery wreck.

Wes climbed down onto the Mound floor. He took

in the pews, the partially destroyed ceiling, the altar he'd been lying on. "I guess I found religion," he said.

"That's not all we found." Ash stepped to the side so he could see little Rose, who was now tottering and walking up and down a pew bench as though she were a tightrope walker.

Wes let out a long breath. "And now it gets interesting."

With the explosion that had killed Thorne, Ash knew it wouldn't be long before the Villa Vizcaya gardens became a crime scene too. She walked over to the pew where Rose was playing. There was so much to say to her, and Ash had none of the words to explain things. She held out her hand and smiled. "Come on, Rose," she said. "It's time to go."

Rose didn't even hesitate. She grabbed Ash's hand and hopped down off the bench. For the time being at least, it seemed that this little child really *was* a child. For now. "Where are we going?" Rose asked.

The question startled Ash for some reason—in part because she wasn't fully sure she knew the answer to it. She started to say, "I'm going to take you . . ."

But the funny thing about the word "home" is that sometimes it's too big and complex for even a sixteen-year-old to fully understand.

And sometimes the word "home" is too small to fill the spaces left behind by the people who have gone.

THE SIBLING PYRE

One blast of fire from you sends the girl in the monk's robe crashing through the front door of the cathedral.

The old wooden doors buckle and splinter, but the girl just keeps on going. She rolls across the dusty road like a tumbleweed in a hurricane. The motion throws back her hood, revealing her Polynesian face, which is quickly bruising from where you blindsided her with your fist.

It's been years since you last saw Violet, but she looks more like you than ever.

She is *nothing* like you.

Violet takes off into the massive palm grove beyond the steeple. You're hot on her trail as you chase her into the forest. From your childhood days on the farm, and the bank heist getaways in the years that followed, you know that Violet has always been slightly faster on foot than you.

But you're the one with the endurance.

The rain picks up, a cold drizzle at first. The clouds roll over the sky like a train coming into the station. By the time you reach the tree line, the rain sweeps over the forest in heavy, pulsing curtains. The palm fronds form natural gutters that pour water onto your head.

It has taken you five years, four continents, and tens of thousands of miles to find your treacherous sister.

You're not about to let a little bit of rain stand between you and your revenge.

Ahead Violet darts rapidly between the trees, but you can see her growing weary already, her running form faltering, the way her legs look unsteady with every footstep in the watery grass.

You're so focused on Violet's feet and closing the distance that you lose your own footing in a deep puddle. You splash down to one knee. You're quick to get up, but by the time you regain your balance, the damage is done—Violet is out of sight, hidden somewhere among the trees.

You walk cautiously now. The cold rain washes clean any heat trails Violet might have left through the grove. The persistent white noise of the rainfall against the fronds and grass means you have to listen even more carefully for the sounds of any wet footsteps. The sky grows darker by the second as the pregnant clouds amass overhead. The temperature, too, is falling.

As if cold rain could stop your fire.

The lightning bolt hits you in the chest as Violet springs

out from behind a tree. But the electricity pulsing from your sister's fingertips stuns you only briefly, and once you've pushed through the pain, you emerge in a rage on the other side. The fire blossoms out of your hand and strikes Violet in the chest of her monk's robe. She slams headfirst into a palm tree behind her, and drops to the ground, still. A barrage of dates rains down around her like marbles.

You drag Violet by her legs through the muddy grass. She moans something you can't understand. With her only half-conscious, the rain dies to a steady trickle.

Nearby a post has been planted into the ground to support a small palm that's much shorter than the others. Even with the support of the post, it looks sickly and twisted, starved of sunlight by all the taller palms around it.

You make quick work of tying Violet to the opposite side of the post. By the time you're finished, she looks just like the scarecrows the two of you condemned in the fields of Maine. Just like those scarecrows, she'll get the kind of quick trial she deserves.

Violet stirs. "What . . ." She tugs at the bonds securing her to the post. They hold true. Her eyes go from dazed to alert. "I . . . I don't understand. Why are you doing this, Little Sister?"

"Why did you kill my husband?" you demand to know.

"Kill your . . . wait, Colt?" Violet shakes her head. "I didn't—"

Your open hand slaps her across the face, and her

head rotates around as far as it will go without breaking her neck. The slap leaves a welt. Inside, you feel a different kind of sting. The tears well in your eyes. This was supposed to be all about anger, about cold revenge, but sorrow is percolating up with it. "Why? Why did you send the assassin? Why did you do it?" you sob. You hit her again. "Why, damnit?"

"You have to believe me," Violet whimpers. "I would never—I didn't even . . . I mean, you know I was never keen on Colt, and I've always been suspicions of his intentions, but even then, I wouldn't . . . Lucy, you have to believe me!"

It's the first time you feel doubt. For five years you've pursued her with unflagging certainty. You've fantasized about what you would do to her for betraying you. For sending that assassin to murder Colt. For her insistence that, if you weren't by her side, then you might as well suffer as she did. Miserable. Vengeful. Alone.

Now there's something in her voice, in the broken sobs that have rendered her unable to speak, in the way she hangs limply from the post, that makes you want to believe her. This is your sister. There is a feeling inside you—and questions, too—that are growing as you watch her.

But then there is that other feeling. The sinking in the pit of your stomach. The clicking in your ears. You can see the hair rising around your head.

You dive off to the side just as the lightning bolt forks down from the sky. One prong of the lightning bolt sinks its electric fist into the ground where you were standing before. The other rips through the nearest palm tree as though it were made of copper wire. Despite the dampness, both the tree and the grass beneath the lightning strike burst into flames.

You brush the mud off your arms and stand up slowly. If it were at all possible, you feel even more rage now for the girl strapped to the post than you did on your nightmarish wedding night.

"Lucy," Violet whispers. "That was only in self-defense. You wouldn't believe me, so I panicked. I'm sorry. Look me in the eyes, and you'll see that what I'm telling you is true!"

You have no desire to search for truth and penitence in your sister's eyes. Instead you're watching the fire trail left by the lightning. The palm is already engulfed in flames. The circle of fire in the grass is widening rapidly.

Violet notices too. The rain picks up again, but the droplets just hiss and turn to steam when they hit the fire.

"You can stop this!" Violet shouts at you, and you wonder if she's referring to more than just the fire. She wriggles against her restraints, and her apologetic tone caves into anger. "Damnit, Lucy, put this fire out *now*!"

"You started it," you say. You smile at the double meaning.

"I didn't kill your husband!" Violet curls her legs up— the fire has crept all the way around her wooden post.

"You know the funny thing about wildfires?" you say

to her. "Sometimes they're good for a forest. Sometimes they burn up all the little weeds that threaten to strangle and suffocate the life around them." You turn to your sister. "You are a weed, Violet."

The little sickly palm tree ignites behind her. The fire courses up its trunk. Violet's eyes bulge when she feels the heat at her back. "I didn't kill your husband," she repeats, "but . . . but I can tell you who did!"

You pause. "Fine. If you didn't send the assassin, then who did?"

"It was . . ." Violet turns to blow out a small fire on the shoulder of her robe. "It was Gracie!" she finishes. "Gracie did it."

"Let me get this straight. You're blaming this on our dead baby sister?" You shake your head. "Have fun in hell, Violet." You turn 180 degrees and walk away.

"She's alive!" Violet pleads with you. " You're punishing the wrong sister! *The wrong sister!*" But her words will be lost soon, because the cathedral bell is chiming now, and you're walking farther away, and the rain thickens even though it won't save her. Still, between her shrieks, and through the bells and rain, you hear three words echoing over and over again in your mind, three words that you'll never believe but that will haunt you for the rest of your days anyway.

The wrong sister.

The wrong sister.

The wrong sister.

It was a strange thing, having a new sister.

Ash watched little Rose, who was in turn staring through the glass window of Wes's condominium. Whether the girl was watching the torrential Miami rainstorm outside or staring someplace else altogether, Ash would never know.

On top of trying to acclimate to the new addition to her family—and what that would translate to when Ash returned to the real world of school, friends . . . her parents—Ash had a pressing decision to make:

Was she really about to barge her way into the Cloak Netherworld to retrieve her *other* sister?

On the one hand, part of her was tempted to let it be for the moment. It had been more than a month since Eve's abduction. What was another few days, or even a few weeks? Maybe it made more sense to let Rose get her bearings around Ash, one-on-one, before Ash introduced her to the unpredictable elder sister, who was about as calming an influence as fireworks in a room full of sleeping children.

It's not like Ash and Eve had parted with a hug and an "I'll miss you," either. Eve had tried to murder her boyfriend and had nearly drowned Ash herself. Ash had burned her own hands into the flesh of Eve's wrists. And before the Cloak dragged her to hell, Eve spent her final moment on earth conjuring a tsunami to crush Ash and Colt. Their history of attempted sororicide was a lump too big just to sweep under a rug and move on.

Then there was the horrible vision from the prior night. She'd let Eve burn to death in that palm grove, had let the wildfire purge her like some weed. Eve was her *sister*, not just another delusional god who'd had it coming. She was family.

The vision had proven once and for all that their violent sibling rivalry wasn't unique to this lifetime.

It was in their DNA.

But it was reflecting back on the dream that finally made up Ash's mind.

No matter how much Eve may have deserved her fate in the last life—

No matter how much Eve may have deserved her imprisonment in this life—

No matter what Eve being back on earth might mean for the future—

Ash couldn't live with herself if she condemned Eve to death two lifetimes in a row.

The circle of violence had to stop now.

Wes stepped in front of her, fresh from his night's rest and looking surprisingly clear-eyed, considering that he'd spent much of the previous evening in a drug-induced coma. He flipped a chair around and straddled it, leaning on the chair back. "So," he said.

"So," Ash repeated. She slumped back against the kitchen counter and crossed her arms.

Wes glanced at the little girl in his window. "Why do I feel like my bachelor pad just turned into a kindergarten classroom?"

Ash snatched an apple out of the fruit bowl. "Well, heads up, teach." She lobbed it underhand at him.

At first Wes went to take a bite out of it, but something made him stop just short. He lowered the apple and gently balanced it on his knee. "So this is the part where I ask you not to put yourself in danger again. Then you tell me that you have to, that Eve is your sister."

"Is that right?" Ash asked.

Wes nodded. "I come back with a list of very practical reasons why you shouldn't," he continued, "pointing out that you don't even know whether there's oxygen where you're going, or an atmosphere, or a gravity that won't crush you like a sardine can in a trash compactor. Meanwhile I know that everything I'm saying is falling on deaf ears because, if all the volcano goddesses I've ever met share one thing, it's an immovable stubbornness when they've resolved to do something."

"Just one of our many adorable qualities," Ash added.

"So rather than ranting uselessly at you for another half hour, I cut my losses: I tell you that the two of us are going right now. That way you can't give me the slip and make the journey to hell by yourself as soon as I'm not looking."

Ash pursed her lips. "I guess I should also skip the part where I try to convince you that this is *my* fight, and my fight alone . . . and that someone needs to stay behind to fix dinner, because there might be three hungry Wilde sisters ready to eat when we return from hell?"

"Glad we're reading from the same script." Wes stood up and opened the nearest cabinet. "We're out of food anyway, so the four of us can order takeout when we get back."

Ash wandered over to Rose and knelt beside her. While Rose seemed to understand English well enough, it was another thing completely to explain to her that she needed to open up a portal into hell . . . especially when Ash had no idea how it worked. If it weren't for last week's vision, when Rose opened the rift that ravaged and swallowed the pursuing boat, Ash might have believed that Rose's power was something Colt had completely fabricated.

"Rose," Ash said. She reached to brush a strand of Rose's hair that had fallen into her eyes, but checked herself. It still felt too intimate for a sister she'd just met. She did, however, make a note to get the girl to a hair stylist soon after they got back. "I need you to take me someplace that . . . that apparently you've been before. A place with . . ." She fumbled for a word to describe the Cloak. "A place with monsters." She immediately cringed. *Great, Ashline,* she thought. *Let's scare the shit out of her.* Using the word "monster" around a six-year-old wasn't exactly starting off on the right foot.

Rose's expression, however, was nowhere in the vicinity of "terrified." If anything, in the brief moment when she raised her eyebrow, she looked vaguely curious.

This was going to take a different approach. With Wes's help Ash rustled up a piece of paper and colored pencils. She set up a little workstation on the hardwood floor next to Rose and sketched the outline of what she hoped would be recognizable as a Cloak. After a minute of sketching, the scratch of the pencil against the paper finally aroused Rose's attention, and she sat down cross-legged next to the paper.

It was only once Ash had begun to shade in the outline of the Cloak (which, given her dearth of artistic ability, resembled an amorphous oil spill) that Rose made a tiny squeak of recognition. As Ash watched, Rose drew in a deep breath and then exhaled hard against the window. A film of condensation formed on the cold glass. Then Rose took her pinky finger and drew two figures in the dew.

When she was done, even as the condensation faded from the glass, Ash knew exactly what they were looking at.

A row of interlocking machete-sharp teeth.

A flame-shaped single eye.

Rose looked questioningly to Ash.

Ash swallowed and nodded.

And Rose smiled.

As her illustration vanished from the window, Rose excitedly scampered up the stairs leading to the roof and threw open the door.

Of all the times for Rose to show her playful side, Ash thought, *she chooses now?*

Ash followed behind the light-footed little girl, with Wes's heavy footsteps treading the staircase behind her. Out on the roof the rain washed over Ash in a powerful downpour. Thunderstorms this intense were usually reserved for violent encounters with Eve.

How strange that a tempest like this should also signal the start of Eve's rescue mission.

Rose, meanwhile, walked up to the lip of the pool. She descended a few steps until she had waded in up to her knees.

Rose brought both hands over her head and curled her fingers. A miniature vortex of lava formed over her palm, and with a tiny but terrifying scream, she slung the lava ball into the pool.

It burst through the surface of the water and exploded,

showering the roof and its already rain-soaked occupants. After Ash had finished spitting out a mouthful of chlorinated pool water and had wiped the sting from her eyes, she turned back to the pool, expecting a miracle.

Nothing happened. There was no portal, no interdimensional tear like Ash had been waiting for.

Rose tried again, making an even bigger explosion, but to no avail. This time the frustration got to Rose. She pulled at her hair and began to rant angrily in a language that Ash couldn't understand.

Maybe what Rose needed was encouragement, Ash thought. Even half-mortal kids needed positive reinforcement, right? "You can do it, Rose!" she shouted. It sounded lame as soon as it left her mouth.

Rose finally ended her foreign rant and collected herself. This time her fingers were graceful as she used both hands to weave another ball of light and fire out of the air. It hissed and steamed as the water poured down on it.

Rose's fingers tightened. She heaved it into the pool.

And when this one exploded, it took part of the world with it.

The air might as well have been made of tissue paper. The explosion gouged an enormous tear in the fabric of time and space, as if a big fist had punched through this dimension into the next. Dark scraps dropped like confetti onto the surface of the water and dissipated into a thousand microscopic embers.

Rose motioned for them to follow her toward the dark,

jagged hole in the universe. Ash was about to ask why she'd opened it in the pool, but Rose splashed through the opening with an excited squeak and was gone.

Already the edge of the tear started to bleed closed, as the barrier between worlds repaired itself. Ash and Wes exchanged looks and sprinted for the opening. Ash beat him there by a stride and did her best lifeguard dive through the tear. When she immediately felt a falling sensation on the other side, her first thought was, *We are all going to die.* She'd jumped blindly into a slice in the universe created by a six-year-old, and now she was going to splatter on a canyon floor in hell.

But as it turned out, she didn't have long to fall. Ash didn't have enough time to gain her bearings in this strange new world before she plunged into its stormy seas.

She sank down into the frothy water. Wes dropped in right after her, missing crushing her head by only a few feet. They both kicked to the surface, and Ash immediately began searching the ocean for her sister, who was nowhere in sight. It was night here in the Netherworld—if they had a day at all—and visibility was poor. But there was one thing Ash could see:

The crumpled and scorched hull of the boat that Rose had destroyed the week before, its flattened prow jutting out of the water like a mangled tombstone. And now Ash could see bodies floating all around her, the frozen, burned, and broken remains of the ship's crew.

"Rose!" Ash screamed. She started to yell for her

again, but a wave crashed down, filling her mouth with sweet-tasting water and garbling her words.

When she emerged choking from the other side of the wave, barely treading water, she spotted a figure several spans from them. It was Rose, calmly dog-paddling for a dark shore, weaving her way through the corpses, even as the swells lifted her tiny body up and down.

Eventually Ash forged her way into the shallows, assuming she'd made it through the last of the white-caps . . . until one final wave surprised her from beneath and lifted her up into the air. It dumped her off its crest onto the black sand beach as if to say, *And* stay *out!*

Wes crawled out of the shallows and collapsed next to her. "Miami waters . . . not quite so turbulent . . . ," he panted. "Should have taken . . . that lifeguard course."

Ash pulled herself up so that she was leaning on one elbow, although the fine black sand was soft enough that she was tempted to rest her head for a few. "I guess we get to spend our time in hell wet and cold. There's irony for you."

"You're a volcano goddess," Wes reminded her. "Can't you just dry your clothes?"

"Yeah, if I want to burn them off." She caught him grinning. "Lose the smirk or you'll lose something else, Towers."

Rose had plopped down below a small dune not too far away, where her curly hair and gaunt face were backlit by this world's moon, a moon that was threateningly low and took up half the sky. She was busy gathering wet sand into a heap. *We're sitting on the shores of the Netherworld,* Ash thought, *and my little sister is making sand castles.* Since Rose spent much of her time acting like she'd been possessed by a demon, it was all the more creepy when she acted like a real six-year-old.

After some coaxing to get Rose to abandon the black sand, the three of them approached the wall of indigo vegetation on the fringes of the beach. "What's with the Jurassic ferns?" Wes asked.

"Not ferns," Ash said when she was close enough to reach out and touch the soft velour of the ten-foot-tall plants. "They're lilies." In fact, they were monstrous versions of the same black calla lily that Ash had tossed onto Lily's watery grave the night before. . . . Had the Cloak been watching her? "I can't be sure, but something tells me that they decorated the beach just for me . . . which means they're expecting us."

"Could be worse," Wes said.

"Oh, yeah? How's that?"

"They could have left a death trap for you instead of an enormous flower arrangement." He walked up to one of the black callas, wrapped his thick arms around one of the tubelike petals, and tugged hard to no effect. "She loves me not," he grunted.

"You're lucky it didn't turn out to be a Venus fly-trap," Ash snapped at him, although she was happy to see his good spirits temporarily restored.

On their journey down the snarling path, Ash felt like she was beneath a black light, as the glow of the enormous moon filtered through the translucent indigo petals. It was pointless, she realized, to wonder why anything was the way it was in this world—the beach, the sand, the moon—because she got the impression that this was just how it looked *today*.

When they emerged from the end of the path onto a circular stone plaza, the first thing Ash noticed was the tree.

Then the snow.

Then the cliff.

Ash was used to tall trees, having gone to school in the redwoods. This single tree, however, imparted to her an unparalleled sense of awe. Between its thick baobab trunk, and the gnarled, twisting limbs, the tree formed a towering mushroom cloud. Ash gauged it to be at least a hundred feet tall, but it could have been even higher. With the moon looming in the background, she was having a tough time judging space and distance in this strange universe.

A steady curtain of snow fell onto the plaza. It was too beautiful for Ash to even remember to be cold. Rather than switching on her internal furnace to warm herself, she simply let the feathery snowflakes accumulate on her wet clothing without complaint.

Then there was the endless cliff, on all sides. With the exception of the flower forest from which they'd arrived, the stone simply dropped off into nothing. Ash figured at first that there must be ground below them *somewhere*, but when she passed under the magnificent tree to the far edge of the circle, she discovered this presumption to be false. There was no base to the cliff, no canyon floor below.

There was only oblivion.

Nothingness.

Nonexistence.

The three of them stood at the stone periphery, looking out and down. The oblivion induced a gripping fear in Ash that, even as a goddess, even embroiled in her ongoing saga back on earth, she was far less significant to the universe than she could have ever realized. That even with reincarnation, nothingness was *always* a possibility.

Just like the body, maybe even the soul was a destructible, corruptible thing.

Ash might have gazed into the abyss for hours had she not seen the fiery blue flicker against the falling snow. Even though she'd come to the Netherworld fully expecting to meet with the Cloak, the blue flicker still sent dread coursing through her veins like an icy poison.

The Cloak had gathered in a semicircle around them, with a single Cloak standing out in front. Together they formed a monstrous fermata.

However, the Cloak looked different here on their own turf. Their flesh was the same oily coat with the floating blue flame dancing where the eye should be, but they'd traded their usual bulky and amorphous shape for bodies noticeably more svelte. Two arms. Two legs. Humanoid. Like the three-dimensional shadow of a man, only steeped in something primordial and dangerous.

"You're right on time," the Cloak in the middle said.

"You speak English," Ash replied.

"Among other things," it countered. "You sound surprised."

Ash instinctively stepped in front of Rose, although the thought was laughable. If the Cloak meant them any harm, Rose was probably the most dangerous god there. "I guess I should have expected it, since the instructions you sent to me were in English. But the last few times I've run into you, you've squawked, and roared, and smashed lanterns, and eaten people, so I guess I'm not used to seeing you quite so . . . eloquent."

The Cloak all laughed identically and in unison. Still, it was just the humanoid in the center who spoke. "That will make sense to you in time."

Ash sized up their "spokesperson" in the middle. When one of the Cloak had appeared to Serena, the Greek siren at Blackwood Academy, and delivered the personalized instructions that she was supposed to pass along to Ash and her friends, the Cloak creature had identified himself with a human name. "Are you Jack?" Ash asked.

The laughing stopped. "We are all Jack."

Ash shuddered. There was something truly chilling

about dealing with an entity with a collective conscience—many vessels, one central hive mind. "Then I guess you know why I've come."

"Ah, yes." The Cloak purred in its chasm-deep voice. "You're here for the stormy one." As one the Cloak all turned and lifted their heads to the tree above. "You're here for *her*."

What Ash had failed to notice until the Cloak brought it to her attention was that the tree was made of more than just wood and leaves and plant fibers. As she wiped the snow from her eyelashes, she could now see that there were people in the tree—many people, all woven into and camouflaged by the plant matter around them. With their limbs slack and their heads bowed, they were like apples dangling in an orchard, waiting to be plucked. Their eyes were open but showed no signs of movement or awareness.

A rustling sound came from the upper limbs, moving downward, like an object was tumbling through the foliage. A few telltale leaves floated to the ground beneath the tree, and then a female form dropped out of the bottom branches. Her body stopped just shy of a bloody death on the stone platform, suspended by a mess of plant fibers.

Eve looked a bit worse for wear than the last time Ash had seen her. Her hair was longer and unkempt, matted to her forehead in wet strands. Her skin was mottled—pale in places, and flushed with red in others, like calico patches of flesh and crimson. Even in whatever comatose trance she'd slipped into, a feverish dew glazed her skin, steadily dripping from her brow to the stone below.

And then there was the lifelessness in her blank eyes. Even in her most malicious days, Eve had for better or worse carried herself with a vivaciousness, a verve for life and its unpredictability. Now it was as though someone had unplugged the drain to her basin, and all that life force had funneled out with a loud and despairing gurgle.

"What have you done to her?" Ash asked. She knew it best not to grow enraged at the Cloak, especially in *their* world, where she had to play by *their* rules. The fire bubbled up anyway. The snowflakes hissed and turned to steam when they hit her skin. She gestured to the others who were also "plugged" into the tree. "What have you done to *all* of these people?"

"All in due time," Jack said patiently. "But in order for me to explain, we must speak privately, *one-on-one,* as they say." Again the thirty blue eyes around the semicircle flickered with laughter. Jack pointed a finger at Rose, and then at Wes, who was nervously cracking his knuckles. "You have done well to escort Pele here," Jack said, "but now you must take the child and go."

"I think I'd rather stay right here," Wes replied. He took a protective step closer to Ash.

"We mean the fiery one no harm," Jack said. *"Cross my heart and hope to die."*

Wes shook his head. "I'm not going any—"

"Very well," Jack interrupted him. "Back to earth you go." He flicked his fingers.

Two small portals opened in the stone beneath Wes and Rose, and with a yelp, they each succumbed to gravity and fell right back into the other world. Ash dove for the rifts to see where they'd gone, but they closed before she'd even landed. The last thing she heard were two splashes on the other side. *Please,* Ash prayed, *please let it be that they landed in the pool on the roof and not in the middle of the Atlantic.*

But Ash had to worry about herself as well, because with Wes and Rose gone, she was now alone, in hell, with the creature that had transformed her sister into a human acorn. There was no way they were going to make Ash the next decoration in their twisted landscaping.

"Do you like the snow?" Jack asked. "We know it's still summer, but we thought it would make you feel more at home. What is it about snow and big green trees that your people find so comforting around Christmastime, anyway? "

Ash willed the fire inside of her to cool. "Very thoughtful of you, but we celebrate Hanukkah in the Wilde household."

Jack's gray teeth flexed upward in a Cheshire smile. "Noted for your next visit."

"Don't do any major redecoration on account of me. The enormous bouquet of lilies you left for me on the way in was flattering enough."

"It's no trouble at all. This world is far more malleable

than your own. There is always the ocean, there is always the tree, and there is always the darkness beyond. But all that lies between"—Jack swept his arm back toward the forest—"transforms to soothe those we welcome, and to expel those we do not."

"Good thing my name's on the guest list," Ash said. "Now can we skip to the part where we cut my sister down from this tree on steroids?"

"Patience never was one of your virtues, Pele," Jack countered. "Besides, are you really so anxious to flee with Evelyn that you would throw away your chance to ask some very important questions?"

It was disturbing to know that the Cloak had probably spent so much time observing humans that they'd integrated maxims such as "Patience is a virtue." But Jack still had a point. The people in her life until now—Eve, Colt, even Wes—often chose to remain mysterious and selective with the truth. While she had no guarantee that the Cloak wouldn't just feed her *even more* lies, they'd let her pass safely through to their world when they could have easily killed her. Assuming that she could trust them to tell even half-truths, she had a free pass for answers, if she could come up with the right questions.

The real question, though, was where to begin.

Fortunately, Jack must have sensed that she was overwhelmed, because he began for her. "This world we inhabit is a beautiful and magical one, to be sure." Jack knelt down and, using his obsidian hands, gathered a palm full of snow from the stone plaza. "It should be everything that we want—contained, peaceful, responsive to our touch—but even *we* grow weary with time. And because of this, we have lately felt a growing restlessness. An urge to . . . fly away." He cupped both hands around the snow in his palm and then launched it up into the air as though he were tossing confetti. But instead of snow, what emerged from Jack's hand was a raven with two flaming blue eyes. It cawed and beat its wings. It circled the great tree and disappeared into the upper branches.

"We have watched over your world for longer than you know," Jack continued, "and we have grown to respect it, to admire it. It has all the makings of what we wish to call home. The unpredictability. The coexistence of so many different climates and landscapes and organisms, all stitched together like a patchwork quilt. And because we have been charged with overseeing your people, it would certainly facilitate our efforts to cohabit the planet with you."

"Or it would at least shorten your commute," Ash added. Jack cocked his head to the side. "Never mind," she said. "So what's keeping you from making the big move? You seem to already enjoy haunting forests, high school campuses, and airport bathrooms when you feel the urge. If you're worried about what the humans will think if you reveal yourself, I'm sure they'll eventually warm up to being neighbors with an oil slick who has a blue bonfire for an eye."

"Perhaps," Jack mused. "But we have one big problem. Something happens to us when we are around your kind. What your people do not recognize is that your propensity for violence—the humans, yes, but specifically the gods—creates an atmosphere that is poisonous to us."

Ash squinted into Jack's flame. "You're allergic . . . to hate?"

"In a word. It corrupts us. When we stay for long, we lose our sentience, our *eloquence* as you so *eloquently* put it. We transform from what you see now into the shadows of your vengeful hearts. Wild. Confused. Snarling. Wrathful. We drown in it. *And we have had enough.*"

The way that Jack said "enough" sent Ash reeling back a few steps. She could feel the lip of the platform under her heel, and reminded herself to be more careful. One wrong step, and she could tumble right off the edge of the world and into the great void.

"In the beginning we thought that since the gods retained their memories from life to life, so too would they retain their wisdom. We thought that they would return to your world with an even better understanding each time, and guide the mortals who had only one life to live, one life to learn. But it worked just the opposite. Instead of acquiring wisdom, you simply acquired grudges. Memories of past grievances turned to century-long feuds, which generated violence and seething hatred. So a few centuries ago we attempted to remedy this the best way we knew how."

"You took our memories from us," Ash said.

"We gave you the gift of a fresh start. But even that failed to end the violence . . . in part because one of the worst perpetrators of lies and hatred managed to hold on to his memories. Colt Halliday is a virus. Without your memories you gods might live your whole lives without ever tracking each other down, but every time he comes back, he spins a new web that snares old rivalries and ignites extinguished fires. And *you*, Pele . . . well, he can't help but make you the centerpiece to his grand web."

"Do you think I asked for that?" Ash yelled. "Do you know what I'd give to have never met him?"

"Good." Jack nodded. "You are angry. And you should be. Because if Colt is not stopped, he *will* destroy your world in due time. This I promise you, Ashline Wilde."

"Oh, I'm angry." Ash's voice trembled. "But not just at him—at you, too. You could come to our world and grab him, plug him into this freaky little tree of yours, and be done with it. Instead you sent a blind girl with a bunch of cryptic nonsensical messages to get *us* to do the heavy lifting for you. Then you give me visions of my little sister with no instructions, when you could go protect her yourself. It's like it's some kind of *board game* for you."

In a flash Jack had glided up to Ash. He leered down at her. "There are *rules*, Pele. Rules more ancient than you or us. We have been charged to watch over you, to be your gamekeepers, but there are lines even we will not cross."

"As sanctioned by *whom*?" Ash shouted. "You have all this power, and you're trying to tell me that I've watched two of my friends die because you're afraid to cross some imaginary line?"

Jack leaned even closer. As he grew angry, his body was starting to lose its humanoid shape and revert back to the monstrous Cloak she recognized from earth. "The Cloak are meant to oversee the gods. The gods are meant to oversee mankind. Our charge is to watch and protect, but not to intervene. Your people have degenerated into violent chaos precisely *because* you meddled with the humans. You mated with them, you hurt them . . . you killed them." Jack finally took a hold of himself, and the edges of his body narrowed back to its humanoid shape. "We will gently guide and mentor your people, but we will not—what is your term for it?—*take out your trash for you*."

"Well," Ash said, "at least we can both agree to call Colt Halliday trash."

"There is, however," Jack said, "one exception we've agreed to make, where we *will* cross that line." He placed his hand on Ash's shoulders and guided her around so she was looking at the tree again. She shuddered under his touch; it felt as empty as the oblivion behind them. "This is the Tree of Life. It is what renews us from the poisonous hate of your world. It is our oxygen. It is also the only thing strong enough to imprison those gods and goddesses that we have chosen to—how do you say it?—*take offline*.

Those like Evelyn who have, over the years, proven themselves consistently carcinogenic to your world. Here, they are given a chance to exist in tandem with life rather than destroying it, to toil and feed into the tree. It is our hope that in existing for the good of another creature, these gods will eventually be *rehabilitated*."

Jack toed a line in the snow as he continued. "There is a boundary that a god like yourself must cross first before we will finally touch you in your own world. You must first have become such a malignant life force that someone who loves you actually desires you harm. In Evelyn's case she did enough psychological violence to you that you were finally willing to stop her, at any cost. Only then were we able to take her."

Ash kicked snow over the line Jack had drawn. "Good luck applying your rules to Colt; I'm not sure anyone could ever truly love him." But that wasn't true, was it? She'd felt strongly enough to marry him the life before, had doted amorously over him when he was alive, had grieved deeply after he was murdered. If he hadn't revealed himself after the car accident, and they'd continued on that motorcycle ride up to Vancouver uninterrupted, she could have easily developed deep feelings for him in this life as well. After all, she'd let her guard drop completely after their romantic photography trip in the woods.

"In fact, we did try to rehabilitate him," Jack said. "Just once, nearly two centuries ago."

Ash gazed up at the towering tree, and tried to picture Colt wired into it, his hair matted against his forehead and his eyes hollow. "What happened?"

"The tree began to rot and wither. Rather than nourishing it, his mere presence flowed like a slow poison into the branches and down the trunk."

"I'm not surprised that Colt doesn't have a green thumb," Ash said. "He's toxic to people, too."

"Then you also realize how important it is that you carry out the mission we have charged you with," Jack said. "You are remarkably powerful, and perhaps the only one capable of getting close to Colt. For that, we have chosen you as our emissary and our chief hope. Should you fail, then your world and your people . . ." Jack whistled. Above, the raven in the tree cawed and dove for Jack's waiting wrist. Just as it was about to land, Jack swatted it with his other hand. The raven exploded into a thousand snowflakes.

Jack didn't finish his sentence. Ash got the picture just fine.

"Listen," Ash said. "I want to help you out. I do. You've been far more inviting and helpful than most of the other people in my life. But as dangerous as I know Colt is, I would be every bit as monstrous as he is if I didn't put family first." She pointed at Eve's body, and she was surprised when the tears welled in her eyes. "That's my sister. She's not perfect and she never will be. But I'm not leaving without her."

"Very well." Jack glided toward the tree and motioned with a curled finger for Ash to follow. The line of Cloak parted to let them through. "But there is one final thing you should know before you decide whether we release Evelyn Wilde to you."

Ash frowned. "I've come this far, haven't I? What could you possibly tell me that would change my mind about freeing my sister?"

Jack paused. "That Evelyn Wilde is not your sister at all."

It felt like a major league baseball player had taken a sledgehammer to her stomach. "What?" was all she could manage.

"Did you ever do any research on your namesake, Pele?" Jack inquired. "With all the technology your people have now, there's really no excuse."

"It's kind of hard to justify sitting down with an encyclopedia or a Polynesian mythology text when people are dying around you. I know that Pele was the goddess of volcanoes, but I don't know what that has to do with Eve."

Jack shook his head. "Volcanoes are only part of it. If you'd done your research, you would have known that Pele was the goddess of volcanoes, yes, but she was *also* the goddess of storms and explosions."

Another blow to Ash's gut. This time she actually staggered on her feet. "Are you telling me that . . ."

"We see one where you see three. We say 'you' where you say 'we.'"

Ash trembled. "This is *not* the appropriate time to speak in your cryptic rhymes and riddles."

"We call you *the Candelabra*," Jack explained. He held out his hand, and the snow levitated off the ground and congealed over his palm. When it had finished molding together, it formed a white three-pronged candlestick. "Three heads, three flames . . . one vessel. You see, Pele was once the most powerful god to walk the planet. But she was *too* powerful. Too destructive. Too wild to contain. Because of this, two lifetimes ago we finally had to cross the line and do what we thought was best: separate Pele into three pieces, three abilities, three personalities. An unpredictable summoner of storms. An impetuous, destructive wielder of explosions . . . And a cunning volcano goddess."

"No," Ash whispered. "I am not her. She is not me. We are *not* the same." The last part came out as a growl.

"A branch may produce two apples, one flawless and one rotten to the core," Jack mused. "That does not mean they aren't still fruits of the same tree."

Ash could feel her sense of individuality withering away by the moment. It was as though she'd lived her whole life trying to blaze her own trail for herself, only to find out that she wasn't whole at all. She was just a fragment, a shard of a whole being. "You have a look-but-don't-touch policy with everyone else, but it was okay for you to cut my soul like a ten-dollar pizza? What gives you the right?"

The Cloak had formed a ring around her at this point. She could only guess that they were banking on her taking the news poorly. "We thought we could save you from rehabilitation. Pele made this fate for herself. Colt Halliday has romanced your last five incarnations not because opposites attract. Intact, Pele was just like him. Worse, perhaps. By separating you into three parts—the Spark, the Fuse, and the Flame—we have given you each a chance to redeem your past."

Ash's knees no longer felt sturdy beneath her, and she almost collapsed into the snow. "What else can I possibly do to redeem myself?" she asked weakly. She'd completely given up her normal life. She'd saved some friends, and watched others die. She'd survived a tsunami, car accidents, a fall off a skyscraper, and even a lynching.

She wasn't sure how much she had left to give.

"That question brings us to the business of Evelyn's *bail*, as your people call it. We will let the Spark go only on the condition that you fulfill the mission we have assigned you. And so we ask you now, Ashline Wilde, do you promise to stop the trickster Colt Halliday?" He extended his black hand and waited.

In the previous week Ash had taken the lives of three gods. But those had all been in self-defense, for the purposes of her own survival. Did she have what it takes to seek out a man, a man whom she'd known intimately over many lives, and rip his life away from him? His scheming had facilitated woe and tragedy, but Ash had never witnessed Colt commit an act of murder himself.

It took only one look at Eve for Ash to make up her mind. She had no choice but to agree for now, even if she had no intention of carrying out the Cloak's wish. If what they had said was true, there wasn't much they could do to Ash unless she was harmed by someone who loved her. "Consider it done," she said. She seized Jack's hand, and under his touch the nerves all the way up her arm lost their sensation for a moment.

With a sound like wet paper tearing in half, the fibers supporting Eve's body snapped at once. She was spluttering and coughing only moments after she hit the ground. Her retching made her whole body convulse into a ball while she vomited a green concoction onto the virgin snow.

When the vomiting turned to dry heaves, Eve finally looked up and noticed her audience—thirty blue flame eyes and Ash. She snarled and backed up toward the tree like a cornered rabid dog, waiting to attack.

"Eve, it's okay." Ash treaded carefully toward her and pumped the air brakes. "You're just a little disoriented."

Eve didn't say anything, but she held up her arms, examined the tender burns scarred into her wrists.

"There will be time to play the blame game later," Ash said. "For now, do you want to get out of here and back to earth"—she motioned to Jack and the crowd of Cloak—"or would you rather these gentlemen turn you back into a tree ornament?"

Eve remained tense for a few more moments. Then her body relaxed and slumped against the tree. She let her back slide down until she was sitting against the base of the trunk. Then she pressed her face into her hands and began to weep.

Ash sighed. Fantasies of Eve trying to electrocute the Cloak and subsequently being cast into the oblivion faded from her imagination.

She joined Eve beneath the tree and sat beside her. Weird as it felt for her nurturing instincts to take over, she wrapped her arm around Eve's quaking shoulders. "Everything's going to be okay now, Eve."

Eve stopped crying long enough to peel her face from her tear-soaked fingers. Her bloodshot eyes studied Ash. "You came for me," she said finally.

"You would have done the same for me," Ash offered.

This actually evoked some choked laughter from Eve. "Like hell I would. You know better than to credit me with any selflessness. But you . . . After all that happened between us, why would you come for me?"

"Because . . ." Ash glanced at Jack just briefly before she gave the only explanation that made sense to her right now:

"Because you're my big sister."

Ash knew she shouldn't have expected the Wilde sisters to have a family game night around the fireplace for their first Monday evening reunited, but this was ridiculous.

After the Cloak had released them from the underworld, the three sisters had camped out on the roof deck to Wes's penthouse, where the fickle Miami weather had gone from stormy to spotless in a matter of hours. Rose always seemed more at home when she was outdoors, and Ash figured that Eve was probably feeling fairly claustrophobic after being cocooned in a tree for the last month. At the very least the weather goddess was probably anxious to be back in an atmosphere that she could control.

Now Rose stood ankle-deep in the roof pool, staring down into the water. Eve was leaning on the glass railing with her attention turned to the sky. Whenever she snapped her fingers, lightning bolts would flash between the fluffy clouds overhead.

Ash, meanwhile, was having trouble finding any words to say to either of her sisters. With Eve the problem was that they already had so much history between them. With Rose the problem was that they didn't have *any* history.

Finally Ash couldn't bear the silence any longer, so she climbed out of her pool chair and stepped into the shallow end with Rose. She placed a tentative hand on the little girl's shoulder. "Did they have pools where you lived before?"

Instead of answering the question, Rose frowned and pointed at the water. "Where are the fish?"

"They're in the sea." Ash's eyes suddenly lit up, and she knelt next to Rose, ignoring the water that seeped through her jeans. "If you like fish, how about I take you to the aquarium tomorrow?" The word "aquarium" only got a blank stare from Rose, so Ash started to pantomime a box shape with her hands. "It's a big, uh, cage that you can see through, where they take fish of all sizes and color from the ocean and put them on display, so people can watch them swim around."

"They take the fish from their home?" Rose asked sadly. She turned away from Ash and whispered, "They should put them back."

Ash sighed and retracted her hand from Rose's shoulder. She should have known better than to think Rose would want to see animals in captivity, after she had been treated like one for the last few months.

Ash wandered over to Eve, who had had almost no words for Rose since the two had finally met, which was strange and frustrating, since it was originally Eve's idea to track down their third sister. "Easy on the thunderbolts, there, Zeus," Ash said.

Eve bristled. "Sorry," she said. "Guess I got carried away thinking about what I'd like to do to a certain supernatural tree. And its oily black gardeners." Even as she said it, Ash could scarcely hear any of the typical edge in her voice, as though the will to fight had fled her altogether.

Ash had been struggling all day with whether or not she should tell Eve about the Candelabra, about how the Cloak had carved the soul of Pele into three "siblings."

But Eve had barely had time to adjust to being back on earth, and selfishly Ash wasn't ready to untangle how the news might further complicate their already thorny relationship.

"You asked me two months ago," Ash said finally, "after our tennis grudge match—before the Cloak took you—whether I thought the two of us end up like this every time we're reincarnated."

Eve clucked her tongue. "You mean right before you told me that you were done speaking with me for this lifetime?"

Ash cringed. "Good memory. I'd sort of hoped that being plugged into the tree would make you forget some of the things I said."

"No amnesia." Eve wrinkled her nose. "But it did leave me with the strong taste of lettuce in my mouth." She fished around in the jeans she'd borrowed from Ash until she found her mints, and then popped one into her mouth. "God, I hope it's not a permanent side effect."

"What I wanted to tell you," Ash continued, "is that if we keep worrying about all the bad shit we did the last time around, or what will happen to us in the next life, sooner or later we're going to completely forget to live this one. So we can go on living like two self-fulfilling prophecies, two forces of nature that can never coexist . . ." Ash turned Eve so that she was facing Rose, who was now floating faceup in the pool. "Or we can at least make a stab at being a happy, slightly creepy family."

Eve laughed for the first time since they'd returned from the Netherworld. "Let's just hope Rose grows up to have my fashion sense instead of yours." She plucked at the pockets on her borrowed jeans. "Where did you buy these, out of the back of a truck?"

Ash ignored her. "Speaking of family . . ." She slowly held up her cell phone and flipped it open. The word "home" blinked next to the first speed-dial slot. "There is one thing you *can* do for me." Her thumb reached up to press the send button.

"Don't." Eve's hand wrapped tightly around Ash's wrist. Thunder clapped in the clouds overhead. "You rescued me—on many levels—and I owe you a great debt. Don't ask me for something I cannot give."

When Eve withdrew her trembling hand, she left a white imprint in Ash's flesh—exactly where Ash's own handprint was burned into Eve's.

"You don't need to go home right now," Ash said. "You don't even need to make promises. . . . But, Eve, you need to give them hope. Hope so Dad doesn't stay up night after night on his laptop, searching police blogs and obituaries. So I don't come downstairs in the middle of the night and find Mom at the kitchen table with her face buried in your old tracksuit." The phone vibrated in Ash's hand just then, and Ash added, "So they will *stop calling me* every damn five minutes."

Eve let out a long breath, and a sea breeze blew in from the Atlantic with it. Then she reached out and took the phone from Ash's hand. "If I answer this call, we're even. No more playing the 'But I rescued you from hell' card from now on." She clicked the button, and the voice on the line—clearly Gloria Wilde's—immediately started rattling off like a machine gun, a week's worth of anxiety from Ash dodging calls and text messages.

It all stopped as soon as Eve said, "Mom?"

A profound and heartrending silence followed on the other end of the line. Ash was unconsciously holding her breath.

Eve stared penetratingly into Ash's eyes as she said her next three words:

"It's me . . . Eve."

Ash found Wes exactly where she expected he'd be. The Spanish monastery was easy enough to find, and the magnificent weeping willow in the courtyard was far too large to possibly miss.

The morning's rain clouds had gratefully blown off to sea, and the dusky sun peeked just over the monastery walls, casting the courtyard in an orange light. A few final tourists were wandering the grounds with bulky cameras and bored-looking children in tow.

Ash brushed aside the curtain of leaves. Wes was sitting cross-legged between two protruding roots, staring out through the veil of drooping branches.

Wes looked mildly startled by her appearance, and she saw with a sinking heart that he smiled only weakly when she took a seat next to him. "I thought you were going for some retail therapy and sibling bonding downtown," he said.

Ash shook her head. "Strangely enough, even after being comatose and attached to a giant tree all that time, Eve decided that she needed a big nap before she was ready to face the public again. And when I tried to explain to Rose about cutting her hair, I think she got the wrong idea, because she started running laps around the kitchen." She sighed. "Maybe it was too much to expect that everybody would be ready to do 'normal' things."

Wes patted her knee. "Well, you get bonus points for trying to get everyone to jump back in with both feet. In the meantime, the Wilde sisters are all welcome to board at my place for as long as you need. Consider it your four-star hotel."

"Hopefully Eve left her angst back in the Cloak Netherworld, because if not, it might feel more like a sorority house than a hotel."

Wes pulled aside the veil of willow leaves so Ash could see out. The facilities people were beginning to set up rows of white chairs, all facing the tree. "There's a wedding tomorrow morning. The happy couple has chosen to get married beneath this tree. Tourists have been sporadically filtering in and out all day, because of the 'science fiction broadcast' last night. They all seemed to think this tree was some kind of elaborate publicity stunt for some new television show. Not *one* of them actually believes that there is really a person beneath all this wood and bark. A handful of people dead, some of them because of gruesome murders, all in the name of the Four Seasons' new religion . . . and in the end everyone seems to think it was a viral advertisement for a new TV series."

"It wasn't all for nothing," Ash said. "Sure, no one believes it now. But if we hadn't stopped them, the Four Seasons would have traveled from city to city killing until there was enough blood pooled in the streets that people would have been *forced* to believe them."

Wes barely seemed to hear her. "This little girl who couldn't have been older than four or five stopped in front of the weeping willow and couldn't take her eyes off it. She finally said to her mother, 'It's a miracle.'" Wes let the willow leaves go. "I can see nothing blessed or miraculous about this."

"It might not be in this lifetime, Wes, but you'll see Aurora again one day. That's one of the small blessings of being half-mortal." Ash turned to admire the tree, let her gaze climb the trunk to the lofty limbs above. "And as much as I hate Lily for taking her from us, Aurora couldn't have asked for a more beautiful monument or resting place."

"Don't try to make something beautiful out of this," Wes snapped. His hands trembled. "This isn't some happy arboretum—it's a tomb." He stood up. "You may have gotten your two sisters back, but I've just lost mine."

A bocce ball might as well have been lodged in Ash's

throat. She could barely swallow. "That's not fair," she said quietly.

Wes bowed his head. "I'm sorry. . . . I can't believe I actually said that. It's as though this whole city has become venomous to me." He leaned on a branch for support, and a few rogue willow leaves fluttered down. "That is why I have to leave now."

"You really think that if you immerse yourself in the anonymity of someplace else, you'll find a release for the pain you're going through?" Ash asked. "That the white noise of another city is going to help you to forget?"

"I will *never*," he said, "forget. But I don't need to stay where I can see her face etched into every restaurant table, every patch of sand, every bird that flies overhead."

Ash stood up and stepped in front of him. "Then take me with you."

Wes said nothing.

"Oh," Ash said. "I see. So I'm just some scenery that will remind you of her as well."

"Don't you think that I'd love to be able to separate you from all of this?" Wes demanded. His eyes flickered black. "I've known you for a week, but you're already like a craving, like some elixir I can't stop drinking. But I don't know if I'll ever be able to look at you through a clear lens and not see the horrible things that happened here. The memories of her and you aren't like oil and water. I can't just burn the oil slick off the top and leave just the purity. Believe me, if I could retreat to the memory of you and me holding each other in the ocean without reliving everything that happened after that . . . I would give anything."

"So you take it one day at a time," Ash argued. "And you make new memories. And you learn to smile and laugh and love and live again. And one day, once you have perspective and her memory is a distant ache, that horrible night will no longer be the first thing you think of when you wake up, or the last thing you imagine before you fall asleep. Or the first memory you think of when you look into my eyes."

He sighed and bowed his head. "Don't you see, Ash? Maybe one of the reasons we can't remember our previous lives is because we're *not supposed to find each other.* I thought I saved Aurora when I carried her away from that awful relationship, but in the end it was being around me—being around other gods—that killed her." His pointer finger darted back and forth between the two of them. "People like you and me weren't built to lead peaceful lives together in the suburbs. Two of us together in one place is as inevitably fatal as running around a stack of dynamite with a torch." He looked away. "And that's why you need to let me go. To let *me* let you go."

She grabbed his face and forced him to look at her. Her voice shattered into a thousand shards as she spoke, and the tears streamed freely. "Damnit, Wes, don't you run away from me. You've got a shot at meaning something to me, a shot at me meaning something to you.

Instead you're telling me that you'd rather just be the next person who buys a one-way ticket out of my life? Don't be that guy. Don't be just another thing that couldn't last. Don't leave." Still Wes made no reply, so she let go of his face and pounded hard on his chest once, then again even harder, hoping that it hurt. Her temperature rose. "Are you not man enough for it? You'd rather not let the bad in with the good, so you're just going to shut everything and everyone out? You're a coward, Wesley Towers. You're a damn . . ." She broke off into such hysterical sobs that she couldn't finish her sentence.

He wrapped his arms around her, pulling her tightly against his stone chest. Instantly her internal temperature bottomed out and she buried her face in his sternum. "Shh," he whispered soothingly to her. He guided her over to the tree, and together the two of them lay so that Wes was propped up against its trunk while she clung tightly to him.

As Wes held her, he stroked her hair and lowered his lips to kiss her forehead. "Rest now," he whispered. She was mildly aware that his touch was affecting her with some type of magic, but before she could fight it, a calmness swept over her. The troubled seas within her grew still as the winds died from a howl to a whisper. She yawned. Part of her wanted to open her eyes, to stretch her limbs, to fight it, but part of her saw a window to a few minutes without pain if she would just let go, if she would just let go. . . .

It sounded like Wes was speaking to her through a lengthening tunnel, and when she woke later, she would never be totally sure that she hadn't dreamed it. "In a world that's forever uncertain, there is one thing I know in my heart: We will meet again, Ashline Wilde."

When Ash opened her eyes next, it was well after dark. She was curled up in a ball in the cold grass beneath the weeping willow. And she was very much alone.

In the end Wes had left her with two things: the key to his condo, tucked into the pocket of her jeans, and a spreading, numbing cold that even lava couldn't thaw.

After watching fifteen minutes of the seven o'clock news, Ash determined that she was somehow involved in just about every story.

The untimely death of noted tycoon Lesley Vanderbilt, discovered mysteriously frostbitten and afloat in the Venetian Pool, along with the body of a second female victim.

The explosions on the Lincoln Road Mall—that had left many businesses damaged, yet no one injured—and how the FBI was "exploring the possibility of terrorism."

The unidentified corpse encased in glass on the beach, who authorities believed to be the victim of a freak geothermal anomaly. (A portion of the beach had been closed to the public while volcanologists investigated).

The trail of blood and death throughout the overgrown gardens on the Villa Vizcaya grounds, and the strange structure that had been constructed over the

Mound, like some nightmare that had spawned out of radioactive fertilizer.

And then the final, puzzling conclusion that tied all the stories together: The bodies recovered at each crime scene belonged to the strange "fantasy broadcasts" that had aired this past week. The newscasters could offer nothing more than a wild, nonsensical guess that a publicity stunt for an unaired television series had somehow gone awry, leaving six people dead, and the gory remains of a seventh unidentified.

The single weeping willow tree that appeared overnight in the courtyard of the city's Spanish monastery didn't even make the news.

Ash watched just long enough to be certain that her face or name didn't pop up in any of the newscasts. Apparently no one had captured any footage of her firefight with Rey on the Lincoln Road Mall. She finally muted the television and pulled her feet up onto the long chaise longue in Wes's apartment. In her hands she cradled a camera. She had taken it—along with all of the others that she could find—from Lily's botanical arena at Villa Vizcaya.

Unfortunately, this wasn't a camcorder where she could just eject the tape and fling it into the fireplace to destroy the evidence. She flicked the antenna on the bottom. Somewhere in the world there could be a recording showing Ash using her abilities, from multiple angles, probably in high definition—enough to identify her face.

Maybe this recording was sitting in an empty room, on a dusty computer, waiting for Lily or Thorne to come back to it. Maybe her secret was safe.

Or maybe . . .

The buzzer startled her. She dropped the camera onto the floor, and the lens cracked.

When the buzzing at the front door happened again, Ash deduced that it must be the condominium's equivalent of a doorbell. She staggered over to the intercom beside the front door, where she pushed the blinking blue button.

"You have a guest at the front desk, Mr. Towers," the female concierge said immediately over the intercom.

"Very well," Ash said in the deepest voice she could muster.

Ash pressed her ear to the door to Wes's room, where Eve was staying, and then checked on Rose, who was sleeping in the guest room with her arms and legs sprawled out in an *X*. Ash had discovered the night before that Rose slept with her eyes open. Even in slumber, the little girl was a little creepy.

On the elevator ride down to the lobby, Ash wondered whether she was violating house guest etiquette by greeting a guest who'd come expecting to see Wes. She was potentially placing herself in a position where she'd have to explain to a stranger that Wes was on an indefinite leave from Miami to deal with his grief. But between Aurora and Ixtab, Ash had only ever met two of Wes's friends—one now dead, the other missing. The curiosity of meeting someone else who was a part of his life triumphed over her better judgment.

As it turned out, however, the visitor was there for Ash.

The elevator chimed in tranquil monotone, and Ash stepped cautiously out into the lobby. Getting ambushed every day for the past week had made her jumpy. Even greeting guests in the busy lobby felt like she was walking into some sort of death trap. So it was a pleasant surprise when she heard the familiar voice call her name from the row of floral-cushioned armchairs by the faux fireplace.

"Ashline?" Raja said. The Egyptian girl stood up slowly, as though her knees were arthritic.

It took all of Ash's restraint not to tackle Raja in happiness when she crossed the lobby to hug her. Ash kept her back hunched when she wrapped her arms around her, just in case there was any chance of crushing the baby she knew was growing inside Raja. The two of them had never been best friends at Blackwood—or friends at all until that fateful first week of May. But after all they'd been through . . .

They both had tears in their eyes when they finally pulled away to look at each other. Raja had cut her hair so that her bangs came almost down to her eyebrows, but that couldn't hide the thick, dark bags beneath her eyes. Her olive skin was mottled with red. Her face looked rounder, and her curves more accentuated than

Ash remembered. It was hard to believe this transformation had happened in only the short span since Ash had last seen her.

Ash laughed between sobs and wiped the corners of her eyes. "I don't know what to say," she said. "It's just . . . really nice to see a friendly face."

Raja squeezed Ash's arm. "You don't know the half of it."

Ash shook her head. "But how did you know which condo I was staying in, or who to ask for, or . . . ?" Ash had to reflect back on the last week just to double-check that she'd never contacted Raja. "Wait, or what city I was even in?"

"What do you mean?" Raja pulled out her smart phone and held up the screen—a virtual notepad was open with an address and Wes's name written on it. "I know I wasn't the most fastidious student at Blackwood, but I'm smart enough to take notes when I hear something important."

Ash felt that fog of joy, the one she'd been swimming in since she'd first seen Raja, fade into a dark mist. "I meant, who told you where to find me?"

"Is . . . this a trick question?" Raja cocked her head to the side. "Ash, *you did*."

Ash swallowed. The Four Seasons had located Ade with Colt's help—so who was to say they hadn't tried to reel in Raja by using some sick trick as well? "I don't know what to tell you, Raja. Whoever it was on the phone wasn't me. But I promise you're in no danger if it was who I think it was—"

"No," Raja interrupted her. "It wasn't a phone call. It was a video chat on the computer. *I saw you.*"

The night before, once Ash had finished crying and had accepted that Wes wasn't coming back, she had watched television with her two sisters. An awkward silence had clung to the room until, finally, Eve had started laughing under her breath and pointed out the irony that they were watching a sitcom about three misfit brothers living in the same house. Then the three of them had collapsed in laughter, a contagious mix of relief and exhaustion, even though little Rose didn't seem to have any idea exactly *why* she was laughing. That moment was the first time that Ash thought maybe, just maybe, her life was taking baby steps toward someplace more comfortable, predictable, and safe.

In three words Raja had catapulted Ash right back into the land of the inexplicable, disconcerting, and weird.

She could see that Raja, too, had gone quite pale, which made the blush spots on her cheeks far more pronounced. No use causing the girl a panic-induced miscarriage. "Listen," Ash said, "I don't know what's going on, but the important thing is that you're here, and you're safe, and you're healthy." She took Raja by the arm and started to lead her toward the elevator, even though Raja resisted. "Come on. Let's get you up into the air-conditioned apartment before the heat sends you into labor seven months early."

Raja opened her mouth.

Then the baby cried.

Ash stopped tugging. She peered around Raja and noticed for the first time the baby carriage that had been tucked in the shadow of the coffee table.

And the baby who had just woken up inside of it.

"Tell me you didn't, Raja," Ash pleaded with her. "*Please* tell me you didn't."

Raja avoided eye contact by ducking down next to the carrier. She made several soft "shushing" noises and tucked the yellow blanket snugly beneath the baby. It didn't stop crying until she pressed her lips to its forehead and held them there for several seconds. Gradually it's sobbing faded to a gurgle, then silence. Ash could see the infant's eyes flicker closed as it drifted back into pacified slumber.

"You don't understand," Raja said in a hushed voice. "You *can't* understand what it's like . . . what it's like to have the father of your child killed the day after she was conceived. What it's like to stare at your stomach in the mirror and know that you have to wait nine months to make sure the baby's okay too, all the while wondering if she's going to share the same fate as her father. What it's like to feel more alone when you're eating and breathing and living for two people than you ever did when you just lived for yourself." She rocked the carrier gently back and forth. "I just needed to know that she was okay for me to be okay myself."

Ash felt compelled to scold Raja for her recklessness. Harnessing her powers over life and death to speed up a pregnancy could have easily killed the child, or caused it to come out of the womb already old and deformed. But the damage, if any, was already done. And to be fair, Ash had been in possession of her little sister for only twenty-four hours, so she wasn't exactly in the position to dispense parenting advice.

Ash knelt down beside the carrier. "What's her name?"

Raja offered a sleepy smile. "I wanted to name her something strong and Norse like her father . . . so I call her Saga." The baby's eyes blinked open just for a moment when she heard her name.

"It's a beautiful name," Ash said. "*She's* beautiful." And she was. Ash could already see features from both of the baby's parents. The long, shapely nose from Raja, along with her Egyptian skin tone. The expressive robin's-egg-blue eyes from Rolfe, and the early beginnings of what might turn out to be blond hair.

"She laughs a lot, and she almost never cries." Raja's eyes glimmered wistfully. "Wouldn't it be nice if we could all be so strong."

Ash took Raja's suitcase, and the three of them rode the elevator back up to the top floor. The adorable infant served as a welcome distraction to the questions that threatened to run wild in Ash's brain—mainly, who had impersonated Ash? And what had her doppelganger said to Raja to make the girl travel a thousand miles to Miami with an infant.

Raja continued to chatter excitedly (though in soft tones so as not to wake the baby), but she trailed off midsentence as they came through the entrance to Wes's condominium. Eve was sitting at the kitchenette, and had stopped in the middle of a big bite from a McIntosh apple.

The looks the two girls were exchanging said it all. Raja looked ready to drop her own child just for a chance to dive murderously at Eve's throat, and Eve looked like a fox caught with its teeth clamped around a hen's neck. Ash had been so preoccupied with all the other pressing questions that it hadn't crossed her mind until now that Eve was partially responsible for Rolfe's death.

"What the hell is she doing here?" Raja growled. "I thought the bitch was dead."

"Hey," Ash said. She placed her hands on Raja's shoulders and forced her to make eye contact. "I know what you're thinking. I know that you're feeling the lust for revenge, and that Eve might seem like a sensible target for all that rage. But this moving-on thing works only if *all* of us agree to second chances, second chances for everyone."

Raja's body was trembling so much that baby Saga stirred and gurgled. "You'll forgive me," Raja said, "if I don't feel very forgiving."

"It's okay," Eve said. She wiped the juice from the

apple onto her pants and stood up. "I would never ask you to forgive me for the unforgivable. I can tell you that I never meant for anyone at Blackwood to get hurt. I can tell you that I didn't know that Lily would sour and curdle into a monster the way she did. But that won't bring your boyfriend back." Eve walked over to the guest bedroom. "For that," she said over her shoulder, "I don't deserve a second chance." Then she closed the door softly behind her.

Raja and Ash both stared at the closed door. Raja finally broke the silence first. "There's one other thing you should know."

Ash withheld the urge to say, "Oh, God. What now?"

Raja unzipped her suitcase and rummaged through the clothes until she found what she was looking for. From beneath the mound of underwear and jeans, she produced a familiar-looking scroll with a braille label on the edge.

After her trip to the Cloak Netherworld, Ash had already had just about enough of the oily black creatures and their prophecies. "Don't these things ever go away?" she moaned.

"When Serena originally handed it to me, I couldn't make sense of the instructions, but I felt this strange tickling in the back of my mind telling me that when I finally understood what it was that I had to do, I wasn't going to like it." Raja cautiously handed the scroll to Ash. "And I was right."

Ash took a deep breath and unfurled the scroll. Raja's instructions had five words:

DO NOT AGE THE CHILD

This is bad, Ash realized. This could be *very* bad. As much as she didn't want to buy into Jack's prophecies, she knew that the overseers had a far deeper understanding of what the future held than Ash or anyone else did.

Ash folded up the scroll, pried open the metal lid of the trash can, and dropped the prophecy in with the other refuse. She hoped she could scrap her misgivings with it. She pointed to the baby asleep in the carrier. "You did the right thing, Raja. Nothing this beautiful could ever be wrong."

Raja smiled. But then she looked around the room like she was searching for something. "Hey, what happened to your trip to Canada?" she asked. "Where's Colt?"

Ash snorted. She collapsed back into one of the empty bar stools at the kitchenette. "Oh, Raja," she said. "We're going to need a couple of cocktails before I can catch you up on that story."

Ash had never slept worse in her life.

Maybe she was getting sick, or maybe it was just a headache from too many cocktails with Raja, but her sinuses blazed with a hot fire—and not the type of fire she could control, nor the kind of heat that made her feel at home. A fever had ignited in her skull. While she waited for the aspirin to kick in, she rolled over on the futon and pressed her sweat-soaked face deeper into the pillow, as though she could smother the feeling.

It only intensified. As the pain swelled, she began to experience that out-of-body sensation that consumed her whenever she had a vision of a past life.

A memory was clawing its way to the surface. If what Colt had said was true, about her brain prioritizing her memories, then whatever was trying to leak out might be important for her survival. Now if only she could fall asleep so she could experience it . . .

Ash took slow, deep breaths and waited for her consciousness to fade,

waited for the dark curtain to drop,

waited for the scalding fever to subside,

waited for the calm of slumber to—

You lean on the ship's railing and look out over the dark sea. Night clings to the Atlantic like an impenetrable shroud. The clouds are suffocating the moon, and only a few choice stars on the western horizon have punctured the darkness. The temperature feels nearly arctic, and even though you could easily produce a bubble of warmth around yourself, you don't. Somehow the chill feels right tonight.

The transatlantic cruise is taking you home from Spain, "home" to America. But with Colt dead, and no family, what the hell is "home" anyway?

Anywhere is home.

Nowhere is home.

You've lived your last five years subsisting only on the bloodthirsty promise of revenge, believing that finding and catching and hurting and maybe killing Violet would be the antidote to this venom surging through your veins.

Now you know the truth.

The anticipation of the act was the only thing keeping you alive. Even if you had the will to start from scratch, you have no idea where you could go for a fresh start. There's nothing left for you in New Orleans . . . but where else can you go?

"Lucy . . ." The wind whispers. "Lucy . . ."

It's not the wind.

It's the voice of the ghost standing behind you.

She could easily be Violet's spirit come back from the underworld to avenge her own death. This girl, barely into her teenage years, looks just like your older sister did more than a decade ago. The lightbulb nearby buzzes and flickers, making all of the girl's movements look jerky between strobes, like she's teleporting forward inches at a time.

After the initial rush of panic, you realize that this is no wraith at all. She doesn't have the same broken, slightly crooked nose that Violet had her whole life from falling in the cornfield when she was five. The tattered black dress, the gaunt, malnourished face . . .

This is not Violet.

"You left me on the farm," she rasps. "You left me for dead. Alone. I was four years old. I killed that bad man for you, blew him to bits, and you two repaid me by leaving me for dead."

"Gracie?" you whisper, and take a step toward her. "My little Gracie?"

Gracie's whole body vibrates, and the lightbulb next to her explodes. "Not *your* Gracie," she says. "Not *anyone's* Gracie."

You're so overcome seeing your sister for the first time in more than a decade that you don't heed her anger. You move in to embrace her.

The back of her hand sends you reeling back. You nearly topple over the stern's railing and into the water below. Your mouth fills with the metallic taste of blood.

"Don't touch me," she roars. Spittle flies from her mouth. "It took years to find you two in New Orleans. Years of wandering, miserable and alone, only to discover the two of you living a life of luxury and hedonism, grinning like I never even existed."

"We thought you were dead," you explain. "With the explosion, and the roof just ripped right off the barn, we figured—"

"*Figured?*" Gracie echoes. "You left the farm without me because you *figured* I was dead? You dropped me in a pile of hay in the rafters and then ran for your life. Like a coward. The truth is that whether I was alive or not didn't matter. It was just *easier* for the two of you to go lead a new life where you didn't have a little girl to weigh you down. I was your sister, and you treated me like some unwelcome burden."

You start to lose your patience. "You found us and you said nothing?"

"No, it was too late for my happiness." Grace runs her fingers along the side of the cabin to her right. "So I took yours from you instead."

You hear Eve's final words again.

The wrong sister.

That's when it hits you.

That's when you snap.

"You delusional little wretch," you growl. "What have you done?"

Gracie smiles for the first time. A weary smile. A deranged smile. "What *haven't* I done? I had your husband killed. I made you kill our sister." She holds out her hand, and a little prick of light blossoms over her palm. "And now I will leave you for dead in the middle of the Atlantic."

You lunge for her, but the explosive orb in her hand hits you in the chest before you can even make it two steps.

Up is down. Down is up. The fall is quick. The water is cold.

You plunge through the surface. It's so dark and you are so disoriented that you're not even sure you're floundering in the right direction until you break the surface.

The dense salt water stings your eyes, and you splutter for a long time before your lungs clear. And by the time you've recovered your bearings, the ship is already fifty yards away. The boat's stern retreats into the cave of night. And standing at the railing is the silhouette of a girl who has taken everything from you and is laughing from the shadows.

You try to ignite your furnace, to warm the frigid Atlantic waters around you. But calm, cool despair sets in like a painkiller, and you simply let the cold anesthetize your body. You tread water as best you can while you wait for the end, and tilt your head to whisper to the hidden moon, the only one that will listen.

"The wrong sister.

"The wrong sister.

"The wrong—"

Ash tumbled off the futon and onto the hardwood floor. She was still half-delirious from watching her own hypothermic, watery death, but adrenaline rapidly cleansed away the fog. Her internal danger indicator was graphing off the charts.

Something terrible was about to happen.

And she needed to find Rose.

Half-blind in the dark, and still feeling partially like she was afloat in the Atlantic, Ash tripped over the coffee table, sending an avalanche of magazines onto the carpet. She hopped in pain on her good foot across the living room until she came to Wes's room. She flung open the door.

The bed was empty, with only the vaguest impression in one of the pillows where Rose's head had recently lain.

Ash hastened over to the front door, nearly tripping over the coffee table again. She prayed that she wasn't going to have to go searching through the streets of Miami after midnight for an escaped six-year-old.

The door, however, was shut and locked, with the dead bolt still in place.

The door to Aurora's room, where Raja and Saga were sleeping, was ajar. The mother lay sound asleep next to the baby's makeshift crib. And even though Eve's door was closed, Ash couldn't imagine the two sisters were in bed spooning or braiding each other's hair.

Unless Rose was hiding in one of the kitchen cabinets, that left only one possibility.

Ash found the door ajar at the top of the spiral staircase, propped open by an apple. The sound of the wind over Biscayne Bay whistled lightly past the opening.

Ash stepped out onto the roof deck. Rose was nowhere in her direct line of vision, at least in the vicinity of the pool. Ash was about to turn the corner to continue her investigation on the other half of the roof, but she heard a man's voice.

"You don't remember me, do you?"

It was Colt's voice, so Ash immediately whipped her head back and forth, assuming that the Hopi trickster was perched somewhere, talking to her.

But then Rose's voice replied first: "No."

Ash peeked around the corner. Colt and Rose stood at the roof's edge. They were both looking out over the downtown Miami skyline, with Colt leaning on the balustrade and Rose, much shorter, staring out from below.

Ash was instantly sickened seeing the two of them together. Her first instinct was to charge toward Colt, to insert herself between them and demand to know how he'd gotten up to the roof, and why he'd lured her sister up here.

Ash, however, was coming fresh off the memory of Rose leaving her for dead in the last life. For now, a flashing beacon in Ash's mind was telling her to wait, to watch, to listen . . .

"This may be hard for you to believe, Rose," Colt was saying, "but we knew each other once, very long ago. Knew each other *very well*, in fact."

The way Colt said "very well" made Ash feel dirty in a way that no bath could ever make clean again.

"I want to tell you a story." Colt fixed a crick in his neck. "It's a love story. Do you like love stories?"

Rose said nothing. Slowly she nodded.

"Once, in a time long before this city was even here"—he made a grand arc over the skyline with his hand—"when all this was just a rolling swamp, before the newcomers even landed their ships on this land . . . there was a man who loved a woman very much. They were both born of this earth, people of the clay, but they came from opposite ends of the world. Still, their love was so strong that, life after life, the two of them found each other, each mag-netized specifically to the other so that no ocean could leave them unbound. Each so attuned to the other's frequency that they could feel each other across conti-nents."

Ash ducked down and quietly padded her way behind a row of the air-conditioning units to get closer. She stopped in a crouch behind the base of a tall satellite dish.

"For centuries these two loved each other. Death itself couldn't even separate them. They had one of those mighty loves that is so rare to this world—cosmic, stead-fast, and eternal. Just like any real cosmic love, some-times the passion was so strong that they hurt each other. Sometimes they destroyed the things around them, the people around them. But even in fiery ruins they ended right back in each other's arms, and that's all that mat-ters, right?"

Ash couldn't be sure from her angle of view, but she thought she saw Rose smile a little.

"Unfortunately, these two lovers weren't without enemies. There are some people who are so miserable that they'd prefer to see everyone else miserable as well. One day these wild but powerful monsters, with hearts and souls as black as their oily skin, grew weary of see-ing the boy so happy and gleeful . . . so they split the girl into three pieces. And because she would never be whole again, the boy felt like he would never be whole again either."

Colt dropped down onto one knee and put his hand on Rose's shoulder. "I bet you've gone your entire life feeling like just a piece of what you could be. Feeling like a shard, like you're incomplete."

Rose looked down. Her tiny hands fell limply to her sides, and she released a little sob.

"You don't have to cry anymore," Colt whispered, barely loud enough for Ash to hear where she was crouched. He pounded his chest over his heart. "Because I feel the exact same way that you do . . . and because I've found a cure. I've found a way to reassemble your pieces and glue them back together. Then we will *both* feel whole again."

It was all Ash could do not to vomit onto the rooftop. So *that* was Colt's plan.

He didn't want to just exterminate the Cloak to end their embargo on memories from past lives.

He wanted to reunite with the Pele he'd loved for centuries.

To melt Ash, Eve, and Rose back into a single person.

Ash had to grab on to the air-conditioning unit to keep from toppling over. All this time, she knew that Colt had some dark agenda, and that it somehow involved the Wilde family, but how could he really consider trying to force her soul and those of her sisters back into a single goddess? All his lying and scheming, a string of gods and humans dead in Miami, and Ash hadn't been just another pawn on Colt's chessboard.

She was his endgame, too.

When Ash turned back to the railing, Colt was fishing around in his pocket for something. "Before I can make you feel whole again," he said to Rose, "I need your help." Colt pulled out a crumpled postcard. He flattened it out and then held it in front of Rose's face. From Ash's position, she could just make out a church steeple with a white top and a brick base. "Everywhere that you go, in every life you live, you leave a special trail, and the portals—the doors you open in the air—they can take you any place that you've been before." He tapped the church in the picture. "You remember this, don't you?"

Rose took the postcard from him. She examined it closely. She nodded.

"Well, in a few minutes I'm going to ask you to take us there. Before we can kill the monsters that split you into pieces, we need to pay a special visit to someone who hangs out at this church."

Ash had listened to enough. She revealed herself from behind the satellite dish. "You're not taking my little sister anywhere, you sick freak."

Colt didn't even look surprised or apprehensive at Ash's sudden appearance. "You cannot stop this, Ashline. You'll thank me for what I've done once I've reconstructed your soul. Once you are Pele again." He actually sounded like he believed it, like she should be *grateful* that he wanted to smash Ash and her sisters back into a single, volatile entity.

"I would die a thousand times over before I would let you touch my soul."

Colt gave her a weary smile. "Fortunately, you'll only have to die once."

Ash didn't even sense the man who had snuck up behind her until his fist blindsided her in the face. She'd fought her share of fights and taken her share of blows over the last few months, but this punch felt like she'd been smashed with a brick. She hit the roof on her back and groaned.

While her world was struggling to right itself, the

blurry image of a familiar Greek man loomed over her body. Proteus cracked his knuckles, which transformed from gray stone and mortar back into soft flesh.

"Careful," Colt warned him. "You are *not* to harm my past and future bride any more than is necessary."

Proteus held up his other wrist, with the still fresh burn of Ash's hand imprinted in his skin. "The bitch had that one coming."

Ash sat up and massaged her face. "Guess I don't have to wonder any longer who was impersonating me on video chat."

"Guess you don't," Proteus said, mimicking her voice precisely.

Raja exploded out of the apartment door and into view. "Saga?" she shouted. "Saga?" Her head swiveled rapidly, frantically searching the pool deck before she realized that there were other people on the roof behind her. "Where is she? Where is my baby?" Finally she discovered Ash struggling to her feet, dazed, and it registered that there were other sinister things afoot in addition to her missing child. "Ash, what the hell is going on?"

Before Ash could even begin to explain, Eve emerged from the other side of the roof, where she must have been listening the entire time. In her arms she cradled baby Saga, who was bundled in a white shawl and was fast asleep.

Raja visibly relaxed. "Thank you, Eve." She held out her arms. "Bring her to me now."

Eve ignored Raja. Instead she carried the child over to the railing, where she joined Colt, Proteus, and Rose.

Both Ash and Raja recognized the treachery that was occurring, and converged on Eve. Eve, however, spread a hand over the sleeping child and let electricity crackle over her palm and fingers. The approaching girls stopped dead in their tracks. "I don't want to do it," Eve said quietly, "but I will if you make me."

Raja dropped to her knees and whimpered. "Please . . . ," she whispered. "Eve, please . . ." She held out her empty arms.

Ash couldn't believe it. "I save you from an eternity of living half-conscious as fertilizer for a big tree . . . and this is how you repay me?" Her voice broke. This she couldn't swallow. "I give you a second chance, and instead you kidnap an infant and start batting for the douche bag team all over again?"

"Did you think that it would be that easy?" Eve shook her head. "That we could all just go back to mixing mint juleps at Mom and Pop's house in Scarsdale, go handbag shopping at the Galleria, catch a movie in Times Square, and everything would be just freakin' dandy? That the two of us would take Rose to the ice cream parlor and send her off on her first day of kindergarten, and that would make everything normal again?"

"I thought you could at least try something for once that didn't involve ruining the lives of everyone around you," Ash snarled.

"If everyone does what they're supposed to, no one has to get hurt. Except the Cloak," Eve said. "I need purpose and direction. I need to move from blindness into knowledge. I need to see my old memories so that I can know that life was better in the lifetimes before, that things can get better from here."

"I can tell you from experience," Ash said, picturing Eve burning alive in the Spanish palm grove, "that things haven't always been peachy. You don't need to resort to terrorism to find out."

"You call it terrorism. I call it activism."

"Enough." Colt stepped between them. "See how you're bickering? See how having your soul butchered into three pieces has made you self-destructive? I've watched you two slowly eat each other alive—watched, chained from a rock, as you, Eve, nearly drowned Ashline, before she cast you into hell. It pains me to see the Pele I knew and loved for so many centuries wage war against herself now. As soon as I melt you back into one, you'll be at peace, I promise you."

Ash pointed at Colt. "Are you listening to this psycho, Eve? Just a month ago you strapped him to a boulder and tried to force-feed him an ocean, and now he wants to throw your soul—our souls—back into the clay to make some supergoddess so he can play house with her."

Eve shook her head. "I didn't know who he was at the time."

"Of course," Ash said. "You tried to murder him

when he was an innocent human, and now you're his willing concubine after discovering that he's actually your unhinged, manipulative ex-boss."

"You used to love how manipulative I was," Colt whispered. Then his face hardened. "Let's get on with this. You—" He jabbed a finger at Raja, whose face was slick with tears. "We need you to add a few years to young Roselyn here."

"What?" Raja sniffed, and her eyes kept darting to the baby in Eve's arms. "You *want* me to age Rose?"

Colt patted Rose on the head. "As a child Rose is dependent and vulnerable, even as explosive as she can be. But as a teenager she won't be quite so cumbersome on the journey we have ahead of us."

"Just because her body matures ten years doesn't mean her mind will do the same," Raja protested.

"If you make her do this," Ash said, "then you'll be igniting a fuse that not even your trickery will be able to extinguish. Putting a six-year-old mentality into a sixteen-year-old body is like handing a sailboat captain the keys to an oil tanker."

Colt set his mouth in a straight line. "Do it now, Raja, or Eve is going to pump baby Saga with enough juice to power Miami for a year."

"I—"

"Do it!" he shrieked, and his voice formed the awful, singing chords that could pluck at the mind.

Ash tried to intercept Raja. "Don't do this. You know what the scroll said. *Don't age the child.* Eve is just bluffing. She'd never actually . . ." She couldn't even finish her sentence. She no longer knew whether there was a limit to the evil her sister was capable of.

"I have no choice." Raja brushed past Ash. When she reached Rose, who was peering curiously up at her, Raja cupped her hands around either side of the girl's face.

The transformation happened rapidly, fueled by Raja's anguish. Rose's limbs lengthened, the creak of the growing bones audible from across the roof. Her thighs thickened, her legs widened, her breasts grew full and round. All the while her clothes ripped and snapped until they were just tattered rags draped half-modestly over the brand-new curves of her body.

When all was done and Raja stepped away from her creation, the Polynesian girl standing at the railing was the very same one Ash had seen on the boat in her last life, right before Rose cast Ash overboard to an icy death in the Atlantic waters.

Rose held her quaking hands in front of her face, trying to come to terms with the sudden lengthier, fuller body she'd been given. She dove for one of the metal air-conditioning conduits and stared at her warped image in the half-reflective steel.

The scream that poured out of her open mouth was so horrible that Ash wondered if she would ever feel warm again.

The next moment Ash would later remember as one of the worst in her life.

Rose turned to face the others. Her eyes narrowed

and her open mouth trembled. Raja had turned to Eve, unaware of what was about to happen next, focused only on having Saga returned safely to her arms. "I've done what you asked," Raja said. "Now give me back my—"

Rose's explosive burst hit Raja in the chest and catapulted her body over the railing and out of sight, leaving the Egyptian goddess to plunge thirty stories to the street below.

For the third time in as many months, Ash watched helplessly as one of her friends died a sudden and horrible death.

"No!" Ash howled. "What have you done?" Her arms were already burning as she stomped toward the newly teenage Rose, ready to inflict severe pain on her, even though Rose was her sister, even though she was really still a little girl, even though *nothing* could bring Raja back.

Rose spun and hit Ash with an open palm. The explosive orb that detonated against Ash's torso knocked her over the row of air-conditioning units onto the roof beyond. Even with the friction of the rooftop tearing into her skin, her body didn't stop until it struck the railing on the opposite side of the roof.

Ash used the railing to lift her battered body off the ground. Across the deck she watched as Rose cast another explosive ball off the roof. This one detonated just beyond the railing, taking out part of the balustrade with it. Just as it had when they'd traveled to the Cloak Netherworld, the explosion carved a rift in the air. Only through this one wasn't an ocean, but a dark cobblestone street lined with brownstones.

Eve was the first to jump through, with Saga still in her arms. She stepped up through the mangled hole in the railing and glanced down at the Miami streets below before rocking back on her feet and then leaping through the portal.

Ash sauntered across the roof toward them. A sharp pain drilled through her ankle, possibly a sprain, but she cared only about making it to that portal before it closed.

Next was Proteus, who looked far more frightened of the short leap of faith he needed to make than Eve had. Colt, however, gave him an impatient shove from behind, and after a stutterstep and a squeal of terror, Proteus disappeared through the portal.

Ash limped forward faster, then broke into a trot. She could already see the edges of the portal starting to shrink and fray.

Then Rose dove through the rift awkwardly, like a little rag doll without full control or understanding of her new body. That left just Colt, who lingered on the roof's edge long enough to watch Ash coming toward him. "I will find you again when it's time for the merge," he yelled across the roof. "You're not ready to follow me now, but my one hope is that by the time we meet again, you'll understand that I did all of this because *I love you*."

Ash screamed and began an all-out sprint. There was no pain now, only the hope of catching Colt before he made it through the portal, the promise of throwing him headlong off the building to his death.

By the time she reached the air conditioners, she had enough momentum to hurdle over them using her hands. Colt, who had misjudged how fast she was coming, took off toward the rapidly closing portal a little late, and Ash grabbed hold of his wrist long enough to slow him down. A sharp kick from Colt, however, put enough distance between them for him to tear away.

He reached the hole in the railing and jumped just a half second before her. She didn't even slow down for a moment as she set her foot near the edge of the roof and hurled her whole body off. Her hand extended, straining, until she could feel the cloth on the back of Colt's T-shirt—

Colt threaded the needle into the portal.

Ash, in midair over the Miami streets below, watched with horror and despair as the rift in the air sealed behind him.

For the second time in a week, she entered into free fall off the edge of a tall building.

Only this time there was no winged goddess to slow her fall.

There was no night god to catch her.

There were no angels to save her.

There was just an ember falling fast in the night.

With the rift gone Ash was left to plummet toward the Miami street, twenty-four stories below her—a fall that even a sixteen-year-old Polynesian volcano goddess would not survive.

But as the air rushed past her, she didn't see all the places she'd been, or all the things that she'd never get to do.

In the end all she felt was the desire for retribution.

If she died, she would never be able to stop Colt—

From exterminating the Cloak—

From merging the Wilde sisters back into Pele, the Polynesian volcano goddess who'd proven too powerful and volatile to exist as a single entity.

Death meant that, when she woke up in the next life, there might be no more Ashline Wilde.

Ash wasn't about to share a head space with violent Eve and crazy little Rose for the rest of eternity.

She would not die today.

As her body started to pick up speed, her blood boiled into magma.

Her skin cracked into panels of igneous rock, no longer just flesh but heavy, durable brimstone.

Her body ignited, the temperature skyrocketing a thousand degrees in less than a second.

And when she held out her hands, a stream of molten fire spewed from her palms, two twin jets that changed her momentum midair. She shot backward into the apartment complex behind her.

The impact with the glass hurt, bad—but the new stony panels of her skin were solid enough to crack the window and for her to keep right on going.

Her burning body landed in an apartment bedroom, rolling hard through the nest of glass and into the chest of drawers against the back wall.

The couple that had been fast asleep in bed bolted upright. When they followed the fire trail of smoldering carpet from the shattered window to the girl in flames, they both started shrieking in unison.

"Enough!" Ash growled, the volcano goddess in her instinctually taking over. The couple instantly shut up and froze in place, with the woman reaching for the bedside phone. "No need to call the fire department," Ash said as she pulled herself to her feet, leaving a trail of charred handprints on the cherry dresser. "I'll just put myself out." The corona of fire around her flickered off, and her igneous skin cooled back into soft flesh. She nodded to the lovebirds, well aware that most of her clothes had been burned off, and she marched out of their bedroom. Thankfully, the fire alarm in their apartment waited to go off until Ash was halfway down the hall to the elevator.

She rode up twelve stories—the distance she'd fallen—back to the top floor. There she cut through Wesley's penthouse and took the stairwell up to the roof.

The item Ash was looking for lay half-crumpled near the roof's edge, near where Rose's portal had ripped apart a large section of the railing.

It was the postcard that Colt had shown to Rose before she'd opened the gateway.

It was the only clue Ash had to discovering where Colt had taken her two sisters, along with Proteus, the villainous shape-shifter, and Saga, the now-orphaned infant of Rolfe and Raja.

Holding the postcard up to the moonlight, Ash recognized the iconic white steeple of the historic church in the postcard. The caption beneath the photo confirmed its location for her:

"The Old North Church."

"Boston, Massachusetts."

It was just a city.

It was just a church.

But it was a start. When Ash had been eavesdropping on Colt, she'd heard him say that there was someone at the church he needed to "pay a special visit to" before he could kill the Cloak, before he could glue the Wilde girls back together.

Well, if there was someone in Boston that Colt needed for his evil agenda, Ash would just have to get to them first. If this person was an ally of Colt's, Ash would stop him. If this person was someone Colt needed dead, Ash would protect him. And if Colt needed to die in order for his symphony of deceit and bloodshed to finally end . . .

The trickster's body might be able to regenerate, but thanks to the visions from Ash's previous life, she knew Colt had one weakness that prevented him from being completely invincible.

His heart was human.

The irony wasn't lost on Ash.

Ash stepped up to the roof's edge, through the gap in the mangled railing. Below, she could see the flickering lights of an ambulance and police cars arriving on the scene, where Raja had just fallen to her death. Now that Ash was no longer plummeting to a similar demise, the grief caught up with her and she dropped to her knees.

She sobbed so hard that only a wet sound escaped from the back of her throat. Raja had been one of her only remaining friends from Blackwood Academy. Now, thanks to Colt's plotting, Eve's treachery, and Rose's instability, Raja had met a horrible end before she could see her newborn daughter grow up.

Who knew what wicked plans Colt had in store for baby Saga.

A familiar rage rose in Ash, and her internal temperature climbed again. The tears evaporated off her cheeks. She still had the postcard clutched in her hand, but now it ignited.

So Colt wanted the old Pele back—the dangerous, murderous, destructive volcano goddess he'd fallen in love with for the last five hundred years.

Well, Ash would show him a piece of the old Pele. And then he would learn to be careful what he wished for. Because it no longer mattered to her that she and Colt had spent the last five lifetimes in love.

If the time came and she really needed to, she would do what the Cloak had asked of her . . .

. . . and pluck the heart from the trickster's chest with her own burning hands.

Ashline spread the petals of her fingers, and watched the postcard smolder in her palm. Then she crushed it with an animalistic growl, sending a plume of hot ashes and embers up around her, before she tilted her head back and screamed:

"I'm coming for you, Colt Halliday!"

ACKNOWLEDGMENTS

First and foremost, to my mythological advisor, Daniele Cudmore, whom I stupidly forgot to thank in the first book for introducing me to Pele. May the Midgard Serpent devour me for such insolence.

To my grandparents Lloyd and Ellen Knight, for letting me borrow our two-hundred-fifty-year-old family farm in Maine for a scene that is far from historical.

To my grandfather James Murphy, because I seem to have inherited your dry wit, and in turn, so have a lot of my characters.

To the city of Miami, for allowing me to wreak fictional carnage on places true and imaginary within your city limits. Consider it payback for the sunburn you scarred me with during my last "research" visit . . . to your beach.

To Anna Staniszewski, for agreeing to mentor Ashline and me for a fourth semester in a row. You must be the goddess of patience.

To my superagent, Mary Kole, for being a constant source of encouragement no matter where you are in your world travels (which, on any given weekend, could literally be anywhere).

To my editor, Courtney Bongiolatti, whose literary wisdom I still revere despite your unwavering allegiance to the Giants.

To Justin Chanda and the whole team at Simon & Schuster, for your continued support of my mythological musings, and especially to Lydia Finn and Colin Riley, for reminding me that you don't have to look hard to find Patriots fans in New York City.

And to Mom, Dad, Kelsey, Erin, Ray, and baby Victoria, all of whom have taught me about the importance of family, and one of whom has taught me the indispensable value of a singing stuffed octopus.

ABOUT THE AUTHOR

Karsten Knight has been writing since the age of six, when he completed his first masterpiece: a picture book series about an adventurous worm. In the two decades that have followed, Karsten worked as a proofreader, a bookseller, and a college admissions counselor before finally deciding that his true calling is to be a volcano goddess biographer. He resides in Boston, where he lives for fall weather and football, and is on a far-too-successful quest to visit every restaurant in the city. *Wildefire* was his first novel. For more information on Karsten or to watch his video blog, visit karstenknight.com.